DRAGON'S BLADE

VEILED INTENTIONS

Michael R. Miller

ISBN 978-1-911079-76-7

🐦 @iamselfpub
www.thedragonsblade.com
www.iamselfpublishing.com

CONTENTS

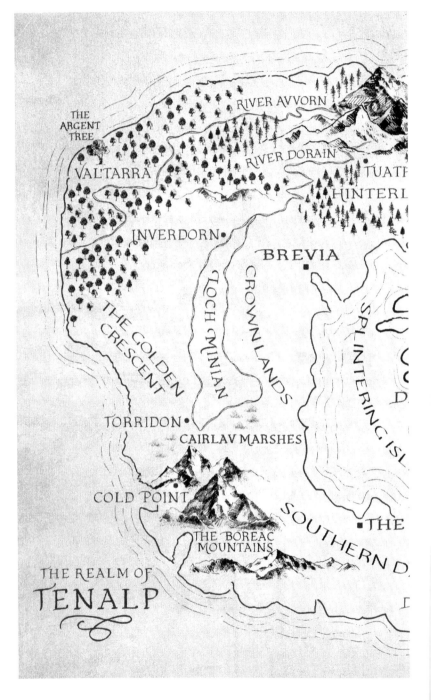

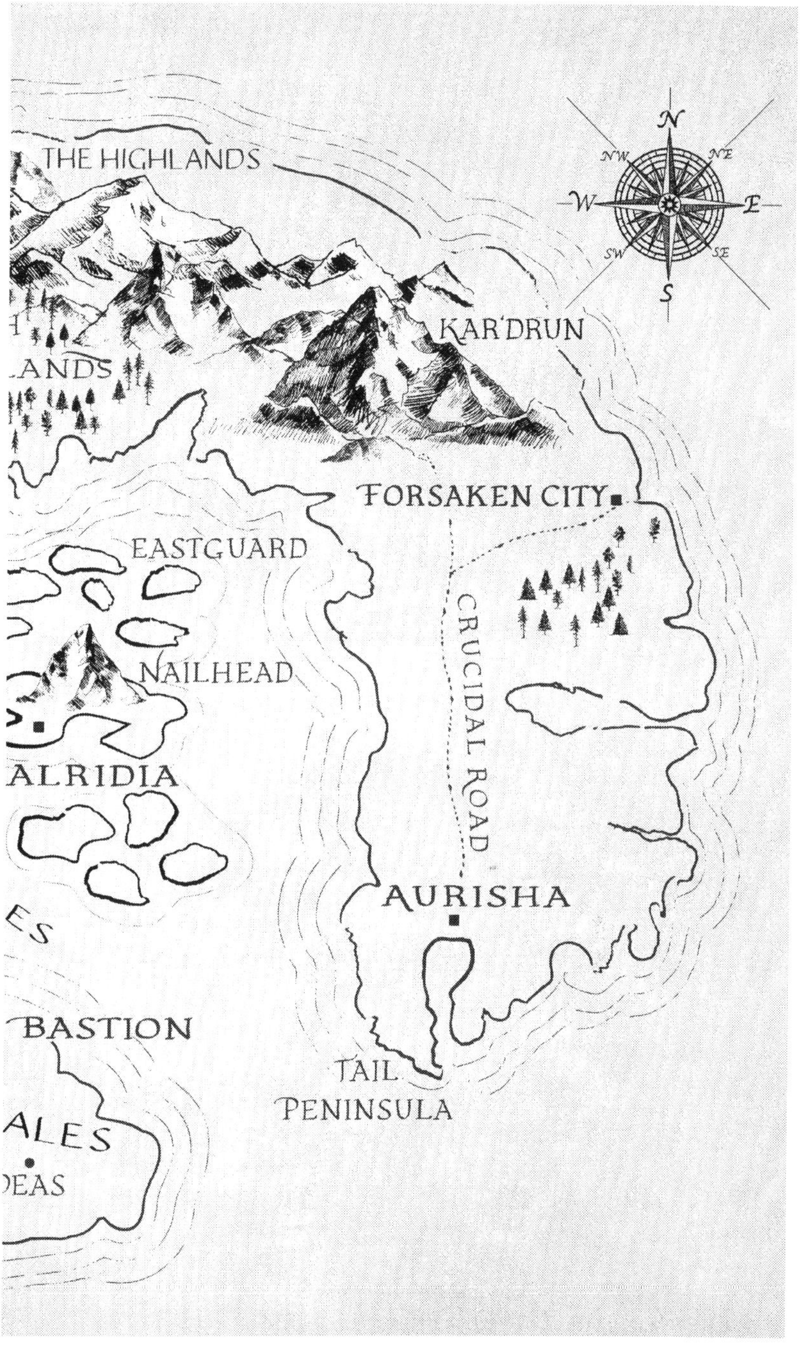
N
NW
NE
W
E
SW
SE
S
THE HIGHLANDS
KAR'DRUN
H
LANDS
FORSAKEN CITY
EASTGUARD
NAILHEAD
ALRIDIA
CRUCIDAL ROAD
AURISHA
ES
BASTION
TAIL
PENINSULA
ALES
DEAS

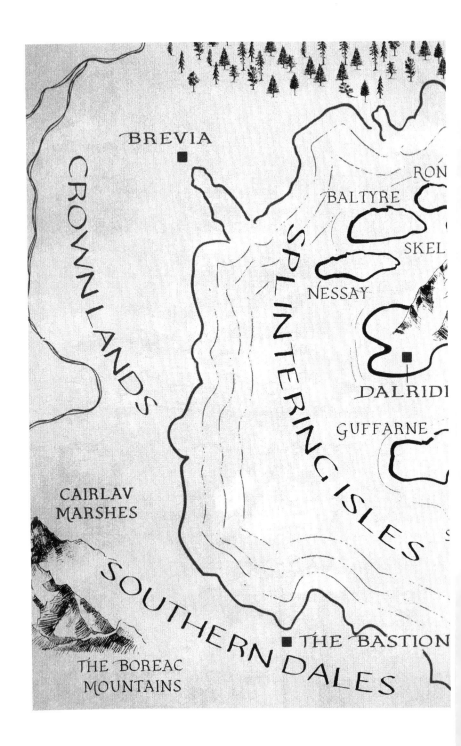

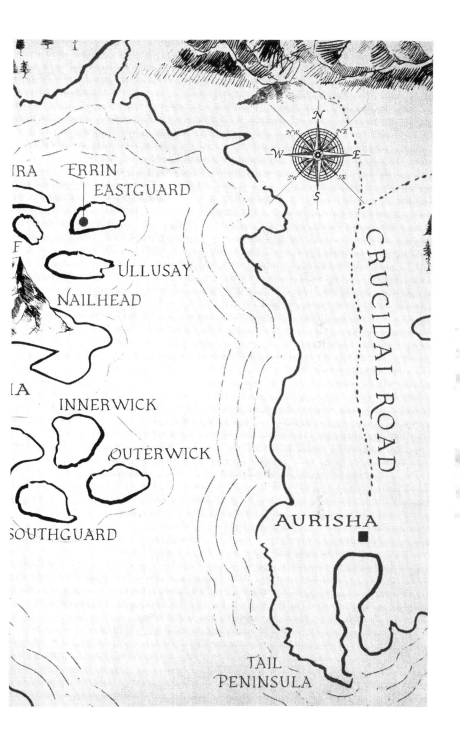

PROLOGUE

Grigayne – Island of Eastguard – Splintering Isles

EASTGUARD HAD FALLEN.

From his longship out at sea, Grigayne watched the old fort upon the cliff burn. It had stood for centuries, keeping watch for dragon war galleys in ages past. Today, it had taken the demons mere hours to destroy it. The flames now licked towards the dense clouds, waving wildly in the wind.

We were undermanned, unprepared and taken by surprise.

Grigayne rehearsed that line in his head. But no matter the reason, it was still a defeat. His father, Somerled Imar, the Lord of the Isles, would slump in disappointment all the same.

Grigayne tasted blood. It was trickling into his mouth and he dabbed at his injured head with a wad of cloth while the oarsmen around him heaved against the angry waves. Water splashed onboard, wetting his clothes, which were already damp from sweat. Some of it entered his mouth as well, mixing unpleasantly with the blood on his tongue: a salty, tangy, metallic taste. Foul. Though not as foul as their defeat had been.

"It wis hard fought," someone said from behind. Grigayne did not recognise the speaker. A coarse voice was a common trait amongst the inhabitants of the Splintering Isles. The salt was said to rub at a man's throat, a woman's as well.

"We should have sailed the moment we saw the demons approaching," Grigayne said. His own voice was lighter, his letters better enunciated. Lord Somerled had desired Grigayne to blend in at the Lords Assembly in the capital of Brevia, and ensured he learned to speak properly.

"And gie up the fortress without a fight?"

"More lives would have been spared," Grigayne said.

"Most of the townsfolk in Errin got away, that's sumin'."

"I suppose."

Grigayne turned to get a look at the man. He must have been in his fifties, with a patchy brown beard and the gore of battle on him. His only noteworthy feature was the stump on his left wrist.

"Do I know you?" Grigayne asked.

"Doubt it."

"Well, who are you?" In the chaos, Grigayne had jumped aboard this boat without much thought.

"Oh, I'll be the Captain. Names' Cayn."

"You don't sound certain, Cayn."

"Well, I'm sure I saw the last Cap'n on fire during the attack. Then his first mate died with a spectre's blade in his belly, and then his closest mate died n'all. Seeing as it's only a small ship, that just leaves me in charge."

"And a fine captain you'll make."

Cayn shrugged. "Might do, though only reason I'm sat here is cause I cannae row." He waved his stump in demonstration.

Grigayne closed his eyes at that. More water splashed up and seeped through the cloth over his wound. It stung powerfully but he held the cloth in place, knowing the salt would help clean the cut.

"So, Captain Cayn, do you think you can take us to Dalridia?"

"I thought we would be stopping at Ullasay," Cayn said, giving his beard a good scratch. "Much closer than the capital. The weather is against us, and we don't have much in the way of food."

"Forget the weather. Every demon that Rectar has at his command seems to be set against us, and we do not have time to stop. My father must be warned as soon as possible."

Cayn's expression was downcast, as if the aged man did not feel any amount of warning would suffice. "Aye, then. We'll make for Dalridia."

Grigayne took stock of the oarsmen he had left. Although many of them bore signs of the recent skirmish, thankfully, they all looked experienced. Most had a small axe or sword at their belts, but nothing compared to the larger war axe resting on Grigayne's own lap. He would have carried his strong round shield upon his back, but it had been cloven in two by the razor edge of a spectre's shadowy blade.

Grigayne would not call what had just unfolded a battle. The demons had come on so fast, there had been no warning.

"Ironic really," Grigayne mused aloud, "that a fortress built to ward against dragons should fall so easily."

"Not enough men," Cayn said simply. "Place was a bit old too."

"Built at the same time as the Bastion," Grigayne said.

"Bastion has taller walls," Cayn said, with another shrug of his shoulders. "And stone. We could've used more stone."

With the blazing fire in the distance, Grigayne could not disagree. The neighbouring islands were no better equipped to resist attack and would not last long. Ullusay, Ronra and the little island of Skelf would surely fall before he could return with aid. All the Splintering Isles were in peril.

All of Tenalp will be in danger from such a force. We'll merely be the first to fall.

He kept such thoughts to himself, however. Despair would hardly drive the men to Dalridia.

"Let us row with all our strength, Captain Cayn."

"Aye, milord. Hard at 'em oars now lads. Heave 'n ho. There's a shark at yer arse, so heave and ho."

Grigayne settled in beside a rower who lacked a mate beside him. The man was shivering, though whether from fear or the cold Grigayne could not tell. He took the end of the oar and began to rock forward and back, forward and back, feeling the ocean resist his efforts. His head still rang from the blow he had taken, and his thoughts jumped from one uncertainty to the next. *Why now? Will Brevia send support in time? Will Brevia send support at all?* Grigayne didn't know the answers and so, for now, he focused on the rhythm of his arms.

Forward and back, forward and back, forward and back.

Will the dragons emerge to fight alongside us?

Forward and back, forward and back.

One thing, at least, was certain.

Eastguard had fallen.

Dukoona – The Island of Eastguard

A human was trying to scuttle away on a broken leg. When Dukoona reached him, he placed one of his shadowy feet upon the human's chest. His victim stopped squirming, then attempted to raise his small, round shield to cover his face. Now that Dukoona could see him, he seemed so young. Not much more than a boy. A crying boy.

Better a clean death.

A blade forged from the shadows swirled into Dukoona's open hand, ghostly purple and sharp enough to cut down through the wooden shield with ease. The boy lay still. He had been the last of the islanders left on Eastguard. The small band here had proven easy to remove. Dukoona's landing had surprised them, as he had intended. A few ships, however, had gotten away. Dukoona had intended that as well.

Kidrian appeared at his side, looking out to the longships heading south and west.

"They will alert the rest of the islanders," Kidrian croaked.

"As they should," Dukoona said. "Come, walk with me." He moved away from the boy's body and drew up short of the cliff edge facing south. Just beyond the horizon lay the island of Ullusay, and beyond that would be Dalridia, lying in the shadow of the Nail Head Mountain. If Dalridia fell, all the Splintering Isles would follow. Yet Dukoona was in no hurry to conquer it. Furtively, he checked his surroundings and then the sky. Dense clouds prevented any shadows from spreading across the land, so he needn't fear being overheard here. He could not place faith in all his spectres, only his Trusted.

"We may discuss matters here, I think," Dukoona said.

"What would you keep from the Master?"

"Most things, but right now, I'd withhold how easily Eastguard fell. Rectar may expect quick progress if he knows how fast we took a foothold here."

"A foothold would require a more permanent base."

"I think you might be correct," Dukoona said, turning to face his companion. A wry smile crept up the side of Kidrian's face, starkly white against the dense flesh-like shadow of his body. The cold purple embers on Kidrian's head burned lowly. Somehow, the wind did not affect them as it would normal flames.

"A Shadow Spire should be constructed," Kidrian said.

"A wise move. One that would take a great deal of time, I'd imagine?"

"It may delay us by a month, maybe more."

"A necessary precaution."

"I quite agree, my Lord."

My Lord. He looks to me. I only wish I could do more for him, for all the spectres.

"Is there something more on your mind, Kidrian?"

The leader of the Trusted shifted uneasily. "The disappearances of some of our people at Kar'drun, my Lord. They worry me still."

"I have not forgotten," Dukoona said. "But, as always, we can only be patient. Go now, before those we do not Trust grow suspicious."

Kidrian bowed and took his leave. Dukoona lingered for a while, surveying Rectar's vast fleet as it swept along the ocean. He could not turn the demons back; only play for time. He needed that now – time to think, time to plan – but there was none. He did not know what he could do to save his spectres from extinction. They were caught between the Three Races and Rectar, as though exposed in a great expanse between two shadows.

Something stirred within his mind. In a split second, the endless presence of his Master glanced towards him, then looked away. Rectar said nothing, perhaps he was satisfied to see the burning fort and dead humans sprawled around it. With the moment over, Dukoona relaxed.

He desperately needed time. But he could not delay for long.

Chapter 1

A POOR START

Unlike previous eras, the Transformation of the dragons, the Third Flight and the forging of the Three Blades is the earliest period of what we can consider history; though it is still blurred heavily in legend. Sources from the time are scant but confirm just enough to allow us to speculate further.

From Tiviar's Histories

Garon – North of Val'tarra

A WEEK HAD PASSED since Garon's expedition had left the tranquillity of the Argent Tree, and two days since they had left the forest of Val'tarra altogether. The Ninth Legion marched, three thousand dragons strong, along with a thousand hunters and as many fairies on their way northwards to safeguard the Highlands and aid the Kazzek Trolls.

Garon had kept their column close to the west bank of the River Avvorn. Its crystal water was clean and energising, laced with hints of Cascade energy from the Highland Mountains. Garon might have found it harmonious, had it not been for his gnawing fear.

He could still hear the pressing worry in Darnuir's voice when he had pulled Garon in close and whispered, "Be watchful for those with red eyes." The words had not been written among the orders on the scroll he had given to Garon, but it was an order nonetheless. He kept that scroll close. It was a reminder to Garon of who was counting on him. It reminded everyone else that he, a human, was in charge of this expedition. Garon thought it a bit of a joke that it had been left to him. The kind of joke that makes you wince and suck in breath through clenched teeth. Yet he was in charge, and so long as that was the case, he intended to stay alive and keep it that way.

Beware the red-eyed men. Suppose I should beware the red-eyed women too.

The threat of these unknown red-eyed traitors loomed over him. He couldn't meet a strange hunter from the Cairlav Marshes or the Golden Crescent without staring awkwardly into their eyes, weighing them up, judging whether they had joined Castallan and been enchanted by his magic, as that red-eyed Chevalier at Torridon had been.

Even those from the Boreac Mountains, he gave a second look; people he'd fought and bled alongside for years. All of them, apart from Griswald and Rufus. If he couldn't trust them, he couldn't trust anyone.

"Not like ye tae be so quiet," Griswald barked beside him. "No seemed yerself since we left the forest."

"I'm mourning the loss of that sweet fairy girl," Garon said airily. He reached into a deep pocket of his leathers and pulled out a thin block of silver wood. "This is all I have to remember her by." He showed the block to Griswald – two painted patterned lines, one pink and one blue, wove halfway along the piece.

"Pretty. She forgot tae fill in the rest, though."

Garon tucked the wood away. "It's supposed to represent our time together. "Passionate, but cut short."

"Ha," Griswald laughed. "Young Pel better watch herself then."

"Wing Commander Pel," Garon said, strongly emphasising her rank, "is off limits."

"I won't hold my breath. If ye had a block like that for each of yer girls, you could build us a new station."

"Oh, come now, Griswald. A small hut perhaps, but not a whole station."

"Well, hold on tight tae that wee momento. I don't reckon there will be many more women where we're going."

"The Hinterlands aren't so far away. I'm sure there are women there."

"I hear they grow 'em tall and blonde in the Hinterlands. I could be tempted. Sure, I cannae persuade ye to change course?"

"I'm afraid I must dash your dreams of tall women to match your enormity. We'll be following the Avvorn northwards. That is how Ochnic came down. It is the fastest way into the Highlands, or so he says."

Griswald gave a loud tut of disappointment. "Where is the troll?"

"Further ahead with Rufus. They are scouting the best path for us to take."

"You trust that creature, lad?"

"Darnuir does," Garon said, tapping a finger against his scroll. "And so does Cosmo. That's enough for me."

"Aye, I'll take Cosmo's word for it. Even if the royal git hid who he was from us all these years."

"Would you call your prince that to his face?"

"Might be best to refrain when I next see him," Griswald admitted. "Expect he'll be wearing thick fancy robes and a crown tae boot by then."

"I hear those girls in the court at Brevia grow very pretty."

"Aye? I'll march faster for that lad."

And march they did.

At dusk, Garon called a halt. The warm amber light of a summer's eve was a perfect end to a far too affable a day. *Something is bound to sour it.* Garon's thoughts immediately jumped to Legate Marus, Commander of the Ninth Legion, and the snide remarks he'd make for halting their march before they keeled over in exhaustion. For now, Garon had managed to avoid Marus, claiming he wished to sup in peace. Though he had not protested when Griswald had taken up a space by the fire. A large space, it was Griswald after all. The man's beard more closely resembled a thicket and a fair bit of cheese was tangled in it.

Griswald belched. "Woah, beg yer pardon."

"Denied," came the low voice of Rufus. Although not as large as Griswald, the cropped, black-haired hunter was still impressively broad.

"You're supposed to be scouting us a path with Ochnic," Garon said.

"The troll said I ought to return," Rufus said, taking a seat on the dry grass by the fire. "It wasn't looking promising, I'm afraid."

"So, where is he?" Garon said.

"Checking other routes," Rufus said. Garon eyed him, but Rufus just shrugged. "Apparently, he'd be quicker without me. Way that troll moves I'm inclined to agree."

"I'm not sure if you've really earned your dinner then," Garon said, pushing a basket of food over with one foot.

"Not a hot one, it seems," Rufus said, exaggerating with a grimace. Garon rewarded him with a smirk. Whilst their fire was warm, their food, sadly, was not. Still, it was not without pleasure. Whatever the fairies did to their bread kept it tasting fresh for weeks, it even retained that fresh baked smell. Garon picked at the small brown loaf, topped with seeds, and ripped chunks from his stash of cheese. As much as he had liked life at the Argent Tree, he could not have lived there forever. That venison served during the council had been his first bite of real meat for far too long. His mouth watered at the memory of it. His stomach knotted as well, though not entirely at the thought of slow roasted deer.

I should have said no. I should have looked Darnuir squarely in the eye and told him, "No, bugger this, I'm staying."

He wasn't a leader. Sure, he had led hunter patrols, but that was different. And Cosmo had been there for him. He'd always been there. Garon had been so young when he had stumbled ragged into the Boreac Mountains, he had no memory intact from before that time. Perhaps his mind had blocked them out to save himself the ache. He remembered the oozy black blood upon the door to his old home in the Dales; remembered pushing it gently in. Remembered seeing the bodies—

He shook his head. *Why ruin a perfectly nice night thinking about that?*

He swallowed down the last of his sharp yet creamy cheese, oddly satisfied with his meal. A cup of shimmer brew to finish was tempting; the very thought of its bitter fragrance wafting in the air made him rummage into the supplies. It had to be rationed carefully, but one cup could be spared. He was on the verge of setting some water to boil, crouched over, his back to the rest of the camp, when he heard the footsteps.

"I thought I was clear," he said. "I do not wish to be disturbed."

"Unless it is these two, I see," came the irritated voice of Legate Marus.

"You will want to know dis, Garon pack leader," said Ochnic, discernible from his earthy voice.

"Something tells me I won't enjoy hearing it," Garon sighed. He turned to be greeted by a frowning Marus. The dragon had such thick dark-blond eyebrows that Garon was surprised he could see at all when frowning like that. Marus' red plumed helmet was tucked under one arm.

"What is wrong, Ochnic?" Rufus asked.

"We cannot travel through da glens dis way," Ochnic said, his icy eyes piercing Garon's gaze.

"And why not?" Marus asked. "You made it down easily enough before, troll."

"Ochnic was alone before," Rufus said. "The terrain is winding and rough. It will slow us down considerably. Likely we'll be single file in places."

"Too slow," Ochnic said, drawing out the words in a long breath.

"And you had no idea of this beforehand?" said Garon.

"Do you know of every rock of your own mountains?" Ochnic said.

"I was aware of spaces a bloody army might pass," Garon said. "Still, we must press on."

"It will take too long, Garon, pack leader," Ochnic said. "We must reach da kazzek before da rains come; before de lochs rise too high; before de winds blow us back."

"We are aware that autumn and winter approach," Rufus said, "but we still have plenty of time."

Ochnic seemed to ignore Rufus. He stepped closer to Garon, drawing himself up to his full and impressive height. He looked down with wide eyes, the white fur on his torso furrowed and Garon glanced apprehensively to the large dagger at the troll's side.

"I worry for da kazzek," was all Ochnic said, softly, almost pleading.

Garon relaxed and spoke softly in return. "I understand your concern for your people but—"

"Last hope, I am," Ochnic said, thumping a hand onto his white furred chest. His thick, grey skin wrinkled around his eyes as he fumed at Garon. One might have mistaken it for anger, as Marus seemed to do, reaching a hand for his sword. But not Garon. He'd developed an instinct for knowing when a person's anger was really directed elsewhere. Perhaps it came from years of hearing angry fathers' curse his name.

"We'll get there, Ochnic," Garon said, reaching up to grasp the troll's callused elbow. Ochnic squinted down, perplexed at the gesture. "I don't intend to fail," Garon assured him.

"We must find a faster way," said Ochnic.

"And we shall," Garon said. He gave a friendly squeeze on the troll's arm.

"Thankful, I am," Ochnic said, taking Garon's upper arm in imitation and squeezing overly hard.

Garon winced. "You're welcome. Griswald, you've sat enough, might you go fetch Wing Commander Pel. It seems we are in need of a change of course."

"That cheek will get ye intae trouble someday," Griswald said, but lumbered off all the same.

Garon, left uncertain of how to proceed, indicated that all should be seated around the campfire. An unpleasant silence followed. Marus removed his helmet and stared into the orange glow, Rufus fidgeted, and Garon half opened his mouth several times, trying to say something, but failing to think of anything. Ochnic didn't seem to mind. He just sat picking a strand of meat out of his teeth with a chipped nail.

"Shimmer brew, anyone?" Garon asked. The response was less than enthusiastic, but with little else to do he returned to his pot and dumped the silver leaves in. A tidal wave of sympathy for Darnuir crashed against any lingering annoyance he had for being given this job.

How much harder must his task be? This is just a mere taste of it and it's already going awry. He tapped his scroll again by way of tribute. *And if I fail, then we all fail. If I fail, the Highlands fall and Val'tarra and Brevia are vulnerable from the north. We'll be fighting outnumbered on two fronts. We'll lose. All if I fail to get this lot to work together.* He glanced around at each leading member of his expedition, who were all sitting grumpily, not looking at each other, arms folded, and was eternally thankful that Griswald returned promptly with Pel.

"I am told our mission may already be in jeopardy," said Pel. She was unable to hide the happiness in her youthful violet eyes, nor the flutter of excitement from her wings. Her silver hair was pulled back in a single long tail and a blue tunic with an emblazoned silver tree cut off at the shoulders revealed lean muscular arms.

"A small snag, Wing Commander," Garon said.

"Perhaps we should return to the Argent Tree?" Pel said.

Ochnic growled.

"You would gie up so easily?" Griswald asked.

"There is a greater fight waging in the south," Pel said.

"We have been given a task and we shall see it through," said Garon. "I was at that council meeting, Pel. Your own Queen approved of this mission."

"We have never been friends with the trolls and General Fidelm —"

"Is outranked by Queen Kasselle," Marus said. "As is King Darnuir. I shall not return in disgrace, having barely begun."

"One more interruption and I'll fly off," Pel said. "You, Legate, should treat me as an equal and you, human," she scowled at Griswald. "I don't even know who you are."

"Griswald," the big man said with a nod of his great shaggy head.

"Griswald," Pel began. "Shut up."

Garon ran a hand through his hair. This was swiftly getting out of hand.

"How mature of you, Wing Commander," Marus said. "You are young, but that does not mean you should act your age."

"Marus, please," said Garon. "General Fidelm selected her for the mission. I'm sure he thinks her capable."

Pel laughed, an angry little titter of a laugh.

"What is it?" Garon said.

"Oh, I'll be blunt," Pel said. "Few of my kind wish to waste time wandering lost through the Highlands to save Frost Trolls. So few, in fact, that I was the only Wing Commander he could press into it, mostly by promoting me the day before we left." Marus and Griswald looked as stunned as Garon felt. Pel shrugged. "My people want to defend Val'tarra, our home. Not theirs." She flicked her hand at Ochnic.

Ochnic himself made a loud sucking noise as he finished picking at his teeth. He uncoiled his gangly body and began to slope off. "Call me when da fairy girl is more reasonable."

"Come back here, troll," Pel said. "You've even said it yourself, I'm told. We cannot go any further this way."

Ochnic stopped. "Always der is ways. Garon, pack leader, said so."

Garon smiled pleasantly at Pel. She did not return it.

"If the River Avvorn will not lead us, perhaps we could follow the Dorain instead," offered Rufus.

"Into the Hinterlands?" said Marus.

"The Bealach Pass is known to be wide," Garon said, drawing on old hunter lessons. "The town of Tuath lies at its end, or its beginning, depending on how you view it. Am I right, Griswald?"

Griswald scratched at his beard. "Rings a bell, but getting over to Tuath from here will take time, lad."

"How long exactly?" asked Marus.

"A week, maybe more," Garon said.

"Perhaps longer," Pel said. "We're on the wrong side of the Avvorn to reach the Hinterlands with ease. Doubling back or moving forward to find a crossing will take up yet more time."

"Den we should be movin'," Ochnic said.

"Is there an agreement?" Garon asked hopefully; too hopefully.

Pel snorted and Marus droned on. Twilight turned to night and still there was no decision.

I was a poor choice, Darnuir.

Garon knew he had been picked to lead this expedition because Darnuir trusted him, but that meant little out here. How could he make this fairy listen, when her own General had admitted his resentment of this mission? How could he make a dragon listen to him when Marus could break him in two? How could he do any of it? Then, he started to have dangerous thoughts. *Perhaps those who've gone over to Castallan have good reasons after all. That red-eyed Chevalier at Torridon did more than stand up to the dragons. If I was that strong, I might make them listen…*

His thoughts were interrupted by a sudden silence. Ochnic was acting strange, creeping towards Marus and sniffing loudly.

"What's wrong?" Garon asked.

"Smoke," Ochnic said. "Burning." He leaned forwards a little more and gave the air another great sniff. "Fresh blood. Can you smell it, dragon legate?"

Marus' expression darkened. The legate sniffed the air as well, then reached for his sword and shoved his helmet back on.

A distinct crack of steel on steel reached them. A roar of a fight. Cries of pain.

"I don't think we need tae smell what's happenin'," Griswald said.

Be watchful for those with red eyes…

Pel flew off into the dark without a word. Marus and Ochnic bounded off at a speed Garon could never match. He joined Griswald and Rufus as they ran towards the noise of the skirmish. Hunters looked on perplexed. They were all mixed together, a vibrant blend of white, grey, mud-red and grainy yellow leathers, illuminated by small pockets of light from campfires. Garon saw a glimmer of a larger fire to the south, towards their baggage train.

They ran into the dragon's camp, with all their white tents lined in neat rows. Most had removed their armour for the day. There was a surprising number of hunters here as well, mingling with the dragons, it seemed.

"Arm yourselves!" Garon cried to them.

Beware the red eyes…

And he began to see them; close by, in the semi-darkness, red eyes opened with a furious intent. Eyes like true predators. It was hard to believe that behind each pair was a human like him.

Knives were used to slit the throats of unsuspecting dragons. Some gouged at their bellies or backs from behind. Muffled screams barely left the dragons' throats.

A huntress in yellow leathers from the Golden Crescent weaved her way towards Garon. Her eyes flashed red as she wiped out her sword.

"I'm with ya lad," Griswald said, hurtling his bulk at the huntress. Griswald was a bear of a man, but she knocked him back effortlessly and charged towards Garon. He dropped flat on his stomach and the huntress bawled in annoyance as her blade swished at empty air. Garon rolled to one side to avoid her stamping feet. Still prone, he cut at her ankles, then her shins, then her thighs as she was brought low. It wasn't sporting but these traitors had changed the rules. She twisted around and Garon rolled again without thinking, hearing his leathers tear as her blade narrowly missed the skin on his back. Flipping onto one knee, he stabbed deep into her exposed side to end the fight. Then, a broad figure was over him; grabbing him.

"Up you get," Rufus told him, blood running from his crooked nose. "They're popping up all over."

Griswald staggered over to them. He seemed winded but unharmed.

The camp of the Ninth Legion descended into chaos. The red-eyed men and women had taken the advantage with their surprise attack. In many places, it was hardly a fight. Half a minute past, or half an hour or half a heartbeat. Garon just tried to keep his head. Red eyes flashed in the night, running at him, as though he were their main target. He supposed he might be. He was the leader of this expedition, after all. Yet most were speeding southwards, towards their supplies where the fire grew brighter. He was only in the way.

A hard buzz grew overhead, a noise like a thousand murmuring people. *Fairies. About bloody time.*

Some of the red eyes began to ascend upwards, lifted by two or more fairies. They climbed higher and higher until the darkness swallowed them. Then they dropped and their eyes extinguished when they hit the ground. Garon stuck close to Rufus and Griswald, as the three of them together offered a better fight to each traitor. Tents were aflame now too.

"We must reach the baggage carts," Garon spluttered, shielding his own face from the smoke. "Or we'll have nothing left to eat."

Griswald roared his displeasure at that, taking a swipe at an approaching red-eyed hunter. The traitor from the Golden Crescent avoided Griswald with ease, making the giant seem sluggish.

"Bastard," Griswald yelled as his quarry disappeared into the darkness and smoke. A moment later, the Golden Crescent hunter came flying back, clean off his feet. Legate Marus followed, his face red with fury, and buried his sword down through the man's stomach.

"Marus," Garon implored, "the supplies—"

"Come," Marus said. As they ran, the tide of the skirmish turned. Fewer red eyes could be seen in the night and many were taking flight.

By the time Garon reached the baggage train, the destruction of their supplies was already a full-blown nightmare. There was singed cloth and leather, ashes from burning shimmer brew leaves and the smell of burning bread – all that fresh fairy bread. Weapon carts were upended, swords and daggers stolen, arrows snapped or tossed into the fires. Dragons and fairies lay slumped against carts or strewn on the ground. Many had their throats slit.

Marus spat at Garon's feet. "I'd spit on your whole race if I could." The flames lit his face in fractured lines, giving him a maddened look. Garon had no words. Even if he could think of some, he was struggling for breath.

"This isnae our fault," Griswald said. "Naebody's but Castallan's."

"Be reasonable, Marus," Rufus said.

"We were sent north on a fool's errand," Marus bellowed, not listening to them. "Sent north to care for some backward race and get stabbed in the back by humans."

"Marus—" Garon began, but Rufus threw out an arm to stop him getting closer to the dragon. He crept closer in Garon's stead.

"Those who have joined Castallan have betrayed us all," Rufus said, stepping very delicately. "We have all suffered here." He stretched a hand out to Marus. The legate looked disgusted as it touched his shoulder.

"Get off, human." His heave sent Rufus reeling; staggering into the path of a red-eyed straggler; a Cairlav huntress with sword in hand. She ripped through Rufus' chest, through the muscle and the fat to chink off his ribs.

"No," Garon cried, but it was nothing on Griswald's howl.

Marus stood aghast at Rufus, frozen, reacting slowly for a dragon as the huntress made to strike him next. All thought of her escape seemed forgotten. Marus parried but only just. Garon started forwards but before he could reach them, the huntress had her skinning knife in hand and was making quick work of the weak spots on the legate's upper thigh.

Marus crumpled.

Blood sprayed from the wound; colourful, scarlet blood that spoke of a cut artery. It splattered the huntress and her bright eyes turned on Garon. She advanced, wielding both sword and knife. Garon's block saved his life but the force behind her blow sent him crashing to the ground.

So, I've failed already. I'm sorry, Cosmo, Darnuir. Rufus is dead, likely Marus, and now me.

He didn't even think to shut his eyes.

Another figure rammed the huntress. It balled out of the night, all grey and white haired. Ochnic knocked her sword from her grip and spun in the air to land on his great hand-like feet, producing his own large dagger from his waist. For a moment, they circled each other. Then they wrestled; a savage brawl of scraping metal, tearing clothes and biting. They crashed and both lost their knives. The huntress was stronger but Ochnic was more agile, more flexible.

He got hold of her neck from behind.

He twisted hard —

And with a ringing crack it was over.

Griswald crawled over to Rufus's body. Garon didn't have the strength to look at their fallen friend. He groaned as he tried to stand and found a large grey hand helping him up.

"I was warned of such humans," Ochnic said. "But I did not think dey were dat strong."

"Marus is hurt," Garon said. His wits were just returning. He staggered the short distance to the legate. There was a lot of blood. "Hold him, Ochnic." He struggled with Marus' armour but managed to get the upper leg guard off, unstrapped his own belt and tied it around Marus' upper thigh. Garon buckled it and yanked down hard to clamp the blood flow.

"Ah," grunted Marus. "Get away human. You too, troll." He thrashed, throwing Garon and Ochnic backwards. Garon landed onto his back with a thud. He was getting fed up of that this evening.

"Do you want to die?" Garon said, getting up. He tore off layers of leather and pushed them down on Marus' wound. He lay most of his weight on the dragon to apply pressure. Ochnic joined him, gnashing his teeth angrily. Marus let loose a pained whimper like a wounded beast; too tough to let himself scream. He tossed again but Garon held on, hating dragons for their pride.

Would he rather die than admit a human saved him? But it dawned on Garon, as he fought to save the legate's life. *He's more ashamed that a human has almost killed him.*

Something hummed nearby. "How bad is it?" asked Pel, landing beside them.

"Nicked an artery, I think," Garon said. Marus rustled again, knocking Garon on the chin. His tongue jolted in pain and he tasted blood.

"Lift the material," said Pel. She bent low and produced a small box like many fairy healers had carried at the Argent Tree. "This should stem the worst of it," she said, dabbing a generous portion of a thick silver paste to the wound. Marus stopped thrashing.

"Dat will still need fixin'," Ochnic said.

"He needs a surgeon," Garon said, rolling off Marus. "Griswald," he called, hoping the larger man could carry the dragon. "Griswald!"

But he did not respond. He did not even move.

"Griswald, da pack leader calls," Ochnic said. Some moments passed before Griswald reacted. Hunched over Rufus, he rolled back his great shoulders, which looked like small snow drifts in his white leathers. At last, he walked mechanically over to them. One foot. Then the next. All in silence. He picked up Marus' limp body and trudged off.

Pel's face showed nothing; nothing that Garon could read at least. Without a word, she took off, beating wind back into Garon's face with her wings. Then it was just himself and Ochnic. And the body. Poor Rufus lay as crooked as his nose.

"In da north, we burn our dead," Ochnic said. "Der is no tellin' what will happen if dey go into da ground."

"What?" Garon said, his head spinning. "No. We bury them here. I'll bury Ruf—" his voiced snapped. The word died. And then he felt a strong squeeze on his upper arm.

"Den I shall help you, Garon, pack leader."

Chapter 2

HELPING HANDS

Aurisha and Dranus were brothers. Together they ruled the dragons, but a discord arose. Dranus thought magic would better serve the gods while Aurisha thought they should serve through faith. While Aurisha dwelt in solitude in the Highlands, Dranus contrived to speak to the gods themselves. He flew to what was then the largest of the Principal Mountains, where the city of Aurisha now stands. There he called upon the Cascade in such strength he managed to touch their minds. In doing so, he brought down their wrath.

From Tiviar's Histories

Darnuir – The Crownlands

"**N**OT EVEN I could jump that," Darnuir said, gazing out across the breadth of the River Dorain.

"Be a shame to waste time finding a bridge," Brackendon said. "I'll make one."

"That won't be too much magic at once for you?"

"Not with this," Brackendon said, twirling his staff affectionately. Perhaps it was the magic in the silver wood, but its tip somehow shone diamond bright in the light. "Stand back," Brackendon added.

The ground around them began to shake. Darnuir stepped away as instructed, returning to the rest of their company. Forty young dragons, the beginnings of his new personal Praetorian Guard, were refilling their waterskins in the river. Beside him, Lira, Prefect of the Guard, splashed some water into her own face. She sighed in relief as the cooling water hit her and pushed her ebony hair off her face.

"Have you caught your breath?" Darnuir asked.

"Enough, my Lord."

He smiled and said softly. "Lira, what have I told you?"

"Darnuir, sorry, sir," she said flustered. "I'm still not sure I feel right in addressing you by name alone."

The vibrations in the ground intensified. Brackendon slowly raised his free hand and clumps of soil, grass, flowers, small stones and unfortunate insects orbited his extended palm. Then Brackendon brought his hand swooping down.

The earth fell into position; piece collapsing upon piece, creating a curving arch up and over the river. About halfway, Brackendon dropped his staff to raise his other hand, bringing in more earth to pad out the bridge to reach the opposite bank. When it was done, Brackendon swayed a little by the riverbank. His right arm shook and his knees wobbled.

Darnuir ran to his side. A lot of colour had left the wizard's skin.

Damn it. I should not have allowed this.

To Darnuir's relief, the wizard was fine. Brackendon snatched up his staff, and even chuckled lightly when he saw the look on Darnuir's face.

"No need to look so panicked. I just required both hands for a moment." His health was already returning to him. His skin brightened, his silver eyes sparkled although his hair remained short and grey, and his blackened hand would forever be damaged.

"Is that staff truly so powerful?"

"I have yet to find its limits."

"Powerful enough to deal with Castallan?"

"That remains to be seen."

"Hmmm," Darnuir mused. "You won't be alone at least. I'll—"

"Come nowhere near that fight. You'll recall what short work I made of you back in Val'tarra?" Darnuir did. The cage of wind and taste of damp leaves was still vivid in his mind. "We should move on," Brackendon added.

"Yes," said Darnuir. He faced his budding Guard. "Over the bridge." They hurried, three abreast, across the river. Once they were upon the other side, Darnuir heard a colossal splash. He glanced back to see

Brackendon's earthen bridge had vanished. He looked to Brackendon, who gave him a wink.

"You didn't think that mud heap was stable on its own, did you? Eyes forward now."

Darnuir retuned to face the Crownlands before them. It was the most heavily populated region of the human kingdom and the capital city of Brevia lay on the coast to the east. Darnuir had to get there with all haste. The sooner he got to King Arkus, the sooner humanity's full strength could be summoned for the war to come.

First, we deal with Castellan, and then we scramble to counter this invasion Rectar is sending. We're always a step behind.

He braced himself, sucked in a deep breath and yelled, "To Brevia," before settling into a slightly uncomfortable run. Dragon or no, his new kingly golden armour, trimmed with starium stone, was thick and heavy. The carved bestial dragon that draped over his shoulders felt particularly heavy and made it sorely tempting to draw on Cascade energy, to creek open the door in his mind and let a small current through. A wandering hand inched towards the hilt of the Dragon's Blade and it was with some effort that he withdrew it. He had drawn on plenty during his duel with Scythe at the Charred Vale and his body had made him aware of it the following day. The cut he had taken on his leg throbbed gently and the bitter aftertaste of the Cascade still lingered in his mouth, no matter how many sips of water he took. He settled for grunting loudly.

"Are you alright?" Brackendon asked.

"For now. Come, let us concentrate on running."

And run they did. On and on and on, across green fields, past towns and villages. They generally tried to keep clear of people, but it wasn't easy to hide forty running dragons. Not when they hurtled by, scattering livestock and causing farmers' dogs to bound after them, barking at their heels. They took what roads and paths they could for the sake of speed. Hurried stops to take a bite of their limited food or fill up their waterskins was all the rest they took. They ran some more. Even at night they carried on, being able to see better in the dark; forty twinkling pairs of eyes picking up the light that spilt from Brackendon's staff. They drove on until the earliest signs of dawn came upon the world.

Dew covered grass wet Darnuir's boots and a fresh day filled his nostrils. He breathed it in deeply, as if the air could clean him from the inside out. At the first sign of real light he heard the many feet behind him slow to a stop.

"Is something wrong, Damien?" came Lira's voice. Darnuir thought she sounded more confident in front of her charges, which was good. He turned to see what the matter was.

The outrunner Damien stood by Lira, looking a little anxious. Unlike the rest of the dragons, he was barefoot, wore looser linens for comfort and was in better control of his breathing. For an outrunner, a run like this was second nature.

"It is dawn, my King," Damien said. "Will we not stop in reverence to D'wna?"

Darnuir did not understand D'wna, nor any of the gods that Blaine held service for. He hadn't in his past either. It was one of the few consistencies that spanned both his lives.

"I do not follow the Way of Light," Darnuir said, keeping his tone neutral. He did not wish to offend Damien, but he had not known the outrunner was a believer in the old ways.

"You... don't?" Damien asked, looking around as if to check he had heard correctly. When Lira and the Praetorians did not look shocked, he turned back. "I only thought... as king... your father always—" but he stopped there, cautious perhaps on how far he should go.

"Draconess, yes, he did believe," Darnuir said. "I have some memory of that. My old self thought it was what brought the dragons such hardship. He – that is to say – I felt my father spent too much time on his knees; saying words rather than taking action. I admit I am ignorant of the gods of our people. Yet my father spoke to them every day and under him our kind were forced from our lands, our city and our homes; nearly wiped from the face of the world."

"There is truth in what you say, sire," Damien said.

"If you wish to take a moment, please do," Darnuir said, gesturing with open hands. "I will not rebuke those who follow Blaine's way. Who am I to judge? I've only known that I am a dragon for months, not even years. I don't want division, and I certainly do not want to cause one amongst my own people." He made sure to look over to his new Praetorians, catching a few in the eye. "But I am not going to start saying praise either, especially when these gods never seem to answer back." He was pleased to find that Damien did not look disheartened.

"I was never fully convinced by the old ways," Damien said. "Though some say it is our lack of faith that has gotten us here."

"Gotten us where? On the way to Brevia?" Darnuir said. "I believe that Brackendon saved me, not some god. I believe Blaine saved us at Torridon by gathering the dragons. I believe in everyone here and we cannot rely on a greater power to save us."

"If we abandon the gods, what will we do?" Damien asked.

"We must forge a new way. All of us. Dragon, fairy and human together. Will you help me, Damien?"

"I watched you charge into an entire demon army alone and come out alive. Of course, I shall follow you."

Brackendon cleared his throat loudly. "I might point out that, apart from me, it is only dragons here."

"For now, that is how it must be," Darnuir said. "Humanity is divided. Castallan has poisoned the minds of many against dragons. With the memories I have now, and after seeing how our elders talk about humans, it is small wonder. How can we expect anything to change if we will not? You are not just my new guard. I hope you will be the new symbol of our people. A bright new future, free from old hatred and prejudice." He hadn't meant this to become a speech but it felt right.

"My father married a human," one called out.

"My mother and I were saved and taken in by humans," said another.

Lira spoke next. "I would never have been granted this position, were it not for you. Humans allow their women to be captains and hunters. Why not us? We're all in your debt, Darnuir." The other young women amongst his Praetorians nodded along at that.

"There is no debt you owe me for that," Darnuir said. "Let's continue. We have paused for long enough."

They ran on.

By the second evening, Darnuir's lungs and legs were beginning to give. At least he thought it was the second evening. His mind felt muddled and he blinked fiercely in the dying light. It felt like nails were driving into his feet and knees with each step. It was far worse than the run from Torridon, what with this armour and their lack of proper breaks. At least then they had taken shifts, and gotten food and sleep.

A large inviting barn lay on a quaint estate ahead. It looked warm, homely and big enough to house them all. As his thoughts drifted towards the comfort of sleep, his legs stopped moving of their own accord. His mouth was dry, yet he felt sweat under the armour of his arms and torso.

"Something the matter?" Brackendon asked. The wizard looked and sounded perfectly fine.

"I think I'm done," Darnuir said, a little breathless. A series of loud gasping and coughing came from behind them. "I think we're all done."

"We should rest for a while."

"Think anyone is in?" Darnuir asked, pointing towards the little farmhouse by the barn. "It looks quiet."

"I don't imagine the farmer will try to stop you."

"Unless he has a host of red-eyed men hidden in that barn."

Brackendon shrugged. "We'll find out. None of you can continue like this."

Feeling utterly spent, Darnuir agreed.

As Darnuir lead his Praetorians to the farmhouse, he caught sight of an old woman staring gormlessly at them. When spotted, her eyes popped and she snapped her wooden shutter across the window, as if this would make Darnuir forget she existed. He thought, therefore, that there would be no need to knock on the door with the chipped orange paint. But no one came to greet them.

Anger began to coil within him, gathering like a clot around that piece of his old self he had taken from the rubies of the Dragon's Blade. He pushed the feeling down.

Darnuir knocked lightly upon the door.

Nothing.

Huffing, he knocked again. This time a little harder.

No one answered but he heard voices this time.

"They're at the door, Walt."

"I gathered that, Belinda dear."

"Don't open it!"

"If they're here to rob us or kill us then a door will hardly stop them." There was another muffled and hurried exchange. Then, at last, the door creaked open and half a face peered at Darnuir from the other side. The man's skin was brown and leathery – evidence of years toiling in the field. "Hello," he said.

"Please, there is no need to be afraid," said Darnuir.

"No?" gulped the man, presumably Walt. "Dragons, yes?"

"All of us except for my friend Brackendon, here. Though he is a wizard."

"A wizard?" Walt said, rather highly.

"My name is Darnuir, King of Dragons. We've run long and hard, and recently fought an army of demons. I'd like to speak with the owner of this estate, if you could point us—"

"I'm the owner," said Walt. "Foulis, is my name. Walter Foulis. You might have heard of my family?"

"I'm afraid I cannot say that I have," said Darnuir. "But if you would allow my Praetorians and I to take shelter in your barn for the night, you would be doing us a kindness."

"I… I err, well," Walt stammered. "I shall, um, just check with my wife." And he disappeared, leaving the door ajar. A squeak of a whisper soon followed.

"Check with me? No, no, no. Just say it's fine – it's fine and maybe they'll leave us—"

The door opened a fraction more and the full face of Walter Foulis appeared.

"The barn, you said? Yes, I think that should be fine."

"My thanks to you," Darnuir said.

"But it ain't perfect," Walt qualified. "Holes in the roof, and some of the bays are cluttered."

"That won't be an iss—" Darnuir tried to say.

"And part of the enclosure nearby is broken, so we had to move the sheep into the barn," Walt rambled on.

"It need not be luxurio—"

"I admit to not being able to afford the repairs, but it isn't the first shame brought on my family. It's been impossible to find extra manpower since the King called up all able-bodied men to fight."

"All of them?" Darnuir said. "King Arkus has taken every man?"

"Those who can hold a spear or pull a bow," Walt said.

"He has," came the voice of his wife. The door was jerked wider, the little woman seeming to have found her spirit. "All of them. All the boys from all our tenants and they've had it hard enough already, just like everyone. So many, called up to fight again. Fight your battles," she added pointing a shaking finger at Darnuir.

"Belinda," Walt said, aghast.

Darnuir was unsure of the pair. As they had a family name and tenants, they must have been some minor nobility, although very, very lowly judging from their surroundings. Whoever they were, they were angry with both himself and Arkus. That gave Darnuir an idea.

"What your own King does or does not do is no fault of mine," Darnuir said. "But perhaps a deal can be struck? I have many strong dragons with me. We could fix your barn, your enclosure and other small jobs in exchange for a place to rest and a hot meal, if you can spare the food?"

"You – what?" Belinda began, evidently caught off guard by the offer.

"We shall earn our keep," said Darnuir.

"They are quite handy," added Brackendon.

"Oh, well that's very generous of you, my Lord Dragon," Belinda said, completely taken aback, her cheeks growing a shade pink.

"Very gracious indeed, my Lord," said Walt. He made a clumsy bow. "We thought that… well, it doesn't matter."

Darnuir smiled at the couple. "Perhaps you could show us what needs doing?"

Despite their fatigue, the Praetorians set to work within the hour. Some hammered up on the barn's roof, others repositioned the stakes of the enclosure's fence, and the heavy clutter in the barn itself was cleared. The hardest task was given to Lira, who attempted to encourage the shorn sheep back into their pen, but the animals ran enthusiastically in any direction but the open gate.

"A good farm dog might have served better," Brackendon said.

"You could help," Darnuir said.

"As could you."

"Yes, but I want to speak to you about Castallan. You keep saying it is a fight I must stay out of. But there must be something I can do? Surely you cannot duel him alone."

Brackendon frowned. "Your kind aren't suited to magic. That sword of yours might process the Cascade quicker than a hundred staffs for all I know, but the energy is a poison, and dragons are made weak by it. There's a reason you can't handle your ale."

"I am aware of that," said Darnuir. "But what do you expect me to do? Wait as a bystander while you tackle him alone? I cannot let you do that. Besides, I feel I have yet to push myself to my real limits. Perhaps I would fare better than you think."

"I admit, you seem capable of drawing on more power than I would have thought," Brackendon said. "Your battle against Scythe was impressive. But Castallan is leagues beyond—"

"If I cannot help you to fight Castallan, then how am I or Blaine or any of us going to tackle Rectar one day?"

"On that, I'm not certain." Brackendon sagged a little. "Tell me, why are you so insistent on this? One might almost think it was personal."

Darnuir had to wonder whether Brackendon was just observant or clairvoyant. The wizard couldn't know about how Darnuir had aided Castallan in his past life – could he?

Gold, and time, and volunteers… what a mess I made.

"Well?" Brackendon asked. Darnuir's mouth twitched involuntarily and he looked anywhere but at Brackendon. Over by the enclosure, Lira had resorted to simply picking up the poor sheep and dumping them over the fence. The noise of the animals' protests cut right through him in his wearied state. And then he felt hunger. Was that roasted meat he could smell, or was his imagination merely wandering as he looked at the huddled sheep?

"Darnuir?" Brackendon said.

He could take the Dragon's Blade, pour out flames: take a bite.

"Darnuir," Brackendon said more sternly. Finally, Darnuir looked towards him, still not quite able to meet the wizard's eye. "That silence has told me all I need to know. What did you do? It isn't about Cassandra, is it?"

"No, not her," Darnuir said, his throat suddenly dry. *Though I've been such a fool there as well. Why did I kiss her? Stupid of me. It's my fault she fell. She was too close...* He coughed. "My old self left me a memory of Castallan. In it, I helped him. I came to him, even, looking for a new way to fight Rectar and his demons." Brackendon blinked silently at him. "Castallan promised he had some solution to the war. Something he was working on. Clearly, I was wrong, duped, reckless," he said at a pace, hoping Brackendon might latch onto one excuse or another.

"Anything else?" Brackendon asked. "About Castallan. Anything about what happened at the Cascade Conclave?"

"Nothing. It was before he turned openly as a traitor. I don't think he'd attacked the Conclave yet."

"That's disappointing."

"Which part? What I did or the lack of information on your old order?"

"Both," said Brackendon, looking lost in his own thoughts. Further discussion was halted by the emergence of Walter Foulis, carrying steaming bowls in both hands.

"We've made supper for you," he announced. "If you want it. If you like this sort of thing." Belinda bustled out behind him, more bowls in hand. The Praetorians eagerly dashed over.

"Just a moment," Darnuir told them.

"Nothing fancy I'm afraid," Walt said. "Just some of the stores we won't be able to eat through with just the two of us." Darnuir took one of the bowls and inspected it. A dark watery gravy swirling around chunks of meat, carrot, mushroom and onion. He sniffed deeply, practically tasting the lamb, searching for any poison. There was nothing untoward in it, so far as he could tell.

"Just a precaution," said Darnuir, handing the bowl back to the nearest Praetorian. She began wolfing it down with a grin. Darnuir turned to speak to the farmer but he had already dashed off, leaving his wife behind. "You have my thanks, Lady Foulis," Darnuir said.

"Least we could do," Belinda said curtly. "You're helping us after all. A damn sight more than King Arkus ever has."

"You are not fond of your King?" Darnuir asked.

"My husband's family has been struggling for generations," Belinda said. "King Arkus cares not." She sniffed. "I have some bread baking. It should be ready soon." With that, she stalked off. Walt reappeared shortly after, struggling with a large steaming pot. Darnuir went to him.

"Let me take that."

Walt let go without protest. "Thank you, my Lord."

"I hope we have not offended the Lady Foulis?"

"Forgive her, my Lord," said Walt. "Arkus calling up the army has brought up old memories. Terrible memories. We lost our eldest boys in the last war twenty years ago. They died in the east, we were told but we never received their bodies."

"She blames me," Darnuir said.

"She blames dragons."

"Do you blame me?"

"It used to be all I thought about," said Walt. "But I'm getting on, I've nearly broken my body trying to keep this estate in order, and I've brooded for long enough. We have Ruth now, such a sweet girl and my youngest boy, Ralph, is in Brevia with the hunters. Smart boy. A good boy. He'll rise up and make things right again. I won't ever love you or your kind, mind."

"We aren't perfect," said Darnuir.

"If I may say, my Lord Dragon. You're nothing like I expected."

"And what did you expect?"

Walt paused, weighing his words. "A bit more aggressive, I suppose."

A part of Darnuir yearned to say, "You have no idea, human", but he managed to ask for more bowls instead.

By the time everyone had a bit of food in them, the repairs completed and the sheep forcibly returned to their pen, night had fallen and eyes began to droop. The Praetorians threw down a thick layer of straw on the barn floor and curled up on their bed rolls. It was pleasantly warm with the lingering heat of day still thick in the air.

"We'll sleep till dawn," Darnuir said. "Then we must be on our way." He noticed that Brackendon was out on a bank of grass, staring blankly ahead of him, his staff lying to one side. Darnuir picked himself up and walked to join him. "You should get some sleep as well," he said as he slumped down beside the wizard.

"I'll live," said Brackendon.

"You've been through worse."

"A fate I would never wish on anyone."

"Even Castallan?"

"Even that bastard. Be careful how you use the Cascade, Darnuir. You must tackle early signs of addiction quickly. The longer you leave it, the more energy you may feel you need to satisfy your craving in one burst. The risk of breaking grows exponentially."

"Were you addicted, before you broke?"

"I was, in my own small way. We all are to some degree. We just have to keep it manageable."

Darnuir looked at Brackendon then. Really looked at him – at the crease lines of his face, at his prematurely grey hair, and finally at his blackened, scaly fingers. Despite the stark warning of what might come, Darnuir's hand twitched towards the hilt of the Dragon's Blade. He clenched his fist just above the pommel.

"I've never thanked you, Brackendon. Not properly. Not in the way you deserve." Brackendon raised an eyebrow. "I mean it," Darnuir said. "You sacrificed so much and not just for me, for the whole world. And I'm sorry it had to be that way."

"I was glad to do it," said Brackendon.

"I probably didn't deserve to be saved," Darnuir said. "Even now. What I did to Balack… if you hadn't been there."

"But I was there," said Brackendon. "On both occasions. Fate has a miraculous way of placing us where we are needed."

"I'm trying to apologise," Darnuir said. "For everything."

"Don't take the whole world and everything in it on your shoulders. Even for you, it's too much. Still, I appreciate the sentiment. It's always nice to know one's hardships have been recognised." He smiled more kindly.

"Would you still have saved me if you had known I had helped Castallan?"

"I didn't save you out of affection. You're too important. That sword of yours is too important. So no, it wouldn't have changed my decision. In fact, knowing the truth might have been useful. All these years I thought Castallan had acted alone; one selfish, power-crazed man. But you helped him along. Perhaps others did as well, either voluntarily or through trickery. Perhaps I have been thinking about this too simply."

"What do you mean?"

"I mean, I have a nagging feeling there is more to this. In attacking and destroying the Cascade Conclave, Castallan took a great risk. Back then, he was one wizard with one staff. It makes no sense for him to have attacked the Inner Circle. So, why did he? And how did he manage to succeed?"

"We'll never know," Darnuir said. "Unless we take him alive, and then it's only his word."

"The Conclave tower is still in Brevia to this day," said Brackendon. "I kept my distance on my brief visit earlier this year. People say it's cursed along with all the land near it. They call the borough the Rotting Hill now, but if there is a chance I might learn anything, I should go, as painful as it might be to re-enter that place. If I can find some clue as to how Castallan succeeded in defeating the rest of my order, then perhaps I can use that against him in turn."

"I will come with you," Darnuir said.

"No. I feel this is something I must do alone."

Unsure of what more to say, Darnuir settled for, "I understand. Please, try to get some rest. We can't afford to stop like this again."

"I think I will sit a while longer," Brackendon said, and returned to gazing blankly across the estate grounds. A light was still on in the unadorned farmhouse and Belinda Foulis was peering out at them again through the lattice of the window. When Darnuir and Brackendon both caught her in the act, she slammed a shutter across.

"Good night, Brackendon."

Darnuir returned to his own straw pile and bed roll. He curled up, too tired to even bother removing his armour, but sleep eluded him. Beads of cold sweat clung to his brow and along his arms, his right arm especially. A thirst grew in him for more than water. *Brackendon would stop me if he saw me do it, but I just need a little – just enough to help me rest tonight. That won't be so terrible.* In silence, he reached for the hilt of his sword; in his mind, he pushed down on the handle of the door.

His sigh was soft and long. And then he fell asleep.

On the morning of the third day of their run, the vast city of Brevia loomed into view. Darnuir had never seen anything so massive; not in his current life at any rate. Brevia looked as though the entirety of Cold Point could fit inside it a hundred times over. It curved around the bay like a great horseshoe, enveloped by thick walls, with tall towers, like rolling black hills. Further off, closer to the mouth of the bay, an enormous white bridge spanned the banks of the city, its cresting peak visible even at this distance.

"Black limestone," Lira said, drawing up to him. "Nearly all of that will have come from the Hinterlands. Maybe even from quarries near Tuath."

"Imposing," noted Brackendon. "Though far from cheery. Used to be a light brown stone that made up the walls."

"So why the change?" Darnuir asked.

Lira shrugged. "The King's wishes. For nearly ten years, Arkus ordered all black stone hewn in the Hinterlands to be brought to Brevia. I saw them hauling it off in mile long wagon trails."

Darnuir thought on the only other great city from his choppy memories. Aurisha, the city of gold. Brevia looked startlingly different from it.

"A statement, perhaps," Darnuir said. "One we must bear in mind. Arkus sets humanity apart from dragons, even in the colour of his city."

"And there is Arkus' army," said Brackendon. "Look southwards," he added, pointing for them. Another city lay in the distance, though this one of tents, carts and ditches. Like Brevia, the human army's camp was the largest Darnuir had ever set eyes on. Yet there was more than just humans assembled there.

"Then we can march on Castallan that much sooner," Darnuir said. Something in the camps caught his eye. "Are those palisade walls?" he indicated with a waving finger, drawing a line around a portion of the camps in the air.

"I'd say so," said Lira. "I think we have found the rest of our dragons."

"There could be thousands still out there for all we know," Darnuir said. "Unsure where to go, lost, hunted by Castallan's red-eyed servants or perhaps oblivious to events. Everything has moved so quickly."

"I also think we've been spotted," said Brackendon. Darnuir looked out again, seeing many black-clad figures moving in and out of the main camp. A small group appeared to be coming straight for them.

"Hunters," said Darnuir and Lira together.

"They wear the black leather of the Crownlands," said Lira.

"And now I understand why," said Darnuir, glancing once more at the hulking walls of Brevia.

"Well, we must make ourselves known somehow," said Brackendon, tapping his staff on the hard earth. He took one step closer to the city then winced loudly, taking his head in one hand.

"Brackendon?" Darnuir asked in concern.

"It is nothing," Brackendon said. "A fleeting pain. Lack of sleep." The wizard gave nothing away.

"Just a little further now," said Darnuir and he called the same back to the Praetorians. "We shall be comparing the food and lodgings to that of the Argent Tree soon." The Praetorians smiled gratefully through their fatigue and followed him and Lira towards the human capital.

Chapter 3
EVENING BY THE LOCH

It is said Dranus angered the gods and they cursed many dragons for his sin, warping their bodies into a weaker, human form. The mountain shattered, breaking a corner of the world and leaving behind a bluff of rock crumbling into the sea. Dranus himself was left scarred, his once golden scales charred black from the Cascade.

From Tiviar's Histories

Blaine – Inverdorn

Blaine smelled Inverdorn before he saw it. A potent mix of smoke and fish, reminiscent of Torridon, with the added stench of a city suffering from siege. He had expected a faint aroma of sweetness to accompany it, but there was none.

They are no longer afraid. Fidelm must have succeeded.

The town itself soon came into view. Lying where the River Dorain entered Loch Minian, it might have looked serene in the late afternoon light, were it not for the piles of bodies. Smoke rose from smouldering mounds of demon corpses. Inverdorn itself seemed relatively unscathed, but he could not account for its inhabitants. Blaine's concern lay with the dragons that had been trapped there. In the aftermath of the ambush at the Charred Vale by traitorous hunters, his concern for humans was limited.

His focus was on his dragons. The Second, Third, Fifth and Sixth Legions were with him. It had been from the Third Legion that the bulk of his new Light Bearers had come from and he favoured their company.

45

Indeed, when they had searched Scythe's encampment after the battle it had been members of the Third who had brought him the Scrying Orb from Scythe's possessions. Sensible of them. Such a powerful instrument had to be held with caution.

The legions made camp outside of Inverdorn and Blaine approached the walls with a score of his Light Bearers in tow. A dark figure with inky skin stood on the parapet above the gate. Fidelm flew down gracefully before Blaine, a lean arm outstretched.

"It is good to see you safe, Guardian."

"And you," Blaine replied, taking Fidelm's arm. The fairy had a few small cuts but nothing serious. His long, braided, silver hair had avoided harm.

"Your timing is not so good," said Fidelm.

"What's the matter?"

"You interrupted my painting," said Fidelm. "The light this afternoon has been exquisite. I fear I shall miss it."

"There will be other occasions," Blaine said. "I see the city is now ours."

Fidelm nodded. "To be fair to the boy, his plan worked remarkably well. Dragons and hunters from within Inverdorn joined us in our attack. The demons were taken from both sides." Fidelm cast his eyes around. "Where is Darnuir?"

"He runs to Brevia," Blaine said.

"Alone?"

"The wizard is with him," said Blaine, "as is that girl and those younger dragons she has been gathering." He didn't like speaking of Lira by name. Darnuir's disregard for tradition would be a dangerous combination with that hothead of his. Still, Darnuir had proved himself. He had killed Scythe, won the day, and Blaine had given him the King's armour. The rest, he prayed, would come in time. Fidelm seemed to be mulling it over. "I thought we might allow our men to rest here before moving to Brevia," Blaine continued. "This day is done at any rate."

"Rest would do everyone some good, particularly the humans," Fidelm said. Blaine clenched his jaw with a low growl. "Is something amiss, Blaine?"

"Are there many hunters within the city?"

"A few hundred," said Fidelm.

"Have them brought out to join their fellows," Blaine said, waving a hand behind him. All the hunters left after the battle of the Charred Vale were wedged together between the legions. If any of the wretches tried to betray them now, they'd be swiftly crushed.

"I do not underst—"

"I shall explain but when we have more privacy."

Fidelm nodded again, though slowly. "Open the gate," he yelled. The sound of chinking chains and mechanisms followed, and the thick oak doors swung inwards. Blaine threw up a staying hand to the legates who were awaiting their orders. His Light Bearers knew to follow, however, and walked with him and Fidelm into the city.

"Stay vigilant," Blaine told his Light Bearers. "Our enemies could be anywhere."

Fidelm shot him a wary look before muttering to some nearby fairies. They flew off and Fidelm spoke quietly to Blaine.

"I shall take you into the fairy quarter, Guardian. We may trust the ears there."

Blaine kept close to Fidelm, and his Light Bearers fanned out in an arc behind them. He took in the scene of Inverdorn. In his long life, he had travelled to most places in the world, even if only once. Inverdorn was no exception. On their way to the fairy quarter, they passed the shores of Loch Minian. A small harbour, although far larger than the rundown jetties of Torridon. It lay in silence.

Blaine remembered it as a bustling place, stuffed with fishing boats, merchant and passenger barges, taking goods and those with the coin quickly across the loch. Now it seemed a watery graveyard of forgotten ships. The market strip at the harbour's edge was also dead. There ought to have been the smell of sweet or bitter shimmer brew stalls mixed with the pang of fish and their purveyors yelling about their freshness. He recalled the barges being loaded with grain from the Golden Crescent and the comforting smell from the bakeries nearby. There had even been a fairy painting market-goers for a few coins. She'd get her subjects to sit on a stool in front of her while she worked them up. It had been a very different place back then, whenever that had been. A slower time; a peaceful time.

Is it my fault the world has turned to this? Death and mistrust. War and more war. My failure; my fault?

"Many people escaped before the demons cut the town off," Fidelm said, as if sensing Blaine's morose thoughts.

"It is not the city I remember," Blaine noted. There was one easel set up at the edge of the embankment, half a picture of a glittering loch sketched out, as if it were a ghost of former times.

"Perhaps I will have a chance to finish this tomorrow," Fidelm said, collecting his equipment.

"I have not seen you paint in many years," Blaine said.

"I find it cathartic to create something after a battle." Fidelm held up his work to inspect it briefly. "A little rough. I might be out of practice." Yet the general did not seem perturbed and motioned to Blaine they should continue.

They veered off the shoreline and wove back through the narrower streets, where the shopfronts and homes steadily became more colourful. Painted patterns and trees had been brushed up; some silver, some burnt black, some brown and green, just like the forest of Val'tarra. Fairies had made this area of town feel a bit more like home. Val'tarra had been Blaine's home for so long now that he found himself feeling more comfortable as well.

Fidelm paused to let a band of Crescent Hunters march by, with fairies at the front and the back of their column. The Crescent Hunters were hunched and wide-eyed, and looked to Blaine as they passed. He saw their eyes take in his armour; thick, starium reinforced plate, with pauldrons shaped into large halves of a radiant sun. Blaine lifted his chin and pursed his lips. These hunters could be friend or foe. Better to keep them afraid just in case. Best to show them the might of the dragons. They passed soon enough and Fidelm continued.

"Are you sure this is necessary, Blaine?"

"Quite sure. Have you known me to do things without reason?"

"No. But I know you can be... extreme with your feelings."

"Extreme?" Blaine said. Fidelm faced him, one eyebrow raised. "Keep it to yourself for now," Blaine told him. How much Fidelm knew, Blaine could not have said. Likely he knew too much. The general was confidant to his Queen in many matters. Why not her past relationships as well?

Thinking of her was a mistake.

Kasselle's voice drifted unbidden into his mind, *"I don't think you should come back."* Unbidden, Blaine's hand curled inwards – searching for hers.

"Let us talk here," Fidelm said, leading them into a crammed garden square. Grass replaced the dirt and cobbles underfoot, and in the centre of the space grew a lone silver tree.

"I was not aware this area was so strong with the Cascade," Blaine said.

"The Dorain runs from the Highlands as well," Fidelm said, walking up to place a hand upon the silver bark. "The waters aren't as potent as the River Avvorn but they still carry some energy. When fairies first took this area for our own, they carried water from the river and wet the earth, hoping a piece of home would grow."

"It is as good a place as any to talk. Light Bearers," Blaine said, rounding on his men, "watch the streets and alleys. I will not be disturbed."

"Yes, Lord Guardian," they chanted. Fidelm gave a silent nod to the fairies in the vicinity and they trotted off.

"Your men seem to be in good spirits after the battle," said Blaine.

"Casualties were low," Fidelm said. "Not much the demons could do. They fought hard though, and something peculiar did occur."

"With the spectres?" Blaine said knowingly.

"Indeed. You experienced something similar, I assume?"

"If the spectres here also abandoned the battlefield, then yes."

"It was as well they did," said Fidelm. "During the battle, the number of spectres we were fighting suddenly swelled and I thought the demons might hold. Hundreds of spectres joined the battle at once, yelling at each other. Yet as quickly as they appeared, they left, every one of them. Victory came easily after that as the demons went wild."

"They also fled at the Charred Vale," Blaine said. "According to Darnuir they scarpered after he killed Scythe."

"Scythe?" asked Fidelm, perplexed. "The dead Captain of the Boreac Hunters?"

"Turned out he wasn't as dead as we'd assumed," Blaine said. "Stone cold now though, his red eyes extinguished."

"What happened up there?" Fidelm said. "I've not failed to notice that Cosmo, or should I say, Prince Brallor, is not with you either. Has he run onto Brevia with Darnuir as well? Why would he leave his son behind with you? And what of this battle you speak of? I thought the plan was to harass the foe, not meet them in the open field."

"Cosmo is dead," Blaine said stiffly. "And I have his son. Cullen will be cared well enough for."

"He's dead?" Fidelm said, sounding crestfallen. "Of all the things to have gone wrong…"

"A lot went wrong," Blaine sighed. He explained everything as best he could; how the hunters, who had vanished as they marched east through Val'tarra, were red-eyed traitors in service to Castallan. He told Fidelm of their strength, their speed, their burning hatred for dragons. He left nothing out; not even Darnuir injuring that human boy, Balack. Cosmo's death was explained; pinned up against a tree by a sword. "There was even an incident with Cassandra," he added, darkly.

"What of her?"

"She was taken by a group of those red-eyed hunters. Back to the Bastion, I assume."

"Why take her?" Fidelm asked. "To lure Darnuir? The boy has a soft spot for her, that is clear at a hundred paces, but Castallan must know we would come for him eventually."

"It transpires she is really a princess, sister to Cosmo—"

"Brallor," Fidelm corrected.

"Dead, either way," Blaine said. "Cassandra's Arkus' daughter. Taken by Castallan when Aurisha fell."

"For what purpose?" Fidelm said.

"Leverage, presumably."

"Perhaps once," said Fidelm. "Yet Arkus remarried. He has a new son; a new heir. I cannot imagine Arkus being held in place for fear of a daughter he never knew. Not after all these years."

"You'd know better than I," Blaine said.

"And you would know if you took a greater interest in the humans," Fidelm said.

Blaine ignored him. "Arkus cannot be the best of leaders, if he has allowed his people to become so fractured; willing to turn to a traitorous wizard who fraternises with Rectar."

"Arkus has lasted this long. There must be something to him. Handling that Assembly is no easy feat. Takes both subtlety and a good measure of cunning." Fidelm stared at Blaine for a moment, then looked up. Blaine had heard it too. It sounded like something had landed in the branches, but he saw nothing other than a few silver leaves fluttering down.

"And you sent Darnuir to Brevia?" Fidelm continued. "On his own? Humanity will shut its gates to us."

"Of course, I didn't," Blaine said, snapping his eyes back from above. "He went of his own accord. Yet they might be more willing to listen to him, given his upbringing amongst humans. And I'm hopeful Brackendon will guide hi—"

There was a squawk from above and Kymethra descended from the upper branches in a storm of feathers, morphing from eagle to woman. Her green robes flapped around her from the force of the fall and she bore her eyes into Blaine's "Brackendon? I've not seen him with you. Blaine, tell me. Is the man I love—"

"He was quite well last I saw him," Blaine said irritably. "This was meant to be a private discussion, Kymethra." She visibly sagged with relief.

"I'll leave you be," she said. "Just tell me where he went."

"To Brevia with Darnuir," said Blaine.

"Then I'll go now," Kymethra said. She stood poised, ready to jump back into her eagle form. "Any message you'd like me to take?"

"Only that I have arrived at Inverdorn," said Blaine. "Tell Darnuir I will allow the men to rest, then rendezvous at Brevia as planned." With that, Kymethra leapt into the air. Her body transformed into the tawny eagle in one fluid motion, the white tips of her feathers shining brightly as she caught the setting sun.

"Well," Fidelm said with an air of finality. "The humans will be watched for now. I shall let you take your rest, Guardian."

"I need no rest. I rested for decades. It is time I made up for it. What of the dragons that were held up here before you lifted the siege? Were any injured or killed?"

"Yes, as often occurs in battles. We set up a field hospital at one of the larger dry docks."

"I shall visit them. Their faith is likely to be lacking after their ordeals."

Fidelm gave an exaggerated bow. "I shall have you escorted there. We shall speak later, I'm sure."

The fairy who led Blaine and his Light Bearers to the field hospital was quick and quiet. That suited Blaine just fine. The evening was nice enough after all. A clear sky meant the odds of a spectre attack were minimal, if the spectres were even coming back. The water on Loch Minian was flat and glassy, reflecting Inverdorn like a mirror; each building, each boat and each pebble on the shore. And then he saw them, reflected on the water's surface: barrels.

So many of them. Scores of them, strung out in stacks along the wharfs. Blaine looked up and saw they ran up to the edge of the building his fairy guide was entering.

Blaine's heart missed one long beat.

"Wait," he called out to the fairy. "Do you know what is in these barrels?"

The fairy looked confused in the direction Blaine was pointing. "No, Lord Guardian," he said. "At least, not all. Many were scattered throughout the city. Some have fruit from Val'tarra, many grain from the Crescent. Some contain a strange black powder no one recognises."

Blaine felt a chill. Black powder; dragon powder; the substance that blazed a trail of destruction on their run from Torridon. He turned to his Light Bearers. All had been on that run. Their faces showed they understood. "We must separate the barrels of black powder," he told them quickly. "They mustn't be close to each other or the city. Take them out to the shore or into the loch itself. I don't want them anywhere near the army."

"Yes, Lord Guardian," they said in unison and hurried off.

"Take no risks," Blaine called after them. "No flame must come near the powder. Work fast to beat the dying sun." The fairy guide looked apprehensive. "Are there any more within the city?"

"Possibly, sir."

"Possibly?" said Blaine, his voice rising. "Return to General Fidelm at once. We must find every single barrel of black powder and move them to a safe location. I should have warned Fidelm of this danger but how was I to know…" he trailed off, speaking more to himself. The fairy stood stock-still, unsure. "Well? Go!" Blaine told him and the wingless fairy scarpered. Blaine took a deep breath before entering the dry dock that doubled as a field hospital.

Cranes, pulleys, saws and other tools had been pushed against the walls to open out the space. Dragons, fairies and humans lay bedridden in various bloodied states. Fairy healers glided elegantly around, supported by some hunter colleagues. And was that one of his Light Bearers amongst the sick dragons? It was either that or another dragon had stolen one of their shields. He had his back to Blaine, leaning over a dragon whose head was covered in bandages soaked with dark blood.

"You there," Blaine called. "Light Bearer." The dragon turned, but his expression was not guilty. Blaine recognised those light brown curls, olive skin and a presence Blaine could not quite explain, yet it was there. Irrefutably so. Blaine had been keeping his eye on Bacchus since the Charred Vale. The young Light Bearer was now one of the most enthusiastic in his duties.

As Bacchus stepped away from the bedside the wounded dragon grabbed his hand. "No. Please," he said. "Don't leave — the pain…"

"I shall return shortly, brother," Bacchus said and gently kissed the injured dragon on the brow.

A little tender, perhaps. But it does have a comforting effect.

"Lord Guardian, I thought there would be dragons here in need of N'weer's blessing," Bacchus said. His voice was measured and steady.

"I would not have neglected them," Blaine said.

"I did not envision you would, your holiness. I only sought to serve while you attended other matters. Forgive me."

Blaine noticed that nearly every dragon was looking their way. More specifically, they were looking to Bacchus.

"You are forgiven, brother Bacchus," Blaine said. "But know that I trust my Light Bearers to many important tasks, not only in the work of the gods. You were on duty to guard Cullen for a reason."

"Four Light Bearers seemed sufficient for an infant human."

"An infant human that finds itself the heir to the throne of Brevia."

"I only wished to help our own people. Forgive me, Lord Guardian."

His earnestness cooled Blaine. "We defend our race's faith but we guard it in other ways as well. You acquitted yourself well in the battle. A talented warrior and devout believer such as yourself holds great promise. Trust in me and you will see the Light."

"How may I serve?" Bacchus asked.

"Return to comforting the wounded for now. I—"

"Lord Guardian," a voice said from behind. Blaine turned to see three Light Bearers.

"I thought I gave clear instruction?" he barked at them.

"We'll need more help to move all these barrels before sundown, sir," the leading Light Bearer said. That worried Blaine. Healers around the dry dock were lighting candles already.

"I shall aid you," Bacchus offered.

"Very well," said Blaine. "One of you run and fetch more of your brothers with all haste. As many as you see fit, but ensure a strong guard is kept on the child, Cullen. The rest of you go to help with the barrels." They all dashed off, drawing stares from the wounded and the healers. Blaine was on the verge of leaving to deal with the barrel issue when something stopped him, or rather someone.

Though he was at some distance, one of the hunters seemed familiar. He was in white leathers from the waist down, but his torso was bare, revealing his bandaged chest. He favoured one side as he carefully got into a battered bed, helped along by a healer. Blaine was sure it was Balack.

Something came over Blaine when he saw him. It wasn't pity, not exactly. Darnuir had been brash and foolish in striking him, but all Blaine really knew was the two had once been firm friends. Likely, that was no longer the case. Still, Balack knew Darnuir in ways that Blaine did not, and if Blaine shared his secrets with Darnuir, he would get to know Darnuir's in turn. It would be painful enough for Blaine. His heart ached at the thought Arlandra. How had he let such horrors befall his only daughter? Instinctively, he reached for the necklace and lightly touched the little A upon it, under the apple of his throat.

The crowd parted before him as he made his way towards Balack and the air grew sweet.

They are afraid of me. Good.

"Are you the hunter named Balack?" Blaine asked.

"I think you know that," Balack said. His voice was hoarse, as though it pained him to draw breath. He winced as the healer made a W shape with her hands and gently pushed her palms on the bruised area of his chest.

"Breathe in for me," she instructed, shooting an apprehensive look at Blaine. Balack breathed in, but gasped midway.

"Gah. I'm sorry."

"Don't be," said the healer. "A damaged rib is no minor thing." She pressed the palms on the healthy side of Balack's chest. "Again, if you can." Balack breathed in, slower than before, and managed to do so without stopping this time. Blaine saw the pain in the boy's bloodshot, watery eyes.

"You're doing well," the healer said. "Expansion is up from a few days ago. I just need a quick listen." She brought out a small brass device, like a horn. She pressed the larger end against Balack's injured side and her ear to the other.

Balack groaned again. "Strong aren't you. You dragons. Could crush us all with your bare hands." Blaine looked the boy in the eye and Balack did not turn away. Blaine sniffed gently at the air. The sweetness had grown, but he doubted it was from Balack. "I'm as fine as I'm going to be today," Balack told the healer. "You should tend to people who need you more."

"Make sure you move as little as possible," the healer said. As she left, the potency of the sweet smell diminished.

"She's afraid of me," Blaine said.

"Of course she is," Balack wheezed. "You've treated every human at the Charred Vale like a criminal. We're not the enemy."

"How can I possibly know that?" asked Blaine. "When your own Captain Scythe turned out to be a traitor. Not only a traitor but the leader of Castallan's forces, no less."

"People are good at hiding their true selves, I'll grant you that, Guardian."

"I've wondered where Darnuir got his insolence from. Maybe you were the bad influence on him."

Balack made a pained smile. "What do you want?"

"To know why Darnuir struck you?"

"Not out of concern for me, I'd wager," said Balack.

"I will be blunt with you. There are things about my past that Darnuir wishes to know. One day soon, I shall have to tell him. But I find it most unjust that he should have things hidden from me. We are linked Balack, Darnuir and I," he unsheathed the Guardian's Blade, "our swords are linked. If he is to be at my side when we face Rectar, I'd know everything about him."

At last, Balack turned his gaze away from Blaine. The boy wasn't hesitant to speak, just saddened. "Why did he hit me? Well, a painful secret was revealed to me, and I said some rather nasty things to him in return. And then he lost his temper… all over something rather pathetic in the end." His gasping voice finally broke.

"There was a girl," Blaine said. It was a statement, not a question.

"He told you? Heh," Balack's laugh was blunted and pained. "Suppose he told everyone before me." Another gasp. "And he never even told me."

"He didn't tell me," said Blaine. "But I'm old, boy. When you've lived to see generation after generation grow, you see the same patterns repeating. A common way for two friends to come to blows."

Balack closed his eyes. "I loved her, she did not love me. Darnuir knew, but that did not stop him."

"Yes. I've heard that tale before."

Balack reopened his eyes, a colder fury in them now. "You want loyalty? Don't rely on him."

"I'm afraid I'll have to," said Blaine. He looked Balack over again and the pity he'd felt changed. Something in Blaine compelled him to say, "I understand the pain you're feeling."

"I don't need your false sympathy," Balack said.

"It's not false. I told you, I'm old. You don't get to my age without losing a lot. Like those you love the most." *What's come over me? Why am I talking about this with him?*

"Does it get any better?" Balack said.

"Barely, but you learn to soldier on anyway. You learn to throw yourself into your duty or find something to wake up for besides the person who's forever gone."

And I must learn to let Kasselle go. I have my purpose again. Prepare Darnuir, restore faith to the dragons. Defeat the Shadow. Enough to get on with. Despite this, his hand curled in. When it found only air, he had to fight back a tear. *Not in front of the human. Get a grip on your emotions.*

Balack rubbed at something in his eye. "Is there anything else you need, Guardian?"

"Not now. N'weer speed you to health, human."

"I thought your gods only —" he stopped, staring behind Blaine.

"What's wrong?" Blaine asked, spinning to see for himself. Not far away from them, at the main entranceway to the dry dock, fairies were moving equipment to make space. As Blaine watched he saw them uncover four dark barrels. One lifted the lid to see what was inside, waving at his fellow to come over. The companion held a torch.

Blaine's blood turned to ice.

His heart stopped.

Then came the flash.

It seemed to take forever for the bang to reach him, an ear-splitting roar.

Something in him reacted and he threw himself between the blast and Balack. He felt the impact on his back, his starium reinforced armour absorbing the blows of debris. Intense heat followed and Blaine thought he would cook alive in his metal casing.

He looked down at the human he was shielding. Balack's eyes were white in shock. He'd curled up into a ball despite his broken rib.

Blaine held on.

He realised he was screaming but couldn't hear himself. Then he choked, gasping in pain as something hot and sharp pierced the back of his knee, between the joints in his armour. He buckled but kept low over Balack.

He just held on.

Chapter 4

THE COURT OF BREVIA

When Dranus returned, he claimed the gods were using the dragons as tools in an endless fight against the Shadow. Furious, Aurisha dubbed his brother a heretic, exiling him and those who had been cursed into human bodies. Out of brotherly love, Aurisha allowed them to go in peace, thinking that they would wither and die in time.

From Tiviar's Histories

Darnuir – Brevia – The Throne Room

"**N**ERVOUS?" BRACKENDON ASKED, as they waited to enter King Arkus' throne room. The door in front of them was immense. Painted black, it was patterned with white gold and had sliding openings that allowed the attending servants to mutter quietly to colleagues on the other side.

"Not at all," Darnuir said. "Some rest would have been welcome, but it cannot be helped." He yawned and strained to keep his eyes open.

Arkus wouldn't have been difficult to deal with if Darnuir's memories of his former self had born any accuracy, but he hadn't been left full memories of the Human King, so much as feelings and impressions he had of Arkus back then. All were laced with derision and scorn, making them far from intimidating.

"You seem half asleep," Lira said.

She's right. I need to be more alert than this.

Darnuir touched the blood-red hilt of the Dragon's Blade with the tips of his fingers, opening the door to the Cascade by a crack. Energy dripped into his system, staving off the worst aches of his muscles. He felt lighter, even glad, as the residue drained down his right arm.

"You shouldn't rely on that," Brackendon said so only Darnuir could hear.

Darnuir let go of the Dragon's Blade. "It was only a little."

"A little is how it begins. A lot is how you break."

"I am about to meet another king," Darnuir said. "I hope to show Arkus that I am a changed dragon. It won't do for me to fall asleep in the middle of the conversation."

"Being polite won't go amiss either. Mind your manners." Nearby, a servant wearing a black velvet doublet over a white shirt coughed loudly. "See, he knows what I mean," Brackendon said.

"Does Arkus usually keep guests waiting this long?" Darnuir said.

"His majesty will call for you when he is ready," the servant said laboriously.

"He knows there is a war on, right?" Darnuir said. The servant provided no response, which irked Darnuir.

Is this some power play? Making me wait while an invasion looms upon us, while Castallan is still at large – while Cassandra is still hostage…

He breathed gently through his nose and calmed. He shouldn't get wound up before even entering the court.

"What about you, Lira?" Darnuir asked. "Nervous?"

She bit her lip, thinking for a moment. "As nervous as when I met you. Kings can have that effect."

"I feel that was due to Blaine's ever-soothing presence."

"The Lord Guardian was certainly intimidating," Lira said.

"Still, you held your ground," Darnuir said. "You won me over that day and this time you have the company of forty loyal dragons." The stony-faced servant, who had an ear against one of the openings, coughed again.

"Can we be of assistance?" Brackendon asked.

"Will all of your company be entering the throne room?" asked the servant.

"Certainly," said Darnuir. "I'm sure the court will not object to the presence of my Praetorian Guard." More muttering was exchanged at the door. To his side, Darnuir heard Brackendon wince again.

"Are you sure you are alright?"

"It's not sore, it's…" but whatever it was Brackendon seemed reluctant to say. He held his head and scrunched his eyes shut. "It's nothing. I think I just need to sit for a moment," he said, dropping into a plush high back chair with a footstool. "We ran a long way after all." He sighed and stretched out luxuriously.

"You may enter, Lord Darnuir," announced the servant. Brackendon grumbled as he got back up.

"Form ranks," Darnuir ordered and the dragons snapped into place.

The huge throne room doors opened silently, revealing a long hall with polished benches, facing each other in rows along the high walls. At the distant end sat a black throne on a raised white stone platform. On the upper benches the people were finely dressed, the extravagance of the garments diminishing with each level to those standing in attendance. Black walls continued high up into an arching roof, as though the throne room was draped in a dark cloak. And above, a system of shutters directed light to bathe the clean white floor before the throne.

"Announcing Lord Darnuir, King of Dragons," the servant called and audible murmuring swept through the court. "The Reborn King, wielder of the Dragon's Blade." The murmuring grew louder. "Also announcing," the servant went on, straining to be heard, "Brackendon, The Last Wizard."

"If only it wasn't so," muttered Brackendon.

"And the dragon Lira," the servant added. "Prefect of the Praetorian Guard."

Darnuir heard Lira gulp.

"Head up now," he told her, then took his first steps into the warm, stuffy throne room. Thick wafts of lavender and honey clogged his nose. He wondered whether the perfume was for his benefit or those on the benches. Such a sweetness would mask any sickly sweet scent of human fear.

He focused on the great chair at the end of the runway, kept his face passive and walked with confidence. He was a dragon; the King of

Dragons. In military matters, he held command of the Three Races. Even Arkus must answer to him.

But Arkus was not sitting on his throne.

Arkus wasn't there at all.

A line of guards stood before the steps to the throne's platform, but Darnuir struggled to see due to the angle of the light that was now shining into his eyes. Entering the pool of light made it worse. What lay at the top of the stairs was now a mystery. Yet the dark-steel armour of the guards was familiar; their faces hidden behind closed visors. Darnuir stopped as close as he dared to them, within arm's length.

All was still. He could hear the breath of the closest Chevalier. Ahead, a door opened with a swish, followed by a pit-patter of soft-soled shoes along the platform.

"Halt there, my Lord of Dragons," a voice announced. The speaker had a distinct pomposity about him.

I know that voice. It's the Chevalier from Inverdorn.

"Raymond?" Darnuir said.

"Silence while you await his Majesty," said Raymond. Yes, it was most certainly the Chevalier.

More time passed.

More silence.

Come along, Arkus. We do not have time to wait on games and posturing.

Yet more time drifted on and still the hall was silent.

Then, without warning, the light shifted.

Shutters over the windows were repositioned and the platform of the throne was thrown into relief. The black chair was simple but arresting, and a smaller version stood beside it. The change of light must have been a signal to the court because Darnuir heard everyone in the hall get to their feet.

Finally, a door at the back of platform opened with a bang and King Arkus strode into view. His feet were hidden beneath his long black robes with white trimmed edges. Darnuir's memory of Arkus was of a man with black hair to match his attire, yet the years had greyed him, his stubble was now a beard and his eyes, though small, were probing.

Arkus made a meal out of sitting down, sinking slowly into his throne. When, at last, he was settled, the shutters above snapped loudly, changing the direction of the light. A few faint rays converged just above Arkus' head, illuminating his crown. Arced and falling, like crashing waves, the crown looked to be pure white gold. It was a speck of radiance amongst the darkness of his robes, his throne and his expression.

The silence held a while longer.

Darnuir lost his patience and said, "How long must the King of Dragons wait? How long mus—" But Arkus threw out a hand towards him.

Darnuir felt a hot prickle on the back of his neck. A little heat even crept dangerously up his throat and he felt the Dragon's Blade warm at his waist.

No, I must show that I have changed.

"The court will remain standing for the *King's Lament*," Raymond said.

From the front of the crowd, two minstrels made their way onto the platform: one all in black, the other in white. The minstrel in white produced a flute and began to play sombrely at a high pitch, as though a deep and devouring sadness was whistling on the wind. The minstrel in black began to sing, his voice light yet tinged with melancholy:

> *There once was a black haired beauty,*
> *With starlight in her eyes,*
> *There once was a black haired beauty,*
> *Her smile was my demise,*
> *There once was a black haired beauty,*
> *Whom I loved with all my soul,*
> *There once was a black haired beauty,*
> *Now there's no one there —*
> *At all.*

The singer's voice cracked poignantly on the final words, as though the full weight of his grief had become unbearable. Both performers gave a small bow and then hurried off.

Two more people walked onto the platform. A pale woman came first, wearing a tiara of white gold on top of her elaborately tied blond hair. She took the smaller seat beside Arkus. Darnuir assumed she was the Queen, although he had no memory of her.

Am I looking at Cosmo's mother? If so, she will be Cassandra's mother as well, although they look nothing alike.

Behind her came a man, and one singularly out of place. He had a wind-beaten, squashed face that was coated in a reddish fuzz. His figure was slender, his movements fox-like. Short in stature and short on adornments, his only jewellery was the longship broach pinned to his chest. He stood on Arkus' left, between the King and Raymond.

Arkus, who's hand had remained outstretched for the whole song, finally brought his arm back in. He paused to cover his eyes, as if he were crying. Then, at last, it was done. Those gathered in the hall sat back down.

"My good king," Darnuir said, forcing down the heat in this throat. "We have run far and hard for days to reach you."

"No one asked you to." Each word Arkus said was well measured to ring throughout the hall. "You have come unannounced. You have come without invitation. You have come seeking the blood of my people."

"Bodies, bought and bled," came a soft echoing chant from around the room. It wasn't said by all but it was said by enough. *This isn't going to be easy.*

"It is Rectar that seeks to bleed your people dry," Darnuir said. "I only ask that some is spilt. All the Three Races will suffer before the end. I request that humanity's armies join me in destroying Castallan at the Bastion. I ask they join me to meet a demon invasion I have warning will come from the east."

"Yes, this invasion," Arkus said airily. "Raymond dutifully informed me," and he waved a hand at the Chevalier. It was only now that Darnuir realised Raymond was not in armour like the other Chevaliers. Instead, he was in more courtly attire, a black velvet jerkin over a white shirt.

"I am glad to see you heeded his warning," said Darnuir. "Having your armies gathered will save precious time."

"Ha," squawked the man beside Arkus. "Time's oot, am afraid." He had a sharp voice, as though he was permanently biting into a lemon.

"My Lord Darnuir," Arkus began, with barely concealed bitterness. "May I introduce to you Somerled Imar, Lord of the Splintering Isles. He arrived not two days ago, with harrowing news."

Darnuir's stomach knotted, knowing fine well what that news would be. The Splintering Isles lay between east and west.

"A pleasure, Lord Darnuir," Somerled said, bowing. "The Splintering Isles are already under attack. My son, Grigayne, leads a desperate defence of our lands." A great deal of murmuring then rose in the hall.

"Silence," Raymond called.

The knot tightened in Darnuir. "I am deeply troubled to hear that, Lord Somerled. My thoughts are with your son and your people."

"I'd rather have yer sword and yer dragons," Somerled said. "What good are thoughts?"

"My dragons are still scattered," Darnuir said. "Although many have arrived outside Brevia, I noticed. It grieves me to hear that the fight has already come on two fronts but Castallan has to be removed first before we can aid the Splinters."

"On that I agree," Arkus said. "The wizard has remained at large for too long. Yet I am hesitant to move, Darnuir. That fortress will not fall easily. You ask for some blood to be spilt, yet, if we throw ourselves against the Bastion, then blood will surely gush."

"Nor will the Splinters last if ye have tae lay a siege," Somerled said.

"We'll be forced to assault the fortress," said Darnuir. "But I am hopeful it will fall without us wasting lives."

Darnuir knew that Cassandra had escaped through some secret tunnels. If they could be found again then countless lives would be spared. Arkus, of course, knew none of this, so he added, "I can explain this to you in private."

"Oh, can you?" Arkus said. "I'd listen more closely if you had more to offer than vague promises."

"Offer you?" Darnuir said, fighting down a fresh rage. *Calm. I must remain calm. This is just the exhaustion.*

Yet Arkus' smug look reignited the heat in his throat. Pressure built at the door to the Cascade in his mind, looking to fuel the fire.

I must be better than I was.

"Yes," said Arkus impatiently. "What do you offer me in return for my armies and my fleet? Dragons alone cannot win this fight. Dragons die the same, after all."

That did it.

"Offer, Arkus?" Darnuir roared. In doing so, he lost control of the door in his mind; it slipped ajar and a stream of cascade energy surged into him. It magnified his voice to dominate the throne room. "I am the King of Dragons. Commander in Chief of the Three Races, am I not? I do not offer, Arkus. I demand." Outrage erupted from the audience. Hearing swords slide from sheaths behind him, Darnuir spun to reassure his Praetorians, gesturing they lower their weapons. Brackendon groaned, audible even over the outpouring from the crowd, but Darnuir knew what would quieten them. "What I will offer you is news," he yelled. "News of your son, and daughter." The crowd settled. The Queen gasped, looking stricken.

"They are alive?" she said, half-shaking, though whether from fear or happiness Darnuir couldn't tell.

"Hush now, Orrana," Arkus said softly, offering her his hand. Orrana took it and seemed to settle. Then Arkus rounded on Darnuir. "My son is dead. My daughter was lost to me too or do you not recall that?"

"My memories from my past life are few but, yes, I remember that," Darnuir said. His voice had returned to normal. He did not wish to mention that he had failed Cassandra a second time.

She was too close.

"Yet I promise you Cassandra is alive," Darnuir said. "Taken hostage by Castallan. I swear to you she lives." Arkus didn't even flinch at the words. He seemed unmoved. "I must also tell you of your son, Brallor, though I knew him as Cosmo." This time Arkus' features snapped into focus, as he peered down at Darnuir.

"If you are here to open old wounds then I must caution you. The last time I laid eyes on you, Darnuir, you held my infant daughter in your arms. And the contempt I saw in your eyes panicked me. I feared you would simply dash her head upon the rocks that separated us. It worked out the same. You failed to make it through Aurisha to me and my daughter was lost."

The hall murmured once more, as though they had rehearsed this timing.

"And you were never to see my grief, my woe," Arkus went on. "As if you would have cared. It was almost too much to bear, to lose a second child. The pain – you cannot imagine. My first wife could not weather it.

Her heart broke first and her body followed." Arkus paused. The Queen beside him, his new Queen, squeezed her husband's hand. "My son is dead," Arkus said flatly. "Do not think some memory of him will help me now."

"Arkus, painful though it is, you must hear this," Darnuir said. "It has bearing upon you all. Your son lived. Brallor lived. He spent his years in the Boreac Mountains as a hunter."

"It is true, majesty," Brackendon interjected. "I must admit I was the one who took him from you. He asked me to take him away from the city, as far away as I could. I took him to Cold Point, where my staff tree once grew."

Arkus got up from his throne. "Will you make a mockery of my court with these stories? Demand your armies Darnuir and be gone!"

The crowd grew more restless, shouting, taunting and jeering.

"Sire," Lira cautioned Darnuir, but he pushed on. This wound Arkus bore still had poison in it. The man needed it drawn. He needed closure.

"He took a new name, Cosmo," Darnuir bellowed, "and he took a wife. They had a son."

This time the silence was so complete that Darnuir felt he had gone deaf. Arkus' face froze, his mouth half open. Queen Orrana paled even further, turning as white as the floor on which Darnuir stood.

"A son?" she said shrilly.

"Cullen is his name. Your grandson."

"How old is he?" snapped the Queen.

"Mere months," Darnuir said. "Only a baby. But an heir all the same."

"Silence," Arkus cried, all his stiffness gone.

"My king and husband has an heir," Orrana said tartly. "Our son, Thane, a boy of eight years. A good and strong prince."

"And unlikely tae make it tae his ninth year if that cough keeps up," Somerled said. Orrana shot him a look of pure venom. "Oh, it's terrible sounding," Somerled added, a cunning smile playing on his lips.

"Enough," Arkus said, looking first to Somerled, then his wife, then Darnuir. "You dragons and your tempers. You have my full attention now, Dragon King. I hope that satisfies you. We shall speak later. The court is dismissed."

"You will rise for the King," cried Raymond, but his voice was drowned by the crowd.

"Bought and bled. Bought and bled. Bought and bled."

"Order," Raymond yelled but it had little effect. The Chevaliers around the platform braced themselves, hands flying to the hilts of their weapons.

"Bought and bled. Bought and bled. Bought and bled."

Chevaliers were moving to encircle Arkus and Orrana, waving urgently, and attempting to take them away. Somerled Imar had quietly slipped away in the confusion.

"Bought and bled. Bought and bled. Bought and bled for dragon wars."

Darnuir felt something smash off his heavy pauldrons. Shards of glass littered the white stone at his feet and an amber liquid dripped off his armour. Soon more items were being thrown down on him and his Praetorians. They drew their swords in response. Darnuir didn't stop them. He'd just put an end to it.

Pulling forth the Dragon's Blade, Darnuir launched a blistering lance of fire into the air. He sent it up to the ceiling then split the flames and sent four strands arching against the roof of the hall. The noise of it covered even the shrieking crowd and after holding it for a few moments, Darnuir killed it, bringing a silence once more. His throat felt hot and raw, but he barely even felt the residue from the Cascade flow down his arm. A gentle kick hit the back of his head and he felt very satisfied. A grin broke out across his face.

I must be getting more used to it. I can handle more.

In the eerie quiet, not a soul stirred in the hall other than Arkus.

The Human King got back to his feet. "The court is dismissed."

Chapter 5

THE CASCADE CONCLAVE

Despite their exile, Dranus and his Black Dragons flourished. They found a new home at Kar'drun, building the world's first great city on the eastern coast and burrowed into the mountain itself for extra safety. Aurisha became concerned that Dranus would use the Cascade under Kar'drun to try and reach the gods again. More than that, he worried that Dranus had fallen to the Shadow. And so Aurisha convinced the fairies to aid him in transforming the rest of his true dragons into human form, in order that they might root out the Black Dragons from their mountain home. This was the Third Flight and the start of a long, devastating conflict.

From Tiviar's Histories

Brackendon – Brevia – The Rotting Hill

AFTER THE EXCITEMENT of the throne room, Brackendon was more than happy to seek a little quiet. Though whether that quiet would benefit him or not was another matter. While Darnuir had chased after Arkus, Brackendon had excused himself. He had some personal business to attend to. He was going to the Cascade Conclave.

The tower of the Conclave loomed upon a hill in the north-west of the city and could be seen from any point in Brevia. Only the enormous white bridge that spanned the far banks of the city could rival its height. From a street near the edge of the borough, Brackendon glanced at the tower and pulled up the hood of his cloak against the drizzling rain. The weather had turned foul since their entry to the capital that morning, it was now muggy and Brackendon's robes were sticking to his skin. No one paid him any attention as he walked; city dwellers hurried about their business or went indoors to escape the unpleasant weather.

As he approached the borough of the Conclave, he wondered what had become of the botany shops, bookmakers, and especially the bakers who made their living from the Conclave's existence. Within another street or so he saw his answer.

Closed.

Closed, boarded up or looted. And this was just one street a fair distance away.

There was something akin to mist before him, a blue and silver fog floating unnaturally at waist height. It halted abruptly halfway up this street, creating a border with the rest of the city. He looked once more towards the tower.

And he heard the whisper again.

Brraaaccck-eendon.

It was the feeblest of voices, but a voice nonetheless. He thought he had first heard it when he'd reached the outskirts of the city and then again outside the throne room.

Brraaaccck-eendon.

It sounded uncertain, as though the speaker were learning a new language. Yet there was also an agony in it that chilled his blood more than any demon ever had. Whatever it was, his instincts told him it came from the tower.

He took his first steps into the swirling vapour.

"Wait," a small voice said. Brackendon turned slowly and found himself facing a group of young children, too young to be out on their own. A bold boy in baggy clothes spoke to him. "You can't go that way. It's haunted."

"Haunted by what?" Brackendon asked.

"A demon," said a little girl.

"No, it's a ghoul," another girl said. Both were shivering in the cold.

"It's a spirit of an ancient dragon," said the boy at the front. "My brother says it's what causes the smoke."

"I don't see any smoke?" said Brackendon.

"Comes at nights sometimes," said the boy. "Some nights there's lots and others there's none. Depends on how angry the spirit is, least that's what my brother says."

"Well, I'll keep an eye out for this spirit," Brackendon said. He stepped into the mist.

"You can't!" shrieked one of the girls.

"I know a dragon who can get especially angry," said Brackendon. "I can handle this... whatever it is. I can handle any ghoul or nasty thing." The children looked horrified. "Here take this or you'll freeze." He unfastened his cloak and wrapped it around the two smallest girls. He then pulled out a plump coin purse and tossed it into the middle of the group. "You spend that on food now." Delighted, the children gathered up the money and ran off. Brackendon tried to clear them from his mind before continuing his journey towards the tower.

After a few more deserted streets he'd seen no sign of any evil spirit, but he could feel the Cascade energy in the air. Not pure energy, such as it was when he called upon it, but rougher, worked, stretched thin and worn: more dangerous. He smelled a faint trace of smoke. It was sulphuric, as though from a large wood fire. Presently, there was no smoke but then it was growing darker and the children said the smoke came at night. With so much twisted Cascade energy affecting the borough, he supposed that small wildfires could start and stop without much reason. Though for it to happen regularly enough to require an angry spirit as explanation would be surprising, but not impossible.

I should have returned long ago. I might have done something.

Though what he might have done to spare Brevia this magical fallout he didn't know. Witches or wizards of the Inner Circle might have known yet the old order was dead. Literally. Only the tower remained. Only Brackendon remained.

And Castallan! I shouldn't have fled. I should have stayed to help when the fighting started.

But he hadn't. He'd run.

Not again. Never again.

As he trudged up the hill to the base of the Conclave tower, full of regret of his previous inaction, he saw that the earth between cracks in the paving slabs had turned a reddish colour and seemed dry.

Before long, the doors to the Conclave lay before him; broken, unlocked and yet entirely uninviting. Brackendon just stood there, staring at the entrance.

He didn't know how long he paused before the tower doors – long enough for the sky to darken and the rain to begin lashing down. He kept the rain off himself, manipulating the air around him. Guilt or fear rooted him in place, though he couldn't say which it was.

Then, something took hold of his hand. It was quite wet.

"I hope you weren't thinking on going in there without me?" Kymethra said. Brackendon's heart, his entire being, warmed at her voice.

"You look drowned," he said, facing her and pushing back a sodden clump of hair. He kissed her. "And you're freezing."

"Heat," she managed through chattering teeth.

"One moment. Stay close."

As she hugged in closer, Brackendon took back possession of his hand and opened his palm. A moment's thought, a nudge more on the door to the Cascade, and a hot ball of fire appeared. He felt a flow of magic through him then, from shoulder to hand, yet it seared so low it was almost pleasant, like the warming feeling of a strong drink. Keeping the fire burning cost little energy after all. Fire could destroy, and like movement it was cheap; for destruction is far easier than creation.

"That's better," Kymethra said. She clung to him and after a while stopped shivering and began to breathe normally again. Her hair dried and fluffed up, the white tips curling upwards in their usual flick. "Ready?" she asked, nodding to the Conclave doors.

"I am now," he said, extinguishing the orb of fire in his hand. Together they made their way inside.

The chill was the first thing that Brackendon noticed as they entered. It was unnaturally cold for the season, miserable weather outside notwithstanding. His breath rose in great clouds before his eyes.

"I think you'll need to relight that fire," Kymethra said.

Brackendon took some tentative steps down the dark, dank corridor. "I don't think so. It's unbearably hot here." He tugged at the collar of his robes.

Kymethra stepped to join him. "Ugh, we'll sweat to death like this. The Cascade is twisted here. Why come back?"

"I felt compelled… We don't know what really happened."

Brraaaccck-eendon, came the strange voice again, louder than outside the tower.

"What's there to know?" Kymethra crept past him. "All we'll come across are terrible memories. Bad memories or likely something dangerous – ouch, my knee. I can't see a thing. Hurry up and light the way."

"Sorry," Brackendon said, distracted. "Can you hear anything?"

"All I'm hearing is you are not giving us some light."

"Like a voice," Brackendon said. "Like a whisper."

"No… Come on now Brackers. Don't leave us in the dark."

Brackendon shook his head and lit up the end of his staff. The corridor was suddenly illuminated. Parchment was strewn everywhere, cushions lay ripped, furniture snapped, drawers pulled out of cabinets, and a trail of debris led into each room. He checked each one and found the shelves were completely bare, not a book or scroll was left on them. He thought that perhaps some brave looters might have taken them along with items of more obvious value.

At the end of the hallway was a winding staircase that would take them nowhere. Navigating the Conclave wasn't obvious. You had to know your way.

Brraaaccck-eendon. Up…

"There it is again."

"Not that I'm jealous," Kymethra said. "But why is it speaking to you?"

"I have no idea. It is saying 'up'."

"Up?" Kymethra said, rolling her eyes upwards as if she could see through to the top of the tower. "Well, let's go." She took a few more steps down the corridor, as though heading for the stairs, and sighed with relief. "Oh, it's not so hot here and mmm, it smells like alderberry pie."

"Kymethra, maybe we ought to turn back. I thought it would give me closure to come here; give us both closure. I thought I might find something to aid me against Castallan but there is no way he would have allowed anything valuable to be left behind."

Kymethra gave him that look that only she could. "Scared?"

"You're not the one hearing voices."

Up…

"I'm frightened too," Kymethra said. "This place used to be our whole lives. I'm terrified of what might be up there. We might even find your old hat." She shuddered at the thought. He smiled and then stepped towards her, happy to be out of the hot zone. Here the air really did smell deliciously tangy.

"That hat is what got your attention," Brackendon said. He kept on walking, veering into a side room that hid the real way to the higher levels of the tower.

"What got you my attention was my desperate need for help on elemental control."

"Shame you never really mastered it," said Brackendon. He twisted the inkwell at the special desk clockwise one full turn and a ramp descended from above. They began to ascend.

Up...Up. Brackkkkkkendon.

"Or maybe you were just a bad teacher," said Kymethra. "Good thing I make up for it with my mind tricks." She pressed three fingers over her ear in demonstration.

"Do you ever regret not completing your training?"

"A part of me does. I could be helping more than I am. But then—"

"You've seen what it did to me," Brackendon said. "I can't blame you for wishing to have nothing to do with the Cascade after that."

"Actually," she began, sounding slightly annoyed, "I was going to say that, had I completed my training you might not have come for me that day."

"Of course I would have," Brackendon said. "How could you say such a thing?"

"Stop interrupting," said Kymethra. She halted before three doors. "Wait a moment. These are the shifting doorways, aren't they? There used to be a method to figure out which one is real."

"Yes, there was," Brackendon said, racking his mind.

Left... something hissed. Brackendon twitched his head around. *Left...* The voice seemed to be getting stronger.

"I think it's that one," he said, pointing at the left-hand door.

"What's the trick?"

"I'm getting some help."

"Or you could be being led into the void."

"I'll go first then," said Brackendon. He pushed on it. "Stairs. I think we're safe. And I'm sorry for before, what were you trying to say?"

"That I'm glad I hadn't received my staff, when it — when it happened. Otherwise, you wouldn't have come to take me away when the fighting started. And don't try to pretend like that isn't true. I could see it in your eyes. I remember. I've never seen you so torn."

"It wasn't an easy choice. But that doesn't mean I regret coming for you. Not one bit."

"I know," Kymethra said and this time it was she who kissed him. "Nor do I regret smashing Malik's face in with my alchemy tome when he tried to stick that glass dagger into you."

"Malik," Brackendon sighed, remembering the young apprentice. "He was only seventeen."

"He was trying to kill you," Kymethra said.

"It sickens me how Castallan twisted their minds. He must have been working on the youngest apprentices for a long time to get so many to join him."

"Didn't sway me."

Brackendon realised he had never asked before. "Did he ever approach you or try to persuade you to overthrow the Conclave?"

"Not directly," said Kymethra. "He came to speak to us all often though. A lot about how we should be using our powers to help humanity become stronger; about how we could end the war and make a better world for humans; a world where we weren't at the mercy of the whims of demons or dragons. I'll admit, he was charismatic."

"But you weren't convinced?"

"Many seemed to listen but it sounded like madness. He was talking about changing the whole world; overturning everything."

They emerged from the staircase into a new corridor where the wall turned sharply away, as if back on itself. Brackendon remembered this zigzagging set of hallways where their dormitories used to be. No room ever seemed large enough from the angles of the walls but they were always spacious once you entered.

Hurry... the voice urged, echoing as though a crowd of people were whispering altogether. The air was thick with the Cascade. It looked clear to the naked eye but Brackendon could feel it as he began to walk. It was like wading through water – stinking, murky water that tried to pull him down. A noise followed him every step down the jagged hallway, like someone gargling their last breath.

"Can you feel this haze?" he said sluggishly.

"Y-Yes," Kymethra struggled.

The Inner Circle's council chamber... come...

"Would the fighting that day really have caused all this?" Kymethra asked.

"It's not just the Cascade at work here. We should go to the Inner Circle's council chamber. I think we'll find our answers there."

They fought through the quagmire of Cascade energy higher up the tower to the council chamber of the Conclave. This was where the Inner Circle, the eldest five members of the Cascade Conclave, used to meet. The door to the chamber lay in splinters against the opposite wall.

HURRY.

Brackendon steeled himself. He crept forward, Kymethra behind him and they stood outside the room, backs to the wall. His breath came in short bursts, his heart beat a little quicker and the hairs on the back of his neck prickled into life.

"I do not know what we will find in there," he said.

"Come on," Kymethra said, squeezing his hand. Together they twisted around the corner as if bursting into battle. Brackendon held his staff forward and light flooded the room. He gasped as foul stale air caught in his throat and Kymethra shrieked. There, at the large round table, were five skeletons.

Some lay bent and broken; one of the skulls was pressed down upon the table itself, completely caved in. Another had a short dagger lodged in its eye socket. Another held its jaw open in an eternal silent scream.

"The Inner Circle," Brackendon said softly. "This is where it started."

"Why is there a dagger?" Kymethra said. "Brackendon, they look like they were killed with brute force, not magic. And what's with the rest of the place?"

He glanced around, tearing his eyes away from the bones. It was immaculate. Not a patch of dust or dirt could be seen.

You have come, the voice said.

"I can hear it now," Kymethra said hoarsely.

"What are you?" Brackendon called out.

We were the Inner Circle... five... now one. In the chamber, the voice was at its strongest, yet a distance remained to it. It was jarred and tangled, as if five voices were speaking in unison.

"Are you not dead?" Brackendon asked.

We wish we were, rattled the voice.

Brackendon felt a shiver run through him. "What dark magic did Castallan weave here?"

Full of anger. Full of fury...

"Castallan's going to answer for what he's done," Kymethra said. "For this and for everything."

Not his magic, not his anger... ours.

Brackendon looked to Kymethra. She looked as confused as he felt.

"This wasn't caused by Castallan?" Kymethra asked.

Impertinent, the voice rumbled. *Castallan would not listen. He would not accept our judgement.*

"So, he attacked you?" Brackendon said.

Not him... us, hissed the voice.

"I don't understand," Brackendon said. He felt a dark cloud of doubt enter his mind.

We felt there was no other way. We demanded he hand over his staff. He refused. We had no choice...

"You attacked him?" Kymethra said, her voice high with surprise.

We had no choice... the voice moaned in terrible pain. *Even the apprentices would not listen. They tried to help him. Stepped between us... we cursed him more for that.*

"Y-you caused all of this?" Brackendon said. "You hurt the apprentices who got in the way?"

He was strong, stronger than we realised... And his experiments... scarlet eyes... such strength... such speed.

"So Castallan stood where I am now?" asked Brackendon. "Presenting his red-eyed men to you all. What did he want?"

Kill us.

"What did he want?" Brackendon asked again.

KILL US.

"Answer me," Brackendon demanded.

He wanted approval. He wanted our help. Said he needed more power to end the war. He wanted humanity to be strong. Through magic... the dragons would never have allowed... He was mad...

"And you reacted by attacking him?" Kymethra asked softly.

Too much change... he would not listen. KILL US.

Brackendon felt a chill in his heart. So Castallan had not conspired against the Conclave after all, not truly. He had intended for the whole order to join him. Brackendon wasn't sure if that changed things. He decided it didn't. Whatever injustice had been done to him here, he had paid back tenfold to the world. He'd consorted with demons and used foul magic to enchant those who he brainwashed in joining him...

Yet Brackendon was forced to stop this line of thought. The apprentices had stood in the way. They had believed enough in Castallan, more than just from coercion. Scythe must have truly believed as well.

"Are you all aware of what has happened since?" Brackendon said. "What Castallan has done?"

We are one... the voice croaked. *And we are aware of little beyond this room. The Cascade haze has prevented our spirits from departing the plane of this world. Trapped... trapped... KILL US.*

"Brackendon," Kymethra said, taking hold of his robes. "Do it. Free them. Please."

"If you know nothing beyond this room, how did you know I was in Brevia?"

Where the Cascade is strong we can connect to the world. This tower... your staff... such power. Like lightning rods to the mortal realm. Pleaseeeeeee – RELEASE US.

"I do not know if you deserve it," said Brackendon. "Castallan turned to Rectar after the Conclave fell. I thought it had been his plan, but perhaps he didn't have a choice. Your actions pushed him that way."

He had to be purged...

"The blood of thousands is on your hands. Fairy, human and dragon alike."

"Brackendon, please," Kymethra wailed. Then he felt her grip loosen. He turned away from the skeletons and found Kymethra with her head in her hands. "They're hurting me."

"Stop this!"

KILL US, the voice boomed and the whole tower quaked. *Trapped. Trapped. Torment and pain. KILL US.*

Kymethra screamed so hard that Brackendon thought her throat would rip.

Brackendon bellowed in turn, slashing his staff in an arc before the table. A thick purple light ripped from his staff and blew the skeletons to pieces. He felt the light residue from his destructive magic rush towards his staff and panted; not from the magic, but from the cry that had emptied his chest. "Kymethra are you—" he froze in horror. Her eyes had rolled up into her head. Blood oozed from her nose and ears, and her skin had turned as pale as milk.

NOOOO, shrieked the voice. *It did not work. End us. END US.*

Brackendon ignored its pleas. Whatever hellish existence the Inner Circle were in was too good for them now. He reached out to the Cascade, yanking the door in his mind wide open. He filled his body with strength and speed and Kymethra felt lighter than a feather as he tore from the chamber with her. He streaked back down the Conclave tower, even as it began to collapse around him, trying to ensnare him.

The three trick doors appeared again.

Brackendon blasted them off their hinges and the correct way was revealed. He spat out a gob of bitterness building in his mouth.

Come back. Kill us or we'll kill her.

Brackendon did not listen. He ran on as fast as he could, not stopping, not even when a chunk of the floor gave way before him. He simply leapt, landing with bone shattering force. His enhanced body shrugged it off.

The Cascade washed over him now, pulsing down his arm. Movement and strength were cheap in bursts but this was prolonged. He could have probably pulverised even Darnuir like this. Soon he was hurtling back down the ramp towards the tower exit, weaving between falling stones. He took a short cut by shouldering his way through the walls of the ground floor.

KILL US

Brackendon burst out of the Conclave into the pouring rain. Night had fully descended and the city flickered with torches. He could feel vibrations in the ground from the tower. Kymethra grunted in his arms and coughed blood.

He was enraged, angrier than he had ever been. He wanted revenge, he wanted the tower and everything to do with his old order erased from the world.

And he knew he could do just that.

He placed Kymethra down, praying she would last, and raised his staff high at the tower. After building up Cascade within his body, feeling the euphoria take him, feeling like he was a god, he began to close the fingers of his free hand into a fist. He did this slowly, for the tower offered some resistance. But piece by crumbling piece it fell.

He caught those pieces in the air so they would not fall into the rest of city and sent them hurtling back at the tower.

Rain lashed, stones cracked and Brackendon's fingers finally closed over. A small pile of gravel was all that remained.

Despite the din of the wind, the rain, and his own ragged breath, Brackendon thought he could hear an echoing sigh of relief, as though the voice was in ecstasy.

Thannnkkkkk youuuuuuuuuu…

Brackendon dropped to his knees. With a great effort, he closed the door to the Cascade. The pain of it felt like venom in his veins. Such levels of destruction would have been impossible without his new staff. It hummed loudly and the diamond bright wood shone as it processed the magic. He clutched onto the staff desperately, his eyes shut against the rain.

"Brackendon. Brackendon," Kymethra said. He felt her hands take him by the shoulders. "Are you okay?"

His eyes blinked open. "Are you?"

"Yes, I'm alright. No harm done." She too was kneeling, right in front of him. Her bloody nose was gone and the colour had returned to her face. "You brought the whole tower down." She just stated it as fact. Brackendon fell forwards to lean on her and they knelt, embracing in the rain.

"The world is better off without it," Brackendon said. His throat was dry, his mouth was bitter. It took some time for his thundering heart to steady and the flow of magic down his arm to ebb.

"Are you going to be alright?" Kymethra asked.

"Oh, I think so," Brackendon said. "But perhaps we should head for the nearest bakery and kindly request a loaf or cheese roll to soak the magic up. Wherever that may be."

Chapter 6

THE 'KING' IN THE SOUTH

Although our current Aurishan dragons will contend that they won the Third Flight, in truth it was a stalemate. As one of the last dragons still able to take their true form, Aurisha confronted his own brother in the final battle and both perished. The Black Dragons returned to Kar'drun and attempted to rebuild their lives. The followers of Aurisha moved south to build their own city on the site where their gods had spoken to one of their kind. It was holy to them, despite the actions of Dranus. Legend says they brought three of Aurisha's talons with them.

From Tiviar's Histories

Cassandra – The Bastion

WHEN CASSANDRA CAUGHT sight of the Bastion she felt sick. She would be a prisoner once more. Already she lacked freedom, being latched to this man's back as he ran at an inhuman pace alongside the other red-eyed hunters.

As the prospect of returning fully dawned on her, she emptied her stomach.

"Ugh," grunted the hunter carrying her.

"Are you ill, Princess?" Freya asked. She was a red-eyed huntress in yellow leathers.

"Extremely," Cassandra gasped. Her mouth tasted of bile. "If you want to cure me, you better take me far away from this place."

"Nonsense," said Freya. "The Bastion is strong and safe. Castallan can help you. He has helped all of us."

"You keep calling me, Princess," Cassandra said. "Doesn't that mean you have to do as I say?"

"Castallan is our true ruler," Freya said. "We chose to follow him and—"

"Quiet," grumbled the hunter. "Clean her up and let's go. We're all exhausted."

Freya mopped Cassandra's face gently with a clean cloth. "That's better," Freya said and the group started to run again.

Cassandra closed her eyes to avoid having to look at the Bastion and those impossibly high walls. With any luck, she would fall asleep and not wake until Darnuir and his army had brought Castallan down. That is if Darnuir and the others were still alive. She had seen the demon horde moving towards their camps as she was sped away. But she tried not to think too much on Darnuir either. It made her too uncomfortable.

The incident atop the hill at the Charred Vale refused to leave her mind. He had half dragged her down the hillside afterwards; that had been how she'd fallen in the first place. She didn't want much to do with him after that.

Her captors began to cough loudly, then the smoke hit Cassandra as well. It was putrid and burnt. She opened her eyes to a mountain of demon bodies, piled high and burning.

"About time we did away with those creatures," the hunter carrying her said. "The spectres never kept them well enough in line."

"What will Scythe do with the army he took to the Charred Vale?" Freya asked.

"Who cares," said another man who wore the dark green leathers of hunters from the Southern Dales. "We won't need them if he succeeds."

"And what if he hasn't?" Freya asked.

"If he was fool enough to fight the Guardian and Darnuir, he won't have," Cassandra said. The hunter brought up his hand and slapped her. Her head snapped to the side at the blow, her cheek grazing the hardened leather on his shoulder.

"A dragon lover eh? Might be literally for all we know." He spat on the ground. "Come on. We're almost at the main gates."

Cassandra assumed she'd be thrown in the dungeons of the Bastion, but she was wrong. After being hauled all the way to the top of the Bastion's inner tower, she was finally dumped into her old accommodation and left alone. Several juddering slams echoed as the door bolted over.

She glanced around. Her once lavish quarters had been gruffly searched. Tables had been upended, heavy drapes torn down, drawers pulled out and their contents scattered. In her private chambers, her bed had been shoved against the wall, left battered in some fury. Sections of wall and floor had been hammered at or taken away. She dashed through to Chelos' room.

He wasn't there.

She had known he wouldn't be waiting for her – arms wide and smiling – but not seeing him still cut at her.

Hot tears rolled down her face. She sniffed, rubbed at her eyes and tried not to think about what might have happened to him. Something terrible, she imagined, for their great secret had been revealed. Chelos' bed lay broken and the trap door to the passageway beneath had been covered with iron bars. She backed slowly out of the room, as if a dead body lay there.

So here I am. Right back to where I started.

Fresh tears began to well up, blurring her vision, but these were tears of rage. She was angry; angrier than she had ever been in her life. She screamed until she had no more breath. She kicked everything she thought she could break. A table leg buckled and then cracked on her third strike. She picked it up, wielding it like a mace, and began bludgeoning anything and everything she could.

Her makeshift club finally broke against an upturned chair, so she picked it up instead. Heart pounding, arms straining, she spun and lobbed the seat at one of the windows. It didn't go right through, but it smashed several panes, sending shards of glass and lead out onto the balcony. Cold wind blew in and she regretted her actions.

Cassandra stood panting, trying to collect herself. It had felt good, even if the temperature was now dropping. Then she noticed the library door was closed and unharmed. When she entered, she could hardly believe it. It was all there; everything – every book, every scroll, and every note was just as she'd left it. A volume of Tiviar's *History of Tenalp* lay where she had last put it down. Old instinct made her reach towards it. When she placed her hand on it, she glanced over her shoulder, feeling this might be some cruel trick Castallan was playing on her. Cautiously, she picked up the weighty tome.

Nothing happened.

Tension unwound from her in relief. She ran a finger through the pages of the tome and suddenly felt a crippling fatigue come over her. Feeling defeated, exhausted and truly alone, Cassandra returned to her old bed. It had already been made. She'd been expected to return, it seemed. She reached the bedside and fell limply on it.

Sleep eluded her.

Despite having closed her bedroom door, a chill was gathering from the broken window in the room beyond. She curled up against the cold under her sheets and propped up Tiviar's History. This was his volume on the Second War between humanity and dragons. She flicked it open to a random page and began to read.

I have gathered over three hundred and twenty-two accounts of Dronithir's movements in and around the Boreac Mountains when he supposedly discovered the mythical Champion's Blade. Aside from vast contradictions in dates, locations, timings and spellings – the Guardian at the time was not named "Noobano" – there is one constant element. It seems Dronithir spoke much about hearing a "guiding voice" within the mountain range. To my mind, the likeliest explanation is that Dronithir helped himself by claiming divine favour…

After a few pages, Cassandra began to lose focus. She blinked, trying to stay awake, but she was warmer now beneath the covers and tired. She was just so tired. She tried to read one more line, but realised she was reading the same line over and over. And then, mercifully, sleep came.

She couldn't tell how long she lay curled up in that bed. She woke sporadically then drifted off again, never quite sinking into a deep, restful state. Food was brought to her regularly, delicious food, but she ate little of it. Bossy women with tubs, soap, hot water and brushes came to clean her but she lashed out at them until they left her. She would wake at dawn, she would wake in the darkest hours of night. She read a little, but mostly slept, trying to make time go faster.

Some days later, she couldn't say how many, she heard the bolts on the main door shift once more. Her stomach groaned loudly and she hopefully sniffed at the air. Smelling nothing Cassandra braced herself for another row with the matrons, but paused as the chink of chainmail reached her ears.

"Princess Cassandra," called a man's voice. "Lord Castallan requests your presence in the throne room." Cassandra drew herself upright, her muscles protesting with lethargy. She gasped as her bare feet touched the cold floor and then slinked out of her bedroom on tiptoe.

"I deny my presence."

The man's eyes flashed red. "He also requests that you wear this for the occasion," and he stepped aside to reveal a red-eyed woman holding up a rich pale green gown with golden thread. "To match your eyes," he said indifferently. "Lord Castallan has been entertaining very important guests and requests you to appear as one, if seen. You'll find it is a perfect fit." The dress was handed to her. Cassandra looked down at the rough white and grey leathers she was wearing, ripped and dirtied in places. She dropped the ornate gown to the floor and ground it against the stone with her foot.

"No."

The man rolled his eyes. "Very well. Take her."

"I'll walk myself," Cassandra said, shrugging away as the woman moved towards her. "I've got enough bruises already." There was some muttering between the pair. Cassandra glared at them. "What?"

"Your face, Princess," the red-eyed woman said. "There is a mark—"

"Courtesy of the thug who carried me here."

"Perhaps we ought to cover it," the woman said, more to her companion than Cassandra.

"No time," said the man. "Come along now."

Cassandra followed without fuss. They kept close to her, but she had no inclination to try and flee. She was tired, hungry and worn. After years of being patient, waiting to be free, she had foolishly got caught up with warring wizards and kings. She really should have run and hid from the world. Yet, she had made a promise to Chelos to warn Darnuir of what was to come. She'd done that at least.

Next time, I'm gone for good. I'll just need to figure out where to go…

A part of her was tired of wanting to run as well. She wanted a home. She wanted to feel as safe and happy and as part of something as she had during their weeks at the Argent Tree. With Balack, Brackendon, Kymethra, the occasional visit from Cosmo and his smiling son, it had almost felt like a family. She wanted that again. She wanted to belong. Where she might find that was another matter entirely. Her real family had abandoned her long ago.

Walking through the corridors of the Bastion she passed finely dressed guests, even some older hunters from the Southern Dales with grey stubble. Half were drunk, keeping one hand to the wall or stumbling. The rest were enjoying some natural high, smiling broadly, talking loudly and happily. Cassandra wasn't sure who to hate more – Castallan, for hosting a party while sending demon hordes to ravage the land, or these people who seemed perfectly at ease to join him.

Entering Castallan's so-called throne room was a strange experience. She had spied down upon it from the passages above so often over the years, but had never stepped foot inside before. It seemed even larger in person. To her right was Castallan's self-proclaimed throne, raised on a newly built platform to look down on the hall. Ten silver staffs fanned out behind the chair, the source of Castallan's power.

The wizard himself was not up there. He sat alone at the head of a long table, big enough to accommodate fifty people. The table was laden with the remnants of a great feast. Pickings of suckling pigs with cold grease stains, hollowed cheese wheels, whole fish that only had their bones sticking out, flagons of ale, pitchers of wine and heavy black pots of barley broth. Like Castallan's robes, the table was dressed in purple cloth, trimmed in silver.

Cassandra was directed to the seat opposite Castallan and she dropped into it, making sure to scrape the floor with her chair as she dragged it in. Everyone left and she was alone with the wizard. Castallan looked especially smug as he lovingly eyed a piece of parchment before him. Then he looked to her.

"Did you not like my dress?"

"Where is Chelos?" she asked, ignoring his comment.

"Your dear old dragon is alive."

"I want to see him."

"Then you may go on wanting. He won't be seeing visitors."

"What did you do to him?" Cassandra asked, envisaging Chelos screaming on his knees before that throne.

"I had no need to harm him. Not as much as I thought."

"He's stronger than you think," Cassandra said with a sort of fierce pride. She noticed a sharp, serrated knife on the table by a breadboard, just within reach of her hand. With one finger, she caressed the base of it, feeling the cold metal against her skin, wondering if she would dare to take it.

"Strong but old," Castallan said, "and I think he realised I wasn't going to believe anything except the truth. And what a truth it was. Secret tunnels throughout my fortress?"

"You'll have had them all caved in now," Cassandra said. "Is that why you're so pleased?"

"As a matter of fact, I've kept them intact. Does that surprise you?"

"Just tell me what you want."

Castallan breathed in through this nose and ran a hand through his swept back, ashen tinged hair. "I want, what I've always wanted. A safe world. A better world. A strong humanity that can stand on its own feet."

"And what do I have to do with that?"

"No need to be so flustered, Cassandra. I have no intention of harming you. I never have. I am sorry my followers cannot always orders to the letter. Who did that to your face?"

"I wasn't saying nice things about Scythe."

"Ah… you know?" he said solemnly. "It grieves me that he is dead. Slain in combat by Darnuir."

Cassandra perked up, and sat a little straighter. "Did you expect him to win?"

"He was one of the first to join me, and one of the strongest. My technique was not so refined back then, but Scythe survived it and was more powerful for it. He was a sly, cunning one, if a little cautious because of it. In the end, that might have been his downfall. He ought to have pushed matters at Cold Point before Darnuir could become stronger. My greatest regret is that he did not live to see our plans fulfilled." He tapped the piece of parchment.

"Did that involve slaughtering all your demons?"

"In part, though I hadn't planned on disposing my demons so soon. However, I am told by my followers who fled the Charred Vale that the spectres took flight after Scythe fell. The demons went wild after that, completely useless. Before long the spectres I had closer to home abandoned me as well, and the regular demons left behind had to be put down. It's meant stepping up my plans but Darnuir has forced my hand." He brandished the piece of parchment. Waxy seals dangled beneath a screed of minute text. "Signed by the Lords of the Southern Dales, including Lord Annandale himself. Their soldiers will arrive soon for enchantment."

"Why would they do that?" Cassandra asked, unable to keep the bite from her voice.

Why are so many swayed to him?

"Because many believe as I do," Castallan said. "Many want what I want. An end to Rectar; an end to war; and an end to human suffering."

"But not an end to my suffering?"

"I've never actively made your life hard, Cassandra. You really shouldn't feel all that special. You are just a piece to be played. An asset of value. And there is no point hiding who you really are now, Princess."

"Yes, I've heard," Cassandra said. It was unsettling all the same. "So, it's true?"

"I carried you from Aurisha myself. I took part in that attack to acquire the Dragon's Blade. I failed in that regard, but the trip was not a complete waste."

"No one wanted to pay my ransom?" Cassandra said. Her stomach twisted a little. She blamed the hunger but her thoughts betrayed her, flitting to the idea of a mother and father she had never considered until recently. Yet, they had left her here. With all the power of royalty, she had been left caged. *What good were they?*

"You act so brazen and strong but you cannot hide your pain from me. Sad, isn't it? To think you were so unloved. If it helps at all, I shall put your mind at ease. Your parents did pay handsomely, or rather your father paid. Your mother, the once Queen Ilana, passed shortly after you were presumed dead." He paused for a moment, looking at Cassandra to gauge her reaction.

"So she's dead," Cassandra said, though her voice was oddly high. "I never knew her."

"Terribly tragic," Castallan said. "But in the aftermath of Demon's Folly, it proved advantageous to me. You see the death of your mother placed Arkus in a very difficult position. Without an heir, stability was threatened. I informed him and enough of his lords quietly that I had you to avoid a civil war. All I wanted in return was a guarantee that Arkus would not bring an army down to take you. I threatened to kill you of course, as I was not then strong enough to resist the might of Brevia, not even here. The threat of strife in the Assembly and potential bloodshed over succession kept him in line for a long time. I also got a little financing out of it, of course."

"I thought Darnuir gave you plenty of gold?"

"He remembers that, does he? I had wondered. The rebirthing spell had never been used practically before. I'm impressed, in truth, but then Brackendon was a great wizard."

"He still is," said Cassandra, thinking fondly of the man.

"His staff tree was burned."

"Queen Kasselle herself granted him a staff, carved from the heart of the Argent Tree."

Castallan raised his eyebrows. "Kasselle must be feeling desperate indeed to gift such a piece of her people's heritage. Well, I shall have to add this powerful new staff to my collection. Tell me, did Darnuir also remember trying to carry you to safety when Aurisha fell?"

"He does now. It seemed to take him some time. The Guardian helped him to unlock those memories his old self had hidden away." Cassandra wasn't too sure if she fully understood it. "Something about the rubies on his sword."

"Ah yes the Dragon's Blade, I had forgotten the gems held that power," Castallan said. "Oh, how I have longed for that sword." He narrowed his eyes at Cassandra, studying her. "You ran to him when you escaped. Did you grow close to him?"

Cassandra narrowed her eyes right back but her insides squirmed. Castallan kept focusing on her eyes, smiling broadly at her discomfort.

"Hungry?" he asked. Without an answer, he clicked his fingers and servants hurried in carrying several fresh platters. The smell of roast chicken made her mouth water. The servants had barely taken the lids from the dishes before she lunged for the food.

"I'll take that for a yes," Castallan said lazily.

"Holding me hostage won't save you now," Cassandra said thickly through a mouthful of chicken.

Castallan laughed a cruel little laugh. "Oh Cassandra, Arkus hasn't been deterred by the threat of losing you for many years. He took a new wife, the Lady Orrana, daughter of Lord Clachonn, chief family of the Hinterlands. And would you like to hear the sad circumstances of that marriage?"

Cassandra shook her head and thought she might now take the knife while he droned one. Her fingers gripped the steel, she raised it —

But something in her faltered and she excused her sudden motion by carving a thick slice of crusty bread instead.

"Arkus decided he was in need of a great deal of black limestone from the Hinterlands," Castallan was saying. "In some fit of grief, he chose to rebuild much of Brevia. He needed so much stone, in fact, that his treasury couldn't bear the cost of it. Yet Lord Clachonn agreed to supply enormous amounts at minimum cost, in return for Arkus marrying his daughter. The official story paints a more... romantic picture of our reigning royalty. But my what sad a tale it is."

"You seem to know a lot about this."

"I have friends all over the Kingdom," said Castallan. "While Arkus was busy building himself a black city to match his black heart, I was gathering those with sense to me."

Cassandra chewed more slowly, thinking that the best thing to do would be to let him ramble on, and maybe she would get her chance. She put the knife down but kept it close. He seemed to be enjoying himself, which seemed odd to her. He was a very relaxed man for one who must know his time was short.

Maybe he doesn't see Arkus as a real threat. Time to find out.

"So why keep me after all that?"

"It gets worse, I'm afraid," sighed Castallan with clear exaggeration. "Their only son is a sickly child – problems with his chest. Coughs so hard that his carers fear his ribs will break. So, while you are no longer the official direct heir, you are a likely spare."

Cassandra was about to tell him about Cosmo and his son Cullen, but managed to stop herself at the last moment. She half choked in doing so, coughing and spluttering into her sleeve.

"Could be it runs in the family," Castallan quipped. Cassandra continued to have difficulty and felt her face going hot with the blood rushing to it. "Now calm down," Castallan said, waving a hand towards her. She stopped gasping at once and her airways felt clear.

"I admit, at times, I wondered whether I should keep you or not," Castallan said. "Marrying you myself would have lent me no extra legitimacy. My followers freely choose me and many think Arkus is a fool. Yet over the years he's become bolder; stopped sending me the gold I demanded. Then he got bolder still, telling me that my magic was not the only way humanity could become stronger, but he does not understand. It is the fastest way. It is the best way. To enhance ourselves; to become as strong as dragons; and once I take the Blades, I will be able to reach out and destroy even Rectar himself!"

"Why don't you just admit you lust for the power?" Cassandra asked. "Why hide behind this façade of—"

"I do not," he said, banging his fist upon the table. When he spoke next, it was quieter, as if he were restraining years of anger. "Always, people have misunderstood my intentions, my vision. The only person I have tried to actively deceive is Darnuir, and then only in part. I doubted he would have agreed with my intentions to put humanity on an equal footing with dragons."

"Not the old Darnuir," Cassandra said, remembering the way Darnuir would sometimes snap in haughty orders, oozing superiority when he did so. "But I think he would listen now."

"It's far too late for that," Castallan said, in that same hushed tone. "So long as dragons remain more powerful than us, we are at their mercy, doing their bidding, fighting and dying in their wars. I said as much to the Conclave but they did not believe me. They were frightened of change too; I could see it in their eyes. I came to them with a proposition, a suggestion, and they answered me by trying to take my staff... my very life."

Cassandra looked into his radiant silver eyes and they did not lie. "You really do believe in what you are doing."

"Of course, I do. I do not force people to follow me. It started back at the Conclave. I spoke to the apprentices first, those not so much younger than myself. Many felt I was right, and they played the price for it: cut down trying to save me from being taken by the Inner Circle. The fools," Castallan added affectionately. "They died for me; for what they believed. They were the first martyrs of my cause, of our cause. I'm glad the Conclave was destroyed for that. They hadn't counted on my volunteers being so strong, and that was before I perfected the magic. Now I have all the power of the Conclave at my disposal. I took their knowledge too, to keep it safe. I'm certain it would have been lost otherwise."

"My library…" Cassandra said, realising what he meant.

"My library, you mean. I'm not some monster, though I am sure many think I am."

"Not a monster?" Cassandra said indignantly. "Not a monster?" She could barely contain herself. Her hand searched for the serrated knife. "You kept me locked up. You kept me isolated. You tortured Chelos. You've killed people, hundreds if not thousands of humans whom you claim to want to help. You worked with demons and kill anyone who you think might stand in your way. What are you if not a monster? Do you think a few books can soak up all the blood you've spit?"

"I kept you isolated for your own good, Princess. Do you think you would have been as safe if everyone in the Bastion had known who you are?" A portion of Cassandra's anger drained at those words.

Might there have been many others like Trask? Is he right?

Her fingers touched the cold metal once more.

"I have worked with demons, yes, I admit it. But I had to learn everything I could from Rectar. I do regret some of the steps I've had to take but what will it matter once he's defeated?"

Cassandra's fingers slowly curled around the hilt of the knife.

"Demons and spectres were a necessary deterrent until I was strong enough to move without them. I welcome their loss at the Charred Vale and their burning bodies outside."

Cassandra steadied herself.

"Sometimes deaths are necessary to build something great. I learnt that at the Conclave. You must be prepared to fight for change. What's a few hundred lives, a few thousand, if Dukoona's invasion is thrown back, if Rectar is defeated and all of humanity made safe?"

Cassandra whipped the knife at Castallan, unleashing a lifetime of coiled fury. Castallan barely flinched as he blasted the knife across the long table. It skewered the remains of a ham as it crunched through it into the wood.

He sighed again, this time irritably. "Sit still will you." Cassandra felt an invisible force push her back down, holding her in place. She couldn't even wriggle.

"They'll come for you," she said softly, the fight leaving her once more. "Darnuir, the Guardian, Brackendon – they'll come to kill you."

Castallan smiled then, as a pure a smile as she had ever seen another person make. "I'm counting on them coming. I'm holed up in an impenetrable fortress, which will be garrisoned with all the troops and hunters that the Southern Dales can muster. And so Darnuir and company will seek me out. They know there are passages throughout the Bastion, even one leading right under the walls."

"Darnuir might know how I got out, but I couldn't tell him exactly where the tunnel lies."

"Oh, don't fear. Chelos' information leaves me confident they will find it. And they will run to me, right into my arms. I shall take Brackendon's staff and graft a piece of it into my own, as I have done with all the others." He gestured proudly at his collection behind the throne. Now Cassandra looked at them more closely she could see small chunks were missing from each one. Castallan's own staff was whole but now she knew what to look for, and being so much closer, she could make out the faintest cracks running up the shaft like scars, as though it had been taken apart and stitched back together.

"I shall take the Dragon's Blade," Castallan continued in full swing, "and the Guardian's Blade for good measure. A new age shall begin, and when we are finally at peace, I shall destroy one staff every year until magic is no longer needed to make humanity strong. This I swear, Cassandra. This I swear."

"I still don't see why I am here."

"To lure Darnuir," Castallan said. "I needed to know if you had one last use and you do. Your squirming at the mention of him told me enough. I want him to come to me, not fight out there on the walls. So, when the time comes, you will wait out the battle in this room with me. I'll make sure everyone knows where you are and Darnuir will bring me the Dragon's Blade. All I have to do now is wait. That, Cassandra, is why you are here."

Chapter 7

TUATH

Three Talons for Three Blades, or so we are to believe. The Dragon's Blade is known across Tenalp. The second is the Guardian's Blade, held by the more secretive Guardian. The third sword is the legendary Champion's Blade, often forgotten by many. Again, the rumours and stories are worthy of their own chapter, though I caution readers against thinking of it as anything other than a powerful myth. It holds allure because there is the chance that anyone might be bestowed great power if they are 'worthy'. However, it seems strange to me that the ancient dragons would make such a weapon when the other two are so specifically designed.

From Tiviar's Histories

Garon – The Hinterlands – near the town of Tuath

THINGS HAD GONE from bad to worse for Garon.

First, there had been the attack of the red-eyed traitors. Second, Marus' injuries had made him no less amenable. He kept the dragons distant, communicating rarely and only through fairy go-betweens, who were themselves in a sour mood about continuing the mission. Thirdly, their journey eastwards into the Hinterlands and towards the town of Tuath had taken three days longer than expected, what with injuries and the need to hunt or forage for a lot more of their food. Those supplies were now running dangerously low. Fourthly, he now found himself at arrow point by about half-a-hundred blue and green clad hunters. It was a mark of the state of things that this did not immediately qualify as his greatest problem.

"We're not demons," Garon said. "There will be no need to shoot us." The hunters had emerged from the wood hugging the base of the Highland range. Rugged heather-topped hills protruded to the left and grew into larger mountains in the distance.

"Just routine," a woman said, emerging from their ranks to greet him. She was curvaceous, he was sure, beneath all that leather. Her face was sharply defined by contrast and she managed to pull off close-cropped hair in a way that few other women would dare.

"Is it routine for a mixed army of humans, dragons and fairies to arrive in the Hinterlands?" Garon asked. He very much hoped that Ochnic would not make one of his surprise entrances and spook any hunter with a weak draw arm.

"Well it's not everyday work, I grant you," she said, extending a hand. "I am Captain Romalla."

"Garon," he said, taking her hand delicately. "The pleasure is all mine."

"Oh please, let's not waste time. May I see the dragon in charge of this 'army'?"

Straight to business, is it? No fun for Garon anymore.

Something fun might have helped to distract him from things, from the lack of a certain crooked nosed person.

"Legate Marus represents the dragons," he said. "But he is not in charge of our expedition. I am." He handed over Darnuir's orders. Romalla looked suspicious but took the scroll. Her eyes darted from left to right down the words. "I should warn you that there is a member of the kazzek race among our number. I'd be most grieved if one of your hunters shot him."

"What? Him?" Romalla asked, nodding to Garon's right.

Garon turned and gasped. "Ah, Ochnic, how do you do that? Twenty years of hunter training and I can't tell when a great big troll comes up behind me."

"I've trained for longer," Ochnic said with a toothy grin.

"You don't seem surprised, Captain?" Garon said.

"Hmm," Romalla said. She finished scanning the scroll and rolled it back up. "Surprised? No. You don't think this is the first kazzek that Hinterland hunters have ever seen, do you?"

"Our people do not wander so far," Ochnic said.

"Perhaps some get lost then," Romalla said. "We send long range patrols north to watch for dire wolves and bears coming down from the Highlands. Many on those patrols claim to spot a troll from time to time."

"Der senses must be keener than da pack leader's," Ochnic said, not unkindly.

"Romalla, we suffered a terrible attack from agents of Castallan," Garon said "I ask that the injured take rest in Tuath and we could do with supplies. My intention is to travel through the Bealach Pass as soon as possible."

"That would be my preference as well," said Romalla. "Come. We shall escort you to the outskirts of town. You'll set up camp a full mile from the walls, mind. No more than fifty of you lot inside at any one time."

"Perfectly understandable," Garon said.

Light lingered for a long time that night. Garon had never seen the sky turn lilac and slowly darken into purple, nor had he thought it would linger for so long. He longed to walk out underneath it and breathe in the fresh pine-scented air. Instead, he was perched at the windowsill in the Captain's regular room at the Carter's Rest in Tuath, with a dragon, fairy and troll, bickering with each other.

"What say you, Garon?" Romalla called to him.

With regret and an ache between his eyes, Garon tore his gaze away from the enticing sky. "There is no question. We go north as instructed. And we'll go with the forces left to us."

He saw fresh annoyance rise in Marus' face. The legate's leg was elevated on a chair while he sat. The fact that he was moving at all was impressive. Such an injury would have left any human in their beds, but through some stubborn dragon stamina, Marus was moving around; puffy eyed and evidently in pain, but still moving.

"I'll add again that I trust all my hunters," Romalla said.

"We cannot take the risk," Marus said.

"I understand," said Romalla. "From what you say, I could be in for rude awakening. You'll have the supplies you need. That much I can grant you."

"That's very accommodating of you, Captain," Garon said.

"Then you may depart as soon as you feel ready," said Romalla. Her position was more than clear.

"And so, our short and thankfully amiable business is concluded," Garon said, with no small measure of sarcasm. Marus got up without a second thought, limping with a great swing of his foot towards the door and his dragons on the other side. Pel rose more slowly, lingering her attention on Garon briefly with a defeated expression before turning to Romalla.

"Thank you, Captain," Pel said. "For being so helpful in our time of need. And thank you, troll, for your scintillating insights."

With his forehead resting upon the table, Ochnic groaned.

"Thank you, Wing Commander," Garon said, hoping to impress upon her that enough was enough. "You heard the Captain. Our discussion is over. Go get some rest."

Pel traipsed out of the room, although her traipse was a human's most graceful glide after ten years of courtly training. Once she was clear of the room, Ochnic dragged himself upright. One of his tusks gouged a small chip in the wood along the way.

"I begin to regret dis great walk," Ochnic said. "Da cold waters of da river will freshen me. Night good, Romalla, hunter captain."

Romalla turned to Garon in confusion.

"It's 'good night', Ochnic," Garon said. "And thank you again for your patience." The troll flashed his fanged teeth in a gesture that Garon decided to interpret as a friendly salute, then he too lumbered off, ducking at the doorframe to avoid injury. With nothing else to do, Garon began to follow.

"Garon," Romalla called after him. "Come back."

Often, Garon had heard that phrase laced with a playful longing. Habit, therefore, prompted him to arrange his face into his best smoulder before turning, but a deep tiredness had come upon him with the evening's bout of arguing done and his lips and eyebrows felt unresponsive. In the end, it was all in vain. Romalla had her back to him, bustling with some papers at a desk she must have kept permanently in the room.

After a while, she turned to check on him. "Is something wrong or do you always look like that?"

Embarrassed, he returned his face to normal and moved to the desk. "Can I help you?"

"By succeeding in your mission," she said. "If this is all true then I will feel better knowing the Highland border is safe from demons."

"I wondered why you had accepted all of this so quickly."

"I accepted it because I have little choice. It's absurd in truth. You, some nobody in Boreac Mountain leathers, shows up with a scrap of parchment with the signatures of two princes long thought dead – Darnuir, now King of Dragons, and countersigned by Prince Brallor, who supposedly died over twenty years ago, as well."

"Both were very much alive when I left them."

"Not only that but you, this nobody human, is leading this joint force and I can barely believe the dragons allow it."

"They do yearn to follow their King's instructions."

"Will you let me finish," Romalla said. He smirked and threw up his hands in mock surrender. To his relief, she smiled back. "Look, it's all so utterly unbelievable that I have no choice but to believe it. Had you come alone with your piece of paper and a troll I'd have thrown you out of the Hinterlands with arrows on your heels. But you have the fairies, you have the dragons, and I don't believe this many people could be so sure of the circumstances unless it was true. That and I can hardly prevent your little army taking anything it needs."

"Has Brevia sent no word?" Garon asked. "There has been chaos brewing in the south for about a year."

"Arkus called his army, and our Lord Clachonn dutifully summoned his vassals in the Hinterlands, and so on. Yet little solid information has filtered through. I had heard of the troubles in the Dales and Marshes affecting the Crownlands, but this business in the Golden Crescent, whole demon armies on the march — no I had not heard. And if the hunters have been compromised, as you say, perhaps it runs to the core of the Master Station, or perhaps some of my own people have been selecting my communications very carefully. It is… troubling."

"You should enjoy the stability of your region," Garon said. "I feel it is the last one left in the Kingdom."

"Stable and drained," said Romalla. "Even before Arkus called to war, I was sending many of my best hunters to Brevia for some unknown purpose. Lately, I've been loath to do so because none have ever come back."

"You're sending away your hunters without knowing why?"

"Indeed. Again, how can I prevent Arkus having what he wants? As for their purpose, you can take it up with Lord Clachonn if you wish. Arkus deals with him and then Clachonn deals with me, bypassing the Master Station altogether. The benefits of having your daughter as queen I suppose. But enough of my woes, I'd like to know a bit about you."

"Me?"

"I don't see anyone else in the room."

"What does it matter? I'm just some nobody, after all."

"You're not anymore. Why you, Garon? Why were you given this task?"

"Darnuir didn't have many options, I imagine. That Guardian fellow was hardly cooperative. I don't think he and Darnuir saw eye to eye."

"Guardian?" Romalla asked, her brow furrowing at this latest revelation.

"It's complicated," said Garon. He puffed out a breath and let it continue into a sigh. "Darnuir wanted someone in charge who he felt he could trust. Someone who would see the matter through to the end."

"And you're the best man for it?"

"I wouldn't have chosen me," Garon said. "But you've seen how they are, the dragons and the fairies. Pel was forced along because everyone senior refused to go. Marus gets on with it because the dragons want to kiss their king's boots, but he begrudges every step he takes. So no, I would not have asked for this. But I was given the job and I shall see it through. I've led patrols; this is just a big one. A great big, shambling, arguing one. In fact, it's worse. At least when the kids are being taken out for the first time they damned well do as you tell them."

"Did you lead Darnuir out on patrols?"

"I did," Garon said, remembering briefly more sane days, even if demons were involved towards the end. Things seemed to make sense back then. "He was a quick learner, fought well, and coped with the effort. Of course, it helped that he is a dragon."

"Lira was much the same," Romalla said. "Tell me did she—"

"She made it to Val'tarra," Garon said. "She even made it to Darnuir's new Praetorian Guard."

"Really?" Romalla said, her eyes lighting up like a proud parent. "Well, her mother will be pleased to hear that. So you know Darnuir, is that it?"

"I was also trained by Cosmo – Prince Brallor that is – during the years he stayed in the Boreacs. I didn't know who he really was. He kept that even from his own wife, poor woman. Grace deserved better than that." He saw Romalla was confused again. He hurried along. "Cosmo helped me when I had nothing. He gave me back my life and a purpose. In turn, I helped him to train Darnuir. My proximity to them is ultimately nothing more than coincidence, but it has led me here."

"So you act upon duty and friendship. Admirable but hardly inspirational."

Garon shrugged. "What do you want to hear, Captain? I'm just a man. I'm not a prince nor king nor wizard, nor even a plain dragon; I don't have a magic staff or a magic sword. I have my bow and my wits, and I've only ever wanted to help people: the way Cosmo helped me. Foolish as that sounds, it's true. Going to save a whole race, well that counts as a lot of help in my eyes and I'll see it through, to whatever end."

"You realise this is all going into my report," Romalla said.

"Make me sound ten times as foolish if you like. All I need is those supplies."

"They won't last long," Romalla warned. "One region's spare rations and arrows can't see so many through a harsh Highland winter."

"Ochnic says his people will provide for us. I trust him."

"And even if you didn't, you wouldn't have much of a choice," Romalla said. She held out her hand again. "Take care, Garon, the nobody from the Boreac Mountains. And good luck." He took her hand with a firm shake. "I will be heading up the Bealach Pass tomorrow to return to our station. We shall escort your expedition that far. After that—"

"We'll be on our own, thanks," Garon said. "I wish you a 'night good', Captain Romalla." He winked once then turned before she could say anymore.

Out in the corridor and out of sight of Romalla, he took a moment to lean against the wall. His heart was beating quickly and his chest seized in pain. He strained for breath. *Am I having some sort of panic attack?* He hadn't had one of these since the last war, when he was fifteen at most. *Maybe this is too much for me to handle?*

He blew out his cheeks and shook his head to try and rally himself. After another deep breath he stood up straight and made his way downstairs towards the chatter of patrons in the Carter's Rest. At the top of the last staircase, the heat of the bar area hit Garon like a warm, damp cloth. Pulling at his collar, he descended. He hoped against hope that Griswald would be sitting at the bar. That he would be roaring with laughter at some mildly amusing joke, out of all proportion, just like the rest of him, and would call Garon over and slap his hand to order another mug of ale.

But Griswald was not there.

There were men covered in dust with hammers and chisels at their belts, but no Griswald. He would be back out at camp, grief still heavy upon him. Garon bit back a fresh wave of his own sorrow.

Don't think on it. You can't think on it. You need to hold up, be in one piece. You've lost men before. This isn't any different.

But this time it was different. Looking around this tavern, in this bar, in this town he had never been to before, Garon knew no one. And of the two people he was closest to on this mission one of them, Rufus – poor, poor Rufus – was dead. He had no desire to return to camp. Not right away. Perhaps a drink or two wouldn't hurt. Cosmo had always favoured that option and it seemed to work, in the main. It was then that he caught her eye.

A tall, blond huntress sat idly at the bar, well away from the quarry workers. Her blue-green leathers were loosened at her chest and her hair fell artfully inwards to cover the gap. She held his gaze for just a second too long to be accidental.

Oh Griswald, you really ought to be here. Just like you said.

Yes, he would stay for a drink, talk to this girl and, well, who knows? He'd take the chance to be away from it all again for one night. Just one night. Just like it had been before all this madness started. That wouldn't be so bad. The blond huntress at the bar glanced in his direction again. It would be an easy form of comfort, one that wouldn't help once the night was over, but he approached her all the same. No stool was free, so he leaned on the bar beside her casually, pushing an iron topped miner's hat on the counter out of his way.

"Rough day?" he said, nodding to the tankard in her hand.

"Back from a two-week patrol on the Highland borders."

"Dangerous?"

"If you run into a silver dire bear."

"And did you?"

"Not this time," she said, taking another sip of her drink. "Doubt there are many left now. Think you could handle one?"

"Oh, it's not animals that frighten me anymore," Garon said.

"What does then?" she asked.

Red eyes in the night, he thought. He saw the huntress rip Rufus' chest open again. Traitors could be anywhere.

"Let me see your eyes," he said, placing a finger gently but firm under her chin. He searched them for some trace of red, for some sign of treachery. He thought if he stared into them long enough he'd find the truth, if it was there to be unearthed. Yet her eyes remained nut brown, with the tiniest flecks of green. Only her pupils changed, widening into onyx ponds.

"You're from the Boreac Mountains, aren't you?" she said. "I've always wanted to see the mountains there. I hear they are so much more beautiful than the Highlands."

"The Highlands hold a certain rugged charm."

"I'd like something a little easier on the eye," she said. Her hand brushed against his free one and a warm finger ran over his wrist. He could feel her breath on his skin. It smelled lightly of ale. He let her go, rummaged in a pouch for some silver then dropped it on the counter. He had some catching up to do.

He awoke the next morning before dawn. After the thrill and fun, Garon had hoped to rest undisturbed, but his sleep had been light and broken, and unrestful by most accounts.

Cold blue light of a pre-dawn Hinterland morning entered the small room. He felt too energetic and too exhausted to move all at once.

Infuriated, he scrunched the edge of the woollen mattress in his fist, over and over, feeling every strand of muscle in his forearm strain. He rubbed his eyes enough to chafe the skin and realised it was no good. He edged himself out of the warm bed and winced as the chill of the morning bit at his skin. Gooseflesh appeared along his arms.

His companion muttered something. He had discovered her name was Jean and she was fully naked in truth, just delicately hidden under the sheets. She opened one eye. "It's not even dawn yet."

"I don't have the luxury of sleep it seems." He finished strapping on his sword belt and grunted as he pulled it too tight. "Go back to sleep," he told her before taking his leave. Carefully, he trod through the tavern, cursed his fortune as each stair squeaked louder than the last on the way down, stepped over an abandoned crowbar on his way past the bar, pushed on the tavern's heavy door and stepped outside, where he was met by a scowling Marus.

"Stay for some fun, did you?" the legate asked. To Garon's surprise he was alone, propped up on a sturdy if roughly hewn crutch.

"What of it Marus?" Garon asked.

"I hoped to find our leader in camp to, now what was it again, lead."

Shame flared inside Garon and burned his cheeks. "I admit this isn't my finest hour."

"How can I be certain you won't be missing at a time of crisis?" Marus asked.

"I won't be missing again, I assure you."

"Can you swear to it?"

"Can you swear you won't be such a stubborn arse all the time?" Garon asked.

"To you?" Marus said. "No. I cannot." He smiled awkwardly, but whether it was in jest or to hide fresh pain Garon couldn't say. He wasn't sure if these older dragons were capable of humour.

"What was so urgent that you had to come into town to find me?"

"The troll wants a word," Marus said. "And as you asked him not to enter Tuath in case he terrifies the locals I have had to—"

"You could have sent an outrunner."

"I can manage just fine," Marus snapped.

"I see what this is," Garon said. "This is your pride killing you." He moved to Marus' left side, which was crutch free. "Come let me help you back to cam—" But Marus snorted and limped on, not giving Garon so much as a backwards glance or a thank you.

Damn you Darnuir. Damn you for leaving me alone.

"You're going to have to learn to ask for help," Garon called to Marus' back. In the silent, smooth paved streets of Tuath, his voice carried far and magnified off stone buildings.

"A dragon does not ask."

"Then a dragon may hobble in pain all the way into the Highlands," said Garon. The pre-dawn light had progressed to an orange haze, enough to see Marus by, as he sped ahead. "Slow down. You'll damage that leg further."

Marus paused and turned, his chest rising and falling heavily. "Would you like me to slow down, human? Are you feeling weak after your exertions?"

"It's a sweet sort of weariness," Garon said more quietly as he caught up. "You might try it sometime." Though looking at the legate's dour expression, Garon felt no one would be interested.

"The only satisfaction I require is service to my King."

"Well, each to their own," Garon said. "But would it be of service to Darnuir to cripple yourself?" No response came from the legate. "I thought not," Garon added. "This whole mission was Darnuir's idea. He won't take it kindly if you ruin it. He might use some of that pent up rage of his on you."

"How dare you speak about the King in such a fashion."

"I knew your King when he was in swaddling clothes," Garon said. "I held him. I even bloody changed him. He could make a right stink when he fancied."

Marus' nose was twitching unnervingly fast. "The troll awaits us," he said brusquely. Yet, in his haste to set off again, Marus twisted around too quickly, pressuring his injured leg. His knee buckled, the crutch slipped out from under his shoulder and Marus collapsed to the ground, armour ringing off the stone.

Garon swooped down to his side. "Damn it, Marus. Are you alright?" The legate clenched his teeth so hard that Garon worried his jaw would shake out from his skull. "No, of course you're not." Marus was struggling to rise, letting loose an unmistakable yelp when he attempted to bend his right leg inwards. Garon offered him a hand but Marus swatted it aside.

"Oh, Dranus take you," Garon said. He got up and stalked away. If Marus would rather his leg fall off than admit he needed help, then so be it. Garon had a hard enough task. He didn't need to tiptoe around Marus' ridiculous need to be a good old tough dragon. He'd made it perhaps twenty yards up the street when Cosmo's voice entered his mind, as though he were sixteen again.

"On patrol, you never leave a squad-mate behind. Dead or dying you bring them home, just as you would want to be. There is no room for heroes or pride, and wounded egos will heal into strong bonds in time."

Damn you as well, Cosmo, Garon thought. He turned back around. Marus was still squirming in silent pain on the ground. It was clear that he couldn't move. Garon spotted a worn wheelbarrow by the side of the road, loaded with tiny pieces of black gravel and propping up a glinting pickaxe. He went to it, shoved the pickaxe aside with a clatter, and was already moving the wheelbarrow over to the fallen dragon when Marus began to call, "Garon? Garon, please." His voice was so laced with pity and hurt that Garon couldn't help but feel a pang of guilt for leaving him.

"I'm here," Garon said, pushing the wheelbarrow, heavy as it was, into place behind Marus to support his back. "Sit up against that. It will give you some support." The legate sat himself up and leaned back against the edge of the wheelbarrow with an audible sigh. One of his hands remained protectively on his leg.

"Thank you," Marus said.

"You're welcome."

Garon sat down by the wheel near Marus, but not looking at him. For comfort, he raised one knee and put his arm over the wheel. He looked like he was tenderly embracing it. In his semi-delirious state of tiredness, the thought made him chuckle.

"Finding it hard to believe where you are and what you're doing?" Marus said, speaking low and slow as though on his deathbed.

"If I could travel back in time and stop this from happening, I would," Garon said. "Romalla was right to doubt me. I'm not cut out for this."

"I can sympathise."

"Come now, Legate Marus. Darnuir picked you. He must have thought you were capable."

"My King did not choose me," Marus mumbled.

"So who—"

"The Lord Guardian."

"And you didn't want to come?"

"I don't think Darnuir could remember who we all were," Marus said. "Not our names, not the legions we belonged to, not our — but I should not be bitter. Nor should I speak ill of my King."

"He's not infallible," Garon said. "That I assure you."

"Fallible or flawless, he wields the Dragon's Blade. None may challenge him. He is our leader and we must do as ordered."

"The Guardian has one of those golden swords," Garon said. "Why not follow him?" For the second time Marus grunted something incoherent. "Why did Blaine pick on you?"

"I never believed much in the old religion, even before we fled Aurisha. My father did, but he died at the hands of three spectres I am told, roaring how N'weer would return his soul to the world to fight on. Perhaps it's true, but I still lost a father. When the Lord Guardian came to select a legate for this expedition I was doomed."

"He knew you were a non-believer just by looking at you?"

"Not quite. Some of us attended his services so he recognised them. But when he gathered us all and announced there was a crucial mission to the Highlands, to lend our swords in service to the trolls, he asked, 'Who here lacks faith?' And I, being so foolish, thought by speaking out I might excuse myself from selection. I thought he would not want to send a non-believer. Turns out he wanted the exact opposite."

Garon felt a strange sense of calm wash over him. "I wasn't tricked into this, but I was pressured to some degree. I think we can understand how one another feels on the matter, especially considering Pel was also forced here against her will."

"I admit it seems unfair."

"Well, I for one say we begin to get along, just to spite them," Garon said. "What do you say to that?"

"I can't just forget the murders at the hands of humans."

"Humans died as well," Garon said. "As did fairies. Probably more will die in the south. I'm not asking you to forgive it all right away, but perhaps, for now, you could stretch to letting me help you to your feet?"

A pregnant pause followed and Garon prepared to sigh in supreme disappointment. But then—

"Very well," said Marus, and to Garon's shock he saw the dragon lift up his right hand from the corner of his eye. Garon forced his own sore legs to work and stood up to take the dragon's proffered hand.

"You'll have to meet me half way now," Garon said, panting as he tried to heave the legate up. With another groan of pain Marus managed to rise and wrapped an arm around Garon for support. And as they held each other up, the first rays of dawn broke, warming their faces from the east.

"Nothing makes the world quite as beautiful as a sunrise," Marus said. Though shocked to hear those words come from Marus, Garon couldn't help but agree. The stonework town suddenly looked fresh again in the pale light, even if the grey stone was drab and overused and each roof was slated in the same sharp black tiles. To the north there was fresh snow on the mountain peaks. It would only get colder now they were on the wrong side of midsummer but, to Garon, it felt a bit like going home.

"Thank you, Garon," Marus said. "Thank you for saving my life. It was remiss of me to wait this long to say it. It's not how a legate should behave."

"Don't mention it," said Garon. "Come, let's go find Ochnic." He scooped up Marus' crutch, handed it to him, and together they made their way to the camps outside of Tuath. Once outside the town walls, Marus let go of Garon to save face and they continued into the woodland beside the River Dorain. Ochnic had mentioned taking up residence there, favouring the trees, moss, ferns and general dampness.

To their surprise, they found Pel by the river, her azure skin clashing wildly with the green all around.

"Marus told me the troll wanted to speak to us," Pel said when they were near enough to hear her. "Though what would be so urgent he had to come ask before dawn, I don't know."

"Well, where is he?" Garon asked. Pel shrugged unhelpfully and Garon continued wandering through the wood. "Ochnic?" he called. But there was no answer.

"I hope that their entire race doesn't hide from us like this," Marus said.

"There," Garon said. He'd spotted Ochnic's leather satchel at the root of a large hazel tree.

"Ochnic?" Garon called again, a little louder. This time there was snapping from above, like twigs breaking. Then, the tall, long-limbed figure of Ochnic slid down from the trees and Garon, still walking, nearly collided with the troll's white furred torso. Water dripped from the troll, rolling off his balding scalp and tusks. "I wasn't aware it had been raining," Garon noted.

Ochnic cocked his head, curiously. "No rains have come, Garon pack leader."

"Then why are you wet?" Marus asked.

"Clll-eeening," Ochnic said awkwardly.

"So it bathes," Pel said quietly. "That's something." Thankfully, Ochnic didn't seem to hear her.

"Climbing da branches or rocks helps dry quicker but is better with more kazzek to chase."

"Naturally," Garon said. "Well, Marus says you wish to speak?"

"Da air from de north grows damper, pack leader," Ochnic said. He sniffed in demonstration. "Already da season changes. We must not delay."

"We'll move as soon as we have our supplies and the wounded have had a chance to rest," Garon said.

"Leave dem," Ochnic said and Garon thought he saw the troll's eyes flick towards Marus.

"We'll need every fighter we can get," Garon said. "We're already fewer in number than when we left Val'tarra and—"

"Leave dem," Ochnic insisted.

"I will not be left behind, Ochnic," Marus said. Garon was about to say something, but stopped himself, surprised at hearing Marus use Ochnic's name.

Promising, Garon thought. *Perhaps he is going to try.*

"We can hardly move faster," Pel said.

"You can try," Ochnic said. It was more of a plea.

"I understand your desire to reach your people quickly," Garon said, "but I promise you that we are moving as fast as we—"

"Last hope," Ochnic spluttered, darting forwards to Garon. Water sprayed from him like a wet dog. He took Garon by the shoulders as if to shake him. "Last hope, I am." He said repeatedly. Steel screeched as Marus half drew his sword, even if he was imbalanced, and Pel's spear cut a swathe through the undergrowth as she swung it up to a guard position.

"Stand down you two," Garon said. "Ochnic, stop." He grabbed the troll's rough leathery arms and tried to gently push him away, but he barely moved the towering kazzek. After a prolonged tussle, and much squirming on Garon's part, Ochnic finally released his grip to bury his great head in his hands. "Has something possessed you?" Garon asked, a little breathless.

"Sorry, I am, pack leader," Ochnic said. He hunched his shoulders and seemed to shrink by a foot in height. "Eager, I am, to return. I have no news of Cadha."

"Your wife?" Marus asked.

Ochnic huffed trying to think of the word. "No, not life mate. My girl." With one palm he pressed down through the air to his knees and with the other he waved at Pel.

"Your daughter?" Garon said. "Child?"

"Dat is da word," Ochnic said, scratching his head. "Da chieftains told me to travel to da silver tree before my clan reached de Great Glen. I had no news."

"I'm sure your clan and daughter made it, Ochnic," Garon said. He patted the troll on the back, squelching against the troll's sodden fur.

"Maybe we could discuss this over breakfast?" Pel asked. "I'm starving."

"You want food?" Ochnic said, emerging from his hunched position. "Yes. You must have a hunger. I brought you here before you sleepy ones normally arise and forget. Sorry, I am."

Pel looked quite taken aback with this level of apology. "I don't... I mean to say... It's quite alri—"

But Ochnic began rooting through the bushes, along the embankment of the river, lifting fallen branches and scouring the earth. He moved around the area in such a frantic haste that Garon could barely keep track as he darted between the trees. In what seemed a matter of seconds he had returned, carrying a collection of wild plants on a giant leaf that was larger than most roasting dishes. He presented it to Pel.

"Food," Ochnic explained. Garon braced himself for another outburst from her, but to his surprise she seemed to well up with emotion.

"You know what plants are edible?" Pel said. "I was never taught that like the other women. Just spear work for me." She reached out for a honey-coloured alderberry, the only item on the flat leaf that Garon recognised.

"I know da wild."

"And you did it so quickly…" Pel continued, chewing the berry with an open mouth and entirely forgetting her fairy etiquette.

"Always der is ways," said Ochnic. "Try this." He handed her a mushroom half the size of his hand with a thousand white strands sprouting up like a hedgehog and placed several delicate white flowers on top. Pel took it with only a small show of trepidation and took a bite.

"It's creamy, earthy and garlicky," she said.

"Feel better?" Ochnic asked.

"I'm starting to," Pel said. Then with some effort she added, "Thank you."

Garon sensed this was an opportunity to seize.

"So, are we all done having our moments?" He asked. "I ran away for the evening. I shall not do so again. Marus learned that sometimes you need help in life; Ochnic confessed his fears to us, and Pel has been fed. I've also learned that that none of us wanted to be here. Marus offended the Guardian; Fidelm forced Pel here; Ochnic would rather be back with his family and who could blame him. And I, your sorry leader, would much rather be with Cosmo and Darnuir because I haven't been separated from them in twenty years and they are the only family I have." He surprised himself with the outpouring. The others were all gawking at him. Garon realised he had best carry on now that he'd started. "There have been deaths and traitors already, and we've each come out with some choice insults for everyone else but I say it ends here. We're all in the shit, and none of us wanted it. Best thing we can do is come together and go help Ochnic's people and his daughter. Now does that sound agreeable?"

"Yes," Marus said, bluntly but wholeheartedly.

"You speak true, Garon pack leader."

They looked to Pel.

"Fine," she said. "Yes, that's agreeable," she added with a little more enthusiasm. Then she took another greedy bite of the mushroom and flowers.

Chapter 8

ON THE SHADOW SPIRE

After the Second War, the humans under Brevia's growing influence received help in constructing the mighty Bastion to help deter against future dragon aggression. One can understand why the humans of the Splintering Isles felt unfairly treated in this regard. The islanders received no such help from the new Dragon King, Dronithir. A fortress on Eastguard was built, but it was no true barrier to dragons. That Dalridia and Brevia entered a form of rivalry is also understandable.

From Tiviar's Histories

Dukoona – Island of Eastguard – The former town of Errin

THE ISLAND OF Eastguard had been transformed. Dukoona had taken the town of Errin on the western coast and created a city for his demons. A sprawling mess of rickety shelters, stacked too high, too precariously and too close together; but what did those mindless runts care? Above it all loomed his Shadow Spire, facing outwards towards the rest of the Splintering Isles.

The Spire was a fortress built for spectres. As shadows gave spectres the most advantage, this is what the Spire created. Each portion of its walls had deliberately large gaps allowing light to enter at any time of day. Criss-crossing beams made from repurposed ship masts connected these walls, which would cast a web of shadows around the Spire and the surrounding lands. The Shadow Spire's twisting walls curled inwards at the top, as though a hand of broken fingers was grasping at the sky. Here, where the gnarled fingers of wood and metal met, was a viewing deck overlooking the grey sea. Dukoona stood there now surveying his fleet with Kidrian and little Sonrid at his side.

"We can delay no longer," Dukoona said. "If what you report is true, Kidrian?"

"I'm afraid so," Kidrian croaked. "I fear we might have lingered on Eastguard for longer than necessary."

"How heavily reinforced are the closest islands?" Dukoona said.

"Large forces on the islands of Ullasay, Skelf and Ronra, my Lord, though the numbers on Skelf are the greatest, despite being the smallest. From what our Trusted could gather, young Grigayne Imar believes we will strike there first, as it the weakest."

"Does he indeed?" Dukoona said. "Fortunate you discovered this information."

"We might have completed our missions sooner, my Lord, but travelling by boat to each island is so slow; and then we had to be careful not to be intercepted."

"You are forgiven," said Dukoona. "Our inability to meld over water is a most inconvenient oversight by our Master." He and Kidrian exchanged smiles of pure white teeth.

"Might we speak more openly," Sonrid said in his half-formed voice. "Only I wish to make my own report and—"

Dukoona silenced him with a wave of his hand. "It is useful, Sonrid, to learn to understand beyond what one merely hears. Just as it is useful to see beyond what only your eyes can see." Yet Sonrid's half-closed eyes was a reminder that he was not as adept as the rest of the spectres. Poor Sonrid suffered daily. He was small and hunched, and his shadowy flesh was wispier than a normal spectre's. As one of the Broken, Sonrid had not been summoned properly to this world by their Master, Rectar.

"I will try my best," Sonrid said.

"You have done well so far," Dukoona said and he meant it.

"I am rarely taken notice of. That is all."

"A trait I wish I had at times," Kidrian said. "Yet all the spectres know I am too close to Lord Dukoona. Those of our kind who are False watch me carefully."

"There have been murmurings," Sonrid said. "Some say the Master will not be happy about this delay."

"And what do others say?" asked Dukoona.

"Some are worried," said Sonrid. "They feel the Master ought to have done something by now. Forced us to move on. They are concerned about his indifference."

Yes, Rectar's indifference worries me greatly as well.

It was as if Rectar simply wanted his demons out of the way, putting a buffer between his lair at Kar'drun and the Three Races. Whilst adding to Dukoona's own unease, the news also offered some opportunity.

"Kidrian, perhaps we could seek out these troubled brothers and see if they are to be trusted?"

"You must be cautious," said Sonrid, and Dukoona was surprised to hear a sternness to his voice.

"I've been doing this for a rather long time," Kidrian said. "Don't concern yourself with me, Sonrid."

"You should be careful around Kraz," said Sonrid. "You say you are watched, well he watches most closely." Little Sonrid even jerked his misshapen head from side to side as if to check Kraz was not there with them.

"Kraz?" said Kidrian in disdain. "That flaunter can barely conjure a blunt sword from the shadows, never mind that double-headed axe he claims to do. Can't trust him with those bright yellow flames on his head."

Sonrid, however, appeared unconvinced.

"Do you fear him?" Dukoona asked.

"He talks of knowing how to better lead this invasion," said Sonrid. "To his own small band of spectres. And he's taken to keep more demons near him of late."

"I didn't ask what you know of him," said Dukoona. "I asked whether you feared him." Sonrid shuffled awkwardly but nodded.

"He often threatens me, my Lord. He speaks of hearing from the Master. That the Master would be glad to see the weakest of his servants culled."

"He boasts," Kidrian said offhand. "He exaggerates and he lies. None hear from the Master other than our Lord Dukoona."

Dukoona, however, was not so sure. "Many things have changed of late, Kidrian. Spectres are dying or disappearing. Great deposits of starium stone at the Forsaken City go missing to some unknown end. We should not dismiss claims like this on a whim. Not anymore. We must hear beyond what we hear," he reminded them both.

"I accept the possibility that the Master may speak to others now," Kidrian said. "Possibly. But surely not Kraz."

"He'd be ideal," Dukoona said. "A puffed up, weak-willed spectre with little reason to question why he was suddenly being spoken to by the Master? A few words and some encouraging nudges and Kraz might really believe he was being singled out for extra power."

"My Lord…" Kidrian began, "do you truly—"

"I do not know what to believe anymore. I doubt everything. That is why we must work carefully. Still, there is no reason Kraz cannot be dealt with."

"Dealt with?" Sonrid asked, sounding both excited and terrified.

"Oh yes," said Dukoona. "If the Master truly speaks to Kraz then I fear how that might develop. If Kraz is merely lying, well… removing an insubordinate is my duty as Lord of the Spectres. I cannot have my spectres second guessing me."

"What can I do?" Kidrian asked.

"You can prepare our ships to launch," Dukoona said. "I shall handle Kraz. Come, Sonrid." He leapt into the nearest shadow and felt the presence of Kidrian and Sonrid close by. A few masts down and Kidrian deviated down a different wall of the Spire. The shadows were so numerous and connected that there was no need to jump from one shadow to another. When they emerged at ground level, Dukoona strode with purpose towards the ramshackle town of Errin. He heard Sonrid pad up behind him.

"I haven't told you where Kraz can be found."

"You'll show me."

"Will we walk there?" Sonrid asked as they entered the chaos of the demon city. The shrieking was almost unbearable.

"I thought so. I know shadow jumping can be difficult for you."

"I am sorry to be a hindrance."

Dukoona swooped around to look at Sonrid. He cast a clear thought to the demons around. *Silence.* Those nearby stopped their howling. He got down on one knee to be at eye level with Sonrid.

"Never say sorry for being as you are. Rectar decided to summon you to this world. You didn't ask for it. He is the one who failed to do it properly; that is no fault of yours."

"My Lord," Sonrid whispered, "anyone might hea—"

"This is something every spectre ought to hear and know. The weakest amongst us need our help, not our scorn. For our Master will do nothing to help you."

Sonrid nodded firmly. "You have given me purpose again, my Lord. I am grateful."

"Thank me by helping me fight back. Now, we must find Kraz. Lead the way." Sonrid shuffled on and Dukoona followed. The demons soon returned to their noise. Dukoona could sense their restlessness. It was well they would be shipped off to fight soon.

It was difficult to weave through the densely packed streets – if they could even be called streets. The entire demon town was becoming a mass grave. Human corpses lined the streets, left where they had fallen and exposed to the elements. Demons were not inclined to move them – they couldn't smell and weren't intelligent enough to care about blocked streets. Spectres could not smell either, but leaving the bodies had been an oversight. Now the Shadow Spire was built, Dukoona would have his spectres clear them.

He watched a crow fly down upon the soft, pulpy body of what had once been a young girl. The crow dove its beak into one of the girl's empty eye sockets and ferreted around for a scrap of meat that wasn't rotten. As Dukoona and Sonrid passed by, the bird yanked up a strip of greying flesh and took flight. Dukoona looked away. Death just didn't please him anymore. Dragons, fairies, humans – they must all feel the same way about their own kind as he felt about his spectres. Every death was felt by someone. He thought of Kidrian lying dead, or even Sonrid, and felt as though a great weight was pressing against his chest.

I will not be able to save them all in this war but I must do what I can.

Eventually, Sonrid stopped outside a tent-like structure made of a torn sail draped across the gap between two earthen houses. Under the canvas, a large hole burrowed into the ground with the entrance uncovered. This was not unusual. When the demons had found it too hard to build upwards they began to dig down instead. They were decent excavators, Dukoona would give them that.

Sonrid had no need to crouch to enter the tunnel; he slid in easily. Dukoona ducked and descended after him. Light soon vanished as they left the entranceway behind. The darkness was total and Dukoona heard Sonrid move closer to him. Spectres despised complete darkness, for without light there could be no shadows.

Patches of coloured fire flitted here and there from the flaming hair of passing spectres. They would be patrolling the tunnels, checking on the demons and keeping the peace. Fiery heads of green, orange and red flames bobbed by, muttering courtesies to Dukoona. All bright in the darkness, except for a Broken, such as Sonrid. The feeble grey embers on the little spectre's head were pitiful, like dying candles.

"It is just up here, my Lord," Sonrid said.

"You go on. Let Kraz and his company see you first. I think you'll appreciate the look on his face when I appear shortly after you."

Dukoona followed close behind Sonrid for the rest of their journey, drawing back only when a luminous cavern shone ahead. Kraz and his fellows must have lit torches. Dukoona thought this an interesting choice; one that spoke volumes.

He let Sonrid continue alone and melded into the edge of a long shadow cast by a supporting beam of the room. He travelled along the shadow and nestled in a finger's width of space. Dukoona stayed there, within earshot and sight of Sonrid entering the room.

"What do you want, scum?" came a voice.

"Apologies," Sonrid said. "I must have taken a wrong turn."

"Clear off then."

"Wait," said a new voice, this one sharper than most spectres. Another figure stepped into Dukoona's view. Yellow flames spiked in short sharp flames over his head.

There you are, Kraz.

"I know this one," Kraz said. "Come to take me up on my offer? Shall I end your miserable existence?" Shadows swirled around Kraz's hand and a long dark dagger materialised there.

"No," Sonrid said defiantly.

"What's that?" Kraz said. "He says no? Look, err, Sonrid isn't it? The Master has spoken to me again. Told me that this war is to be won swiftly and we can't have anything holding us back."

"I am not holding you back."

"No, that would be our mighty Lord Dukoona," said Kraz.

There were murmurs of agreement from around the cave.

"We've been stuck on this rock for too long," Kraz said. "There are humans close by that need killing."

More murmuring, louder this time.

Well, you have a point there Kraz, but I can't stand your tone. Dukoona was about to emerge from his shadow and reveal himself but stopped, as he heard Sonrid speak up.

"You're wrong."

The room fell silent.

"Did you croak something, wretch?" Kraz said.

"You heard me," Sonrid said. "You're wrong. Lord Dukoona is wise and vigilant."

"More like cowardly," said Kraz. "The Master does not appreciate wisdom. Only deaths." He stepped closer to Sonrid, raising his dagger.

Now was the time.

"What is happening here?" Dukoona asked, emerging from his shadow and sweeping into the room. Every dark set of eyes flicked frightfully between each other.

"Nothing, my Lord," Kraz said, his dagger melting away into shadow. "Little Sonrid here was lost, weren't you?"

Sonrid remained silent. Dukoona made a show of looking thoughtfully around the room, letting his gaze linger on some of the torches. "Fire and light? An interesting choice. Did you anticipate needing shadows?" No one answered him. "You are all very quiet. I thought I heard conversation as I made my way here but I must have been mistaken. Were you lost, Sonrid?"

"I may have taken a wrong turn, my Lord."

"I do hope that was the extent of it," said Dukoona, more to Kraz than anyone else. "We have too many battles ahead for our own to be divided. On that matter Kraz, I have an important request to make of you."

"My Lord?" Kraz said.

"I have been trying to decide upon a lead spectre for one of our landing forces. I thought you might be up to the task?"

"Absolutely, my Lord," Kraz simpered. "I would be honoured."

"I am glad to hear it. You shall acquire for me the small island of Skelf."

"The smallest island, my Lord?" Kraz said, unable to keep the disappointment out of this voice.

"A vital mission," said Dukoona. "Take Skelf for me. Then we will flank the humans on Ullasay and Ronra. Succeed and I may grant you command of the assault on Dalridia."

Kraz could barely contain his idiotic grin. "I am thankful you realise my potential. I shall not fail."

Oh, you will, but that will be something which pleases me.

"I hope not," Dukoona said. "Come Sonrid, let me help you find your way."

A day later, atop the Shadow Spire, Dukoona watched the assault force bound for Skelf set sail. The force tasked to take the island of Ronra to the north of Skelf had also sailed earlier that day, led by other spectres he knew to be False. From a deep shadow cast by the curving wall behind him, Kidrian emerged to join him. Hundreds followed, all Trusted; some of their most loyal. He was pleased that he could count on most of his people.

"I reduced the fleet heading Skelf as you requested," Kidrian said.

"Poor Kraz," Dukoona said. "It seems he was not the Master's chosen after all." Although Dukoona had to admit to himself, sending Kraz to his doom wasn't conclusive proof either way. This stunt hadn't even drawn a passing glance from Rectar's enormous presence in the distant recesses of Dukoona's mind. Yet Rectar's disinterest could only last for so long.

"Will we take Ullusay then?" Kidrian said. "Our forces here will overrun that island easily."

"No," Dukoona said. "Kraz is a fool but he and those who sympathise with him have a point. We have lingered long enough. Whatever the Master's intentions, he will not be satisfied if we do not make progress." He summoned his favourite sword from the shadows. Long, curved, impossibly sharp, and a deep purple like the shade of his shadowy flesh. It had been a long time since he'd had a proper battle. Once he would have been excited; now he looked around his Trusted gathered there and felt only worry. Still, he had to encourage them.

"We will not go to Ullusay," he said, raising the shadow blade high. "We will go around it. We will cut to the heart of the islands. We sail for Dalridia!"

Chapter 9

A MEETING OF KINGS

The oldest part of Brevia lies on the southern bank, where the Master Hunter station now stands. Originally, it was a small port that was developed to begin trading surplus grain from the Golden Crescent to the expanding island centre of Dalridia. Since then it has grown, to say the least.

From Tiviar's Histories

Darnuir – Brevia – King Arkus' Palace

"FASTER, PRAETORIANS," LIRA called. "You'll have to push yourselves to find where your true limits lie."

The young Praetorians repeated the exercises, quicker than before, but not quick enough. Darnuir thought it strange to think of them as young, for they were all close in age to himself; but he felt much older. Having the memories of a sixty-year-old dragon merge into his mind had altered his perception on a lot of things.

"I know how abnormal it will feel," Darnuir told them. "I found it hard to unlock my own strength. You've lived among humans all your lives; you're not used to it. But push. Come on, harder now." Each Praetorian drilled again, and again, and again. Their swords rang in the Chevalier training hall that Raymond had kindly offered them. A few of the dragons were visibly breathless now. "That's it," Darnuir told them. "We dragons might be few now, but each of us is worth ten humans. You will all be worth far more than that."

Lira sidled up so only Darnuir could hear. "They weren't the most experienced but their attitude aligned closest with ours. They'll be happy to work with humans."

"Skills we can hone," Darnuir said. "Attitude is far harder to change. They'll need more practice with the bow. How good a shot are you?"

"Decent enough," Lira said. "Captain Romalla always said I was better with a sword."

"Captain Tael told me the same thing. Yet brute strength and extra stamina can do that when sparring with humans. Everyone thought I was gifted."

"You are skilled, sire."

"We fought briefly, Lira. You gave me too good a match for one who wields the Dragon's Blade. But I have learned a lot since then."

"We may have to be patient with them in learning the bow."

"I know," Darnuir said. "I don't expect them to master something that takes hunters years to learn. Although much of that is building their arm strength. These are dragons we're training."

Lira tilted her head thoughtfully, a little grin playing on her face. "Let's see how they do today."

Strength was a hindrance, as it transpired. Quite a few Praetorians whipped back their arms so hard the strings snapped, but eighteen broken bows later, a handful of them were beginning to hit the target more often than not.

"Focus on technique," Darnuir said, walking around each in turn to help. "Feet shoulder-width apart, left foot just in front with your toes facing the mark. Those left handed will do the reverse."

"Find a comfortable position for your hand at full-draw," Lira told them. "This will be your anchor. Try to pull back to the same spot each time."

Darnuir saw one girl pull back her string too far. Her hand was passed her ear, her string quivering with the tension. "Not so tense now," he said, gently easing her hand back towards her face. "Do as Lira says. Find where it is comfortable. Perhaps where your thumb touches your ear or where your knuckles meet your cheek." The girl nodded, concentration etched into her expression. She loosed the arrow and it hit the secondary ring, a little off the centre.

"Yes," she cried, then reorganised her features more seriously after catching Darnuir's eye. "Sorry, sire."

"Don't be," he said, returning to patrolling around the group. "Just keep practising. Demons and red-eyed men aren't going to stand still for you. One day I want you to be able to run and shoot at the same time, as many experienced hunters can." Some of them looked to him as if this was insanity. "It's true. You forget that hunters were trained to kill dragons once. I know a hunter who can even loose three arrows within seconds... well, I knew a hunter..." he said to himself, trailing off. Balack was the greatest archer he knew but he doubted his once closest friend would ever help him in the archery yard again.

I don't deserve his friendship. Not after what I did. Not after dealing a blow to his heart and then his ribs.

"Lord Darnuir," a voice called to jar him out of his reverie. Darnuir turned to see Raymond at the entrance above them. Yet again he was without his dark steel armour and wore a black leather jerkin over a white shirt. "King Arkus will converse with you now."

About bloody time.

"Lira, continue with things here," said Darnuir.

"I am afraid I must ask your dragons to vacate the hall," Raymond said when Darnuir reached him.

"But why?"

"My superiors do not approve," Raymond said. "And I have had my privileges removed." He turned like a soldier to leave and Darnuir followed alongside him.

"I am sorry to hear that," Darnuir said. "Perhaps I could—"

"The White Seven feel I am already too close to you, my Lord of Dragons. If you were to intervene that would only prove them right."

"Close?" Darnuir said, surprised. "I think you got over some of your prejudice at Torridon, but I would hardly call that close."

"That is close enough for many in Brevia," said Raymond, leading Darnuir through the black carpeted corridors of the palace. Darnuir assumed he was going to Arkus' more private council chambers.

"I would have thought their more pressing concern would have been your brother?" Darnuir said. "Castallan's agents and followers are clearly in high positions."

"That is exactly the issue. I should have realised before I opened my mouth to the White Seven."

"Your superiors?" asked Darnuir, not finding the term familiar.

"Yes, the White Seven," Raymond said, a touch of bitterness in his tone. "One for each region of the Kingdom and one for Brevia itself. They have the King's ear in military matters. Telling them of events at Torridon, of Sanders' betrayal," he gulped. "It did not go the way I envisaged."

"Tell me about it," Darnuir said. Something about this unsettled him. *Do such powerful men really work against me?*

"Some thought I was lying," Raymond said. "Told me it was safe to admit the dragons killed my brother. I said that was preposterous." His speech grew hotter as he continued, "I explained, Lord Darnuir, I did; that were it not for your decision and the great effort of the dragons, then all would have perished at Torridon. Alas, it did not help. Lord Boreac in particular—"

"Lord Boreac?" Darnuir said. "He's one of these Seven? What does he have to do with it?" Hearing that name only deepened Darnuir's disquiet. His thoughts raced, and then it came to him: a brief and painful memory of a conversation with Eve at the hunter station. She had asked why Scythe had been chosen as their new captain after Tael's death, and Darnuir had told her Lord Boreac had nominated Scythe for the job.

Could it simply be a coincidence?

"You seem distracted," Raymond said.

"I'm sorry. Continue."

"Certainly. Lord Boreac is one of the White Seven, but that is not unusual. About half of them are old lords who can afford the position. If not them then one of their sons often takes the region's post. I am told that was not the way things used to be, that once anyone could rise through the Chevaliers with bravery, honour and skill, like the hunters. Now, I'm not so certain."

"How did you join, if I may ask?"

"My father asked King Arkus to grant my brother and I the honour," Raymond said. "He and my grandfather made a deal of money in new print methods – enough to aid Arkus in financing his reconstruction of Brevia; enough to make a name for our family. My father thought that

Tarquill would be fitting. Yet we were always looked down upon, my brother and I."

"And you have been trying to prove yourself ever since," Darnuir said. "I sympathise, Raymond. I worried whether I could prove myself as a dragon and now as a king."

Raymond looked taken aback by Darnuir's honesty but nodded. "I can see why Sanders would have been lured by the thought of some extra power. Perhaps he was sick of the jeers, of being given the second rate tasks. But I'll never truly know why or how it happened…"

"You said you had your privileges stripped but you were making announcements for Arkus in the throne room."

"If someone asked you to make announcements rather than don your sword and armour, how would you take it?"

"As a slight."

"Forgive me, Lord Darnuir," Raymond hastened to add. "You must think I'm grousing over trivial things."

"Your temper is nothing compared to mine," said Darnuir. "I'm sorry to hear all this, Raymond. You deserve better."

"The King has been kind to me in truth," said Raymond. "He helped keep me within the Chevaliers when some called for my dismissal. He didn't just grant me my position as a repayment for a debt. Arkus has encouraged men like my father and grandfather – men with ideas, ambition and drive. I think they are jealous of the favours the King shows us."

Raymond slowed his pace and Darnuir matched it. Up ahead was a heavily guarded room, which Darnuir assumed to be Arkus' council chamber. Each man guarding the corridor was heavily armoured in dark steel.

"Are ten Chevaliers necessary?" Darnuir asked.

"Arkus at least has taken my warnings seriously," said Raymond. "Yet I am ill at ease. Something does not seem right in the city anymore. The White Seven handpicked these men but—"

"I understand," Darnuir said, more quietly as they drew ever closer to the group.

"Be wary, my Lord of Dragons," Raymond said in an equally hushed voice.

When they reached the guards, their leader stepped forward and removed his helmet. The Chevalier was a little taller than Darnuir, with a mane of dark blond hair to his lower neck and marble smooth skin. He smiled tauntingly at Raymond.

"Ah, that was quickly done. You'd make an excellent squire, Raymond."

"Gellick," Raymond said curtly.

"Please be seated, Lord Darnuir," Gellick said. "I shall inform King Arkus you have arrived."

"I had thought to tell the King myself—" Raymond began.

"You are dismissed, Raymond," Gellick said without looking at him.

"But, sir, I—"

"Dismissed," Gellick said. "Or must I ask you to brush our steeds next?"

Raymond's face was growing pink but he nodded to Gellick and bowed briefly to Darnuir before taking his leave.

"One moment," Gellick said. He entered the room, leaving Darnuir alone with the rest of the Chevaliers. They still had their helmets on and visors down, making it impossible to see their eyes. Yet, Darnuir had other methods.

Furtively, he sniffed the air, trying to find a trace of fear. There was a light sweetness but from which guard he could not tell. Nor was he truly more informed. *Are you afraid because you are worried about being caught or because of who I am, whoever you are?*

Frustrated that he was being forced to wait, Darnuir dropped onto the plush bench, reaching to adjust the scabbard of the Dragon's Blade so that he could sit properly. The moment his hand touched his sword all the Chevaliers had their own weapons out. Darnuir let go of his sword slowly and deliberately.

"I'm not here to fight," he said. The air was much sweeter now. That gave him some comfort. If they were afraid of him then they couldn't all be enhanced red-eyed men. As the Chevaliers sheathed their swords, not saying a word to him, Darnuir wondered whether he could take all nine at once. He liked to think so. It might take a bit of Cascade energy, but he could do it. Ten humans, armour or no, couldn't hold up to him now. Just a little Cascade energy is all it would take. His hand twitched. He saw a mental image of the Dragon's Blade carving through their steel bodies

like meat and could almost feel the rush of magical residue running hot
down his arm.

What is the matter with me?

He breathed steadily through his nose and calmed himself.

It was important to show Arkus he had changed. Sadly, those outbursts
in the throne room wouldn't help matters. In the days since, Darnuir was
sure that he had been kept at arm's length as a means of establishing the
status quo. Arkus was saying "This is my city, my keep. We'll talk when I
am ready."

Yet time was short and Blaine was still to show.

Darnuir had tried to get Kymethra to go scout out Blaine's movements,
but she refused to leave Brackendon's side. The pair of them had become
reclusive, holed up with heaps of old books and scrolls. Events at the
Conclave tower had set a fire under Brackendon although Darnuir was
still unclear on what had exactly transpired that night. Arkus had been
furious enough to deny seeing Darnuir that morning and now the days
had rolled by.

*What's Arkus waiting for? His armies are here. His fleet ready to sail. We
do not have any time to lose.*

Darnuir rose. "I am weary of this delay." He stepped forward,
intending to push past the Chevaliers if necessary. To their credit, they
did not react brashly. Darnuir heard those to his flanks thump slowly in
behind to surround him.

He reached for the door.

He saw the closest Chevaliers reach for their swords.

"Yer as unreasonable as yer sluggish, Arkus," came a loud, sharp voice
from inside the room. Then the doors swung inward. Somerled Imar stood
there, his face red, arms wide from heaving the doors open. Up close,
Darnuir noticed that Somerled was a good deal shorter than himself. "Do
us a favour, Lord Darnuir, and knock some spirit intae him. Oot of ma
way now." Somerled shoved passed Darnuir and the Chevaliers returned
to their original posts.

"The King will see you now," Gellick said, as though nothing had
happened.

The room was sparse and practical, the only real adornment being a life-size portrait of a rather stunning woman, with long black hair and grass-green eyes, wearing a pale green dress. Her smile was dazzling.

Arkus stood stony-faced behind a large desk, topped with maps, figurines and open books with minuscule text. A great steaming vat of shimmer brew rested by several thick mugs and a bowl containing heaped silver alderberries. Arkus' hair hung loosely due to the absence of his crown, which lay atop sheets of ragged old parchment like the most extravagant paperweight in the world.

"A little privacy please, Gellick," Arkus said, popping a few of the berries into his mouth. Arkus didn't acknowledge Darnuir. The King of Humans seemed preoccupied with his maps and accounts.

"Lord Imar appears displeased," Darnuir noted as he reached the other side of the laden table. The light fragrant bitterness of the brew was energising on its own.

"Somerled feels I ought to have sent reinforcements to his islands already," Arkus mumbled, not looking up from the map. The military figurines were mostly of humans, painted in black and white for Arkus' regular army. Most of them were outside Brevia but a collection stood farther south at the Bastion, along with bow and arrow carvings in dark green.

Has he already sent troops south? If so, why so few?

Arkus sniffed then finally looked up. "Somerled believes I am moving too slowly."

"Understandably so, but we must take the Bastion first and for that we'll need to wait for the Guardian Blaine to arrive."

"Why do you think I've called you?" Arkus said. "This Guardian and his army should arrive at Brevia today."

"Today? Why wasn't I informed immediately?"

"Word arrived late last night and I am telling you now."

"That's hardly the level of communication I require," Darnuir said.

"I've had a lot to manage of late," Arkus said. He indicated the piles of parchment. "Brackendon's bit of vandalism hasn't helped either."

"He learned valuable information," Darnuir said.

"Did he?" Arkus asked. "So, we know it wasn't Castallan who struck first. It hardly helps us. I hope all this studying the pair of them are doing will produce results on how they can weaken him."

"Brackendon's never let me down before," Darnuir said. "I'd have thought you'd be pleased such a blemish as the Conclave tower was removed for you."

Arkus grunted. "It will be once the irregularity of the area clears, I suppose. The city's population could use more room. But enough of the damned Conclave. We have an impenetrable fortress to take."

"It might not be so hard," Darnuir said. "At the Charred Vale, we defeated Castallan's demon army. The Bastion will lie relatively unguarded, unless he has summoned thousands more in such a short space of time."

"Don't be so sure it is demons we will face," Arkus said. He pointed to the figurines around the Bastion. "It would seem Castallan has gathered fresh troops." He poured himself a fresh mug of shimmer brew and took his first sip loudly. "Those are no longer my forces," Arkus added, reaching for a large piece of parchment with a multitude of coloured seals at the bottom. He passed it to Darnuir to read.

To our former King Arkus, the Lords of Brevia and the Kingdom, and every human drawing breath, we, the Lords of the Southern Dales, and those lesser lords signed herein, do by renounce the overlordship of the City of Brevia and the King. We instead pledge ourselves to and proclaim our King to be Castallan, Greatest of the Wizards. King Castallan even now burns his demons in the embers of a renewed faith in humanity, while a resurgent Dragon King attempts to restart a conflict long since left in peace. Dragons thirst for war again and humanity shall suffer as we have always done when dragons draw their swords. Only King Castallan, who wields the power of the Conclave of old, may lead us to renewed security for evermore. We welcome all those who feel the same to join us. It is not a decision blithely made. It is not for power, nor for riches, nor the advancement of person, but for the benefit and defence of all mankind. It is a cause we believe in upholding, even with life itself.

Chief Signatory, Robert Annandale, Lord of the Southern Dales.

Scores of names followed, each with their own curly scrawl and lump of wax. Darnuir's teeth scraped together as he clenched his jaw, the darker reality clawing up from his gut.

'Even with life itself'… more lives will end than will be saved with this madness, Annandale.

"I wished to confirm the truth of it before bringing it to your attention," Arkus said. "If what Raymond says about these red-eyed men is true, then we will need every dragon to take the Bastion now."

"His superiors did not believe him," Darnuir said.

"The White Seven are a conservative lot," Arkus said. "They can barely believe that a book need not be copied by hand alone these days."

"And you?"

"If you can be reborn then why not. Magic isn't something I claim to understand and I've never wished to have much business with it."

"It is dangerous, yet it is the source of my strength and we will need Brackendon if we are to defeat Castallan."

"Brackendon's certainly a destructive force," Arkus said. "In any case, I believe I have a tool equally as destructive. A substance of great power."

Darnuir raised his eyebrows. "Would this happen to be a powder? A black powder?"

"Yes," Arkus said, deflating a little. "How do you know of it?" Darnuir proceeded to tell him of the events of the run from Torridon, when they had piled a makeshift wall across the land and set it ablaze, only to be greeted with explosions all along the line.

"The Head of my Praetorian Guard, Lira, also knew of it," Darnuir concluded. "Told me it is used in the quarries of the Hinterlands. I don't think it is a great secret."

"Few enough know just how strong it is and given the circumstances, I'd be willing to use our stores in the fight to come."

"You plan on making a weapon of this powder?"

"A weapon," Arkus tittered. "My wife's dear father, Lord Clachonn, would baulk at that. He calls it a tool."

"A hammer is a tool, but it can smash your skull."

"A crude if effective method. Right now, the powder is crude but effective at blowing rock to pieces. Why not use it?" Arkus sounded quite jovial, reaching for a handful of silver berries.

Darnuir wasn't quite sure what to make of all this. The powder would give them a needed edge but it was dangerous, hard to wield. It might well explode on their own men. He felt uncomfortable but he couldn't say exactly why – it all seemed too straightforward; too open.

If only Blaine was so clear with me; my, wouldn't that be nice.

"You're being very honest with me, Arkus."

"Because I hope that we might be frank with each other, Darnuir. My people are divided on how they feel about your kind. Events in the Dales make that all too clear."

"The audience in your court seem to hold similar opinions," said Darnuir. "You as well, from what you said there."

"A small piece of theatre, Darnuir," Arkus said. "My rule is not like your own. I must strike a constant balance of having more of my lords and people on my side than against me. Since this chaos began, many have blamed the dragons and you for it. In the past, I too have had my issues; we have even had our issues, but you might not remember."

"I remember enough," Darnuir said. "Enough to want a fresh start, if that can be achieved."

"It gives me hope to hear you say that," said Arkus. "Hope, that we might forge a more agreeable relationship after this war is over. Assuming we are still alive that is."

"A stronger partnership is something I too seek," said Darnuir. "The Three Races should stand as equals."

"I had something else in mind," Arkus said. "Human autonomy."

"Break the alliance?" Darnuir asked, taken aback.

"Only in a sense," said Arkus. "Only to make it seem like I have removed the overbearing dragon lords from my back and, more importantly, from the Assembly. Besides, if we win, if Rectar is defeated, what need will there for an alliance then?"

"Let us agree to discuss this matter seriously *if* the time comes," Darnuir said, extending a hand. It wouldn't be what Arkus wanted to hear, but Darnuir would not make important promises like this too hastily. It was all too quick and polite and smooth. After a moment, Arkus took his hand, if a little reluctantly.

"I'll agree to that for now. My people are the ones currently causing us the headache, after all." Arkus hovered a clenched hand over the figurines near the Bastion on the map, as though he meant to squash them.

"As you say, many blame the dragons. Castallan offers them an easy solution. It's disheartening how many believe in him."

"Castallan can be convincing, but there is something else he desires as well: power." Arkus bent to grasp his crown as he spoke. Picking it up, he balanced it delicately on his palms. He looked down on the white gold circlet with narrowed eyes. "He wants what's best for humanity, I don't doubt. But he also wants this. And I'm afraid I am not willing to give it up."

"Then what makes you so different from him?"

"Nothing in truth. It is just self-preservation," Arkus said, tossing the crown unceremoniously back on the table. "Would you give up what you have?"

"I don't have a choice," Darnuir said. "The Dragon's Blade answers only to me."

"There is always a choice in these things," said Arkus. "Yet it simply isn't in our nature to make ourselves lesser. Annandale's words in his declaration are well put and inspiring, but they are false and mask his longing. Yet such is the way of words."

"People are capable of change," Darnuir said. "It seems you are. You are nothing like the memories I have of you."

"A shattered heart and a shattered people will do that to a king," Arkus said. "I have grown harder, less assuming; that may be the only way in which we can change. Those who don't will slip and fall. I did wonder whether you would be the same, when I heard you had been reborn. It did help to explain why you had disappeared for all those years. The Darnuir I knew wouldn't have had the patience to wait for so long."

"I very nearly lost my patience waiting upon this meeting," Darnuir admitted, thinking of his frustration of only minutes ago.

"And yet you did wait," Arkus said, giving Darnuir a quizzical look, as though he had done something singularly strange. "I confess, I expected you would burst into my chambers one day and make demands of me. But you didn't. In fact, you have shown a considerable deal of courtesy, apart from shouting sensitive information to my whole court."

"For that I am sorry," Darnuir said. "I ought to have shown more restraint but—"

"You were being harassed and abused," Arkus said curtly. "Frankly, I'd have lost respect for you if you had simply taken it. You dealt a strong and deep blow with your words, more than I imagine you are aware of."

"I was simply stating the facts."

"And the facts are distressing to many of my noblemen," Arkus said. "My Queen, in particular, is worried by them."

"You did not seem phased to hear of Cassandra."

"No," Arkus said simply. He did not speak again for a moment or two, perhaps thinking hard on his words. "I have long been aware that she lived, and that Castallan had her."

Where does the honesty end with this man?

"You knew, and still you did nothing?"

"Precisely," said Arkus. "Marrying off politically important daughters requires more planning and strategy than any war. Having her as my sole heir created a tremendous issue for me, Darnuir. I was already staring down civil unrest at sword point when she was lost to me. Nothing has been simple since Brallor ran off." Arkus' tone was dead, flat and cold. No emotion seemed to move him when speaking of his son.

"I am sorry, also, for bearing news of your son so crassly," Darnuir said. "I'm still reeling from the loss myself."

"Are you?" Arkus said more casually. "I am not. I presumed my son to be dead decades ago. That was the first wound and it has had the longest to heal."

"You have a grandson to love instead," Darnuir offered. "And Cassandra, when we save her."

"To love you say? Perhaps," Arkus mused. "What is the boy's name again?"

"Cullen."

"I'll see he is well cared for but for the sake of stability, Thane will remain my heir."

"Very well," Darnuir said. "My priority is defeating our enemies. So long as Cullen is cared for."

"He'll have an easier time of it than Cassandra I'll wager," said Arkus. "Already the vultures circle overhead – Somerled for one. He wishes his son Grigayne to marry her."

Darnuir felt an involuntary twitch at his mouth at hearing that. "You refused him, I assume?"

"I said I would need to think on the matter. Something more favourable may yet turn up."

"I doubt Lord Imar believes anything is more favourable," said Darnuir.

"The Splintering Isles have always been a troubled region," Arkus said, taking another handful of silver alderberries. "I would hate it for Somerled to believe he is getting what he wants. I judge you are not keen on the idea either? Though I imagine for very different reasons."

"Why would it matter to me?" Darnuir said, cursing himself for his indiscretion.

"Why? Well, I only thought that you might also have been interested in her for her position," Arkus said. "I could be wrong of course. You could just have feelings for her."

"You think I would?" Darnuir said, trying to feign some of the old scorn he knew his older self was capable of.

"My Lord Darnuir, if she is anything like her mother, then I'd be shocked if you did not. Tell me, what is she like? Does she have green eyes full of warmth?"

"She is beautiful," Darnuir said, though warmth was not apt for her eyes. Cosmo's yes, but not hers. "Beautiful but distant," he continued, "like the promise of spring in the middle of a long mountain winter." His gaze lingered on the portrait of the women behind Arkus a little too long. It might have been Cassandra, had it not been for the flush on her cheeks and the brightness of her smile. He was certain that Arkus caught him staring. "Cosmo's eyes, I mean; Brallor's, his were warmer."

"His mother's eyes," Arkus said. He turned to face the portrait as well. "Does she really look so much like Ilana?"

"She does," was all Darnuir could say. A part of himself felt ashamed at being affected in such a way by the mere thought of her. *Cassandra seemed to keep most at arm's length. But not me. She confided in me. We are close, right?* But he also knew that half of why he was drawn to her was based on the relief of his head pains. Some intangible connection over his lives that had settled the memories trapped in the rubies of the Dragon's Blade before he unlocked them.

What was that kiss? Was any of it real or was it all in my head?

Arkus let loose a shuddering, tired sigh. "I'm not sure whether my heart will leap or sink when I see her." His voice was suddenly hoarse. "Clever as well, I assume?"

"Of course," Darnuir said. "Intelligent and capable; she escaped from the Bastion after all."

"I had wondered… I don't suppose you know how?"

"There are passages within the fortress," Darnuir said. "Though without Cassandra with us, I doubt we will be able to find the tunnel she used."

"Passages?" Arkus questioned. "Curious. I saw none when I inspected the old plans for the fortress earlier."

"You have the plans?" Darnuir said more eagerly. *Perhaps some other weakness can be found.*

"I do," Arkus said, reaching for the rather old and large sheets of parchment that his crown had been resting on before. "They were deep in the royal vaults, but we found them. However, you will see that there is no indication of any passages under the walls."

Darnuir studied each sheet carefully, noting with some trepidation the thickness and height of each wall, angled in such a way to make it impossible to find a dead zone from defending archers. The detail was intricate, every measurement given, and each method of defence quantified. There was nothing, however, that looked remotely like passages either in the walls or the central tower.

"Are these the only plans?"

"They are. It is possible that later additions were added and the plans have since been lost. It is peculiar." Arkus looked more intensely to Darnuir then. "You only have Cassandra's word about these tunnels?"

"Well, yes," Darnuir said. "I believe her. And finding these passageways will be our best chance at success. I'll dig up half the Dales if that's what it takes to find them. Unless this powder of yours will bring down the walls."

Arkus glanced back at the plans. "My supply of powder isn't vast and these walls are thick, and there are two layers to contend with. We'll deploy it as best we can, but this will likely still be a job for swords and strength."

"And there are few enough dragons left now," said Darnuir.

"Enough to cause a panic when four legions of your kind arrived at the city gates."

"I'd be more concerned about the traitors surely lurking in your midst," Darnuir said. "The man I killed at the Charred Vale was called Scythe and he was one of your hunter captains. There ought to be investigations. Certainly into the hunters at the Master Station here in the city, if nothing more."

"No," Arkus said.

Darnuir half opened his mouth and then stopped, caught off guard by the blunt response. "No?" he said slowly.

"No," Arkus repeated.

"I did not think it to be an unreasonable request," Darnuir said. "Nor did I imagine you would wish such men to continue at large." Arkus swept aside to pour himself another mug of brew. Darnuir watched, perplexed, as Arkus threw back its contents in one extended gulp and his whole body shook a little with the injection of energy.

"I thought this point might be tough for you, Darnuir. If you truly have changed, as you say, then you will listen to me."

"Will I?" Darnuir said, his temper beginning to rise. "I can wait for an audience with you if needs be. I will leave you to run your affairs as you will. But this is a military matter and in that, until this alliance changes, I am not to be denied. These traitors revel in killing dragons. I would see them brought to justice."

"You would see their heads roll," Arkus said. "Don't deny it. I recognise that look about you, that much you have retained from your old life. The anger you turn to so easily. I urge you, however, to rethink. I urge caution."

"Caution? It is caution and planning and waiting that has gotten us into this position. Castellan should have been handled years ago. Blaine should have gathered the dragons years ago."

Arkus remained calm by comparison, staring Darnuir back down. "I find this bloodlust for traitors intriguing when you yourself helped Castellan get to where he is today."

Darnuir choked. "You know?"

"Now I do," Arkus said, a smile playing on his lips. "You just confirmed it. I only suspected before, though I was sure I was right."

"That was an error," growled Darnuir. "I'm not the same dragon anymore."

"Indeed," said Arkus. "A simple mistake of your past life, fuelled by misinformation and perhaps desperation. Could not the same be said of many of those who have joined Castallan?"

"It is hardly the same."

"But it very much is," Arkus said. "Annandale and Castallan have stirred up enough dissent in the south without us adding fuel to the fire. Your traitors are their brave new soldiers. You say you want justice for your people and I understand that. Believe me, I do. But I cannot have my Kingdom torn worse than it already is just to satisfy you. They are humans and under my laws. That is why I plan to offer clemency."

"Clemency!" Darnuir's heart drummed at the thought. "You might not be so quick to forgive if you had seen your son pinned against a tree with a sword."

Arkus winced. "And I presume you have taken your vengeance already. Is that not enough for you? No, Darnuir," Arkus added sternly. "I won't do it. If I allow you to go carving your way through my city looking for traitors, it will cause us both irreparable harm."

"This is a military ma—" Darnuir began.

"This is my Kingdom," Arkus said louder, "and my people. Persecution will get us nowhere. Let us remove the leaders and allow the followers to return quietly to the fold."

There was a knock on the door followed by, "Do you need us, sire?"

"It is fine," Arkus called back, then to Darnuir more quietly. "If you seek a better relationship then trust me on this. Do not give them justification."

Darnuir seethed, snorting air like a bull. He was on the verge of continuing the argument when the door burst open.

"I did not say enter," barked Arkus.

"My King," Gellick said, ignoring Darnuir. "The dragon and fairy armies have been spotted."

"Then I think we can conclude matters here for now," said Arkus.

"We're done for now," Darnuir said. "But the matter is not." He stormed out the room, letting his inflamed anger carry him back to the Chevalier training hall. Lira and the Praetorians stood outside, their way barred by a group of dark steeled guards. "Back inside," Darnuir ordered.

"But Darnuir, the guards, Raymond told us—" Lira began.

"If they want to stop us, they are welcome to try," said Darnuir. "I want a fight." The air grew very sweet as he approached the closest Chevalier on the door. "Well?" he asked, drawing close enough to the man to see his eyes widen behind the slots in his visor. The Chevalier said nothing but moved to one side.

Right move, human.

He heard the footsteps follow him in, down the tiered room to the lowest level. It was like a small arena or pit this far down and an audience would doubtless form soon. Darnuir whipped out the Dragon's Blade, turning it over and over in his hand.

"We need to intensify your training," he told the assembling Praetorians. "Four of you, you'll fight me at once. The rest of you, pair up and spar. No exercises; fight like you mean it. Now."

They began. Darnuir's opponents were better than he anticipated, that was good. Each time he fought them off he demanded they charge again. One managed to land a hit on him and that made him laugh. Soon he was lightly nudging on the door to the Cascade, letting a drop or two in.

That felt better than anything.

Soon he forgot why he was enraged. All he felt was the movement, all he saw was the eyes of those he trained with, all he heard was the thud of feet and the scrape of steel. He didn't stop. He just kept fighting.

It only ended when he saw what surrounded them. Hundreds of Chevaliers, faceless behind their visors, stood silently around the hall. Had they snuck in? Had they crept in like mice scurrying around the feet of wolves? Darnuir looked to them. Raymond wasn't there but Gellick was, the only one to have removed his helmet. He looked down upon Darnuir with a blank, unreadable expression. With one hand, Gellick lightly tapped the pommel of his sword.

"We're done for the day," Darnuir said. His Praetorians were trying to calm their breathing around him. "Come let us go meet our kin."

Chapter 10

THE END OF MAGIC

The wizards and witches of the Cascade Conclave are simultaneously remarkable and worth little attention. Their use of magic is extraordinary but their reserved nature – a necessity in handling magic in such a free manner – has dissuaded them from engaging in major events of the world. Had the Order joined one war or another in full force, the course of history could well have been different.

From Tiviar's Histories

Brackendon – Brevia – King Arkus' Palace

"AND THERE THEY go," Kymethra said. "Darnuir, Arkus, even Lira and enough guards to clog the streets. But not us."

"Not right now," Brackendon said. He didn't look up from his reading.

"Darnuir will want you down there." She rapped her knuckles on one of the tiny glass panes held within the lead lattice. The sharp tapping made Brackendon lose concentration on his page. He looked up and was met with Kymethra's frustrated expression.

"I'm busy," he said, his voice half a rasp. He took a gander out of the window towards where Kymethra had gestured. The palace resided on higher ground than most of the city, and Brackendon's room was high within it. High enough to see beyond the black walls of Brevia and witness the dragon legions approach the city like a wave of molten gold. *And so, we draw ever closer to the Bastion.* His silence seemed to annoy Kymethra further. She was scowling. "You might help me rather than berate me," he said.

"We've been through all these books. There's nothing there. Too much was either stolen from the Conclave or lost."

"There might still be something—"

"But there isn't," she said, her voice half-cracking. His brooding was fatiguing her, Brackendon knew. But it was more. She was afraid, as was he. For each day drew them closer to the battle to come; each day drew him closer to Castallan.

Whatever it takes, it must end. We must end.

"Will you stop acting like this?" she said, a little desperately.

"Like what?" he said, returning to his reading.

"Like a child. It's not like you at all."

"I'm sorry if I've upse—"

"I'm worried, Brackendon. You've barely spoken since the Conclave. Each day you've fallen deeper into this mood. It's like a part of you died. I heard what those *things* had to say as well, but I'm not giving up on the world."

"The Inner Circle attacked him," Brackendon said. "Castallan was forced to act as he did."

"Maybe in that moment," said Kymethra. "But in every moment since? Everything he's done since? I don't see how this changes anything."

"It doesn't," he said morosely. *It doesn't, and yet it changes everything.*

"Are you just going to brood here?"

He nodded, closing his eyes.

"Rather than tell me what really troubles you?"

He continued to nod.

"Fine," she stormed towards the door. "I'll go. Hotheaded dragons sound more reasonable at present."

There was a slam and distant footsteps. Brackendon took in a breath, held it, and then let it go slowly through his nose. He opened his eyes and returned to the page he had been reading.

This one was Mallory's *On the Bitter Taste of Power*. So far it was proving a tedious read and wasn't offering any insight into the limitations Castallan might have. When Brackendon reached a section about the optimum diet for a cautious Cascade user – oddly, poppy seeds were the prime recommendation with most meals – Brackendon closed the book. He added it to one of the many discarded piles with a thud. Landing askew, Mallory's dense tome tipped the balance and sent the entire stack crashing off the desk.

Grumbling, his frustration mounting, Brackendon rose to tidy up the books that lay scattered beneath the window. In his haste, he bashed his hip into the desk corner. Groaning, he bent down to collect the fallen books. It was warmer beneath the window due to light angling in through the glass. One beam burned uncomfortably at the delicate skin around his eye. The vexing heat caused an itch and jerked his head to escape it, only to slam against the underside of the desk.

This time he let loose a growl and tossed the book he had just retrieved back down. He gave up on the endeavour and stood, leaning his weight against the window and watching the dragons draw closer to Brevia. A blue mass crept into view behind them and behind the fairies marched hunters in red and yellow. *We're all gathering. Ready for the pointless slaughter.* It was a shame that Kasselle did not join her forces. Brackendon could have used her advice and knowledge, but then, the toil of marching and war had never been Kasselle's way. She sent others in her stead. Brackendon had been granted a shiny staff and been sent to do the impossible.

For there had been no answers. Not then, nor now on how he might actually win such a fight. Perhaps there might have been within the Conclave but he had brought that tower to dust.

He didn't regret it.

In the days since he'd exhausted Arkus' limited vaults and found nothing. Like Darnuir's rebirth, the situation was the first of its kind. Castallan had possession of all the staffs of the Conclave, save for Brackendon's. As powerful as Brackendon's new staff was, surely it alone would not best such incredible processing power. And where once Brackendon had been fuelled by a sense of justice and revenge, driven by a belief that Castallan was the enemy, he now felt deflated. It was as if his previous conviction had acted as a barrier between him and the reality before him. Yet, since the Conclave, the full weight of the duel ahead had begun to crush down upon him. Slowly. A little more pressing each day. Slowly. Until Brackendon considered that they had all been fools.

Where had this infighting gotten them? To the precipice of disaster. It was too late now for either party to make amends. Brackendon wasn't sure why he ought to fight. He was simply on one side and was stuck there. It wasn't the 'right' side, not anymore, just a side. He supposed it had always been this way, but he had been blind to it.

It was only then that he noticed his hands had bored into fists against the glass. They felt hot – too hot to be heated from sunlight alone.

Perhaps Castallan's intentions had once been noble, but Kymethra was right. His methods left him irredeemable. Brackendon would do his best against him, but not for the reasons he once had. It wasn't to avenge the Conclave; nor for humanity, for it seemed so many had joined Castallan, both then and now.

Something in Brackendon shook and the air around grew even warmer. A tremor ran down his right arm, yet there was no staff in his grasp.

He wouldn't fight for Darnuir either, he decided, looking out at the massing dragons. He knew Darnuir hoped to rectify his own mistakes by killing Castallan. Brackendon reckoned all the dragons were paying for their past. Not even the memory of Cosmo could move him. Yet Brackendon would fight. That was not in question. Though what he would fight for would be very different.

I will fight to end magic.

If by some miracle, he succeeded, then he'd break every staff that remained. He'd burn his own as well, even if he risked breaking to do so. He'd pass on no teaching.

Magic will end with me.

The window shattered, breaking in a shockwave from his fists and pouring down into the palace grounds. The tremor running down his right arm intensified, as did the heat around him. He grabbed his staff and felt the stinging rush of the Cascade.

Loose sheets of paper were whipped towards the breach. Embarrassed, Brackendon tried to grab them out of the air but most of them made it past him and flitted on the wind outside. Cooler air blew in and took the worst of the heat away, leaving Brackendon ashamed of himself. He ought to go down. It was childish of him to lurk up here when there was so much to do. There was nothing else that solitude and books could offer him.

Sadly, Brackendon's mood did not dissipate on his journey down. There was a restlessness within him, mixed with a reluctance to take part in whatever talks were going on between Darnuir, Arkus, Blaine and the rest. The thought of standing in the middle of that argument, for there was bound to be one, was enough to cause a grating headache all on its own.

So, he took his time, drifting slowly through the army camps outside the city. He passed by the palisade wall of a legion encampment and saw a human with a cart being barred entry by grim-faced dragon guards; that is until he managed to convey he was delivering food. Then he was waved on through.

Dragons will take and take, and never give.

Fairies seemed allowed to fly in and out as they pleased, however. One shot over head, drawing Brackendon's eye, speeding to some far away section of the sprawling tents above the rising strands of smoke and steam.

Soldiers laughed, soldiers wrestled in their boredom; some glanced inquisitively at Brackendon as he walked by, while others ducked their heads to avoid eye contact. Hunters and huntresses from the Crownlands patrolled in their black leathers, setting those idle to work and bemoaning the quality of the men's equipment. One pudgy fellow knocked into a stand of spears, nearly skewering passers-by, and hastily tried to pick them up before the hunters saw.

You might have called up many to fight Arkus, but these are hardly soldiers.

As arrogant as the dragons were, Brackendon could not deny that humanity would be at a woeful disadvantage in this war without them.

Somehow, Brackendon found himself before the hastily erected pavilion, positioned at the central point between the camps of the three races. There was a collection of Chevaliers, Light Bearers and Darnuir's Praetorians outside, standing in an awkward silence. One amongst them was not armoured but seated by a crude-looking crib. Auburn hair and the favouring of one side signalled that it was Balack, a little hunched over in his white leathers – well, what passed for white under that dirt.

Are those burn marks and singes?

"What happened to you?" Brackendon asked when he reached him.

"More of that Dragon Powder, or Black Powder, whichever it is," Balack said. He rolled up the clothing on one leg to reveal a series of burns.

"You must be in a lot of pain?" Brackendon said.

144

"Could have been worse. The Guardian shielded me, actually. Kept me in one piece, though I doubt I'll be battle fit in time for the Bastion." He winced and gently put a hand to his chest. "What's wrong with you?" Balack asked.

"Nothing," Brackendon said, perhaps a little too tetchily. "Did you see Kymethra?" He added, attempting to sound more pleasant.

"She flew down a while back. I think she's inside. Are you not going in?"

"Darnuir can make his decisions without me. He always has."

"He's changed," Balack said simply. He didn't seem to want to add any more. Footsteps beat behind Brackendon, and both he and Balack were spared further talk of Darnuir by the arrival of the outrunner Damien.

"Milk for the child," said Damien. "Approved by Queen Orrana's trusted wet nurse."

"He's asleep right now," Balack said, accepting the bottled milk. "But I'm sure he'll be eternally thankful."

"You didn't just bring the wet nurse?" Brackendon said, unable to resist despite his mood.

"She protested," said Damien. "Excuse me, I must return to the King." And he disappeared into the tent. Brackendon observed as Balack filled a horn with milk and lowered it carefully towards Cullen. A wedge of good clean cloth stymied the flow of liquid.

"Why are you playing mother?" Brackendon asked.

"Well, I'm still injured and so won't be able to fight. If I am honest, I feel I lack the will as well."

"What do you mean?"

"It's difficult to put into words. I don't feel as strongly as I did before; a little empty, truth be told."

"Cosmo's death has hit us all hard," said Brackendon. "He and Grace were decent people. I find it cruel that they've been taken."

"Yes, that was hard. I still don't think I've grasped that he's gone. Darnuir seems fine, though. He just ran off. Barely even checked to see whether Cullen was alive, never mind being looked after by anyone who cares."

"That seems a touch harsh," Brackendon said. "He has been concerned about Cullen."

"Concerned but not present. Not here… not the same."

Ah, so that is it. You miss your friend, even if you can't stomach the thought of him right now.

"It's not fair, what happened to you either," Brackendon said. "None of this is fair."

"Back home, even when things got desperate, even before you arrived, I somehow didn't feel as bad as this," Balack said. He hadn't seemed to register Brackendon's words. "We were all together then. All fighting; fighting for each other. And now—" Balack stopped, as though something had stuck in his throat. He swallowed and then busied himself feeding Cullen.

"I feel like I've lost something too. Lost what was driving me, so to speak. I understand what you're going through, I think."

"Have you lost the ones closest to you?" Balack asked. "Were your friends sent far to the north while you stayed here? Did the man you might have called a father die without you being able to do anything? Did your closest friend betray you and crack your ribs?"

"I don't have many friends," Brackendon said, and it sounded strange to say it aloud. "Most of the people I cared for were lost to me when the Conclave fell or have died in some other fashion. Until recently, I thought I was fighting for their memories, to make things right. Now, I've discovered that many were not who I thought they were. Darnuir is far better than he was, but the only one I truly have is Kymethra…" *And I've been pushing her away.*

"I, I'm sorry," Balack said, looking guilty for his outburst. "I hadn't considered that. Still, I can do good by honouring Cosmo and helping Cullen. I'm glad to."

"You might be of more help in the war."

"What can one archer do?"

"What can you do for Cullen that all of Arkus' palace staff cannot?" Brackendon rebutted. Balack opened his mouth to say something, but then seemed to reconsider, burying his face into his hands instead. "We need to keep fighting," Brackendon urged him, kneeling beside the young man. "As hard as it seems, we must. You might not wish to go on for Darnuir, but you can still go on *with* him. We can both help. But in our own way. For our own reasons."

Balack lifted his head up slowly, looking Brackendon in the eye. "What are your reasons?"

"I'm going to kill that wizard, or break him, and I'm going to prevent anyone else ever having the power that we do. With more luck than I dare count on, I might live out my days as just a man. A recovering addict, sure, but just a man." Balack said nothing. "Is there nothing left to drive you?" Brackendon asked.

"Helping a friend is worthy," Balack said. "Cassandra is a prisoner again. Although she can take care of herself, and I think Darnuir will have the rest covered." He thought for a moment. "I'll fight for Cosmo. That can be my reason."

"All you need do is help," Brackendon said. "And I can get you there. How many weeks have you been in recovery?"

"About three," Balack said. "I thought you couldn't heal with magic?"

"You can it's just... ill-advised. May I?" He moved an inspecting hand towards Balack, who obligingly raised an arm. Brackendon hovered his hand above the injured rib, sensing the damage there.

"How is it?" Balack asked.

"Healing well already. About halfway there. Yes, this can be done."

"Are you sure?"

"Half the healing, half the magic," Brackendon said. "And I have a staff from the Argent Tree. I think I can handle one minor to moderate injury." He shut his eyes and reached out to the door to the Cascade. He twisted the ghostly handle, pushed it open and let it flow. That moment of euphoric joy infused him.

He held it.

Savoured it.

Then he set to work, fusing Balack's rib together and easing the swelling. He sensed a minuscule splinter of bone lodged in Balack's lungs and dissolved it. Finally, he reduced the burns enough so that they would no longer cause pain. When it was done, Brackendon felt a powerful rush down his arm as the poison was sucked towards his staff. He held his breath, believing for the length of a heartbeat that he had gotten away with it.

Then he doubled over in agony.

"Brackendon," Balack said in alarm, catching him as he swayed forwards.

"Well it still hurt," Brackendon said through gritted teeth. "Did it work?"

Balack breathed in deep and fast. "I'd forgotten what it was like to not ache each time I drew breath. I feel better than ever."

"Oh, wonderful," Brackendon said, taking shallow breaths himself. He fixated on a trodden patch of grass, so as not to concentrate on anything too overwhelming. From somewhere behind him there came the sound of heavy footsteps on the hard earth, enough for several people.

"What is going on here?" came the unmistakable, disapproving voice of Blaine.

"Brackendon," Kymethra exclaimed. Suddenly, another pair of hands were pulling him off Balack. "What did you do? Your arm!"

"What about it?" Brackendon mumbled.

"There's another black streak," Darnuir said, stepping into Brackendon's shaky vision.

"What were you thinking?" Kymethra said.

"I was thinking that I might actually use my power to do some good," Brackendon said, getting to his feet. He felt a little off balance but nothing worse.

This staff truly is something.

"He healed me," Balack said. "Thank you."

"Thank me by not holding back at the Bastion."

"That was quite reckless," Darnuir said.

"I don't think you can comment on anyone's recklessness," Brackendon said. "Sorry, that was—"

"It's already forgotten," Darnuir said. "Are you alright?"

"I am," Brackendon said.

"Good," said Darnuir. "For we march to the Bastion on the morrow."

"Darnuir, if we may depart for a private word," Blaine said. He almost sounded hesitant. It was only now that Brackendon noticed Blaine was leaning his weight upon his left leg, and had bandages on his right calf, instead of armour.

"Haven't you made things worse enough today?" Darnuir said. He only then seemed to notice that Balack was there. "Balack – it will be good to have you back as well. We'll be in need of your bow," he added, not quite looking at his old friend. A second passed before Darnuir scrunched his lips, unfurled them again, and opened his mouth to say, "Balack… I—"

"I hope that is the last controversy between us, Guardian," Arkus called from out of sight. Everyone turned to see Chevaliers pouring out of the pavilion, and a pink-faced Arkus blustering through their ranks, his long black robes dragging on the earth. Darnuir didn't finish his thought. He glanced between Blaine and Arkus then swept off towards Brevia with Lira, Damien and the Praetorians filing in around him.

Blaine watched Darnuir go, looking disappointed at his departure before turning his attention to Arkus. "My treatment of the humans following the Charred Vale was—"

"Not appropriate," Arkus interrupted. "As I've had to explain to Darnuir. Those hunters are under my rule and my laws. Taking precautions is one thing. Making prisoners of humans out of mere suspicion is quite another. And as for the Dragon Powder—"

"Do not use that term," a Light Bearer with black curls said, drawing in closer.

"It's alright, Bacchus," said Blaine. "Allow me to handle this matter."

"I'll use what name I want, when it is mine," said Arkus, stepping even closer to the Guardian. "I'm sorry about the accident at Inverdorn, more than you are I dare say. That was one of my cities."

"If it is your powder then you seem to have lost a great deal of it," Blaine said. "Barrels in the Golden Crescent, even more at Inverdorn. Where else might they turn up unaccounted for?"

"Clearly, mistakes have been made," growled Arkus. "And I will use all my power to investigate the matter."

"You'll forgive me if I do not feel the substance is safe in human hands for the time being. My Light Bearers will guard your stores as we transport it to the Bastion."

"Darnuir himself has agreed to my plans," Arkus snarled. "The powder is a human tool and should remain in human hands."

"Tell that to the dead of Inverdorn," said Blaine. "And you would do well to watch your tone with me. As Guardian, I seek what's best for the world. This dangerous substance should not be trifled with."

"You guard the world?" Arkus asked, more quietly, stepping within an inch of Blaine. "Which world? This one soaked in blood? I remember Draconess used to mumble about a Guardian; he revered you. Can't say I'm as impressed." It was only then that Arkus seemed to notice Brackendon. "Finished moping wizard?"

Brackendon's stomach knotted. "I had come to join the discussion."

"There is little left to discuss," Arkus said. "Now, I will take my grandson back with me." Five Chevaliers began to close in towards the crib at the King's words.

Balack stepped forward then. "Sire, if I may accompany Cullen with you. I'd like to see he is in good hands and say my farewells."

"And who are you, hunter?" Arkus said, scanning Balack with his shrewd black eyes. "Do you not feel my staff can attend to the needs of one baby? My own flesh and blood."

"Excuse me, sire, I meant no offence," Balack said quickly. "My name is Balack. Your son, he meant a great deal to me. Something like a father, but also a friend and teacher. I'd like to part with Cullen properly; if only because I was robbed of the chance with Cosmo."

Arkus' expression softened. "A terrible name for a Prince… Cosmo," he mused. "Very well, Balack. Walk with me."

"Thank you, sire," Balack said. "And to you," he added into Brackendon's ear as he set off with Arkus and the Chevaliers carrying baby Cullen. Somehow there was just Kymethra, Blaine and himself left. An awkward grouping, Brackendon considered.

"Balack told me you saved him," Brackendon said to Blaine. "That was brave of you."

Blaine seemed to take a moment to decide what to say. "My armour could withstand the blast."

"But not your leg?" Brackendon said.

"A heated fragment of a barrel ring, blown apart," Blaine said, his face blank. "Slipped in the gap between the plates."

"You stood between the explosion and a human?" Kymethra asked.

"I felt no need to watch him die," Blaine said impatiently. "I must take my leave. The two of you will have matters to discuss."

At last, Brackendon and Kymethra were alone in the middle of the vast array of camps. He reached out for her hand, but she withdrew it. Her polite public demeanour changed into a disappointed frown.

"They want me to fly to Dalridia. To check on matters there for Lord Imar."

"Then you should not wait long."

"I can't leave again," Kymethra said. "Not now. We're too close to—"

"You must play your part," Brackendon said, "and I mine. I'm sorry for the way I have been acting. I have been afraid of what I must do." Kymethra nodded. She hit him hard on the shoulder, once, twice, then took a fistful of his robes and fell in against him.

"Everyone is ignoring it," she said. "All of them. They speak of marching to the Bastion and assaulting it, assuming it will all go well. But, how can it?"

"For as long as I can remember, we've all spoken of defeating Rectar as well and Castallan isn't as dangerous as him. We tell ourselves these things because to do anything less is to have already given up."

"These last days, I thought you had given up."

"I thought about it. Yet if Castallan and Rectar were truly invincible they would have no need for men, for demons, for flesh and blood, for walls or mountains. They need these things because they can be killed; even if it seems impossible. If I make it through this then we're done, Kymethra, I promise you. I'll snap my staff and we can quit playing our parts. We'll spend our days at the Argent Tree, eating fruit and walking barefoot through the forest."

"Don't you dare go into that fortress before I come back," Kymethra said. She kissed him. "I haven't quite forgiven you yet."

"Go on," Brackendon said. "Fly, and fly back to me."

Chapter 11

HIGHLAND HUNGER

Of the Highlands, I have nothing to say. The Frost Trolls keep to themselves and I, a fairy, would certainly never be welcomed to journey there. I find it hard to imagine they have even kept records of their history. And there is some of that fairy scorn, so ingrained within me. I shall leave those words in this text, if only to serve the purpose of showing the effect of a lifetime's worth of prejudice.

From Tiviar's Histories

Garon – moving north through the Highlands

"ARE WE LOST?" Pel demanded. "Where are all the kazzek?"
To avoid answering, Garon pretended to have a good look up the wide, deep valley, as though he wasn't sure it was totally empty. Jagged boulders dotted the landscape, poking out above the blooming heather; thatched roof homes sat beside long thin strips of farmland. But no kazzek could be seen. There hadn't been any in the last three glens either. Ochnic was on his right, peering out at the landscape deep in thought.

"Well?" Pel asked again.

"Dey must have gone to da Great Glen," Ochnic said. "A place of refuge for kazzek in times of peril."

"And taken every scrap of food with them?" Pel said.

"Why would dey leave any behind. If we gather in da Great Glen, we don't know how long it will be for." Pel said nothing more but her wings fluttered in some agitation.

Garon bit his lip, unsure what they could do other than trudge on. *What choice do I have?* He gently placed a fingertip on Darnuir's scroll, though it offered him no answers. His stomach rumbled audibly and he found it hard to concentrate. Even the dim grey sky felt harsh against his eyes and he squinted to shield himself.

"Let's move on," Garon said. "Perhaps the kazzek will have left something behind." Ochnic's snort was not helpful. Pel visibly drooped and they walked a little slower. Their speed was not improved by the terrain. It had been arduous progressing through the Highlands. There were no roads, barely anything resembling a path; the wild land had proven a hindrance at every turn. Yet, there was a rugged beauty to it that Garon could not deny. Heather bloomed brightly, ranging from amethyst to orange-yellow, but there were also clumps charred black with the poison of the Cascade, much like the trees in Val'tarra had suffered in places. Upon the mountainside, there was a large cluster of black heather like a scar slashed against the landscape. Garon noticed Pel looking up at it too.

"Do your people not remove those dead plants, Ochnic?"

"No," said Ochnic. "It is natural. Why remove dem?"

"That's what we do," Pel said.

"Da kazzek know de dangers of de blue poison. Burned bushes remind us to respect it." Pel looked confused but held her tongue. Garon smiled at her and nodded. He was thankful that she was at least making a concerted effort to be civil with Ochnic, despite their hunger.

They searched the homes of the kazzek. The trolls had cleared out anything useful, including tools. In one home a basket remained, its lid askew. Garon glimpsed orange as he strode by it and his mouth watered at the thought of one small carrot. Without daring to hope he pushed the lid clean off. It was, in fact, a bundle of carrots and even some onions. He grabbed for an orange delight and despaired at the blue mush where the root once had been. The onions were no better: black and rotten. The smell made him nauseous but he had nothing to throw up.

Giving up, Garon dragged himself back outside and sat down amongst the heather. Pel and Ochnic followed him; she began kicking at the undergrowth, wandering in a small circle, while Ochnic crouched low and broodingly amongst the petals. Garon sighed and looked back on their expedition filing into the glen. The hunters and fairies came first, with groups of flyers already heading east to scout further. One dragon was already limping up to Garon, Pel and Ochnic.

"Nothing?" Marus said without hiding his bitterness. His thick eyebrows were furrowed into a single angry line.

"Ochnic believes the kazzek have fled to a refuge deeper into the Highlands," Garon said.

"How far is that?" Marus asked. "The extra supplies we picked up from Captain Romalla were only enough to help us reach the trolls."

"A week from here," Ochnic said. "Maybe a little more."

"We're already on half-rations," Marus grumbled. "Ochnic, I thought you promised—"

"I said da kazzek would help. Dey will. But I didn't know dey would have called to da Great Glen already… somethin' must be wrong."

"We still have some food," Garon said, trying to prevent any arguments. "And we can still hunt game, I'm sure. We have almost a thousand hunters, after all."

"Then where is our roast deer?" Marus asked.

"You'll struggle to find even a grouse once de clans have been summoned, dragon legate."

"The Ninth Legion marches on its stomach," Marus said.

"And humans and fairies are no different," Garon said. "We're all suffering here."

"Some more than others," Pel said. She brought out her spear and cut a swathe of heather in frustration. "At least your meat is cured. Food fit for fairies is running low."

"You're perfectly capable of eating meat," Marus said. "You'll just have to manage, Wing Commander. It's not our fault your stores got burned by Castallan's traitors."

"Stop it," Garon said. "We're all just hungry. Don't let it get to you."

Pel either ignored him or didn't hear him. "It's not our fault the trolls have all ran off," she said, her voice rising. "Maybe they saw fairies coming and thought they'd take the chance to torture us while they feast up a mountain somewhere. Maybe—"

Ochnic rose a little out of his crouch, growling lowly.

"Pel, that's enough," Garon said, forcefully this time. He stepped between Pel and Ochnic, arms raised against the two.

"Dat won't be necessary, pack leader," Ochnic said, shoving his hand aside. "My daughter says things she does not mean when hungry. Let's hope she is feastin' and not facing a demon horde without me." He stalked off.

Pel's eyes widened. "Ochnic, wait. Please." But the kazzek kept on walking. Pel started forward, nearly taking off after him, but Garon stepped in to catch her arm.

"Let him go. You both need to cool off. We all do," he added, catching Marus' eye as well. The legate's face was unreadable.

"Very well," Pel said. She flew off though in the direction of the other fairies. Garon's stomach ached from its emptiness and rumbled loudly again.

Marus, his gaze downcast, half-turned to leave as well. "I am sorry for adding to that outburst, Garon. Let's hope we reach the kazzek sooner than late, and not only for the sake of our bellies. It might be best if we have a more natural figurehead in this Chief-of-Chiefs." He took his leave. Alone, Garon slumped back down into the heather.

Maybe he's right? Maybe I can't do this after all?

He thumbed the edge of Darnuir's scroll but it didn't help. It never really did.

Chapter 12

THE BASTION BESIEGED

I am assured by military minds that the effort required to storm the Bastion would be incredible, even for the dragons. It is designed to repel them after all. As a deterrent against future conflict between dragons and humans, the fortress works well enough. Yet should war ever come, I foresee this deterrent will decimate generations on both side.

From Tiviar's Histories.

Blaine – Outside the Bastion – Camp of the Third Legion

IT HAD BEEN two weeks of ponderous marching south. They had followed the coast, enabling much of their supplies to be carried by Arkus' fleet. The humans made progress slow, and still Blaine had not found the chance to speak with Darnuir. The boy was giving him the cold shoulder since their less than cordial meeting with Arkus. In a way, Blaine was impressed by it. Darnuir was showing more backbone even if the timing wasn't ideal. And now they had arrived within siege range of the Bastion, time had truly run out.

Evening was fast approaching, so little would be done other than set up a perimeter to the west of the fortress. Troops would be sent to secure the woods a little south of their position. The trees ran until half a mile from the base of the Bastion's south-west walls and would be an easy source of wood for siege engines and towers.

The colossal fortress could have been raised by gods during the world's creation, as though some power had left part of a mountain unfinished. Its mighty walls met at sharp angles like arrowheads to envelop the citadel tower in a star shape. Two sets of walls made two great stars if seen from above: two imposing grey, dead stars. An aura of challenge radiated from the Bastion; its very strength inviting foes to test it. To Blaine, it seemed inconceivable that humans could have made it – although it was with the aid of dragons, he reminded himself. Blaine knew that all too well.

Would Darnuir begin his search for the passageways of the fortress tonight? Blaine hoped not. He needed to speak with him about it, but a service to N'weer would need to be held first.

"Bacchus," Blaine called. The Light Bearer dutifully stepped forward from the entourage. "You have proven yourself trustworthy and diligent since the disaster at Inverdorn. I hope you do not mind me asking some small favours of you?"

"Never, Lord Guardian. I live to serve the gods, and you are their conduit."

"Find the King for me," Blaine said. "Tell him I request an urgent audience. Perhaps he won't be so scornful towards someone else."

"At once, Lord Guardian," Bacchus said and he was away as light as a feather on the wind. Blaine was growing fond of the younger dragon. *If only more dragons that followed the Light were as dutiful, our race would fare far better.* Then again, Blaine had seen what had been done in the name of duty, in the name of the gods long ago. He tugged lightly on Arlandra's necklace.

"We should prepare for service," Blaine said to his remaining Light Bearers. "Multiple sermons across the legionary camps. More attend with each day, and we must not let the impending siege distract us."

"Yes, Lord Guardian," they said together.

Darnuir – Outside the Bastion

"We should begin searching for the passage under the fortress immediately," Darnuir said. A large intricate map of the area had been found and the usual figurines placed upon it. With Darnuir was

Arkus, Somerled and Fidelm, in a central command tent that was at the intersection between the camps of all three races outside the Bastion.

"It will be perilous searching blindly," said Arkus. "Trenches will be needed to protect our teams. It will need to be carefully done."

"Carefully sounds like it means time," Darnuir said. He wanted this fight to come swift and hard.

"It will take five days at least to assemble siege towers," Arkus said. "Maybe more."

"Can't it be done faster?" Darnuir said.

"Those walls are very high and we're hardly used to making such towers," said Arkus. "Few have been needed since the Kingdom united. In any case, island aggression was always by sea, not land." He glanced to Somerled Imar. The Lord of the Isles was picking pieces of chicken from his teeth.

"Didnae need towers to sack Brevia back then did we?" he said. "Shame the Bastion doesn't have a wide open bay."

"If there is any way to hasten the process…" Darnuir said. He imagined the battle, the feel of the Cascade down his arm and the smell of fresh blood filling his nostrils.

"We should not rush our preparations, Lord Darnuir," Fidelm warned deeply.

"No, of course not," Darnuir said. His hand twitched and his thoughts drifted towards the door in his mind.

Fidelm narrowed his eyes. "Is anything amiss?"

"What?" Darnuir said. He shook his head. "No, I'm fine. We should prepare as best we can. My concern is for Lord Imar and the state of the Splinters should we take too long."

"I'm grateful for yer concern," said Somerled. "But what is a few more days now. I await my fleet from my southern islands before I can hope to ship reinforcements back north. I trust yer witch friend travels fast."

"She'll deliver your messages faster than anyone," said Darnuir.

"What of the Dales, General?" Arkus asked of Fidelm.

"My flyers report the lands are quiet. Castallan's forces are entirely holed up in the Bastion."

"So, he has left Deas exposed?" Darnuir said. "Perhaps if we placed pressure on their homes, your southern lords would forget their newfound loyalty to Castallan."

"I recall mentioning my displeasure at exacting harm on my people," Arkus said.

"I said pressure, not murder," Darnuir said. "The mere threat may cause some to lose faith."

"I will dispatch a force to cut Deas clean off from the Bastion if you wish," Arkus said. "I'll likely need a peacekeeping force present once the Bastion is taken."

"Yes, send a small force to threaten the idea of encirclement," said Darnuir. "But not enough men to weaken our chances here. The Bastion will be a terribly hard fight." A part of him was counting on it, hoping for it. He picked up the nearest wooden figurine, this one a dark green hunter carving of the Dales, and clenched it in his fist.

"Oh, Darnuir," Brackendon called from the tent's entrance.

"Coming to join us?" Darnuir asked.

"I was but it appears you have a messenger," said Brackendon. The tent flaps opened seemingly of their accord and Brackendon stepped in alongside a Light Bearer with curly black hair and a plain, unreadable expression. Darnuir recognised this one. Bacchus, he was sure, and he'd been with Blaine at the meeting outside Brevia. "He's very insistent," said Brackendon.

"My King," Bacchus said, with a bow. He did not address the others. "The Lord Guardian wishes an audience with you."

"This again? He does realise I am busy with a war? I'd ask him to join us but I'd rather avoid insulting our human *allies*."

Arkus' face darkened at the very mention of Blaine.

Bacchus seemed unmoved. "The Lord Guardian requests you attend him. As the leader of the faithful—"

"Attend him?" Darnuir asked. In his anger, he crushed the figurine in his hand. The splinters and chunks of wood trickled from his grip onto the map below. Everyone looked to him.

That wound me up quickly, even for me – even for the old me. Am I truly angry with Blaine or is it something else? He hadn't drawn on the Cascade since Brevia. He'd fought against it, but maybe it was time to surrender to it, else he might not make it through these war councils. *I shouldn't, I shouldn't, I can't.* Yet his hands shook at the very thought of the Cascade. 'Just a bit,' some part of him urged. He opened his clenched fist, let the remains of the figurine fall, and dusted off his hands to excuse his fidgeting.

"Very well, I shall see Blaine. Forgive this interruption my Lords."

"We shall begin laying siege," Arkus said. "Good luck, Darnuir." And he smiled. Darnuir returned the gesture, glad for Arkus' understanding. There may well be a good future there after all. Bacchus fell in beside Darnuir as he left the command tent, as did the Praetorians with Lira at their head.

"Is something wrong?" she asked him.

"Just going to pay Blaine a visit," Darnuir said. "Bacchus here says I must 'attend him'. Tell me, Bacchus, how is Blaine's leg?"

"The Lord Guardian has recovered well from his injury," said Bacchus. "He has a slight discomfort, but moves as well as ever, sire."

"Yes, the Guardian's Blade is good at healing, or so he told me," said Darnuir.

"The Lord Guardian will be glad to hear of your concern," said Bacchus.

"I also hope he will be glad to take up my offer," said Darnuir.

"Offer?" Lira said.

"I'd like to challenge Blaine to another duel," said Darnuir. "It's been some time and it will be a good warm-up for the battle to come."

"I do not think the Lord Guardian intends to—"

"If Blaine wants to see me it can be on my terms for once," said Darnuir. "Bit of a show for the troops as well. Surely he won't begrudge me?"

Bacchus took a moment to think. "I am certain he will oblige you, sire."

Blaine – Outside the Bastion – Camp of the Third Legion

Blaine made his way up the via primacy of the camp. He felt most comfortable here where there was a large majority of the faithful. He was almost at the central point of the camp when he spotted Darnuir approaching from the south with his Praetorians, Lira and even Bacchus in tow.

Well done Bacchus. You've proven yourself again.

Now, if only Darnuir would keep his head long enough to hear him out. Sadly, from the look on his face that didn't look likely.

"Thank you for coming, Darnuir," Blaine said.

"Blaine," Darnuir said. Dragons nearby, especially those making their way to N'weer's service, were already beginning to stare.

"I'm afraid you've come just as service is to begin," said Blaine. "Will you await me in my tent?"

"I have another idea," said Darnuir. "What do you say to another duel?" That drew more eyes.

"Now?" Blaine asked.

"Now," Darnuir said.

"I wanted to talk."

"And I want to duel. We can talk after, though I am quite busy with the siege."

And have you ever thought I might have some important information in that regard?

"Your leg isn't ailing you, is it?" Darnuir said.

Blaine felt a twinge behind his left knee. "It is fine. But my service must come first."

"Lord Guardian, I could give the sermon tonight," Bacchus said. He stepped forward and all the onlookers now directed their attention to him.

"You?" Blaine said.

"Why not?" Darnuir said. "Other Light Bearer's conduct your services elsewhere now."

"But this is the main congregation," said Blaine.

"You are the Guardian," said Bacchus. "You should not have to trifle yourself with every matter. Allow me to free your time tonight."

Blaine pondered. The Guardian Sulla never held service himself to increase his mystique, keeping himself hidden from the masses. But that was over a thousand years ago. Their faith was not so strong now. Blaine had to be the one to lead the way. Besides, his leg wasn't fully healed. A duel now would be painful and pointless. Why was Darnuir so insistent?

"I'll go easy on you," Darnuir called.

What is the matter with you, boy?

Then Blaine noticed it – an infinitesimal twitch of Darnuir's hand over the hilt of the Dragon's Blade.

Damned, fool. He's seeking to use magic. This isn't good, but unless he gets a fix soon—

"Well?" Darnuir asked, interrupting Blaine's thoughts.

Perhaps if I make it quick we can move past this and he'll be more inclined to listen.

"I think you've forgotten our last encounter too quickly, my King," Blaine said. "It is I who must will go easy on you for the fight to be fair."

Darnuir's lips spread into a broad grin. "He accepts the challenge. All may come and watch. No holding back now, Guardian." To his right, Lira flicked her eyes between the two of them and shuffled one foot nervously.

"I won't," Blaine groaned. "And I shall follow you shortly." Darnuir and his Praetorians headed northwards up the via primacy, leaving Blaine with Bacchus.

"Thank you for believing in me, Lord Guardian," Bacchus said with a small bow.

Blaine stepped close and placed a hand on his shoulder. "This is a one-time thing," he said quietly. "You may hold sermons if you wish but the Third Legion is mine."

"I understand," Bacchus said. "I meant no offence. I only thought to—"

"There has been no offence," said Blaine. "Go now. Our men require inspiration for the battle to come."

By the time Blaine reached Darnuir outside the camp walls, a small ring of spectators had already formed. The ground was soft underfoot, turning to sand at the far edge of the crowd nearest the coast. The smell of seaweed was thick in the air.

As Blaine passed through the ring on onlookers he unsheathed the Guardian's Blade.

The audience drew a collective breath.

"Best of three strikes?" Darnuir asked. The Dragon's Blade was already in his hand, red and fierce. An orange tint lit the golden metal at the dragon's mouth.

"This won't take long," said Blaine. *I pray it doesn't*, he thought as his knee twanged again in pain.

Darnuir threw himself forward, twisting to Blaine's left at a blur. Blaine easily blocked the attack by pouring some magic into his own reflexes.

That eager to draw on the Cascade, Darnuir?

Blaine drove left with his shoulder, slamming into Darnuir's chest. Their heavy armour thudded dully and Blaine pushed them along the grass. Darnuir dug in his heels. They halted. A moment passed during which neither budged, then Blaine pulled back and the true sword fight began.

Darnuir had improved since their duel in Val'tarra. He was faster, stronger and less obvious. Blaine recognised a feint and nearly had him but Darnuir lashed up at an impossible speed. The sheer force of it pushed Blaine's sword arm high, exposing him.

He saw the blow coming.

Blaine dropped to his knees, slamming his injured leg into the ground and rolled. He heard the sword cut through the air above and struck at Darnuir's midriff with the flat of the Guardian's Blade as he rose.

The crowd remained tensely silent.

"One to me," Blaine said as he got up. His joints protested from manoeuvring in armour like that. His lower leg throbbed horribly and he bit his lip in pain. He risked opening the door to the Cascade to ease it off. A trickle of power that warmed him, comforted him: then he slammed the door shut. Healing too often, even in bursts, would leave him much like Darnuir, Guardian's Blade or no.

Darnuir had already paced back to his starting position. "Ready?"

"I'm not the one losing," said Blaine. But he knew this round would turn sour.

The King came on for a second time.

He didn't feint. He didn't lunge suddenly to one side. He just came head on.

There was a savagery behind the blows. With each block, with each narrow escape, Blaine felt his muscles burn hotter from the strain. He stepped back to the edge of the ring and unleashed a counter attack. He slashed down from shoulder to waist but Darnuir caught his sword on a wing of the Dragon's Blade. This time Blaine wasn't fast enough and Darnuir thrashed his upper arm.

"And one to me," Darnuir said. He gulped visibly as though he were swallowing an egg and winced at the taste.

Not spitting out that bitterness? Blaine thought. *At least you're trying to hide it.*

This time Blaine would not hold back. There was a large audience now and much more at stake than merely the next round. Blaine feared Darnuir would only drift further from him if he thought he was the more powerful. Blaine reassured himself he wouldn't lose. He had experience of fighting one such as Darnuir, after all. So, he kicked the door open.

And he made the first move.

How long they fought for, he couldn't have said. Long enough that he heard Darnuir's breath come in ragged pants. Blaine too fought for air, his chest swelling within the confines of his breastplate. A Cascade infused backflip left him dizzy but out of reach of Darnuir, and able to breathe. Then the Dragon's Blade came soaring towards him. He blocked it and it returned to its master's hand as Darnuir ran at him. Their fight raged on.

Blaine lost the feeling in his mouth as the harsh bitterness of the Cascade welled up. The rush to his Blade threatened to pull his arm off.

But he would. Not. Lose.

"That's enough," Brackendon bellowed. As Blaine was in mid swing, Brackendon whizzed in between him and Darnuir just as their swords would have met. There was a sound like a fairy wings in flight, a whirring that was magnified a thousand fold, and Blaine was tossed backwards.

Face in the grass, he rolled over and blinked up at Brackendon. The wizard's staff shone like a star on the earth, crackling with sparks of blue and silver all along the wood.

"Call it a draw," Brackendon said, his voice returning to normal. "Don't ruin yourselves fighting each other." Blaine sheathed his sword, afraid he'd pushed it too far. "Go on now, all of you," Brackendon added to the spectators. After seeing what the wizard had just done they didn't hesitate. Once the area was clear Brackendon spoke again. "Kymethra has returned from the Splintering Isles. Lord Imar hopes you will join him in discussions."

"You go on, Darnuir," Blaine said. "As I'm not welcome on your councils anymore." And he left, exhausted, leg throbbing, all thought of speaking to Darnuir about the passageways of the Bastion forgotten. Blaine kept up a good show of strength until he returned to his private tent where he collapsed onto the floor.

He lay in a heap for some time until he summoned a reserve of strength to unstrap his armour and take the weight off himself. He didn't even have the wits to place the pieces on their stand. He managed to wash his face then glug an entire jug of tepid water.

Gods but I feel old now.

It was the last thought he had before he buried his head into a pillow and sleep took him.

Darnuir – Outside of the Bastion

As Darnuir watched Blaine go, he felt his body unwind after the battle. He was drenched in sweat, panting harder than a dog in summer, but he felt… good. Relief washed over him. The battle had released some pressure in him like water from a dam. His head felt clear, whereas before the duel it had been aggravated, almost fuzzy. In fact, he could barely remember the moments leading up to the fight: just the fight itself and now this pleasantness. And what a fight it had been.

"You shouldn't have stopped us," Darnuir said.

"I should have stopped you half an hour ago," Brackendon said. He stepped in close to Darnuir. "I thought I told you to be careful with the Cascade," he hissed.

"You did," Darnuir said.

"Then what in Dranus' filthy long tail was that?"

"A duel," Darnuir said, feigning shock.

"It was the duel to end all duels. Do you want to break, Darnuir?"

"Of course not."

"Then don't needlessly waste your body pulling stunts like that," Brackendon said.

"I'm okay, Brackendon," Darnuir said, his voice rising higher than normal. "I'm not addicted," he added, trying to laugh it off. *But I am... I am or I will be. How can I possibly admit that to them and still have them follow me?*

"Denial is the first damned stage," Brackendon said. "You need help. Your fight with Scythe plus that run to Brevia must have affected you more than I realised. I should have known it would. Your body has hardly had a chance to build up a tolerance yet."

"Brackendon, I swear nothing is wrong. I actually feel great."

"You will leave Castallan to me, understand?"

"You cannot be seriou—"

"Yes, I am," Brackendon said. "I didn't save your life all those years ago, so you could break just months after getting your sword. I broke remember? I wouldn't want to see anyone go through that, not even Castallan. Stay away from our fight."

"I will try."

"Try very hard," said Brackendon. "Magic truly is a curse. Now, let's move on."

Grumbling, Darnuir faced his Praetorians and was surprised to find Raymond standing sheepishly amongst them. The chevalier looked a little pale and he was still without his armour.

"It was I who came to deliver the message," Raymond said sounding hoarse.

"Well out with it then," said Darnuir.

"You've had it, my Lord of Dragons," said Raymond. "About Lord Imar and Kymethra's return. I tried to get your attention but—"

"You did more than try," Lira said. "Nearly ripped your throat out shouting to them."

"Then why did Brackendon..."

"Lady Lira ran to fetch help," said Raymond. Lira blushed at the formality.

"And here I am, fetched," said Brackendon.

Darnuir looked around the group. None of his Praetorians gave anything away: they weren't afraid or disgusted, but they weren't admiring him either.

"I have acted inappropriately," said Darnuir. "Forgive me?" Silently they nodded. Lira too, if a little stiffly. "Please, Raymond. Lead me to Somerled."

It turned out there wasn't much to discuss. Kymethra reported that demons had bypassed Ullusay and had landed east of the Nail Head Mountain, on the island where Dalridia was based. Every longship Grigayne Imar could spare was en route to the Bastion to pick up reinforcements as soon as the fortress was taken. Until that time there was little that could be done. Darnuir made his promises that Castallan would fall soon and took his leave. Night had fallen and, as always, Lira fell in beside him when he emerged from Somerled's tent.

"You're allowed to rest, you know," he told her.

"I think you should apologise to Raymond."

"I should. He's a good man."

She seemed to hesitate for a moment. "Are you… are you feeling okay, Darnuir?"

"Perfectly."

"As the Praetorian Prefect, I feel it is my duty to—"

"I'm fine," Darnuir said irritably. She nodded quickly and cast her eyes to her toes. Then she yawned widely.

"If you intend to go see him now I will leave you, if that is your wish."

"That's not what I meant," said Darnuir. "Come with me. You can send the rest of the Guard to bed, however. They will need to be well rested."

Minutes later they had made the short walk to the Chevalier field accommodations beside Arkus' pavilion. The guards didn't utter a word as they approached, nor did they protest as they entered the encampment. They passed a slim boy brushing a horse with its nose in a bucket of oats. The next tent over had a lad hastily polishing steel greaves in the light of a dying fire.

They did not find Raymond until the far end of the Chevaliers' enclosure. He had no youths attending him. His tent was smaller than the rest and he was setting down a pale of oats for his own nut-brown steed when they reached him.

"Lord Darnuir, Lady Lira," Raymond said, bowing low. "I did not think to expect you."

"I came to tell you I'm sorry," said Darnuir. "It must have been humiliating trying to get my attention. You didn't deserve that."

"You were busy, my Lord. One such as yourself need not apologise to the likes of me. I did not acquit myself well at our first encounter, after all."

"I bear no grudge," Darnuir said. "Not to you. Not for that."

"And I the same," said Raymond.

Lira stepped up to Raymond's horse and began petting his mane as it bent over the pale. "What's his name?" she asked.

"Bruce," Raymond said. "T'was the name of my grandfather before our house had a name. Sanders desired to call him Longshanks. I'm glad I went with my own choice now."

"I haven't seen you ride him on our entire march," Darnuir said. "He isn't injured after the stresses of Inverdorn, I hope?"

"Chevaliers who are banned from wearing their steel cannot ride, my Lord," Raymond said. "I keep him healthy in case but alas, I fear I have been reduced to Gellick Esselmont's lackey."

"Is it all my doing?" Darnuir said.

Raymond shook his head. "I returned to Brevia a different man. Sanders' betrayal and your heroics, saving all those people who weren't your own kind, it made me rethink the stories I had been told. The fairies too have surprised me. Taking so many humans into their care, you wouldn't think it possible given what is said around the capital."

"I'm glad you don't think of us so poorly, Raymond," said Lira. She scratched Bruce fondly along his neck and shoulder.

"Perhaps not after my display in the throne room and earlier tonight," said Darnuir.

Raymond shrugged. "Your intentions are noble even if your methods are yet unrefined." His eyes widened suddenly. "I am sorry for that outburst. I don't know—"

"It's quite alright," Darnuir said, waving it off with his hand. "I want my Praetorians to feel comfortable in telling me when I have erred."

"But I'm not…"

"I'd like you to be," Darnuir said. "If Lira is okay with it." Lira looked as stunned as Raymond. "You're the Praetorian Prefect, Lira. You're in charge of recruitment. But I did wish to include all the Three Races in my new Guard. Castallan's infiltration of the hunters has made that difficult, but I can trust you, Raymond. Will you join me?"

"As part of your – *Guard?*" Raymond said as though the meaning of the word had temporarily left his mind. "What good can a mere human do to help you?"

"It's a sign of what I want to achieve," Darnuir said. "You know honour, you are well trained and both you, and Bruce here, would make fine additions, I think. Say yes, Raymond. Say yes and don your steel again."

"I – I accept, Lord Darnuir."

Darnuir shook his hand, careful not to squeeze too hard. "Welcome, Raymond. And please just call me Darnuir from now on."

"And just Lira for me."

"That may take some getting used to, my Lor— Darnuir," said Raymond.

Lira smiled. "It gets easier with time."

Chapter 13

THE BREAKING OF THE BASTION: PART 1

There has been a First War, and a Second. When, I wonder, will the Third War come?

From Tiviar's Histories.

Cassandra – The Bastion

CASSANDRA WAS COILED snakelike on her bed when the knock came. Dranus only knew why they bothered to knock. It was tiring that some of those serving in the Bastion still felt the need for niceties. Some didn't, of course. Some seemed to loathe her for being Arkus' daughter.

Her visitor knocked again.

"Come in," she said, scrunching her face into her sheets. The door hit the wall with a soft tap and heeled boots clicked in.

"Good morning, Princess." Whoever he was, he was highborn for his speech lacked any provincial accent. "The enemy's siege machines are built and they will strike soon. His majesty will be sure to request your presence in the throne room."

"Just get out." She untangled her face from her sheet and craned her neck. He wore a courtier's purple velvet doublet, pulled in tight about the waist by a belt. Something on that belt caught her eye. Something sharp.

"If it pleases you, I have your breakfast and fresh clothes."

Cassandra didn't answer. Her attention had turned to the bowl on the bedside table, where lay the remnants of her dinner the night before. It was a sturdy treen dish. Quite heavy in hand, but would it be enough? Then she looked to the fat volume of Tiviar's *History*.

"Princess?"

"It would please me," she said hastily. "My head is spinning. Perhaps some food will help."

"I don't feel right in the morning until I eat," the man said. He bowed out and Cassandra hopped out of bed. The smell of cold grease from last night's stew made her feel sick as she grabbed Tiviar's tome.

The purple clad man returned with an oversized tray with folded clothes on one side and breakfast on the other. She gave him a smile to disarm him. Now that she saw him properly, Cassandra could not be sure of his age. He sported only two patches of wispy bristle on his chin and cheeks, which had not lost their youthful chubbiness. He must have been even younger than her.

She had the heavy book in hand, feigning that she was browsing it innocently.

I'll have to be quick.

"Now I shall give you some time to get ready," he said, turning his back foolishly to her as he set the tray down.

Cassandra stepped towards him, raising the book high.

"Please do not tarry Princess, as—"

Thunk.

Cassandra felt the blow ricochet up her arm. The boy spun, dazed, his jaw hanging loosely. She struck him again between the eyes and he smacked his head for a third time off the bedpost before he crumpled to the cold floor. He lay unmoving with a bloody nose.

A rush of panic came over her. *Is he dead?* She bent down, placed a finger on his neck and found a pulse. She puffed out her cheeks in relief and collected herself. *It's fine, you've done it now.* She deposited the book onto the mattress and began searching at the boy's belt. Hanging amongst coin purses, keys and vials, she found what she was after.

There we go. Thank you, whoever you are.

The knife was stubby but strong. It would serve. She pilfered the belt so that she could strap the weapon to herself. If positioned at her abdomen, she could probably keep it hidden under her clothes. Upon rising, she assessed her situation.

The boy's limp form was still at her feet. It would be prudent to do something about him before anyone else arrived. Cassandra dragged him to the bedside, his leather boots squeaking terribly, and began stuffing him unceremoniously underneath the bed. Another pang of guilt hit her so she placed a pillow under his head.

Before attending to her food, she inspected the clothes. As usual, they were too courtly. There was a clean smock, which Cassandra was grateful for, and she used the knife to cut out the looser bottom half so it became more like a shirt. Then she belted the dagger to her midriff, put on the modified smock, and placed her hunter leathers back on once more, trying to ignore the smell. No one had thought it necessary to clean off the gore from the Charred Vale; it was likely they were trying to force her not to wear them.

The food was next – chewy brown bread with butter to spread, a plump pear, thick wedges of hard tart cheese and crunchy honeycomb. She wolfed it all down. Cassandra wondered whether all Castallan's prisoners ate half so well.

What grog would Chelos be suffering?

More guilt stabbed at her, and shame. Even as a captive, she could not feel the quiet pride of enduring hardship; of having something active to fight back against. Instead of torture or a cell she had a four-poster bed, fresh clothes daily, food to feed a lord and servants delivering it all. It had always been that way. She was a spoilt prisoner.

Then she saw a smear of blood on her hand. She wiped it away with the ripped remnants of the smock she had no use for. There was some blood on her bed as well, from where she had put Tiviar's book down. She scooped it up like a wounded animal and wiped it clean, making sure it was spotless before returning it carefully back to the library. It was a crime to have used the book in such a manner, yet needs must.

With adrenaline still flowing, Cassandra returned restlessly to the main chamber of her suite. She stood waiting, rocking on the balls of her feet.

Now what, Cass?

Attacking the boy had been impulsive. What she would do with the knife she did not know. Anything she could, she supposed. Someone who searched her might feel it but the leathers were padded and she'd take the risk. Castallan wasn't going to kill her.

But she would kill him if she could.

Chelos was probably dead after all. Cassandra had asked time and again to see him, even just briefly, but she'd never been answered. She hadn't been denied; her requests just fell on deaf ears, as though there was some unspoken agreement to spare her feelings. It hadn't worked. She had thought on it and she'd soaked one pillow with her tears.

Cassandra knew she would fail. It was desperate. Still, she had to try something and was still standing stupidly in the middle of the foyer when they came to collect her.

"I see you're ready," the huntress Freya said. Her eyes were scarlet. "Come along then."

Blaine – Outside the Bastion

Blaine kept low as he crept through the trenches. Lacking his armour and wrapped in a cloak, he prayed he would not be recognised. The digging teams were too busy to notice much beyond the dirt and danger. They had worked day and night, moving ever closer to the outer wall of the Bastion. Shovels rose and fell rhythmically as Blaine passed, piling the soil up on the sides for added defence. Now dawn had passed, archers on the walls resumed taking shots when they could, but the catapults were the greater danger.

"Look out," someone cried, and Blaine whipped around to see a rock impact into the trench behind him. A team of dragons rushed to remove it.

To Blaine's great disappointment the brave digging teams had not been successful in their main objective. He had hoped to avoid this, hoped the tunnel might be found on its own. It would have been far better that way. Each day he had checked, even nudged the teams in the right direction but to no avail. And now they were so close to the walls the battle would come soon, perhaps that very day. The ridge of the trench obscured their camps but he could see their lumbering siege towers were complete at last. He had no choice. He couldn't keep quiet about the tunnels and let thousands of dragons die just to safeguard old Guardian secrets. Arkus would fume in rage, Darnuir would hate him for it, but he had to reveal what he knew.

I've run out of time.

Cassandra – The Bastion

Castallan's throne room was brimming with armed men and women. Many were hunters of the Dales but many more were regular infantry in padded jerkins. Those more fortunate wore some chainmail. Nearly all had glowing red eyes, save for Castallan and a group of lavishly dressed people crowded around him. He stood in front of his elevated throne.

"It will not be long now," Castallan said. "The great battle for humanity is upon us, friends. Will we be forced to follow the whims of dragons or shall we forge our own future?"

A cheer followed with much clanking of weapons. Cassandra's spirits rose as well.

Soon it will all be over; you will be dead.

Freya manoeuvred Cassandra towards the throne. She was close to the wizard, but couldn't reach him from down here. These red-eyed devotees would easily stop her before she made it anyway.

"Victory today is my burden," Castallan said more solemnly. "All the power of Brevia, of Val'tarra and the dragons is set against us. I cannot ask you to triumph through strength of arms but through resolve. I ask that you hold the walls, hold the defences and hold together."

Another round of cheering, even louder than the last. So many voices, and this was not even a fraction of Castallan's supporters. Cassandra never had a hope of killing him. But she had to do something. Thousands of dragons, humans and fairies, were about to storm the Bastion. She couldn't just sit here helpless.

"You have placed your faith in me," Castallan continued, his voice rising, "and I promise I shall not disappoint; when I take hold of the Dragon's Blade and bring humanity into a new age!"

Cassandra covered her ears against the roar that followed this time.

She realised then that these people truly were prepared to fight for him, to die for him too. Did he really stand a chance against Brackendon, Darnuir and Blaine? Surely not. But then he had all those staffs, grafted and bound to his own. Like each lord's signature on the declaration, each staff added legitimacy to Castallan. Power was persuasive and many had been swayed by it. She looked to the throne, lingered on the gleaming silver staffs, and decided what she must try to do.

The uproar had not died down and Castallan was revelling in it. She'd only have one shot to reach the staffs on her side that were low enough. Realistically, that meant two potential targets.

Her heart quickened and her mouth went dry. The idea was insane.

Out of the corner of her eye, she saw Castallan raise his hands for silence. "Bring in the dragon," he called. Jeers and booing answered in preparation as the great doors of the throne room opened. Cassandra couldn't see through the dense crowd but she knew who it would be. It was another full minute before Castallan raised a hand to bring order. Then he pointed an accusatory finger down the length of the throne room. Cassandra stood on her tiptoes to try and see but it was no good.

"Before you stands an ancient dragon," Castallan said. "One so old he can remember a time before Rectar and the demons, a time when dragon fought against dragon and somehow humanity still bled. Tell me Chelos, do you still not see the merit in what I do?"

Cassandra started forwards at the name, her fear confirmed, but Freya held her back with an iron grip.

"Never," Chelos said. His voice wavered but there was still strength in it and that spurred Cassandra on.

"No?" Castallan said. "So, you do not think I should seek to end the war? I have found the means to defeat our great enemy."

"What you make are abominations," Chelos said. "Are you all fools? How can you follow this man who's set demons upon your own kind?"

There came a piercing, echoing slap.

"Do not harm him," Castallan said lazily. "Let him have his say. Let him rant and preach his old ways, even as they burn around him and a new world begins."

Cassandra renewed her efforts to break free. "Let me see." But her captor wrestled her back. "Let me see him. Let me go. Let m—" Cassandra's breath left her as she was hoisted up onto the platform of the throne.

"Settle down, Princess," Freya snapped. Cassandra could hardly believe her luck. She was standing right beside the staffs. Yet she could not move closer for Freya held her in place by the ankle. When her red eyes looked up to Cassandra, the message was clear: not one move. At least from here Cassandra could see Chelos, forced down on his knees with shackles on his wrists.

"Too much power," Chelos said. "So much you delude yourself into thinking you can kill a god. None will be able to defeat Rectar save those with the grace of Dwna, Dwl'or and N'weer." Chelos met Cassandra's eye then and her heart seized up.

I'm sorry. I'm sorry. I'm sorry. She tried to tell him this through her stare.

Castallan followed Chelos' gaze and his mouth twitched when he saw Cassandra behind him. "She is back Chelos and she knows who she is."

Chelos did not break his gaze with Cassandra. He looked to have aged greatly in the time she had been away. The crinkles of his face had deepened and an angry bruise was now spreading across his cheek, but that did not stop him breaking into a smile when he saw her. She saw him mouth out, "Hello, my girl."

"I shall make you a deal, Chelos," Castallan said. "If you, perhaps the eldest of your kind, can admit fault just this once, then I shall be merciful on your people."

"I am not the oldest of my race," Chelos said. "And you will not defeat the Shadow."

"You see," Castallan said. "Even on their knees, dragons will not bend; afraid of change and terrified of losing their power. Even when my intentions have always been for the good of all of Tenalp."

A loud mumbling of agreement swept the room once more.

Chelos finally broke his gaze with Cassandra to glare at Castallan. He drew himself up as far as he could, defiant. "Kill me or send me back to my cell. I will await the true king there, and pray you all dare to get in his way. For it will be the last thing you ever do."

The crowd was now close to pandemonium. There were cries for blood, cries of disbelief, taunts, even laughter. Cassandra felt the tight hand on her ankle disappear as Freya moved forwards to add her own insult to the tirade. Chelos received another blow to the face and Cassandra winced, turning away. Her head almost collided with the tip of one of the silver staffs and there she saw a weak point. The wood was thinner near the top of the shaft where Castallan had taken a cutting.

This would be her only chance.

She slipped a hand down underneath her leathers for the dagger. Retrieving it wasn't as easy as she hoped, but she wiggled it free, cutting her chin as her hand jerked upwards.

Everyone else was still occupied. Castallan was forcing his way through the crowd to reach Chelos.

"Leave him," Castallan was saying, amplifying his voice, yet it had no effect on the crowd.

Cassandra took a deep breath, grasped the staff in one hand to brace herself and brought the knife down upon the weakened segment of wood. One blow did little, the second sent up silver splinters. She hacked again, with all the might she possessed, feeling her shoulder pang with the effort. Three, four, five times she swung until, with a crack, the staff gave way. The gnarled head of it crashed to the platform and rolled, bouncing down each step. She watched it go, her heart racing so fast she thought it would burst.

Instantly, the atmosphere in the throne room changed. A deep booming emanated from Castallan, throwing the attendees into silence. The room darkened almost to blackness and the heat dropped to a chill. Desperately, Cassandra raised her arm again, targeting another staff, but she was lifted high into the air before her stroke could fall. She flew, soaring to slam high up against the far away wall. Steel cuffs appeared to bind her and she looked out across the crowd, as a sea of red eyes glared up at her through the dark.

Blaine – Outside the Bastion

Back in his tent, Blaine held the white gem in his palm. The weight of the memories within it threatened to drag him down. He'd got what he needed from it, so placed it back into the hilt of the Guardian's Blade with a satisfying click.

Perhaps that black powder would be enough to win the day, and there would be no need for Blaine to speak up. But he couldn't waste lives for the sake of holding his tongue, nor did he wish for Arkus and Darnuir to feel validated by using it.

Thankfully, he could always rely on hot water being delivered to him each day, and as expected, his tent flap was pushed aside by two young dragons; one carrying a steaming bowl, the other a scrap of parchment.

"Dwna bless you Lord Guardian," they said.

"Dwna shine upon you both," Blaine said.

"We came earlier but you were not here," said one of the boys. "The water would have been cold."

"Then I am grateful you returned. That will be all."

By the mirror, the water boy looked unsure. "Lord Guardian, I wonder sir, if I may ask wisdom of you."

"You may," Blaine said, intrigued. "Though I shouldn't tarry. I am already late for Dwna's service."

"It is about the sermons, Lord Guardian," said the boy.

"Oh?"

"You often speak of fighting the Shadow," the boy said, "but here we are fighting humans. Will the gods condone this?"

Blaine rubbed his chin thoughtfully, feeling the rough bristles. "Such questions are difficult to answer. Yet I have done you all a disservice by not addressing it. I shall rectify this shortly."

"Will you fight today, Lord Guardian?" asked the water boy. "Brother Bacchus says the battle will come soon."

"Does he? Well, it likely will."

"We only wish we could do more. My brother and I."

"One day you shall. Do your duty, keep to your training in the Way of Light, and you shall both be Light Bearers one day."

The boys beamed. "Thank you, Lord Guardian," they said together, then left Blaine alone.

He moved to the steaming bowl and examined himself in the mirror.

I look a damned mess.

The hazy dawn through the tent's flap lit the blond dusting across his face. His sunken eyes had not quite recovered from his duel with Darnuir. They looked greyer than usual, the amber less bright

He unwrapped the cloth around the shaving tools and instinctively picked up the razor with the blue pearl handle, even though it no longer brought the joy it once had. He could not help hear Kasselle's voice each time he held it, with every stroke of the blade, "I don't think you should come back."

His fingers felt weak as he placed the razor back down. Thankfully, the hot water was reviving when he splashed his face. He dabbed his face dry then stared at himself again in the mirror.

You are old. Might be you're too old, Blaine. But you must go on.

Once he reached the sermon tent, his spirits rose. His audience had swelled greatly since their time in the Golden Crescent. Though Light Bearers held service across the legions, many dragons chose to make the trip to hear Blaine himself. Fresh banners with the symbols of the gods had been made: the three emanating rays of Dwna; the half-seared sun of Dwl'or; and the three spiralling rays of N'weer. These banners adorned the space behind the dais, which now shone with a daily polish.

Then his mood darkened in an instant.

Someone was already standing behind the dais.

"My friends, we prepare for battle this day," Bacchus proclaimed. "It is a good omen that the morning light is clear and warm."

"Dwna shines upon us," the congregation said as one. They were answering him; saying the words just like they would with Blaine. He stood dumbfounded. And furious.

"I know some of you question our actions here," Bacchus continued. His voice was different than usual: a smooth, calming, honeyed voice that could convince a queen to marry a beggar. "These are humans we fight today, not the Shadow. Yet as the grace of Dwl'or is always half shrouded, so too is the service that we must make unclear at times. Rarely are matters so clean cut."

Blaine was astounded. He couldn't have put it much better himself. When Bacchus looked at the audience they looked back, locked eyes. And they were listening so closely. Bacchus was addressing concerns that had taken two bold water boys to bring to Blaine's attention.

I've been too distracted lately.

A member of the congregation spoke up. "Dragons lost the Second War. The gods did not shine on us then. What if the same occurs again?"

There was mumbling around the tent.

"Those red-eyed beasts seek to kill us," someone else noted. "Would we need more reason?"

A louder chatter of agreement followed.

"There is a clear difference," said Blaine, finding his voice at last. "Our predecessors wrongly thought humanity to be of the Shadow, as we are of the Light. This is not so. Humanity is neither Light nor Shadow, favoured by no side. We have not lost sight of the real threat."

He made his way to the dais to take his proper place. Bacchus held his ground for a second before stepping aside.

"Dwl'or also shows us that there are two paths in life," Blaine said. "One of Light and one of Shadow. Though every dragon is born under Dwna's blessing, the gods know that some are led astray; taken by the allure of the Shadow. Dranus was one such dragon. He turned his back on the gods and took his Black Dragons down the other path." Blaine paused, noticing that the congregation were looking to Bacchus, as though for a second opinion.

Bacchus looked nervously at Blaine then turned to face them. "I believe we have reached a pivotal moment in our history. N'weer shows us that all things can be restored. Our king was reborn. I foresee our connection to the gods being repaired as well if we can defeat Rectar, and all who stand within the long shadow he has cast across our world. Inside this Bastion hides a wizard and humans corrupted by our enemy. It is our duty to cleanse them."

"Then Dwl'or grant us strength," a call came out.

"Dwl'or grant us strength," the assembled dragons said together.

"Thank you, friends," Blaine said, hoping to regain control. "Prepare yourselves and steel against your fears. Dwna shine upon you all." As the congregation began to rise Blaine rounded on Bacchus. "What part of 'a one-time thing' didn't you understand?"

"You were late, Lord Guardian," Bacchus said. "And those gathered looked worried. I thought you might be—"

"You thought wrong, didn't you," said Blaine. "When have I ever missed a sermon?"

"I only thought, with the battle so near, you might be in council with the King."

Blaine scowled. "Do not presume to take my place unless instructed. Is that clear."

"Quite."

"Good. Now go prepare yourself for battle while I go see our blessed reborn King."

Darnuir – Outside the Bastion – Three Races' Central Command Tent

Darnuir's agitation was reaching new heights. He puffed an angry breath through his nose and saw it steam in the crisp morning air. It seemed the full heat of summer was already passing.

"We are getting nowhere with this," Arkus said, standing safely on the opposite side of the sweeping war table. "This passage may well exist but we should focus our efforts on the assault."

"What say you, Somerled?" Darnuir asked. "This passage is our one best chance at securing victory." Lord Imar replied with a cold expression.

"Well, yer right about that. But for once I agree with my liege lord."

"Your king," Arkus reminded him curtly.

"Hmmm," Somerled said. "Might be King. Though I don't see any other Great Lords here, almost as if they 'av tae obey ye without question. Or they're over the other side of those terribly high walls I suppose."

"Not for much longer," said Darnuir.

"It's been long enough," said Somerled. "Two weeks it took us tae get here and almost another one preparing. Meanwhile, the demons continue to smash my own people, and are likely to be at Dalridia itself by now.

You two kings have argued plenty about how tae storm this place. I agree with Arkus, nae mer time can be spared."

Off to Darnuir's right, Fidelm's wings buzzed briefly. The General had largely stayed silent on the issue, while Brackendon and Kymethra lingered at the edge of Darnuir's vision, contributing little.

"You are right," Darnuir said, looking to Somerled. "We cannot stay any longer. The Bastion must fall today. Though I shudder at what it will cost us."

"It was not designed to fall," said Arkus. "Even with a dozen trebuchets the outer wall may not give and then there is a second behind it.

"So, we shall use your stores of black powder," said Darnuir. "The Bastion was not designed with such a weapon in mind. Our trenches have at least crept towards the base of the western walls. Sapping teams could begin tunnelling within the day. We could mine down, use the powder, and destabilise the foundations."

Arkus was shaking his head. "The walls are too thick," he said tapping at the dimensions on the unfurled plans. "We'd need our sapping teams to burn every pig in the Kingdom to level those walls."

Darnuir scanned the blueprints again and then it hit him. He cursed himself for a fool to not have thought of it sooner. "We could blow a gate or two open. As mighty as they are, they will be the weakest points along the walls."

"Just the gates, you say," Arkus said, pressing his knuckles down on the table. "We could do that."

Finally, we are getting somewhere.

"We still have a serious consideration," Fidelm said. "Whether the gates are blown open or not, we will likely lose a great deal of troops in the initial waves. Which race is to bear the brunt of the attack?"

Silence reigned.

"I fear there is little either myself or Kymethra can add on this," Brackendon said. "I should like a walk before it begins."

"Of course," Darnuir said. He didn't begrudge Brackendon. Everything would ultimately hinge on his success. "I'll come find you," Darnuir called after them as Brackendon and Kymethra exited the pavilion.

"Well?" asked Fidelm.

"An equal split between the races seems the fairest option, in my eyes," Somerled said. "But as my own people are not part of this army, I feel I too should bow out at this time."

"Very well," Darnuir said. Some minutes passed in awkward silence. Neither Fidelm nor Arkus seemed eager to send their troops first into the jaws of the Bastion's defences.

"Dragons would surely be the most capable of fighting these servants of Castallan," Arkus finally said, a little cautiously. Darnuir sighed though he wasn't surprised to hear it. Sending humans to scale the walls would only lead to a massacre.

"You are right," Darnuir agreed. Arkus looked at him in shock. "Yet, I fear, I cannot only use dragons in this battle, else my people may not understand the point in this alliance."

"The old ways are not entirely forgotten," Arkus said. "With packed spear formations and many archers, we will fare well enough given space."

Darnuir knew of these capabilities all too well. He'd watched what had befallen dragons when they did not treat humans seriously. Caught in the bogs, he thought, remembering vividly the memory Blaine had shown him. *Caught in the bogs… waist deep in mud and bloody water.*

"If the gates can be taken, then your spears could push in," Darnuir said.

Arkus nodded. "Open the way and humanity will take back what is ours."

"As your people will deserve for their efforts," Darnuir said, finding a smile tugging at this mouth. They were actually agreeing and it didn't seem forced.

"I shall direct my flyers against the catapult crews as a priority," Fidelm said. "But archers on both sides will make our work perilous."

"Enemy archers on the outer wall should thin out once our siege towers gain a footing," Darnuir said. "Then, once the dragons and I have cleared a path, I suggest we bring up hunters to begin thinning out their ranks on the inner wall. Perhaps a company of Chevaliers could join the dragons as well at that point?"

"My White Seven are always telling me of their prowess," Arkus said. "I'm sure they will relish the chance to prove it." He ended on a low, satisfied laugh that barely escaped his lips, as though enjoying some private joke. Then Arkus nodded, seeming content. Fidelm nodded as well, cracked his knuckles and stretched his wings as though flexing.

"This will be a hard-earned victory," Darnuir said, heart swelling in anticipation for the coming battle. "But if we use the best of each race I'm certain we will achieve it."

"I fear many will die in taking this place," said Fidelm.

"There will be no need for any slaughter," Blaine said solemnly, entering the pavilion with a heavy stride.

"And why is that?" Darnuir said. "Your input isn't required here, Blaine."

"Lives will be lost," Blaine said, ignoring Darnuir. "Yet fewer will die if we use the tunnels to infiltrate the fortress."

"We can't," Darnuir said, agitated. "We've dug up half the land near the woods that Cassandra described exiting from to no avail. It was always a long shot. Only Cassandra would have been able to find the entrance." Blaine didn't seem to hear Darnuir. He drifted over to the table and began shifting amongst the maps and blueprints.

"The tunnels are not shown on those," Arkus said, sounding both confused and concerned.

"I'll need a quill and ink," Blaine said to no one in particular. Darnuir wasn't sure whether to be more annoyed or worried by Blaine. It would be poor timing for Blaine to have lost his wits or taken ill. *But Blaine cannot get ill, can he?*

"What do you need ink for?" Darnuir asked.

"Did you never ask Cassandra how she found out about the passageways?"

"I did," Darnuir said, gently. "Her carer told her about them. Chelos, his name was."

"And how do you think Chelos knew of them?" asked Blaine, looking relieved as he spotted what he desired at the other end of the war table and moved to take them. When he returned, he dipped the quill tip into the dark liquid.

"Chelos?" Arkus said. "The name is familiar. You don't mean that old steward of the Royal Tower in Aurisha?"

"The very same," Blaine said, peering intently over the maps again.

"What's he got to do with this?" Arkus asked. "You speak as if you know him."

"I do," Blaine said. "Or, I did. It has been such a long time."

"So, you knew him," Darnuir said. "That doesn't explain much."

"Not in itself, but Chelos was once part of my order. He was a Light Bearer."

"Why would a Light Bearer have knowledge of secret passages within a human fortress?" Fidelm asked.

"Why indeed?" said Arkus.

All eyes were fixed on Blaine. Darnuir's instincts screamed at him. Blaine was about to cause another row, a catastrophe. He felt the tension, like a long strained heartbeat before drawing swords. Arkus shouldn't be here. But it was too late.

"Because it was the Guardians who built those passages," Blaine said.

And so, the hammer falls, Darnuir thought.

"Built them?" Arkus said, his voice suddenly high and rasping. "Built them? The Guardians. Built them?" he repeated, as though he had forgotten the meaning of words. "How?" He ended, more coarsely.

"The Bastion was built in the wake of the Second War," Blaine said.

"I know that," Arkus said. "The Dragon King himself helped construct it. A measure to guard against future aggression from his own people. Dronithir was ever the greatest of your kind."

"Norbanus felt otherwise," said Blaine.

"Norbanus remained Guardian?" asked Darnuir incredulously. "After the disaster of the Battle of the Bogs? After Dronithir defeated him?"

"Yes, the Guardian's Blade must be passed on. Norbanus held on for a time," Blaine said. "I told you, Darnuir, that I thought Norbanus to be over zealous. Well, this might be the one thing he actually did right."

"Did right?" Arkus said, turning a shade of red, much like the head on the Dragon's Blade. Fidelm's face was unreadable. As smooth and unyielding as the very walls they were about to assault. His eyes were cast downwards, as though he hoped the earth might offer him some guidance. The only movement he made was a light, nervous fluttering of his wings.

Darnuir wasn't sure what he felt. A part of him, the boy that had grown up the hunter, felt betrayed by the news. The older dragon felt satisfied, as though a very fine meal had just been eaten. His confusion led to a loss for words and Arkus looked at him accusingly, seemingly taking Darnuir's silence as acquiescence to the revelation.

"Norbanus had Light Bearers infiltrate the build," Blaine went on. "Working in secret, placing measures by which the fortress might easily be taken should the need arise. That's why the passages won't show on any plans you possess."

Darnuir closed his eyes but he wanted to cover his ears.

Stop Blaine. Just stop. Please. Stop, stop, stop...

"It was a secret kept even from the King," Blaine said. "Darnuir did not know this Arkus. Only I alone, through memories passed down to me."

Arkus seemed to have lost the capacity to speak as well. He leant his full weight upon the war table, rocking on the balls of his feet, eyes closed, and breathing heavily as if breathless. He let out a few choked sounds that might have been laughter; an unnerving mixture of hysteria and fury.

"I hoped it wouldn't come to this," said Blaine.

After a dangerously long pause, Arkus found his voice. "I do not feel as shocked as I ought to be. Betrayed? No not quite that, for it was neither of you who did this. It is a surprise and yet it is inevitable, isn't it? And just when I dared to hope we might be able to work openly together."

"Arkus, please," Darnuir said. "You said it yourself. This crime was not committed by any here. I swear I would never condone such a thing."

"As awful as this news is, it has at least worked out favourably," said Fidelm.

Darnuir cringed.

"Favourably," Arkus repeated. "True. A good thing that humanity never angered the dragons enough again to cause another war. A good thing we had no need to rely on a fortress we thought would help protect us. A good thing, then, that humanity never stepped out of line."

"Arkus—" Darnuir tried to say.

"Enough," Arkus snapped, rising as quickly as he had spat out his words. "I'll still supply the powder to blow through the gates, if that's possible. After we are finished here you can take my fleets to the Splinters and then eastwards to your Golden City. I want you gone from my lands – all of you. And know this, you will never set foot in my own city again."

And with that, Arkus was gone. He did not even stay to see where Blaine had finished marking the tunnels upon the maps.

"Why, Blaine?" Darnuir asked.

"A siege is out of the question," Blaine said, "and I will not waste lives through assaulting the walls alone. The passages are small though, so we can only pass so many troops through at a time."

Darnuir nodded.

"I did try to speak to you," said Blaine. "Maybe now you will listen to me in the future?"

"Don't use this as some lesson. You've caused irreparable harm."

"Arkus will calm down," said Blaine.

Darnuir couldn't tell whether Blaine truly believed that. "This news changes things," said Darnuir. "If we have access to the citadel tower then Brackendon will have a clear shot at Castallan. I will accompany him along with my Praetorians."

"Allow me to accompany you with my best warriors," Fidelm said.

"No, General. If only because I require a *trustworthy commander* to watch over the assault," Darnuir said pointedly.

"Must you venture inside, Darnuir?" Blaine droned on. "Let the wizards fight it out. It would not be wise in your current state."

A part of Darnuir yearned to duel Blaine again, then and there. Blaine had just cost him a deal of diplomacy and he was feeling too strained to care what the Guardian thought right now.

"I helped to create this mess," said Darnuir. "It seems only right that I help end it. Castallan won't be expecting Brackendon to show up in the midst of battle, and I can help get him there."

"You're not going to listen to me, are you?"

"I'm going," Darnuir said.

Blaine grimaced. "On your head, be it. I shall emerge between the walls with the Third. My Light Bearers are ready."

Naturally. You probably told them all of this before you told me, Blaine. No more secrets I said. No more...

"By nightfall it will be over," Darnuir said, already feeling fatigued. "One way or another."

Darnuir was the first to leave. A darker sky greeted them, the brighter morning having disappeared behind tendrils of ashen clouds, stretching across the sky like grey veins. The wind had picked up from the north, rolling in force from the ocean. It felt unnatural.

Blaine walked off without looking back at Darnuir or Fidelm.

"A shame," Fidelm said, pausing at the tent's entrance. "Not ideal conditions for flyers to do battle in. At least the wind is not blowing from the east against our path." He started to move but Darnuir caught the fairy's arm.

"If I may ask a favour of you?"

"I am listening," said Fidelm.

"Both your eyes will be busy on the battle, but if you can ever spare one, look out for Balack for me, if you can? I'd see him make it through this if I could. I must still make amends."

"I will do what I can," Fidelm said, bowing his head graciously. "We all need the ties of friends in this world. Even kings." And the fairy left Darnuir alone or as alone as one could be when Praetorians were within a few paces.

Horns began to blow, some sharp, some echoing, some distant; and the drums began to beat. The human army was stirring. At a high price, dragons and fairies would win the walls for them, but Darnuir figured the dragons had a debt to pay, even if most of humanity would never know it.

I have debts to pay as well, to Cassandra, to Balack. I'll need to win back some sorely needed favour with Arkus, if that is even possible.

For all their sakes, a bridge had to be built between the two races. If only Blaine could see that. If only it were not up to Darnuir alone to pursue such a dream. It seemed harder than ever; especially here, as they prepared to spill the blood of the Southern Dales.

A flicker of fear spread through Darnuir that it might be impossible.

Chapter 14

THE BREAKING OF THE BASTION: PART 2

Dragons won the First War, and the Second was something of a stalemate. Would humanity rise in a Third to become the new world power?

From Tiviar's Histories.

Brackendon – Outside the Bastion

BRACKENDON HEARD THE horns and the drums, and knew it was time. The defenders of the Bastion answered in kind, roaring the infamous hunter song.

"The wolf may howl, the bear will growl,
And our arrows shall sing."

The combined army of the Three Races began to stir. Brackendon felt the vibrations pulse under foot. There was another kind of tremor in the air, though this one felt like the Cascade. It wasn't faint either, but a fierce tide of energy moving unseen towards the Bastion.

"What is it?" Kymethra asked.

"I'm not sure," said Brackendon. "Though it is Castallan's work."

"What is?" asked a battle ready Balack, armed with a fat quiver, sword, two side knives and swinging his bow over one shoulder.

"Something for me to worry about," Brackendon said. "You keep your keen eyes on those walls."

"Is he making the weather turn as well?" Balack said, pointing upwards to the swirling sky.

For leagues around there was the sun and peace of a fine late summer's morning; however, near the fortress itself the world might have been ending. Ashen clouds coalesced towards the tip of the Bastion's inner tower. Wind buffeted Brackendon. Thunder cracked, and unnatural claws of green light descended towards the citadel tower, lingering for seconds at a time.

"This is the twisted work of the Cascade," said Brackendon. "Though to what end I do not know." He shared a look with Kymethra. It was the madness of the Conclave tower, magnified and brought to the battlefield.

No one should be capable of this. This must end.

"Well we have no choice but to face it head on," said Balack. "This is where Castallan answers for Cold Point, for Grace, for Cosmo and for Eve." He extended an arm. "Thank you for coming to see me."

Brackendon took the proffered arm. "Make sure you live through this."

"You as well," said Balack, moving to give Kymethra a quick hug.

I'm afraid I can't promise that.

The chanting of the defenders grew even louder.

"Still we as men can counter them,
A dragon dies the same.
When arrows fly, the wild beasts die,
A dragon dies the same."

Balack let a deep breath loose then drew in another one. "I better go. Looks like you're needed elsewhere," he added, nodding at something behind Brackendon.

Brackendon turned to find Darnuir, Lira and their Praetorians all assembled. Each dragon wore their plate armour, though with pieces strategically removed to be more agile, like a hunter. They bore two swords each – one regular and one shorter one for shield work, except for Darnuir who carried only the Dragon's Blade and wore his heavy starium reinforced armour. Darnuir's expression was akin to that carved dragon draped across his shoulders.

"You have need of me?" Brackendon asked.

"Blaine knows where the tunnels are," Darnuir said.

Brackendon was sure Darnuir threw a glance to Balack as his old friend headed for the assembling army. He wondered whether Darnuir would say anything, call out perhaps, but no, he did not. Instead, the King of Dragons looked back to Brackendon. "Come. Let us take this wizard by surprise for a change."

"Go," Brackendon said. "I shall only be a moment."

Darnuir glanced to Kymethra. "One moment," he said before leaving them.

"So, you'll be out here?" Brackendon asked her, once they were alone.

"I'll be flying high to relay information."

"There's no such thing as high enough," he said, stepping in to hug her. "You hear me? You can't fly high enough." He buried his face in her hair. He did not want to let go. Eventually, she gently pushed him away.

"I'll be fine," she said and kissed him. It was a long kiss, the longest they'd ever shared. But it ended, as it had to.

"I'll find you the moment it's over," Brackendon said. Kymethra nodded, her lower lip struggling to stay still.

"Just don't age too much alright? The grey hair is enough." She stepped back from him and shifting into her eagle form. She perched briefly upon his arm, skilfully avoided sinking her talons into him, and nibbled affectionately at his blackened finger before taking off into the dreadful sky. Brackendon watched her soar off; then, tightening his grip upon his staff, he set off after Darnuir.

Brackendon joined them south of the Three Races' army, by the edge of the small forest, which had recently been harvested for siege weapons. The Third legion was hidden amongst the trees, ready to follow into the tunnel when Blaine gave his signal. The Guardian himself was moving across the ground, tapping his feet on various spots as he went.

The assault of the Bastion began. Drums beat louder. Horns blew harder. The bellow of the defenders rose to match the howl of the sea and wind.

With its unique shape, the Bastion was difficult to approach. The sharp angle of the western wall split the advancing army like the bow of a ship cutting a wave. Arrows hailed down from the Bastion. Catapults sent stone crashing against the plated siege towers; some denting them, some smashing sections of the towers clean away, taking golden bodies with them. Angling the towers to align with the Bastion's walls was the most dangerous, leaving them more vulnerable as they tried to turn. On the ground, and in the trenches, dragons made their way towards the base of the walls, shields raised against the arrow storm. But there was no respite. Hunters and longbow men atop the siege towers let loose their own arrows but their efforts were akin to pushing against a waterfall.

Brackendon ripped his gaze away from the brewing battle. "Remember, Darnuir, you leave—"

"Castallan to you, yes," said Darnuir. "Let us play our part at least. Are you nervous, Lira?"

"A little," Lira said. "Though I'm glad to finally fight alongside you."

"I'm glad to have you at my side," Darnuir said. "All of you," he added more loudly.

"It is here," Blaine called.

"Open it then," Darnuir said running over. The two dragons stamped on the soil until there came a great crack and the ground gave way underfoot. Both fell with the broken door and Light Bearers and Praetorians rushed over to the breach. Brackendon reached the hole first, moving faster than they could hope to.

He savoured the rush down his arm, that oh so wonderful rush.

He jumped down into the tunnel between Darnuir and Blaine who were still half crouched from the fall. It was pitch black ahead. Only the broken entranceway behind let in dim half-light from the corrupted world outside. The eyes of the dragons flared like cats in the darkness. Brackendon was about to light his staff when a pale beam was cast from his right. On his left a warmer glow crackled into life as Darnuir set a flame licking up the Dragon's Blade. Brackendon added his own light and they began to run.

Cassandra – The Bastion – Castallan's Throne Room

Cassandra's limbs had never ached more than now as she hung from this wall. Not even when she had spent entire days in the crawlspaces of the Bastion; not even when she had stumbled half-dead into the Boreac Mountains. The bonds at her ankles and wrists were biting and her neck screamed in protest. Somehow, she had gone deaf as well, though she was sure that was due to whatever Castallan had done.

The wizard had ripped a hole in the world. That was the only way she could conceive of it. Thankfully, he had done it far away from her, up near the throne: a gaping tear hanging in the very air. She could see nothing on the other side, only blackness. Yet it seemed more than just darkness. It was as if nothing existed within it. Castallan was standing close by it, his shoulders hunched, and his arms shaking terribly with the effort. She saw his entire right hand begin to darken, a few fingers burning black like Brackendon's. It crept up as far as his neck and then to his ear.

"What are you doing?" she cried, though she could barely hear herself.

Castallan didn't acknowledge her. He stood bent over, frozen in place for perhaps half a minute, his robes fraying at the edges. He started moving towards the chasm he had created, as though it were sucking him in. Even the staffs began to tremble in their holders, and she swore she saw the closest one edge a little out of its grip.

"Stop it," she screamed. It felt like her head was under water.

Then, something wonderful happened. Another one of Castallan's staffs, the closest one, flew out of its bracket, nearly hitting the wizard as it entered the dark tear in the world. A good chunk of the staff remained behind, broken and useless.

Castallan's cry of anger sounded distant until, with a painful pop in her ears, her full hearing returned. Castallan's wail reverberated around the throne room, and a deep blue light shone out from the hole in the world. There was something on the other side now; a bubbling, blue substance hanging in the air. Castallan drew himself back up, his chest heaving. His hair and stubble around his blackened ear was singed.

"What have you done?" Cassandra asked.

"I have created a Cascade Sink," Castallan rasped. "I'm drawing all magic for miles around to it."

"You lost another staff for it," Cassandra said with relish. "That's two gone."

"Be quiet!" He limped away from his creation, groaning and clutching at his side. "Have no fear, Cassandra. The Dragon's Blade will more than make up for the loss. Or the Guardian's Blade. Whichever dragon comes for me first. There will be enough concentrated energy in that Sink to bind the Blades to me. Your breaking one of my staffs won't hold me back." Yet from the way that Castallan held himself up, leaning heavily on his own staff for support, Cassandra knew that there was still hope.

Castallan shuffled over to the great doors. "It is done," he called, and the doors swung in. Red-eyed servants swarmed in, carrying baskets of bread and flagons of water. "Any word on Darnuir?" Castallan asked, taking a huge bite out of a steaming roll.

"He and a contingent of other dragons were spotted entering the south-western passage, as expected, Your Majesty," one of the food bearers said. "Forces have been placed between the walls as instructed. We also believe the other wizard is with them."

"Good," Castallan said thickly, reaching for a second roll. "As expected. But I'd rather deal with one of them at a time. Harry them and separate the group, but ensure Darnuir makes it here. Kill the others if you can."

Darnuir – The tunnels of the Bastion

"Which way?" Darnuir asked as they reached a crossroads within the tunnels.

"Straight ahead takes you under the inner wall towards the tower," said Blaine. "I'll go left and come up between the walls."

"Praetorians with me," Darnuir said. Brackendon had carried on without him. He didn't want to leave Lira and the others behind so he pounded down the tunnel at an unenhanced pace, following the distant light of Brackendon's staff.

Before long, Brackendon disappeared upwards and his light dimmed. Darnuir tried to intensify the flames on the Dragon's Blade to allow them to see. Yet, when he nudged the door to the Cascade the flow of energy did not increase. Rather than getting hotter and brighter, the flames on his sword guttered out. *No, no, no…*

"Darnuir?" Lira said.

"I can't draw on the Cascade. It feels like nothing is there." He tried throwing the door wide open but it had no effect. Where there should have been a well of power, there was nothing. Not one drop. His armour suddenly weighed double without the constant trickle of magic to help him carry it. His mouth felt dusty and his heart quickened in panic.

"Darnuir?" Lira said again, more concerned. "Are you—"

"Keep moving," Darnuir said, forcing himself to keep the worry from his voice. "I made do without the Cascade for long enough. Stopping is not an option."

When they emerged from the passage, it was into a dank cell. There was a foul-smelling dampness, straw was strewn across the floor, and the grated cell door lay bent and ajar.

"Brackendon?" Darnuir called, offering a hand to Lira to help her up.

"I'm here," Brackendon answered. Darnuir stepped out of the cell to find Brackendon leaning against the corridor wall near a torch bracket.

"I cannot reach out to the Cascade," Darnuir said.

"I can barely feel it," Brackendon said. "It is as though all the Cascade has been taken elsewhere… but it is still here… somewhere." His eyes flicked upwards as though he could see through the stone.

"Wait," Darnuir called, but the wizard had already vanished up a staircase.

"I don't think he wants you to follow," Lira said.

"I know he doesn't, but without the Cascade what can either of us do?" The rest of the Praetorians began filing out of the cell, clanking loudly in the quiet dungeon.

"You'd never know there was a battle happening outside," Lira said. "Down here we can hear nothing."

"Perhaps we ought to double back and aid Blaine in storming the walls?" Darnuir said, thinking aloud.

"Darnuir, over here," Raymond called. He'd done well to keep up and was now standing by a cell, bending low at the bars.

"What is it?"

"A prisoner," Raymond said. "A dragon."

"How can you know that," Lira asked, moving over. "Oh," was all she added.

Darnuir stepped over, conscious of time slipping by. Inside the cell was a figure slumped to his knees and bound with thick chains on his legs, arms, even neck. Around his neck was a block of wood, the word 'dragon' painted in dried blood. Whoever he was, he was thin, with wrinkles to mark his age.

An old dragon, here at the Bastion. Darnuir had a mind as to who he was.

"Get him out," Darnuir said softly. Lira pulled at the cell door. It was a touch rusted and came free easily under her strength. Darnuir entered and crouched down. The dragon's eyes were closed and his breath sounded ragged but at least that meant he was alive. "Chelos?" Darnuir said gently. There was no response. "Chelos?" Very carefully he rocked the dragon. "Chelos?"

"Darnuir, what are you doing?" Lira asked. "We should not linger here."

"Chelos?" Darnuir asked. He knew it was the old dragon. He knew it.

At last, with heavy drooping eyelids, the dragon blinked and looked at Darnuir. "Your eyes aren't red," he said blearily.

"We're here to end Castallan," Darnuir said. "We're dragons too. I am Darnuir."

"And I am, Chelos." His words were laboured. "It is… it is… you look so similar. We owe thanks… thanks to N'weer."

"I should thank you," Darnuir said. "For sending Cassandra to me. For warning us all about the invasion from the east."

"She's back here," Chelos mumbled.

"I know," Darnuir said. "That was my fault."

"Throne room," Chelos said. "In the… in the throne room."

"I'll get her out," Darnuir said, but Chelos was already slipping out of consciousness. "Chelos? Chelos do you hear me?" But he was gone for the time being. Darnuir took hold of the Dragon's Blade and hacked at the chains. Raymond darted in to catch Chelos in his arms.

"Stay with him," Darnuir said. "There are questions I have for him. I think Arkus will have a few as well. Don't try moving him. He's too fragile."

"Raymond can't just stay here if we return to the battle," Lira said.

"We aren't going outside," Darnuir said. He made for the staircase Brackendon had taken.

"No," Lira said. Her tone was defiant, strong. Not her usual self.

"No?" Darnuir said, turning to face her. The rest of the Praetorians hovered uncertainly. Lira hesitated for a moment but soldiered on.

"You said it yourself. We should help the Lord Guardian. There is a war going on out there and you want us to fight through the tower for some girl?"

She's standing up to me. Not the same Lira I first met in Val'tarra.

"You'd be right, Lira. You'd all be right to not follow me if it were just some human girl. But Cassandra is the daughter of Arkus and our relations with him are now at an all-time low. Chelos there is a part of the problem. Cassandra may be part of the solution. If I have any chance of mending relations with Arkus, I need to bring her safely to him. She's too important to risk."

Lira stepped forwards, stopping between Darnuir and the Praetorians. "That's not your only reason." The accusation hung heavy between them.

No, it isn't my only reason.

But he could not admit it to Lira nor his Guard. He'd failed Cassandra twice before, first at Aurisha when she was a baby and again at the Charred Vale. He'd failed her in other ways too, shameful ways. Instinct told him he was right on that. His guilt felt like a heavy stone in his gut. He'd been wrong but perhaps if he could get her out, perhaps if this time he did not fail, then he could begin to make it right.

"When I said I mean to strengthen the bond between humans and dragons, I meant it. That dream now lies on a knife-edge. This is something I feel have to do and I ask that you do it with me."

He could tell Lira wasn't convinced. She pressed her lips together in a thin line, but nodded all the same and drew her sword. Every Praetorian followed her lead and steel rang in the stony dungeon.

Cassandra – Castallan's Throne Room

Cassandra still hung painfully on the far wall from Castallan. He was sitting on his throne, a heap of crumbs on his robes, and shattered glass at his feet from where he had dropped the water jugs. His groaning had only just subsided.

Any moment now someone will come to fight him. Brackendon, Darnuir, Blaine, I don't care who. Soon. Soon…

The doors burst open and her heart raced, but it was only a red-eyed messenger. He bowed before Castallan and relayed word of the battle. Siege towers had made it to the wall. Fairies were targeting the catapults. Dragons had emerged from underground but were bogged down in a fight between the walls. Arkus' soldiers were taking great care to bring up many barrels before one of the outer gates on the western wall.

Castallan shooed him away with a flick of his hand. "I did not expect the walls to hold forever. Just long enough. Leave. Now." The messenger did not need telling twice and scampered out, leaving the doors wide open.

Any moment now.

Were those footsteps she could hear? She was sure she could hear shouting. Was that why Castallan had gotten to his feet and marched down from his throne? The blue light of the Cascade Sink cast a long shadow of the wizard across the floor and picked out the new blackened streaks on his skin.

The messenger returned. Only he did not return on foot. Through the air, he journeyed, before disappearing into the blue tear in the world. A red mist puffed up as he entered it. Castallan paid the man no mind. His gaze fixed on whoever was approaching.

Brackendon entered the throne room.

Cassandra almost cried. The best of the three had come.

His sapphire robes matched the light of the Cascade Sink, and his greying hair was wild. Beads of sweat glistening on his brow and his chest rose and fell rapidly. Had he run here without magic? Cassandra wondered. Darnuir did not follow in behind Brackendon. Perhaps Castallan's men had done their job well. She hoped not.

"I know what happened," Brackendon said. There was a strange sense of calm in his voice. "I know about the Inner Circle. What they did. I felt their anger first hand."

"So, you went back," Castallan said.

"I destroyed the tower."

"Then for that, I thank you."

"I am sorry. For what it's worth."

"It's too late now, isn't it?" Castallan said, lowering his staff at Brackendon. "This fight was inevitable."

"I'm afraid so," Brackendon said, rapping his own staff off the floor and pointing it at Castallan. The jewel-like wood was radiant in the blue glow. "A Cascade Sink. A good thing I can still draw on energy near the well."

"It's not for your benefit," Castallan said. "I never dreamed I would be forced to where I am. For what it's worth, I am sorry too."

Then it began.

Brackendon struck first, pushing himself to his right at speed and sending a ball of fire at the remaining staffs. Castallan sent his own to collide with it in mid-air. Before the cinders reached the floor, Brackendon had already appeared behind Castallan and lashed out with his staff. Castallan spun to counter it, the two staffs failing to hit each other due to some manipulation of the air. They duelled like swordsmen for a time, adding flourishes of fire, or violet and orange arcane energies when they saw an opening.

This seemed a battle of stamina rather than force. Yet Brackendon looked to be increasingly on the defensive; pushing back rather than attacking himself. Castallan had the advantage. He was just that bit faster, his spells always a little stronger.

Brackendon made for the staffs behind the throne again and very nearly destroyed one. He kept pressure on the staffs and Castallan was the one forced to react, barely keeping some strikes from landing. Then the platform of the throne began to shake. From the look of concentration on Brackendon's face, it seemed he was trying to topple the chair. Castallan looked to be countering it, his face twisting in concentration as he spun his staff wildly in both hands. Neither won, but the platform did buckle, the throne jerked forward, and a couple of staffs were thrown from their holders.

"Arrgh," Brackendon cried as a spear of yellow-green energy sent him spinning. He landed close to Cassandra.

"Don't give in," she cried out, not knowing if he would hear her. New white strands were appearing throughout his hair. The magic must already be taking its toll. By the throne, Castallan paused to recover, spitting to the floor.

Brackendon rose. His right arm trembled and his knuckles turned white as he gripped his staff. He looked up to Cassandra. Blood streamed from his nose. Somehow, he still managed one of his chuckling smiles. He too relieved his mouth of a great gob of spittle, then returned to the fight.

Blaine – Between the walls of the Bastion

Blaine missed death through luck alone.

A blue body fell onto his opponent moments before the red-eyed hunter would have gouged at his own face. Gasping for breath, Blaine plunged the Guardian's Blade through the neck of his foe.

He rose laboriously, feeling weaker than he had any memory of.

The Cascade had abandoned him.

No magic was flowing in at his call, even when he flung the door to it open. He had been unable to send up a beam of light to signal the Third Legion. Instead, Blaine and his Light Bearers were caught and surrounded.

A Light Bearer went down beside him and Blaine took revenge at the human's waist. The Guardian's Blade bit through the chainmail with ease. At least his sword offered some advantage.

Arrows clattered off his breastplate. Thwack-thunk.

Sweat ran into his eyes and soaked him under his armour, which was now too heavy. Gods, but he had forgotten what it was to sweat. His muscles protested, his body longed for rest. He didn't feel like the Guardian right now, just a dragon. It had been a very long time since he had felt like that.

"Closer together," he called. "Reform with shields. Push to the stairs." Yet Blaine, who had never felt a need for a shield before, suddenly felt very exposed. Forced to huddle within the ranks of his Light Bearers, they edged along, backs to the wall.

They must have expected this? Why else would Castallan divert troops from the walls? There had been no fear in them either, no sweetness. And now there was only the stench of the dying.

Two more bodies fell from the wall above, landing amongst the Light Bearers with bone crunching thuds. One dragon; one human.

"The Third will arrive soon," Blaine yelled, desperately hoping they would. He clutched a hand over his pounding heart.

Gods he was old.

And afraid.

Dwna, bless me? Dwl'or, grant me strength?

Their shield wall kept the worst of the arrows off, but fresh defenders on foot were beginning to box them in, red eyes flashing all around, preventing them from reaching the stairs. It wasn't far either – twenty paces at best. The humans might have been less armoured, but their numbers and compact bodies made it equally hard to find any openings. Blaine tried to thrust his sword out but was blocked each time, swatted away as though his strength was nothing to them.

Then came the bang, and for the third time in recent months Blaine heard the explosive force of black powder, as though a door the size of a mountain had been slammed shut. Screaming followed, from both sides of the wall.

The red-eyed humans nearby began to squirm. A panic took them, eyes darting to the source of the noise and cries came from among their ranks.

"To the gate."

"They have broken through."

"Quickly. Quickly. To the gate."

Suddenly, the crushing weight pressing against Blaine and his Light Bearers lifted. Blaine had never thought he'd be glad that humans were coming to his aid. He now had a chance.

"Break ranks," Blaine cried. "Cut them down." Hacking at an opponent's back had never seemed more appealing than it did now. "Up the stairs. To the wall." It would probably be safer than down here.

Though the explosion at the gate had distracted the humans in the courtyard, those still manning the inner wall were alert. Their arrows continued to fly.

Thwack-thwack-ping.

Only Blaine's exceptional armour kept him alive. He kept his head bent low as he ascended the stairs, praying his gauntlet would stop a shaft from piercing his skull. It meant fighting one handed, another thing he was not used to. A red-eyed huntress nearly knocked him off balance when he blocked her strike. The shame of it alone nearly killed him. Yet, in her haste, she over-reached and Blaine struck at her knee with an armoured fist while she was wrong-footed. Bones crunched. She toppled off the stairs into the courtyard below.

Blaine climbed upwards, slowing with every step. By the time he reached the top of the outer wall he thought his lungs would explode. Finding his footing amongst the bodies was the trickiest thing. Luckily, the defenders weren't expecting an attack from behind.

Blood sprayed into his face as he waded across the wall. A siege tower lay broken to his left, just short of the wall. Ahead another tower was being inched into position. At the wall's edge, it paused, then the drawbridges, thickly spiked, crashed onto the parapets. Dragons spilt out of it, even as a thick ballista bolt sailed into the opening.

Blaine locked eyes with his next opponent, some overgrown human with a blood-soaked beard. The man was feet away when a buzzing filled Blaine's ears and a blue blur collided with the human, kicking him in the head. The man stumbled, fell to his knees and Fidelm finished him with a shove of his double-headed spear.

"You seem breathless, Guardian," Fidelm said. Blaine was so exhausted he could barely think.

"Third," he managed to say. "Where is… Third?"

"The legion? You were to give the signal."

Blaine coughed, hacking away until something in his throat snapped. "Can't," he choked. "Go. In the wood. Tell them to come."

"We'll need the help," Fidelm said. "The powder was set off too soon. Only a segment of the gate was destroyed and there's a crush forming at the opening."

"We won't win like this," Blaine spluttered. "Go."

202

Fidelm nodded then took off, just as another hunter from the Dales charged across the wall. Blaine raised the Guardian's Blade high and brought it down, cutting through the man's raised wrist and burying the sword into his shoulder. The effort brought Blaine to his knees, unable to resist the momentum of his own swing.

He spent a dazed moment staring at the fresh green pulse wrapping around the citadel. When the Cascade had left him, so too had the sound of nature. The wind was silent, the ocean sounded still, and every cry of battle sounded thrice as loud because of it.

A hand gripped Blaine by the shoulder but he felt unable to resist it. "Lord Guardian, are you wounded?" Bacchus asked.

That could have been the end of me, right there.

"Only my pride is hurt," he lied. In the courtyard below, Castallan's troops were giving little ground to the humans loyal to Arkus. Hunks of stone continued to be launched by the defenders with very little being repaid in kind. Victory would come at too high a cost. A glance around depressed him further. Even if they took the outer wall, the inner wall remained well guarded. Not far ahead was the gatehouse that stood above the semi-breached gate below. A fierce fight already raged atop it.

"We need to take that gatehouse," Blaine said. "We need it open."

"Are you able to continue?" Bacchus asked. He was looking at Blaine differently than before, with less awe, more concern, and even pity.

"Are you really asking me that?" Blaine said.

"You did not give the signa—"

"I know!" Blaine yelled. Then he was coughing again. Light Bearers were fighting all around him. Their efforts shamed Blaine, enough to force him to stand. "To the gatehouse," he spluttered.

The humans at the gatehouse had prepared a defence, perhaps intending a last stand.

Blaine fell into the brawl clumsily, his arms feeling lethargic. A figure amongst them, a white blur, caught his eye, firing arrows as fast as he moved. The boy was fighting as though the strength of all three gods were at his back.

Is that truly Balack?

Red-eyed humans continued to come up from a staircase leading into the body of the gatehouse below, where the gate mechanism would be.

Blaine caught Balack's eye and the boy gave a curt nod before dropping to one knee, hacking at a soldier's shin allowing Bacchus to finish him. But with every fallen defender another came.

Blaine could barely lift his arm. He needed the Cascade, but it had abandoned him. *Have the gods abandoned me as well?* Darnuir might be dead. That could be why his powers had diminished.

Another hunter from the Dales locked eyes with him.

I can't do this anymore.

The hunter swung his sword.

I'm just too old.

A screech filled his ears and a tawny eagle dove into the hunter's face, raking at his soft eyes. Kymethra's screeches were painful on the ear.

"Lord Guardian," some deep voice was calling. Fairies flew in to support them on the gatehouse, swarming the defenders briefly. "Blaine," the voice shouted again. "The Third have come." Fidelm was in front of him, bloodied. A chunk of his long hair had been cut away.

"Open the gate," Blaine managed to say. Fidelm strode off, barking orders at some flyers. They disappeared down into the gatehouse proper. Balack was still fighting.

How is he doing this?

Balack took the last kill, ripping out a knife and throwing it into a red eye. The flow of defenders finally ceased. Something stirred within Blaine again. It was far from pity this time – more like pride. *The boy has done well to put his despair behind him.*

Below, on the besieging side, the troops were looking up to them as they stood atop the gatehouse.

"This was your doing, Balack," Blaine said, nodding to Castallan's purple standard. Balack seemed to understand and wordlessly retrieved his knife from the corpse of the red-eyed hunter.

"Lord Guardian, are you sure?" Bacchus said, scowling at Balack's back. "Take the victory for your own."

"He earned it. I can't deny that," Blaine said.

Balack stepped up to the parapet's edge and cut the flag down as the great doors began to open underneath them. A cheer grew across the army of the Three Races. It nearly sparked some life back into Blaine, until he remembered that the inner wall still stood and red-eyed defenders still lined it.

We are far from done.

Another explosion ripped across the battlefield.

Blaine looked up to see a large hole in the face of the citadel tower. The debris blasted outwards, raining onto the battle, crushing those on both sides. And from the wound in the tower came light. It spilt in tiny pinpricks against the ashen sky, as though a thousand shooting stars in a thousand colours were hurtling out from the breach.

You better be alive, Darnuir – for both our sakes.

Cassandra – Castallan's throne room

Cassandra thought the heat might cook her alive, somehow it didn't leave a mark. It had blown half the room apart, though. She looked out onto the carnage below; the armies looked like swarming insects. She couldn't tell who was winning and the fight in the throne room was equally indecisive.

The wizards were circling far apart, whirling their staffs and sending pulses of energy at each other. Countless jets of light in every colour – colours she couldn't name. Brackendon fired energy at Castallan and Castallan batted it back; back and back and back, until the room was blindingly bright. Their attacks seemed to have weight as the balls of light blew chunks from the floor and walls upon impact. When several had hit the Cascade Sink at once, the explosion had blown half the wall away.

The circling continued. Brackendon was close to the doors when he launched a ball of greenish-purple energy. Castallan, who was closer to Cassandra, deflected it and then sent a silver jet of his own. Something from outside the throne room drew Brackendon's attention for a split second and the silver wave nearly took him. He dropped to the floor, the silver light shattered against the wall behind him. While prone, Brackendon flicked his staff at the open doorway. The doors closed with such force that Cassandra felt the reverberations in her steel cuffs. A muffled bellow came from behind the door.

"Brackendon, don't do this alone."

Darnuir?

"It won't open. Damn it. Lira, hold them off while I try to break through."

"You'd protect him?" Castallan asked, flicking one hand upwards. Brackendon was flipped off the ground and flung towards Castallan. As he passed the crest of his arc, Brackendon righted himself, gripped his staff in both hands like a mace and brought it down on Castallan. They collided with a bang to rival that of the black powder, sending both wizards sprawling.

Thunk, thunk, thunk, came from the doors, as though Darnuir was trying to hack his way through.

Castallan was the first to recover. He looked a mess; jaw hanging loosely, and his left arm bent backwards at the elbow. Yet he turned even more gruesome as he began to heal. As his bones reset the black lines across his skin slithered further across his neck and up onto his scalp, under a patch of hair whitening to milk then catching fire and smoking.

Brackendon had fared little better. One leg looked crushed and red pools were collecting under his robes.

He wasn't getting up.

"Heal yourself," Cassandra cried out, her throat nearly cracking with the effort. "You can't give in now. Brackendon? Brackendon?"

But Brackendon stayed down. Something rolling across the floor caught her eye. Brackendon's staff, the most powerful staff in the world, was making its way to Castallan's feet.

"No," she sobbed.

Castallan's skin had lost all colour and he looked like a laughing skull as he gently stopped the staff with one foot. Brackendon tried to move, propping himself up on one arm, but it gave way. He slumped down and lay still. Brackendon's power over the throne room doors must have broken for, at that moment, Darnuir stormed in, a bloodied Dragon's Blade in his hand. The sound of a skirmish raged from the corridor beyond.

"And at last, here you are," Castallan said, sounding half dead. "Will you give the sword to me? Or will I be forced to take it?"

Darnuir looked first to Cassandra, then to Brackendon. "Is he—"

"Give me the sword, Darnuir!"

"Never," Darnuir said, taking the Dragon's Blade in both hands. He charged Castallan, who grunted impatiently. Darnuir was halted mid-stride, frozen in place, and the Dragon's Blade was ripped from his grasp. The sword shook in the air, trying to return to Darnuir, but Castallan brought it towards him, an eager arm outstretched.

"And now, the last act I make as a mere man," Castallan said, raising his staff at the Cascade Sink. The blue glow intensified, the substance within it violently bubbled and tossed. The Dragon's Blade started glowing, heat was rising in it; first a pale yellow, then orange, then red, then white. "Yes," Castallan said, a crazed look in his eye. "Yes. Even this ancient magic can be broken and turned."

Is it really over then? They can't defeat him... no one could have. Such a thought should have made her weep, but she felt nothing: just a cold emptiness at the wasted energy. Everything she had gone through, everything they had all gone through; all for nothing.

Then, the Dragon's Blade stopped moving.

It hung for a moment in the air between Castallan and Darnuir, close to the wizard. If Castallan only stepped forwards he might have taken it. But the Dragon's Blade began to move back towards Darnuir, fighting against Castallan's magic. Castallan's eyes popped madly and the glow from the Cascade Sink shone even brighter.

"Come to me," Castallan growled. Darnuir unfroze as the sword drew nearer.

"The Dragon's Blade is mine alone."

"I will save this world," Castallan screamed. "I am the only one who can." And with what appeared to be a final effort, Castallan reached for the sword again. The Cascade Sink produced a near deafening droning, and then, just as the Dragon's Blade was exactly midway between the two, both Castallan and Darnuir began to convulse. Fits came over them. Their eyes rolled up into their skulls. No sane word came from their mouths.

From Darnuir's came something more terrifying – a hint of a forked tongue, and a roar like a true beast. Patches of his skin grew red, hard and shiny. Skin to match the head of his sword.

Cassandra's bonds released and she fell. She managed to roll as she hit the floor, keeping low as the horror unfolded before her. This was no place for an ordinary human.

What do I do? What do I do?

The bestial roar from Darnuir grew louder.

Cassandra forced herself to look anywhere but at him. She whipped her head towards Castallan instead and there, at his feet, she saw it, just lying untouched. Brackendon's staff. She bolted for it, picked it up and tore back to Brackendon. She fell down at his side, shoved the shaft into his hand and closed his fingers around it.

"Brackendon, get up. Fight. Please," she said desperately, shaking the wizard by the shoulders. His eyes were closed. "Brackendon. Please get up. Please. Brackendon." And with a great gasp, as though he had been drowning, Brackendon opened his eyes. He tried to stand but his leg was too badly hurt. Cassandra placed herself under his free arm, and he leaned heavily upon her.

"Thank you," Brackendon said weakly into her ear. "Castallan," he said, raising his staff with an air of finality. "You are just a man."

The Dragon's Blade flew back to Darnuir's grasp as Brackendon broke the bond. Castallan's eyes rolled back down to face them, one pupil now black. Nearly all his hair had burnt away. It looked like there was no life left in him. Even with all his power, he had failed. It hadn't been enough. The Dragon's Blade had one master.

Castallan did nothing to resist Brackendon's magical push, perhaps he wanted to die. Cassandra would never know. Brackendon sent him back, right into the Cascade Sink. A puff of red mist, a blinding blue light, and both Castallan and the Sink were gone.

Brackendon became a dead weight, letting out a rattling sigh as he slumped onto her. She couldn't keep him upright so tried to lay him gently down. All his hair had turned white, his right hand entirely black, and a little bubble of blood gathered at the corner of his mouth. He was mumbling, but nothing that made sense.

She pressed the staff firmer into Brackendon's grip, closing her eyes and feeling the hot, salty tears descend. She didn't want to open them again. Every emotion was flaring at once; joy, horror, distress, and despair. Cassandra didn't know what to feel, so she just let herself cry. Brackendon was still breathing, that much she could feel from the shallow rise and fall of his chest. She didn't know long she knelt beside him. Time simply passed until a soft hand closed over hers.

"There's nothing we can do," Kymethra said. There was no life in her voice.

208

Cassandra sat back, wiped her running nose on the back of her sleeve, and didn't know what to do. Darnuir looked to be stirring. He'd be fine. So, she sat there with Kymethra, as the witch lay down beside Brackendon, embracing him in a silent hug, and wetting his robes with a downpour of her own tears. It seemed that no sound was fitting for her grief.

Only silence.

Chapter 15

AFTERMATH

In Val'tarra we bury our dead under the cleansed earth of blackened trees. When the first flower blossoms on that ground, we know our loved ones have found peace.

From Tiviar's Histories.

Darnuir – Castallan's throne room

DARNUIR FELT LIKE he'd been beaten to death. He never wanted to move again. This floor felt like a feather bed, and the stone was cool on his cheek. It was quite a come down from the godlike high of only moments before. Every pore of his body had been seeped in magic, then. But it had been sucked out too soon. It had been so good.

What happened? I shouldn't have that that much Cascade in me. Brackendon won't be pleased... where is he?

Then he remembered where he was, and what he had come here to do.

He slowly opened one eye. A crumpled blue robed body lay across the room, with two women around it: one with long black hair, the other brown with white tips. His groggy mind was slow to process it all. A painful rush down his arm towards his sword had started; it felt like bits of gravel were flowing through his veins.

With some effort, he managed to get to his feet. The Dragon's Blade slipped from his limp fingers but flew back when it bounced off the floor. He forced his hand to tighten around the hilt, trying to drain out the poison. A strong wind battered him and he drifted a little closer to the chasm in the wall. A distant cheer was spreading and, even at this height, Darnuir caught a sweet scent in the air.

"Darnuir," Cassandra said. There were cuts on her wrists, her eyes were puffy and had dark circles underneath; but her black hair still fell in thick shining waves. He'd expected his heart to drum when he saw her again; instead, it slowed almost to a halt.

"Darnuir?" Cassandra said.

"Yes." He found it very hard to speak.

"We need to leave," Cassandra said.

"Yes," Darnuir said again. Instinct told him to walk to Brackendon's side, sheathe his sword, and drop to one knee. Brackendon's eyes were milky and blank; his entire right forearm had turned black and scaly. His hair had gone white. Kymethra had her face buried into his robes, one arm clutched like a vice around Brackendon's shoulder.

"Kymethra," Darnuir said, trying to be gentle with his ragged voice. "We have to go." The witch did not move. More footsteps hammered along the hard stone and Lira and the Praetorians came surging into the remnants of the throne room.

"Darnuir, is everything…" Lira began, trailing off when she saw them.

Cassandra returned, attempting to prise Kymethra off Brackendon. "We need to get out of this tower." Kymethra resurfaced, her face red and glistening.

She wiped at her eyes. "Come on Darnuir. Use that strength." Darnuir made to pick Brackendon up. "Wait," Kymethra said. "The staffs. Burn them."

Darnuir looked to the toppled throne. The eight remaining staffs were scattered, one lying precariously over the edge of the room where the wall had collapsed. Lira and Cassandra helped collect them, and once heaped together, Darnuir drew out the Dragon's Blade and set them alight. He felt no need to watch them turn to ash.

Darnuir picked Brackendon up in both arms. He felt so light and fragile. They walked in silence down the citadel tower, the Praetorian Guard surrounding Darnuir and Brackendon like a golden shield. Followers of Castallan cowered before them now. Only minutes ago they had rushed Darnuir as he fought up the tower, swords raised and eyes red. Before exiting the tower, Lira sent a few Praetorians down to the dungeons to collect Raymond and Chelos.

Out in the vast inner courtyard of the Bastion, the people parted for them, or ran back into the buildings lined against the inner wall. Darnuir found the sweetness in the air nauseating. Ahead, the western set of gates had been opened. They passed through, passed the bodies already being piled, and the prisoners already being split up, towards the gates of the outer wall, which were half blown to cinders. Burnt stone, burnt bodies and a trail of embers ran deep into the Brevian army. No one stopped them through all of it, until about a hundred Chevaliers marched towards them with a man in billowing black robes at their head.

"It is over then," Arkus said. His small eyes flitted over Brackendon. "Is he—"

"Broken," Kymethra said shakily.

"Such an outcome was a risk we..." but he froze, having finally noticed Cassandra. Arkus' mouth hung foolishly open and the colour drained from his face. He gulped, opened his mouth as if to speak then closed it again.

"This is King Arkus," Darnuir said. He wondered if she knew about her parentage. "Arkus, I'd like you to meet—"

"Cassandra, yes?" Arkus said eagerly. "Of course, you look so much like... I — well I would have hoped to meet under better circumstances." He stepped gingerly towards her, all his regal bearing vanishing. Arkus opened his arms, offering a hug. Cassandra reacted by taking a quick step back, nearly knocking into Lira. Arkus' face fell.

Cassandra steadied herself but crossed her arms. "It's been twenty years. Sorry if I don't rush to embrace you. I need... time."

"Yes – yes, I understand," Arkus said. He let his arms drop to his side. "I have arranged a private tent for you, and a hot bath and food can be arranged at once. Would that be agreeable, for now?"

"That would be welcome," Cassandra said. She didn't give Darnuir a backwards glance as she left with the Chevaliers. He watched her go, his heart slowing even further, until he thought it might stop altogether.

The next morning, Darnuir sat at Brackendon's bedside. Tucked under layers of warm blankets, the wizard looked like an oversized and swaddled baby.

"Is there anything that can be done?" Darnuir asked.

"No," Kymethra sniffed, stroking a finger through what remained of Brackendon's white hair.

"Mmbghm," Brackendon mumbled. Kymethra sniffed again and wiped away another tear. Darnuir had never seen someone cry for so long.

"He recovered once," Darnuir said, trying to be hopeful.

"And that took so long," said Kymethra. Neither of them spoke for a while. Darnuir took Brackendon's blackened hand in his own, knowing it would be a long time before he saw the wizard again.

"What happened at the Conclave?" Darnuir asked.

"Nothing that matters anymore. If you must know, we discovered that Castallan hadn't set out to destroy the Conclave. He had loyal supporters even then and wanted to help humanity fight Rectar through his magic. But the Inner Circle were worried what the dragons would make of humans enchanting themselves and things got ugly. Had the Inner Circle not reacted so rashly, perhaps things would have been — would have been, been…" she choked, hiccupped and took a second to recover. "But it's over now."

"Will you try to rebuild?"

"No," Kymethra said firmly. "Brackendon wanted it to end, whether he made it or not. Look what happens when one wizard gains too much power. You will destroy his staff as well. Promise me."

Darnuir looked to the gleaming silver staff by Brackendon's side. "Will it not help him recover?"

"No. When you break, your body is passed the point of flushing the poison out," Kymethra said. "Just burn it. I don't care."

"It's an important artefact of the fairies, Kymethra. I'm not sure if I can simply—"

"Burn the staff," came the reassuring voice of Fidelm. The General stood at the entrance flap of the tent, looking too tall to be there. His hair was chopped unevenly and there was a heavy bandage around one hand. It was hard to tell with transparent wings, but Darnuir thought Fidelm's might have suffered a cut at the edges.

"The Core of the Argent Tree is important to my people. Yet, for millennia, it lay untouched and unseen, kept where only the Queen may visit. No one will miss it and Kasselle will understand."

"Are you sure?" Darnuir said.

"I'd rather there was another way," said Fidelm. "But my people wish to create, while these staffs are capable of much destruction. This will not go beyond myself or Kasselle back in Val'tarra."

"And when a new queen one day reigns?" Darnuir asked.

"A worry for another time," Fidelm said. "But I didn't come here to talk about staffs. Kymethra, I'd like to give this to Brackendon." From beneath his tunic, Fidelm fished up a piece of silver bark, fashioned into the shape of an acorn and looped around his neck by an old piece of twine.

"I can't let you give your life broach," Kymethra said.

"What is it?" Darnuir asked.

"A simple thing," Fidelm said, moving to Brackendon's side and tying the bark around his neck. "A cutting from the first tree my mother saved as an arborist. All fairy children are given one by the closest relative who tends the trees. It is said to foster good health."

"But it was from your mother," Kymethra said.

"My mother is long dead," Fidelm said. "And it is only a piece of bark, though I was always a healthy child. Let's see if it has some power. If I ever desire it back, I'll know where to find it."

"That is very kind," Kymethra said.

"We'll give you space," Darnuir said. "Goodbye for now, Kymethra."

"Goodbye," she said, though she only had eyes for Brackendon.

Darnuir took Brackendon's staff and left with Fidelm. When they emerged from Brackendon's tent the daylight near blinded Darnuir. His head still felt like it was made of iron, and no matter how much water he drank, he could not rid himself of the bitterness. What had happened when Castallan had tried to take the Dragon's Blade terrified him. He could only remember flashes, but he remembered the feel of all that Cascade energy, as though his blood had turned to magic. And he remembered the noise that had come from his own throat: that deep, bone-chilling roar.

He rubbed his eyes to stave off the light, his tiredness and his grief.

"He didn't deserve this," Lira said. A green and purple bruise coloured her left temple.

"We all mourn his loss, Lord Darnuir," Raymond said and the handful of other Praetorians with them nodded in a silent vigil.

"This was his fight to win," Darnuir said. "He gave everything. Now the fight is ours. All of ours." He raised Brackendon's staff – taking in its dazzling, diamond-like quality one last time – and then tossed it to the ground.

"I assume your Guard can be trusted not to tell the world what we're about to do?" Fidelm asked.

"I trust each one like I once did my hunter brothers and sisters," Darnuir said, and Fidelm nodded, content. "Is there anything you would like to say, Fidelm?"

"There is little to say, but each fairy is born into a role, and we serve our purpose. This piece of our people was crafted for a role and has served its purpose. It is a fitting end."

Darnuir smiled. "That was, quite perfect." Then he drew the Dragon's Blade and set the staff on fire. It resisted the flames from his sword for a while, far longer than wood ever should. But soon enough, it crackled, smoked and hissed, and turned to ash under the intense blaze from the Dragon's Blade. There was perhaps half a minute of silence, as if in respect, then Darnuir sheathed his weapon.

"Fidelm, this seems as opportune a moment as ever to ask if you or some of your fairies might join my Praetorian Guard."

"My role deters me from such a thing," said Fidelm, suddenly cool. Something about the fairy's bluntness stung at Darnuir.

"You could join ceremonially?" But Fidelm turned away, pretending to be fixated by something near the Bastion's gates. "Praetorians, give us some space," Darnuir said and Lira and the others moved away out of earshot. "Is something wrong, General?"

"The Praetorian Guard is for dragons," said Fidelm.

"I'm changing that. Raymond has already joined."

"You never seemed warm to me before," said Fidelm.

"I admit, your attitude towards Ochnic and my Highland expedition annoyed me but—"

"My attitude has not changed. I don't believe you made the right decision."

"Kasselle herself agreed to help the kazzek," said Darnuir.

"My Queen has not always made the wisest choices," Fidelm said. He furrowed his brow in some discomfort. "That was improper of me. My Queen is my people."

"Fidelm, I don't see why we can't come to a—"

"How am I to perform my duties and also serve you?"

"I don't need you to serve me," Darnuir said.

"Fairies don't need to be further involved than we already are," said Fidelm. "I couldn't dream of my warriors performing any better than your own. Let dragons guard dragons and let us move on."

"It seems you have resolved to deny me," Darnuir said. He didn't even have the strength to feel angry. "We need to find Blaine and Arkus to discuss our next move."

"Blaine will be in his personal tent," Fidelm said. "I believe he was attending to Chelos."

"Come along then, General," Darnuir said.

They gathered up the Praetorians and marched through the camps, passed wagons overflowing with weapons and armour without owners. It would take days to fully strip and bury the dead, but Darnuir intended to set sail with Somerled Imar long before that; today if possible. There was still a war to win: the demon invasion had to be repelled and Rectar would need to fall before the end. Like their victory after Cold Point, today was a sombre day. Yet there was a cheering coming from somewhere deep within the human camps, although for what Darnuir did not know.

As Darnuir suspected, there was a crowd gathering at Blaine's tent. A score of Light Bearers stood with shields raised against even more Chevaliers. They seemed too preoccupied in their glaring to notice much else. Lira and the Praetorians waited dutifully at the entrance flap as he and Fidelm pushed inside.

"For the last time," said a haggard looking Blaine, "I will not allow you to question him, Arkus. Chelos has been through enough." They did not notice that Darnuir had arrived. Cassandra was also there, by Chelos' side.

She still won't look at me. At least that answers what that kiss was – a damned mistake.

"If there are any other secrets that would impact on the security of my people, I'd know of them," Arkus said. "Perhaps the Guardians dug secret tunnels under the streets of Brevia as well?"

"It was a decision made almost seven hundred years ago," Blaine said. "And you cannot deny that we needed it. Your black powder failed to do its job. Without the passage, we would never have taken the walls."

"And I, Lord Guardian, am informed that without the valiant efforts of the hunter Balack, the gates would never have been taken. I hear you were… less than efficient in the battle." Blaine had no response and Arkus smiled a dangerous little smile, looking very pleased with himself. It was then that he noticed Darnuir. "Ah, there you are. And Fidelm, also. I hope your injuries are not too severe?"

"Not so serious," said Fidelm. "I will not be able to fly for a time, but I'll recover."

No concern to show for me, Arkus?

"Good," Arkus said, briskly. "And, how is Brackendon?"

"Kymethra says there is nothing that can be done," Darnuir said.

"A great pity," Arkus said. "But perhaps ultimately for the best. Wizards have caused us nothing but hardship."

"For the best?" Darnuir said, incredulously. "It's a fate worse than death."

"I sympathise," said Arkus. "And it is no deserving end for another human hero of the Battle of the Bastion. He will not be forgotten and he will receive the best care in Brevia."

"Thank you," Darnuir said. "And, Arkus, I must again profess my sincere apolo—"

"Spare me it, I beg you."

"I do not wish to part like this," Darnuir said. "The revelations yesterday were also trying for me. If there is anything I—"

"No, there is nothing," Arkus said. "You intend to leave at once then?"

"As soon as we can gather the men and supplies," Darnuir said. "Blaine and I will sail with Lord Imar. We'll lift this siege at Dalridia." He looked to Blaine then, and was pleased to see the Guardian nodding in agreement.

"Good," said Arkus. "The supplies you shall have. As for troops, you may take as many as there is space for, although I will reserve five thousand soldiers to keep peace in the Dales. The rest will return to Brevia to be sent on with the remainder of my fleet. I feel it is past time that dragons returned to the east."

"That is generous of you," Darnuir said.

"Well, there is nothing more to say," Arkus said. "I shall take my leave. I have a kingdom to attempt to piece back together. Cassandra," he added far more gently, "you may stay with Chelos for as long as you like. I'll leave a squad of Chevaliers to escort you back."

"Thank you," Cassandra said, not looking at her father.

"Hmmm," Arkus grunted, and with that, the King of Humans left them.

When he was certain that Arkus had marched well away, Darnuir said, "I'd feel more comfortable if we had someone we trusted in Brevia to ensure Arkus follows through with sending more troops and supplies on." He looked to Cassandra as he said this, hoping she'd pick up the hint. Hoping she'd look at him at all.

"I will go," Fidelm said. "There aren't enough ships to take my fairies with you."

Yes, Fidelm, don't risk getting 'further' involved.

"There's barely enough space for the dragons," said Blaine. "I feel we bore the worst of the battle here, let the humans take back their own islands."

"I would agree," Darnuir said. "Though as you saw, we have little pull with Arkus right now. He wants us gone, and I'm loathe to leave any dragons behind when the entire Southern Dales recently declared open hatred for our kind."

"Without Castallan's enchantment, the humans won't dare attack a legion," Blaine said.

"Have you ever considered it is talk like that which infuriates so many?" Cassandra said, though she still looked at none of them. "They wouldn't dare," she said, imitating Blaine. "Keep belittling humans and it's no wonder many push back."

"I'd be more grateful, girl," Blaine said. "It was our strength that rescued you."

"I'm a Princess now, Guardian," Cassandra said venomously. "That makes me important as well. And dragons did not 'save' me. Darnuir may well have burned away like Castallan if I hadn't been there to give Brackendon his staff back. What did you do Blaine?" Blaine sniffed like a bull and Darnuir was prepared for a full row to ensue when Chelos suddenly coughed and sputtered back to consciousness. Blaine bent carefully over his charge, taking Chelos firmly by the hand.

Cassandra took the other. "It is okay, Chelos. You are safe now."

"Cassandra?" Chelos croaked. "Cassandra?"

"He ought to be with the healers," Darnuir said.

"And have Arkus interrogate him?" Blaine said. "No. He'll be coming with us. Back home."

Cassandra looked livid. "You want to take a sick old dragon across the seas with you? What if it kills him?"

"Water," Chelos gasped. Blaine moved to pour a cup and handed it to the wrinkled dragon.

"If we could just, have a moment?" Blaine asked fiercely. "Just myself and Chelos."

"But—" Cassandra began.

"Please," Blaine implored.

"Fine," Cassandra said, getting up in clear umbrage. "I'm happy you're safe," she said to Chelos.

"You too… my dear," Chelos croaked.

"I'll walk with you back to your father, Cassandra," Fidelm said. "I must inform him of my plans."

"Very well," Cassandra said, moving swiftly for the exit without a backwards glance at Blaine or Darnuir. His stomach tightened. She was about to leave and he was about to head east to more war.

Do something you bloody coward.

"I'll expect you on board Lord Imar's ship in time," Darnuir told Blaine hurriedly before darting out of the tent after Cassandra and Fidelm. He half lunged to take her arm, but at the last moment he thought better of it, nearly lost his balance, and only stayed on his feet by drawing on some Cascade energy to snap his muscles into action. Fresh, jagged pain rushed down his arm.

"Cassandra, may I have a word?" She turned and finally looked at him, though it was with deadened eyes. She seemed to consider it for a moment but came closer.

"I'll give you some space," said Fidelm, moving off. To the side, Lira also took the hint and stayed back, throwing out an arm to stop a Chevalier coming any closer.

Cassandra tightly folded her arms. "What?"

What do I say?

"I've been thinking things through," he said. "Thinking about everything that happened. Before Blaine helped to unlock my memories, before I understood what was happening to me, I think being near you helped calm me, because the old me – the memories that is – maybe thought things were right, you know, because you were the last living thing he had proper contact with and I think that… that."

He paused, trying to gauge her reaction. She merely blinked. "Well, I think that it made me think and act in ways I had no good reason too. I'm trying to say sorry. I'm truly sorry." He tentatively extended his arm. Cassandra took some time, looking at his hand as though it were something foul. Then she bit her lip and took it in a very light shake.

"We're fine," she said, even smiling half-heartedly for the first time. Darnuir's heart returned to a more regular rhythm. "Do one thing for me, please. Look after Chelos."

"Of course," Darnuir said. "I hope you find happiness in Brevia."

"We'll see," she said. "I don't know if I want to be Arkus' daughter. I don't know what I want now."

"You'll figure that out," Darnuir said.

"Have you seen Balack yet?"

"I haven't had the chance," said Darnuir, though that was not entirely true. Just then, another resounding set of cheers came from the human section of the camps. "And I have a feeling he is busy right now."

"Well," Cassandra began, withdrawing her hand. "Goodbye for now, Darnuir."

"Goodbye, Cass."

Later that day, aboard the *Grey Fury*, Somerled Imar's great longship, Darnuir watched the Bastion grow smaller as they cut through the ocean. It wasn't just the Southern Dales he was leaving, he was also leaving the west – the human world he had grown up in. The Boreac Mountains had been his home, but they were now abandoned ruins.

Will I ever return? Will I ever set foot in the cold snow again?

One half of him hoped he would, the other knew the hard truth: he wasn't going back.

The *Grey Fury* sailed at the head of their fleet. Around one hundred and fifty feet long, with three rowers abreast up each side, it was big enough to offer covered shelter at the aft. A square sail of woven wool, fastened with leather straps to keep its shape, stretched overhead and a wooden warrior, wielding a heavy round shield and axe, dominated the bow. Lord Imar was still busy seeing to his men and reacquainting himself with news from his lands, leaving Darnuir alone for the first time in recent memory. Blaine interrupted that by appearing at his side.

"I am concerned about Arkus," Darnuir said.

"Do not worry about the rage of one human King," Blaine said. "Humans pass in generations within our lifetime. You may still be the King of our people when Arkus' great grandson inherits the throne in Brevia."

"We may not survive for that long if we cannot work together," Darnuir said.

"He'll work with us," said Blaine. "He just granted us the use of his forces. Defeating the demons works in his favour as well."

"I'm thinking long term," Darnuir said. "After the war, should we win, our people will need ships to ferry them home; we'll need shipments of food until we can begin to regrow our own crops. And I'd rather we were not barred from visiting Brevia."

"That was a throwaway threat."

Darnuir silently hoped that was true. He spent a few seconds picking at a loose chip of wood with a nail before asking Blaine, "What happened to you during the battle?"

"I could not call upon the Cascade."

"Nor could I, but I still fought on."

"Are you suggesting I am no longer capab—"

"I'm suggesting nothing of the sort," Darnuir said.

"Very well," Blaine said. Darnuir didn't fail to notice the slight shake of Blaine's hand. Something about the battle had unnerved him, whether he would admit it or not.

"No more secrets Blaine," Darnuir sighed. "Do you remember agreeing to that, after the Charred Vale? It wasn't so long ago. No more secrets…"

"I remember," said Blaine. He leant over the side of the boat and the chain with the little silver 'A' dangled from his neck.

"What else does Chelos know? Why were you so insistent he come with us?"

"He can help explain me everything to you when he's better."

"If the poor dragon regains his strength," Darnuir said. Chelos looked feeble underneath all the furs. Exposed to the elements it would only make his recovery more uncertain. "I promised Cassandra I'd take care of him."

"He'll recover," Blaine said.

"He'd better."

Chapter 16

DA GREAT GLEN

Garon – West of the Great Glen

GARON WARMED HIS hands upon the campfire. He rubbed them hard, bringing them up to cover his mouth and nose, and breathed out, trying to warm his nose. The lack of food was starting to make him feel numb and his empty stomach gave him a constant sense of sickening nausea. The only one of his company who did not show weakness to the cold was Ochnic, though the kazzek looked no less despondent as he gazed up at the Principal Mountain looming over them. It dwarfed every other hill and crag, a massive blue and grey barrier against the early evening light. Garon wondered if Ochnic was more worried about reaching his people than relieved.

"It's tae the benefit of our stomachs we'll reach our destination soon," Griswald said as he peered miserably into his ration bag. "Basically all out." He demonstrated by shaking the bag upside down and only a solitary portion of salted beef fell out. "What I wouldn't do tae get ma hands on just one small roast partridge." Griswald hunched over a little more. Garon was pleased to have him there all the same. Being around company was a good sign that Griswald was coming around after Rufus' death. Garon just hoped that Griswald's old spirit would return soon as well.

"Oh no, more meat, I beg you," said Pel. She was staring in equal amounts of despair and disgust at her own preserved beef. Perhaps unhelpfully, Ochnic chose that moment to devour his own portion with great enthusiasm. Pel grimaced.

"Is there anything else Pel might eat, Ochnic?" Garon asked. "Maybe some unheard of flower of great nutritional quality?"

Ochnic cocked one of his shaggy white eyebrows. "No. Not unless you want to eat da heather." He reached for a bush, ripped off a purple tip and began to chew. He spat it out shortly after. Pel's wings drooped and she hung her head, looking very much a young girl.

"It won't kill you," said Marus. "I know fine well that flyers and warriors are given more meat in their diet."

"Not this much and it's usually sweeter," said Pel. "I feel unclean, and can smell the stink of it on me. Well, I'm used to the jeers about that." She looked defiantly at each of them, as though hoping to shut down any judgemental set of eyes. Yet, after a scan of the group, her expression softened. "You don't care do you?"

"D'you think he cares, lass?" Griswald said, waving his shovel of a hand towards Ochnic, who had his head deep in the ration bag.

"Human sense of smell isn't that keen," Garon said. "Marus?"

The legate shrugged. "Won't catch a dragon turning down some meat."

"Oh," Pel said.

"Probably a good thing you've gotten out of that forest then," said Garon. "Learn how the rest of the world works and such. I never appreciated how much your kind is averse to a good roast chicken. Would you really be treated differently?"

"I *was* treated differently," said Pel. She shivered and edged a little closer to the fire. "It was hard enough trying to speak to the other women in my family without them holding their noses around me. They were all chosen to be healers, or painters or arborists. Some even served in the Argent Tree. But I was rare and born with wings, so I got handed a spear. No choice about it."

"You would rather be doing a woman's work?" Marus asked.

"I'd rather have friends," Pel said. "I'd rather have my mother understand me and treat me like one of my sisters than like a warrior son."

"But you can fight," Marus said as though that settled the matter.

"Can't do much else, though," said Pel. "We're not taught other useful things of life. 'That's someone else's job' we get told; it's all we ever get told. And sometimes — sometimes I wish I didn't have wings."

"Oh, Pel," Garon said. "Don't say that. They're a gift." But Pel – Wing Commander Pel – had begun to tear up. She tried to hide it, but she couldn't completely cover up her quick breathing, nor the little sniffs. "I know the food isn't what you want, but you should try to eat it. You'll feel a little better." If this were a young huntress or hunter on patrol he would have the group console them and make fresh needle brew. Exertion and hunger were usually to blame for breakdowns. Right now, however, he wasn't sure what else to do. Hugging one of his commanding officers seemed entirely inappropriate. As Pel tried to collect herself, Ochnic emerged crestfallen from the empty ration sack.

"I can teach you some ways," Ochnic said. Everyone looked to him, then to Pel, then back to the troll.

"I'm sorry?" she said.

"Teach you," Ochnic said slowly as though they were all dim-witted. "Ways you don't know. Ways of da plants, da herbs, da wild. Some you can eat and some you use to heal. All kazzek are taught these things."

"You would?" Pel said. "Why?"

Ochnic let out a truly spectacular sigh. "If you are not wanting my help—"

"No, I do," Pel said. "I'm just… surprised. Thank you, Ochnic." The troll growled his approval and thumbed one of his tusks.

Garon beamed. "Well, that's settled then. Now Pel, will you please eat your— Ochnic?" he said, alarmed as the troll leapt to his hairy feet. "There's no need to start your lessons immediately." But Ochnic wasn't paying him any attention. He was sniffing deeply.

"What's wrong?" Garon asked crisply. He, Griswald and Pel rose as well, while Marus clambered awkwardly up, still favouring one leg.

"Silver Furs," Ochnic hissed.

"What are they?" Marus asked. "Some dangerous animal of the Highlands?"

"Dey are the elite who serve da chieftains," Ochnic said. "Stay here," he added, then dashed off into the heather, prone to the ground like a stalking cat.

"It'll be alright," Griswald said. "They wanted us tae come up here didn't they?"

"Ochnic seems worried," Marus said. He shoved his helmet back on and gripped the hilt of his sword. "His kind have left us out here to half starve already. Better to be safe."

Garon peered in the direction Ochnic had departed, but saw no signs of movement. He was considering how hunters could learn an awful lot in the arts of stealth from the kazzek when Pel let out a cry of shock from behind him.

"Back off," Pel said, waving her spear towards two trolls that had appeared near her. Both had silver fur, which was thicker than Ochnic's. Their skin was also grey, but it seemed more vibrant than Ochnic's drabber complexion. Their eyes had a slight glint to them, and even their tusks looked shinier, like marble.

Ochnic emerged from the heather a moment later. "Back off, Silvers," he told the two trolls who had scared Pel.

"Only playin'," said the leftmost of the pair. Ochnic growled lowly again and another five silver-haired trolls emerged from the heather, springing upright to their full heights. The biggest of the lot had foot-long tusks with iron bands around the middle of the bones. Tartan cloth covered his upper body, which was a mixture of light reds and greens across blocks of white. The rest of the Silver Furs bowed their heads and grasped their tusks before him.

"Dis is da Chief-of-Chiefs," Ochnic said, also bowing his head and taking his tusks in hand. Garon gulped as he looked up at the towering chieftain.

"You look like you might be in charge," Garon said.

"Rohka, I am." The chieftain lightly took hold of his tusks and lowered his head to Garon.

"Well, it's nice to meet you," Garon said. He thought it prudent to bow his own head. "Forgive our dishevelled states. We weren't expecting visitors."

"Got any food there?" Griswald asked.

"Food?" said Rohka. "We struggle ta feed our own."

"So then why are we here?" barked Marus. He clambered upright upon his crutch and looked distinctly unthreatening to the large kazzek.

"It was not I who convinced da chieftains to send for Lowlanders," said Rohka. He glanced to Ochnic.

"Ochnic promised us we would be provided for," Garon said. "In return for lending aid to your people. We're hungry out here."

"Some of us are starving," Pel muttered darkly.

"You are da pack leader?" said Rohka, looking to Garon.

"I am," Garon said.

"Da chieftains wish to see you," Rohka said. "Come with me."

"Am I to journey alone or can my companions accompany me?"

The Chief-of-Chiefs and his Silver Furs put their heads together and spoke hurriedly in a language Garon didn't understand. Their native tongue sounded hard on the ear, their low voices flaring in hard rhythmic inflections like a beating drum.

"Da dragon and human may," said Rohka. "Not da fairy."

"Excuse me?" Pel asked.

"Not safe," Rohka said.

"Not safe for who? For me?" said Pel. "I will not be left behind."

"I insist," said Garon. "These fairies have travelled far to help your kind, Rohka."

"She should come, Rohka, Chief-of-Chiefs," Ochnic said.

As tall as Ochnic was, Rohka looked down on him. "You've brought many warriors Ochnic, Shadow Hunter. But dis is not a matter for you to decide."

"I won't come if Pel can't," Garon said.

Rohka took several tense seconds to think. His lips bulged as he ran his tongue around his teeth. Then he flashed his fangs. "Da fairy can come. Leave your weapons here."

"Very well," Garon said. He unstrapped his belt and set his sword on top of the rest of his gear. "Griswald, you're in charge while we're gone."

The Silver Furs set off immediately. Garon chewed the last bite of his beef, gulped nervously and followed. They skirted the edge of the expedition's camp through the heather, drawing rather close to the fairy tents. As they passed, many fairies stopped what they were doing and stared out at the group of trolls and to Pel in the middle of them, their faces stricken with worry, as though she were marching to her own execution.

"I'll catch up," Pel said, before taking off and flying over to speak with them. They really were a young bunch, probably the greenest fighters that Fidelm could have sent. Garon considered it a cowardly move. Cowardly and selfish. Fidelm had sat on that council, heard his own Queen approve the expedition, and he and Blaine had still tried to sabotage it. The more Garon thought about it, the angrier he got. It wasn't just the trolls they might be sacrificing, but Garon, everyone who had come with him, and the whole of the west. Did their pride and scorn run so deep that they'd rather punish their own people, their own young – in Fidelm's case – to get their own misguided way? And it was definitely misguided, Garon had concluded. Ochnic, on the other hand, had been the pinnacle of a diplomat, even a friend.

I hope you can deal with them Darnuir. He tapped the scroll by way of solidarity. *Maybe having Cosmo by your side will help.*

Pel rejoined the company as they approached the base of the Principal Mountain. Garon began to wonder where they were being led. There was no obvious route to the Great Glen on the other side. It became especially puzzling when they arrived before a flat face of rock with weeds and moss that struggled for life between every small crack.

"Dis is not da way," Ochnic said.

"Oh der is ways into da Great Glen that few know," Rohka said.

"Special ways through da High Rock," said one of the Silver Furs.

"Da chieftains did not tell me of this," said Ochnic.

"We tell dem who need ta know," Rohka said. "You succeeded in your mission, you may know. Southerners have never been allowed in da glen before. Da chieftains show you a great kindness. Don't go ruining dat."

"We promise," Garon said on behalf of the group.

"Good," said Rohka. "Open da door."

"Door?" Marus said. "What door." But the trolls had already set about their work. Rohka himself went to pick up an inconspicuous rock, slightly squared at the bottom. It required three of the trolls to lift it. They shimmied themselves up onto a grassy mound and carefully positioned the rock against an indistinct dent in the mountainside. The other kazzek grabbed smaller, longer stones, like oversized sausages from around the area with well-practised efficiency. And in a final cat-like display of agility, the remainder of the Silver Furs bounded onto their colleagues' shoulders, or clung to small crevices in the rock, holding up their own pieces up to make a giant stone hand.

The mountain groaned in approval and the rock face shimmered as though in a heatwave, intensifying and pulsating until miraculously, even impossibly, an archway appeared; tall enough to fit five Griswalds and wide enough to practice archery in.

They entered the archway, stepping from the fading pink-orange evening into the darkened tunnel. Silver Furs collected some pre-oiled torches and flicked flint against steel to ignite them. An instant later, the light from the outside world vanished. When Garon turned he saw the archway that had silently reformed into smooth rock.

"Onwards," Rohka commanded. They proceeded downwards at first, delving deeper under the mountain. Their steps echoes loudly and the faint light from their torches was not enough to illuminate the cavernous space. They kept close to one wall as they moved, the other well out of sight. Garon placed a hand against the freezing stone to help balance himself as the incline down became steeper.

"It's rather hard to see," Garon said. "Couldn't we have lit a few more torches?"

"We won't need dem."

"Human eyes aren't so good, y'know," said Garon. But before the troll could say anything further Garon saw light ahead – a dim blue glow, coming from the walls themselves. When he was closer, Garon saw that the stony grains were so fine he could see through them, like a thin shade over a window. A free-flowing blue ooze swam behind the fine rock, lighting the underground world. Each vein through the rock was dim but combined it was enough to see by and threw relief onto the carved runes upon the walls and floors.

"Raw Cascade energy," Pel said quietly. Garon looked back to her. She was drifting trance-like towards the walls and her sudden change of course nearly caused Marus to crash into her.

"Careful, Wing Commander," said the legate.

"Yesssssss," Pel said dreamily.

"Keep an eye on da fairy," Rohka snarled.

"What?" Pel snapped. "I'm fine."

Other passages peeled off bending out of sight or leading to giant staircases where each step would require a ladder to reach the top. The air was cool, if stale, and Marus' crutch echoed sharply with each step.

Ochnic seemed the most in awe. "So it is true. Der are tunnels of da golems under our feet."

"I fear my imagination won't be wrong in picturing them," Garon said.

"Living rock," said Ochnic.

"Naturally," said Garon.

"Living rock?" Marus repeated in disbelief.

"You do not have dem in da south?" Ochnic asked.

"Never heard of them," said Garon. "And I used to live in a mountain range similar to this one. There are two Principal Mountains in the Boreacs, but I've never come across such creatures."

"Dey need a lot of da blue poison," said Rohka. "Even here it is not enough for dem anymore. Dey 'av been dying out for many years and—"

"Pel, no," Marus called. She had wandered closer to the wall again.

"Just one touch," Pel said. Her violet eyes were wide and bloodshot. Some of the Silver Furs tried to shove their way towards her but they were too late. She placed her hand upon one of the thin veils of stone. She screamed wildly, sounding both in pain and ecstasy, and Garon reached for his sword to find only air.

No weapons. Just as well.

Ochnic was the first to reach Pel. His grey hand clamped onto her shoulder but she shrugged him off effortlessly. She tore her hand away from the wall to swat away the other kazzek as they tried to subdue her. Her eyes were completely red now, as though filled with blood from lid to lid.

"Pel, stop this," Garon yelled, but she either could not hear him or ignored him. Marus stood there helpless, his great strength neutralised by his bad leg. A Silver Fur managed to grab her hands behind her back but she bent and flipped him over.

There was nothing Garon could do. He was too weak – just a human.

With a cry, he lunged forwards anyway, throwing his weight behind his shoulder and into her legs. He locked his arms around her knees and pulled. She wobbled for a moment and he held on; he held until he felt a blow to his head and his vision spun in a daze. The next thing he knew, Garon was being tossed through the air, landing softly at Marus' feet, but the impact not as hard as he had feared.

"Da power is draining from her," called Rohka. "Let her settle."

Pel took several more clumsy swipes as the trolls who inched towards her, but her eyes soon began to return to normal. Ochnic brought her down, pinning her flat against the floor with a hand on the back of her neck.

"Calm, Pel," Ochnic said as soothingly as he could. "Calm. Calm…" He kept his eyes locked with hers and after a few moments of struggle, she finally returned to normal. Tears filled her eyes immediately.

"I'm sorry," she sobbed. "I don't know — I don't know…"

"No harm was done," Ochnic said. "Put dat away," he added to an approaching Silver Fur. "She is not enraged or crazed." The offending kazzek snarled but sheathed his long dagger.

"Let's get you to your feet," Garon said. With Ochnic's help, he got Pel upright and gave her a steadying arm.

"We should hurry," said Rohka. "No more *accidents*." They hurried along after that. With Garon on her left, Ochnic on her right, and the kazzek around them, Pel was at the centre of a wall of bodies ensuring that she could not drift. Yet she did not seem interested as she had before and kept her head low as they passed through the golems' tunnel. As they progressed upwards the blue light of the raw cascade faded from the walls and only the torches guided them.

Finally, they reached the end.

The kazzek placed another set of stones against an indent in the wall in the shape of a large hand and an archway to the outside world appeared. The stars were so bright and numerous above the Highlands, Garon could see well enough. Leaves crunched underfoot as he staggered outside and there was a chill in the air.

"Are you okay, Pel?" Garon asked.

"I'm just so hungry," she said weakly. Garon's own stomach rumbled. No matter what came of this meeting he would have to secure food, first and foremost.

"You might have warned us," Marus said accusingly to Rohka.

"I tried," said Rohka. "Now you know why you might listen to me in de future. Come. Da chieftains await."

The Silver Furs kept them moving at a brisk pace, pushing through the wild growth towards a small ridge directly ahead. As they cleared the top of it the Great Glen stretched out in its enormity before them. It might have been the starlight but nearly all of the heather here looked silver; those patches, at least, that were visible amongst the kazzek packed into the valley. Even at this distance, a whiff of smoke reached Garon from countless campfires outside the tightly packed, dry stone walled homes with high thatched roofs. The Great Glen looked to be more of a permanent settlement, with enough buildings to make a city.

"Like smoking dunghills," Marus said quietly in disgust.

"Marus," Garon warned.

"No wonder we've been left in the cold when dealing with savages," the legate muttered. "I swear we—"

"Stop it," Garon said. "This is just coming from hunger. Don't let your temper unravel weeks of good relations with Ochnic."

"I'll try," Marus said.

"You'll try your hardest," said Garon.

The Silver Furs led them towards the heart of the valley. Kazzek began curiously following them and a muttering grew in tandem with the crowd. Horned cows with shaggy red hair chewed grass methodically and slowly turned their heads to follow Garon as he walked past. He even caught sight of a kazzek child, wrapped in red-green tartan cloth, trying to keep up with the procession – a young girl, judging by the length of her hair. She squealed at the sight of Pel and ran off crying. Pel looked too drained to care. The blue of her skin was dangerously pale.

"How much longer?" Garon asked.

"De First Stones stand in de centre of da glen," Ochnic said. "Not much farther, pack leader."

The First Stones turned out to be an enormous triple-ringed circle of standing stones, erected on the flattest piece of land in the valley. Garon craned his neck to see the top of the stones as they drew closer. The outer ring was the tallest and descended in size towards the middle. Where each of the giant outer rocks stood, there was a large house to accompany it, ten in total. These had the luxury of a second story.

"Homes of da chieftains when in da Great Glen," Ochnic explained.

"Quite the auspicious position," Garon said.

"Da chieftains will have gathered in the stone ring," Rohka announced.

"That's good," Garon yawned. "Any chance they will bring something to eat with them?" Rohka flashed his fangs. "Look, if not for me, can you fetch something for Pel? She'll collapse if she doesn't put something in her stomach soon." The Chief-of-Chiefs eyed Pel, who was propped up only by Marus, who was propped up himself by his crutch.

"Da fairy touched da blue poison," Rohka said. "She attacked my kazzek."

Ochnic gave a grunt of impatience. "I shall find food."

"I wish you ta be present, Shadow Hunter."

"I won't be long," Ochnic said. He seemed flustered and eager to get away. "Can you eat fish?" he asked Pel. She didn't seem to understand and was unable to make proper eye contact with him.

"Fish is fine in small doses," Marus said. "Better hurry, Ochnic." And he did. Quick as a flash their kazzek guide was pushing his way back into the gathering crowd.

"Be gone now," Rohka shouted to the kazzek. "Away to your fires. Da chieftains shall converse with da Lowlanders. Der is no need to fear." The crowd seemed unwilling to move and it took the menacing Silver Furs to disperse them. Garon waved an encouraging hand to Marus and Pel, and together they gingerly followed Rohka into the middle of the standing stones. At the centre, eight older kazzek had arranged themselves around a circular stone table. *Eight here, plus Rohka is nine. Nine chiefs and ten houses. Someone is missing.* A noticeable gap had been left for Garon, Marus and Pel, and they moved into it.

No one spoke, not for an uncomfortably long time.

Exhausted and starving, Garon tried to keep his eyes open. He hated feeling so unprepared for this pivotal moment and yet, here he was; as unready as he'd been at seventeen, approaching nineteen-year-old Fiona from Ascent at the station one misguided evening in late autumn. This was an early autumn night, and he was now thirty-six, but he felt like the boy he'd once been. Out of his depth. And probably out of his mind. Still, he'd learned after Miss Fiona that confidence was the key and so he mustered as much phantom self-assurance as he could and said, "So is this it?"

"What is dis 'it'?" asked Rohka.

"This," Garon said, flapping his arms to illustrate the situation. "You request help to be sent into the Highlands, we're told the demons are knocking on your doorstep and then you allow us to walk next to blind through the difficult mountain terrain with no additional food or wildlife to live off. To cap it all, we reach your magnificent glen and you have absolutely nothing to say."

"We have a great deal to say," said Rohka. Garon was about to reply but the chieftain cut him off. "When kazzek receive guests we always wait for dem to make the first greetings. Your greeting was a strange one."

"Ah," Garon said, feeling foolish. "I suppose it was. Hello, then, great chieftains of the kazzek."

"Hello," the chieftains chanted in unison.

"Allow me to introduce Legate Marus, leader of the dragons on our expedition," Garon said. Marus winced and clutched at his leg. "And Wing Commander Pel, the lead flyer of our fairy forces." On cue, Pel swayed into Marus' shoulder.

"You brought da fairy through da mountain?" one of the chiefs asked in shock. Her colleagues grumbled around the table, audibly grinding their teeth.

"Dey insisted she come," Rohka said.

"I insisted," Garon said. "We three will not be divided on this mission. The Three Races have agreed to help in your fight against the demons, and we will do so together. My orders," he proclaimed and produced Darnuir's scroll, placing it upon the stone table. "From the King of Dragons."

"Lowlanders cannot enter da Great Glen, Rohka," said a chief. This one had tusks that curled upwards and wore a tartan of yellow and black. Garon whipped his head from side to side and peered exaggeratedly down at his own body, then to Marus and Pel.

"There seems to be some upset then," Garon said. "For we are 'Lowlanders', as you call us, and we are here."

"Exceptions had to be made," Rohka said slowly.

"Clearly, it is possible for us to enter the glen," Garon said. "What you mean is that you do not allow it, by which you mean you do not wish it."

"Pack leader," Rohka said loudly. He was suddenly stern and drew up to his full and towering height. "Da Great Glen is a refuge in times of crisis. Da kazzek are scared when dey come here. We did not wish to frighten dem further. And our food stores are not as full as you think."

"Then how were you planning to feed us?" Garon asked. All the chieftains exchanged nervous glances.

"We did not expect you to come," Rohka said. "We did not believe Ochnic would succeed."

Garon sighed. "There has been a lot of ill-will towards this mission. But if you would struggle to feed an extra five thousand mouths, then you must be in dire straits indeed."

"We might have made it through da winter," said Rohka. "But now you Lowlanders have arrived…"

Garon's heart sank. "So what are we to do?"

Before Rohka could answer a familiar voice cried, "Where are dey?" And Ochnic came bounding up to the stone table with a steaming bowl in his hands. "Where are dey? My clan." His voice shook as did his hands and a portion of the bowl's contents spilt onto the earth. Marus reached to take the bowl and Ochnic relinquished it without protest.

"Trapped in da east, Shadow Hunter," said Rohka. "Cut off by demons."

"Dey were coming," Ochnic said. "Dey were to leave just after I…"

"Demons came from da Black Rock glens faster than expected," said Rohka. "Too many for us to fight dis time. Even da golems are trapped with your people in da Glen of Bhrath."

"You abandoned them?" Marus asked.

"We left great food stores in da east behind as well," said Rohka. "We had no choice. Until now."

Ochnic turned to Garon and took his arm frantically, squeezing far too hard. "Pack leader. Please. Go we must."

"Ah," Garon grunted in pain. "Loosen that grip there, Ochnic. Of course we'll go. As Marus said, that's why we're here, regardless whether anyone in the world cared if we'd succeed; that's why we're here."

"Thhh-ank you," Ochnic said weakly.

"I'll help save your daughter, Ochnic," Pel said. "Even if I have to fly her away myself, I swear." Everyone turned to her, the chieftains in shock and Garon in concern. Spoon in hand, she'd clearly been wolfing down whatever Ochnic had brought her. It looked like a creamy soup with flakes of white fish, leeks, translucent onions and chunks of a golden vegetable that Garon did not recognise. Vigour had already returned to Pel's skin.

"Thank you, too," Ochnic said gratefully.

"Da fairy would swear oaths to a kazzek?" asked the incredulous chieftain in pink and green.

"We've had it rough but we're learning to look past our differences, for the most part," Garon said. "Maybe you all should as well." He let that settle in the air for a time. "Now, chieftains, if you will kindly resupply our forces, we can move out immediately. With your own warriors and guides as help, we'll stand an even better chance." The ring of chieftains closed together to converse.

"Done," they all said together.

"We shall send one thousand warriors and our Silver Furs," said Rohka. "I will lead dem myself. But I must make clear, de food stores are de priority, for all of us. Without dat we shall starve through da snows."

"Chief-of-Chiefs, my clan dey —" Ochnic began.

"Might not be alive," said Rohka. "Dis is hard words, but could be true. If Chief Orrock and your clan survive, dey will surely be with da store. If not, or if der is a choice to be made, I cannot order our warriors to take any risks. Da food is critical."

"But—"

"Do not overstep your place, Shadow Hunter," Rohka said.

Garon felt like he should say something. He could almost feel Ochnic tense with rage beside him and gently placed a staying hand on the troll's rough hide. It was Marus who spoke first.

"A strong leader knows difficult choices have to be made. My dragons will be at your disposal, great Chief-of-Chiefs. My King would wish for trust to build between our peoples."

Garon glanced sideways at Marus. *So you'll follow who's strongest, is that it Marus?*

"We know what to do," Garon said, suppressing his own frustration. He hoped they could leave before anything worse was uttered. "Send along kazzek who know how to make that soup," he said more light-heartedly. "It smells delicious."

When they answered, the chieftains spoke again as one. "Done."

Chapter 17

WHISKY AND PAINT

The sacking of Brevia was swift and brutal. In 1738 AT, Godred Imar, King of the Splintering Isles, showed his might when he sailed his fleet of longships into the Bay of Brevia and seized the city. At that moment, Godred showed that Dalridia was the true powerhouse of humanity.

From Tiviar's Histories

Cassandra – Brevia – The Throne Room

"SHOW YOUR LOVE for the hero of the Bastion!"

The crowd in Arkus' throne room roared in approval.

Cassandra watched on surreptitiously from the back of the throne's podium, not wanting to stand front and centre with Arkus and his family.

They are my family too, I ought to remember. Arkus is my father; Thane is my half-brother. Orrana is… well she's nothing to me really.

Between his parents, Thane looked rather small. She could see him coughing regularly. Arkus patted his back, but his convulsions could not be heard over the announcer's orations.

"I give you Balack, Hero of the Bastion! A human who took the gates where dragon and fairy failed; a human of the ruined Boreac Mountains who took his revenge; a hunter of the finest quality."

Arkus got to his feet, clapping enthusiastically with the rest. He nudged Balack and the hunter raised an arm to wave at the throng of Brevia's elite. The King let the hall quieten before speaking.

"This is a time of celebration. The tyranny in the south has ended. Castallan has been defeated and his enchantment over the people of Dales is broken. Their minds are their own once more and we are joined again in a truly united kingdom."

Cassandra yawned deeply as another round of cheering ensued.

"The dragons paid a high price at the Bastion," Arkus went on. "But a price needed to be paid, for it was dragon lords who first pushed Castallan on his path of madness."

What are you doing, Arkus?

"I have sent the dragons east, back to their home, and I shall offer passage to any dragon still in our lands. Let them know they can find that passage from Brevia. It is time to remove the burden of their people from our shoulders." The crowd responded enthusiastically to that. "One final fight must still be won. The Splintering Isles will not fall. No demon will set foot in our lands again. The heroism of humans, of hunters like Balack here, will be what saves our people from destruction," and with that, Arkus took Balack's hand and raised it high in his own. "Humanity will stand up for itself. Humanity will not cower!"

Another round of cheering followed.

They'll shred their own throats doing that.

Before it was over, she turned to leave. She'd heard enough bravado for the day. There had not even been a mention of Brackendon, the real hero.

They'll never know, and so he'll never be remembered. The truth of it will die and this rhetoric put in its place.

She wondered then how much had been lost across time. How much of what she had read was true?

I will not forget.

Trumpets blew behind her as she left the throne room. She took the staircase leading directly back to the royal apartments, and had barely emerged onto that floor when four Chevaliers blocked her path. They no longer seemed to wear helmets, she had noticed. It made them less intimidating, but their eyes were always visible.

"Move," she said. They stood still. "Move, please."

Still nothing.

"Your father wishes a word with you, Princess," said Gellick lazily. He ran a hand through his mop of blonde hair. "We will take you to his council chambers."

"I know the way," Cassandra said. She had been mapping out the palace in her mind since arriving three days ago. After the Bastion, it was easy.

"Your father asks—"

"Fine," Cassandra said, hoping they would lead her there in silence.

She found it uncomfortable when people referred to Arkus as her father. It just didn't feel real yet. Nor did it feel completely true, as if she wasn't the baby girl who Darnuir had left behind in Aurisha. Nor did she feel settled within the palace or the city. She felt as if she might start running at any moment and never look back. Everything was too new. The boundaries of her new life had yet to be drawn and she was on the precipice between this new existence becoming either another prison or, possibly, very distantly, her home.

The trip to Arkus' council chambers had passed her by and the Chevaliers led her inside. "The King will be with you shortly," Gellick said as he closed the door.

In the bare room, the painting on the wall behind the desk stood out immediately to her. Cassandra blinked and rubbed at her eyes. For a second she thought she had seen herself in it. The woman in the painting had her hair and eyes; the only difference being the colour of their gowns – the woman's was pale green, Cassandra's white.

She looked happy, this woman in the painting.

"If only you could have met Ilana," Arkus said. Cassandra had not heard him enter but kept looking at her mother. As though in a trance, she stepped closer to the frame. From here, Cassandra saw Ilana's cheekbones were a little lower than her own; her eyebrows a touch thinner, and her hair parted differently. Ilana's was to the right and Cassandra's to the left. They might be small things, but they were there.

"I would have liked to meet her too," Cassandra said. "But alas…"

"Cassandra, I am so sorry. I've tried to expla—"

"I know. I know… I'm sorry." It had been a cheap dig at the man and spiteful. She'd heard the full story from Arkus on their journey back to Brevia. He hadn't had much choice. Even so, it still stung.

"This is hard for me too," Arkus said. He removed his crown and let his greying mane fall loosely behind his ears. Placing the crown on his desk, the King moved to sit behind it. "Making time for you is… difficult. I'd like nothing more than to get to know you, but I have a kingdom in tatters. The Cairlav Marshes are more desolate than ever; the Golden Crescent's population is scattered or returning to fields crushed by running dragons; I have thousands of soldiers tied up in the Dales and a war still to wage. To top it all," he added, sounding deathly tired, "Lord Boreac has disappeared."

"One hiding lord seems the least of your worries."

"Boreac's actions show he was clearly involved in the plots against me," Arkus said. "I can't have any ringleaders still at large. He must be brought to justice or I risk it all again."

"But you cannot find him?"

"We'll comb the city for him. He won't last long."

"What makes you think he's still in Brevia, this Lord Boreac?" Cassandra said. It seemed strange to her that, with everything else going on, this one man was on Arkus' mind.

"For one, his regional seat lies abandoned and decimated," said Arkus. "Additionally, it is likely he still has friends and sympathisers in the city. Castallan might be gone, but the networks he built must run deeper than I ever suspected. Then again, I rely so much on information from others who, as far as I know, were part of these plots. I find I am lacking in people I can trust."

"Is that why you are telling me this?"

"No, I have simply been side-tracked," said Arkus, regaining his authoritative air. "You are here on a different matter. One of marriage."

"I think you have more important things to worry about," said Cassandra.

"Were you not of noble birth it wouldn't matter. But you are. In fact, you're the eldest of my children. You could be heir if you wanted?" Cassandra let out a sound that might have been construed as a laugh, something between a snorting giggle and a choking gag of pain. Arkus' expression remained flat. "It's far from a laughing matter."

"I don't want to be queen."

"Your brother had much the same attitude. Fighting me at every turn." His face paled at that point and he cast his eyes on the floor. Cassandra hadn't considered that Cosmo was her brother; her much older brother to be sure, but family still. It seemed so wrong, so untrue; and he'd died trying to save her from Scythe's men. That memory suddenly took on a more painful meaning.

"He was a good man," she said.

"So, I'm told," said Arkus "But, to put your mind at ease, I don't intend you shall ever be queen. Although if both Thane and Cullen die, things would get complicated."

"So why *must* I marry then?"

"Politics. Thane will remain my heir. Not least because that is how the Kingdom has been carefully nurtured these last eight years and because he is promised to the daughter of Lord Esselmont of the Golden Crescent. Doubtless, that kept Esselmont loyal throughout the years."

"So, you're going to open up the bidding for me and gain another loyal house?"

"Do not look at me like I'm some monster. This is a time of war and the Assembly must be kept malleable. Your coming has upset the status quo and all will seek to gain from it. However, I do not intend to indulge any of my fine Lords."

"Then, it is all some ruse?" She was hopeful. Oh, so naively, so desperately, hopeful.

"I'm taking you out of their sights. I would have you marry Balack."

"Balack?" Cassandra said aghast. This she had not been expecting.

"He is the perfect candidate," Arkus explained. "You see, should I grant one lord or rich merchant the honour, then I would face unrest and rebellion. Not openly, of course, not so soon after the Bastion. Yet I would face resistance all the same, particularly from the rivals of whichever family I picked. Choosing one would require me to placate the other in some form and I'd rather avoid playing a continual game of gift giving; as though all my lords were children, each demanding a sweet treat."

"Surely Balack would offend them all, *father*." She struggled with the word, as though learning it for the first time.

"Perhaps some will feel snubbed," Arkus said. "However, they cannot complain too loudly. I have arranged for him to visit each district of the city. The people will be singing tales of his bravery before long. My lords might be discontent by the betrothal but they cannot openly object to someone so beloved by the people. And, as no one house will gain anything from it, it will cause no real damage within the Assembly. It's perfect."

"Except for me," Cassandra said. "And Balack," she added. "What does he think about this?"

"I haven't brought it up yet," Arkus said. "I thought you would prefer Balack over some stranger. He tells me that you grew close before you were recaptured."

"Balack is a good friend," Cassandra admitted. "That does not mean I want to marry him."

"How about Grigayne Imar," Arkus said. "Son of Lord Somerled. The two of you will be of an age – perhaps he's a little older. This is Somerled's idea of course. I think he feels it would help strengthen Grigayne's position to take the islands to full independence one day."

"Is nobody an option? I'm tired of having no control."

"Cassandra," Arkus said, becoming stern, "do you think any of us have full control of our lives? I am a King and yet I must do many things I'd rather avoid to maintain stability."

"But—"

"I am a King," Arkus continued, "and yet I must bow my head to a boy dragon. I am a King, and still I could not keep my son from leaving me; I could not bring you home from Aurisha with me; I could not heal your mother's broken heart nor keep her in this world with me," his voice cracked. "None of us are truly free, Cassandra."

"I have been a prisoner all my life. Am I to swap one jailer for another?"

"You wound me," Arkus said. "If you'd grown up here, you'd understand. But you didn't. So, it will be the hard way. It doesn't matter to me if you love him or hate him. It does not matter to me whether you spend all your days together or merely show up arm in arm when required. But what I do need is the marriage – in ink on parchment."

"You don't care about me at all do you?" she said.

"I care about our family," Arkus said. "This is the best thing for the family."

"I'm not part of your family," she seethed. She turned away, storming for the door.

"Where are you going?"

"For a very long walk." She ripped the door open.

Arkus was calling after her. "I'll have Gellick accompany—"

"I'd rather go alone."

"Out of the question!" He appeared at the doorway to block her, moving fast for an older man. Furious, she faced him but his expression had softened. "I just got you back. I won't lose you again."

She shuffled her feet. "Very well. I won't go alone."

"Thank you," Arkus said. He raised a hand as though to pat her shoulder but thought better of it. "He'll be here shortly. I'm expecting him. But if you'll excuse me, I have much work to attend to." He walked back to his desk and Cassandra shut the door behind her. She waited on the comfy bench and when Gellick eventually appeared he had no fewer than ten Chevaliers and a large crate. She eyed it suspiciously but Gellick's look told her not to ask.

Her hope that a walk through the city might cheer her up was soon dashed. The Chevaliers were a sullen lot, walking with their noses up in the air and clanking loudly with every step. She'd rather roam the streets alone and see the city as it truly was, not how a noble was supposed to see it, as little she saw was authentic. The people ducked or bowed their heads as she passed. Anyone who spoke did so with a nervous politeness. Merchants brought out special wares reserved only for the wealthy and some even tried to give her gifts for free if she would tell the others at court where she got this or that.

It was quite tiring.

At a crossroads, which was ripe with the smell of fish, Gellick came to a halt. "Might we venture down to the harbourside now, Princess?" Soldiers in chainmail and holding spears were trudging past.

"It looks busy," Cassandra said. "I'm not sure I'm in the mood for it."

"We also have business there."

Cassandra looked to the sealed crate. "You're very polite to make it seem like it's my decision."

"As you say, Princess."

Down at the harbour proper, Cassandra took in the fullness of the vast horseshoe bay. A forest of ship masts stretched to the colossal white arch that spanned the distant banks. The wind whistled in the space between the ships, seagulls screeched and she could almost taste the salt in the air. Cassandra followed Gellick's lead as they fought through the crowds. Before long, the rest of the aromas reached her: sweat, horse muck and fish guts. Gellick raised a white silk handkerchief heavily scented with lavender to his nose.

"Put it down over there," he said beneath the handkerchief, pointing to a group of fairy warriors surrounding two easels. At one easel was Fidelm, brush in hand. Opposite him was another painter, a human in overalls with a long, hanging beard tucked into his belt. The Chevaliers carefully placed the crate down before the fairies. "General," Gellick said. "I believe you were expecting this."

Fidelm set his brush down and stretched his arms. "Your timely arrival is most appreciated, Chevalier. My people will take good care of it."

"Take good care of what?" Cassandra asked.

"The scrying orb we recovered from the Bastion," Fidelm said. "Arkus has the one that Blaine recovered. This will grant a method of communication with Aurisha when delivered."

"If Aurisha is retaken," Gellick sniffed.

"That would be a good thing, Chevalier," Fidelm said. "My Queen will be sending all the dragons still in our forest onto Brevia soon. The quicker they can be sent home the better, I'd imagine."

"More dragons, oh joyous," Gellick said. He half-turned to leave but hesitated. "I hope your wing is on the mend, general?"

"Niceties aren't required," said Fidelm. "You've completed your task."

"Very well," Gellick said. "Come Chevaliers, Princess, back to the palace."

"I'm not ready to return," Cassandra said. She had no reason to stay other than to be rebellious and if she couldn't fight Arkus just yet, then Gellick would do.

"I cannot allow you to remain without protection," Gellick said.

"I can have her escorted back," said Fidelm. "My fairies can be trusted. None of them joined Castallan."

"I only accept orders from the royal family," said Gellick.

"I'm the Princess."

"Your father outranks even you," Gellick said.

"And he said explicitly that I could not stay at the harbour and keep Fidelm company?"

"The General appears to have a companion already."

The bearded painter nearly dropped his pallet at being brought into the discussion.

"Douglas isn't much of a conversationalist when he works," Fidelm said. "A true artist."

"Have it your way," Gellick said. "Bring the Princess safely back to the palace or you won't leave this city."

"I'm quaking at the thought," Fidelm said. Gellick muttered something under his breath as he and the Chevaliers stalked off. The moment he was out of sight, Cassandra looked quizzically at Fidelm.

"Why help me?"

"Why stay here?" he asked.

"I just wanted to annoy him," Cassandra said.

"Then we were of a mind," said Fidelm.

"So, what are you doing?" she asked.

"I am acquainting myself with the latest Brevian fad," Fidelm said.

"It is no fad," Douglas squawked from behind his easel.

"I like to capture the scene perfectly," Fidelm said. "These broken strokes you've asked me to attempt are making a mess."

"Perfection is not my goal," Douglas said. "I am studying how light affects the scene. The eye does not see everything in detail but focuses on a single point. The rest is blurred. A mere impression of what is there."

"Ah Douglas, your skills are too great to waste on fleeting fancies. Alas, that is your kind."

"Change can be worthwhile," Cassandra said.

"Why change what does not need to be changed," Fidelm said.

"But how will you know if things are better or worse without change?" said Douglas, sweeping his brush across the canvas until some yellow flicked off the side and splattered Cassandra's white dress.

Change. Something has to change. Can I really settle into a life here?

"You look troubled, Cassandra," Fidelm said.

"What? No. No. I'm fine—"

"May we have some privacy, Douglas?" Fidelm asked.

"And just when the light was at its best," Douglas said glumly. He got up and shuffled off behind the wall of fairy warriors. Cassandra was left with the ink-skinned fairy, a little unsettled.

What does he want?

She found it hard to judge. His deep blue eyes gave nothing away.

"Well?" Fidelm asked, turning to face her. "Why bite at the Chevalier?"

"Why the concern? You don't know me."

"Curiosity," Fidelm said.

"I'm not something to be studied."

"I'm trying to decide whether to feel sympathy for you or not," said Fidelm. "You've been in a foul mood since the Bastion."

"I felt fine until today. Arkus is trying to marry me off."

"So?" Fidelm said.

Cassandra could barely believe her ears. Rage pulsed inside her. She wanted to take his canvas and toss it into the water of the bay.

So? So! How would you like it if Kasselle forced you into something?

Then she remembered that, as a fairy, Fidelm was selected for a role at birth and was stuck there. He likely wouldn't complain.

"It hardly seems right that I should have no say in something like this," Cassandra said, forcing herself to remain calm. "It doesn't seem right either that I should work so hard for my freedom only to get stuck in this situation."

"Then do something about it," said Fidelm. "You're resourceful enough."

"It's more a matter of principal," she said. "Of freedom."

Fidelm shrugged. "Freedom to me is having a choice and you have a choice here."

"No, I don—"

"Yes, you do," Fidelm interrupted. "You can try to act or you can do nothing and complain. At the Bastion, you could have done nothing, but you chose to act. You escaped and in doing so helped to bring about Castallan's downfall. Freedom is relative, Cassandra."

"Is that the fairy perspective?"

"I can see why you think that; however, I've lived for a fair time, and in ninety years you see enough to form a broad perspective. Darnuir, for example, might be the most powerful individual amongst the Three Races and yet he is not utterly free. He cannot do exactly as he pleases. Nor can your father, nor can I and nor can you. To think otherwise is childish. If you don't want to go down the route Arkus has laid before you, find a way to alter it. As a human, you can."

"I'm just not sure how," Cassandra said. "I've lived my whole life for one thing and that's over now…" She trailed off, lost for words.

Fidelm twisted his canvas around. On it was a half-finished picture of the Bay of Brevia, with a beautiful ship at the centre and an array of dashed strokes around it that helped to give a dream-like quality to it. "Before I started this sheet was blank. I could make it anything I wanted." He picked up his colour pallet. "Look at yourself. You're exactly the same." Then he flicked a little green paint at her. Cassandra hadn't the chance to react. The paint splashed across her dress, crossing paths with the yellow left there by Douglas. Fidelm swirled his brush on the pallet then painted a purple stroke along one of her sleeves.

Cassandra found herself laughing. Fidelm handed her the pallet and she started smearing paint all over her once pristine white gown. Red and blue, the brown that Fidelm had mixed for the wood of the ships; her hands rubbed it all over her white satin dress.

Once the paint was gone, she handed the pallet back.

"And people ask why I paint to relax my mind," Fidelm said.

"That was fun. Thank you, general."

"I wish you luck," said Fidelm. "We'll all need it before the end."

Back in her room, Cassandra felt restless. The place was more splendid than her chambers at the Bastion, even the mirror was lined with white gold. But she had nothing to do, nothing obvious at any rate. And with little to occupy herself with, Arkus' threat of marriage weighed dangerously on her mind. So, she took to the long corridors of the palace, poking her head through every doorway, looking for a distraction; hoping for some inspiration.

What she found was none other than Queen Orrana.

The door had been innocuous; the room on the other side, not so much.

It was lush and packed with more cushions than there would ever be a use for. Most striking was just how much colour was in this one room. Where much of the palace was black with the occasional bit of white, this was a medley of bright yellows, warm oranges, greens, blues and pinks. Frankly, it was unsightly.

Orrana, thin, pale and at odds with her surroundings, was sat in an upright, ornate chair with a purple lining. She held command of the room's majestic easterly view of the bay of Brevia. The Queen jumped, startled by Cassandra's arrival and nearly dropped her teacup. A tray of pots and cakes lay on the table in front of her.

"I'm sorry to have disturbed you," Cassandra said. "I'll just go."

"Oh no," said Orrana. She got to her feet and faced Cassandra, waving her in. "You might as well come in now if we've already skipped the formal invitation to my parlour and, well good gracious, you've dressed to match." She tittered. "How about some tea and cake? My maid just brought a fresh tray."

Praying that this wouldn't be deathly awkward, Cassandra stepped lightly over, like a street dog to a stranger's hand. There were no less than four richly patterned pots on a large tray laden with little cakes, fruit pastries, scones, butter and a bowl filled with what looked like raw sugar. She took her seat, eyeing the raisin scones.

"May I offer you something?" Orrana asked, in a voice to match the sugar bowl.

"I'm fine."

"No?" Orrana said, in a pitch slightly too high. "There is shimmer brew and three different varieties of tea. Or perhaps you would like something a little stronger? Some sherry, brandy, or even a touch of whisky. I can have it brought at once. You must be so worn out from your travels and that battle," she gave a little gasp. "A little spirit to lift your own?"

Cassandra wasn't sure what to make of Orrana just yet. She seemed friendly, but perhaps a little too much?

"No," Cassandra said, adding a quick, "Thank you," as an afterthought.

"Well do help yourself, if you change your mind," Orrana said, though she touched none of it herself. She did pour herself some steaming shimmer brew and brought the cup delicately to her lips. Soundlessly, she took a sip. "So, I'm told you were raised in the Bastion—"

"Held captive," Cassandra corrected her.

"Quite so," said Orrana. "I assure you I knew nothing of your imprisonment."

Why is she telling me this? What does it matter now?

"I doubt it was common knowledge," said Cassandra.

"But Arkus knew," Orrana went on, "and I suspect my father knew as well. We women are always the last to know such things, us highborn women at least. People always bleat about the equality, especially in the lower classes, about how we're so much more civilised than the dragons but, sometimes, I'm not so sure. It could be all an act."

"What about Captain Elsie?" Cassandra said. "She was the very first Captain of the Master Station here at Brevia after the hunters were institutionalised following the Battle of the Bogs. Or Lady Margo Foulis, who designed the white arch of Brevia and its defences. Or Queen Flora, who reigned for forty-five years on her own. So many more come to mind."

"But what do they all have in common?" Orrana asked.

"Little that I can think of," said Cassandra.

"Childless," said Orrana. "Yes. All the greats were childless, as though a child shackles a woman. Perhaps it does – children or the lead up to them. For the lowborn blood matters little but for us…" she drew out the word and took another sip of her brew. "I hear Arkus intends for you to marry?" Cassandra thought it a sudden shift in topic but she supposed it was why Orrana had invited her to come in.

Best get this discussion over with.

"I'm sure you know his intentions," Cassandra said.

"Marriage is often a precursor to children," Orrana said rather pointedly.

"He mentioned nothing of that."

"He loves our son very much," Orrana said. "Arkus would do anything for him. I'd do even more."

Oh, so this is what you're worried about?

"I can assure you I want nothing to do with the throne."

Orrana leaned forward. "You know, I think you might be being completely honest with me."

"Why wouldn't I be?" Cassandra asked. "There's nothing I want from you. I'm not playing any game."

"True," Orrana said, before adding in a less sweet voice, "Well, you won't mind if I have a whisky then?"

"Um, not at all," Cassandra said. The words were barely out of her mouth when Orrana produced a small glass seemingly from nowhere and filled it with a golden liquid from one of the pots.

"If anyone ever asks for this one," Orrana said, setting the pot down, "I just tell them it has gone cold and shall taste dreadful." She drank from the cup. "Gracious, that's better." Cassandra stared at the Queen, feeling her eyes widen in amazement. "What?" Orrana said. "You've seen and done more shocking things I wager. Ever tried it?" she said, proffering the tumbler.

"No," Cassandra said, taking it.

"I'm not surprised," said Orrana. "Southerners tried to make it but failed. The best stuff is from the Splinters because each island has a unique type of peat. That one is from my father's own distillery in the Hinterlands. The hint of Cascade in the Dorain gives it a taste of peach." Cassandra sniffed it. She coughed as something rankled the back of her throat, then took a sip.

"It burns," she said, half-choking.

Have I just been poisoned?

"That's why I love it," Orrana said. "Can hardly taste the peach if I am being honest. I'd tell you that I seek the warmth for lack of it from my dear husband. But the truth is I just love it."

"Arkus does not love you?"

"How blunt you are," Orrana said, bringing the cup to her lips again. The Queen cocked her head and eyed Cassandra as though she were an exotic animal. "You truly are new to Brevia, aren't you? You don't come with the expectations - the baggage. Take that dress for a start, how wonderfully different. Around most, I must pretend to be the stoic Queen." She took another sip from her glass. "Arkus cares for me enough, by the way," she added conspiratorially. "But he's never gotten over your mother. He married me for duty, and for some black stone. I advise you get out of your betrothal if you don't want it."

"I'm not sure how," Cassandra said.

"Find a way," Orrana said. "I'd help you if I could, and not just for my son's sake. I don't imagine you would enjoy putting on the same show that I must. Take these abominable cakes for example," and she looked at the tray as though the pastries had done her great harm. "I am forever being offered them, as though a queen's constitution could be sustained on them alone, and out of politeness I must always try one or two. I used to like such sweets as a child, but now I'm sick of them. It's become a trend in Brevia to even sprinkle extra sugar on top, as if they needed any."

"I'll try one," Cassandra said, and feeling the tension had decreased, reached for a raisin-dotted scone. "Without the sugar."

"Quite right," Orrana said. Their discussion died for a time while Cassandra ate and Orrana topped up her shimmer brew. The hot silver liquid let off its enticing bitterness into the air. It was a pleasant sort of silence. The scone was soft, the raisins chewy, and Cassandra felt quite comfortable. She had the uncanny feeling that she actually liked this bony, pale Queen and very much hoped it wasn't due to the contents of Orrana's glass.

"Do you fight, Cassandra?"

"Sometimes. Only with a sword, though," Cassandra said through her last mouthful of scone. "Do you?"

"Such a dear to ask. Yes, I did a little, in my youth," Orrana said wistfully. "I wanted to be a huntress and roam the rocks and forests of the Hinterlands. But there was a war on, and as my lord father's only child I could not be risked in such fashion." Orrana sighed then, slumping from her rigid posture. "I'm afraid I wasn't very affectionate towards my father for much of my life. Now I have a son, I can understand his concern. Though I always fancied a daughter." Her eyes fell on Cassandra.

This is getting a little intense.

"But it is too late for me now and likely too late for us as well," Orrana said. "However, I would like to have one person around here I could talk to without having to pretend to be someone else." The Queen wafted a hand around the parlour in demonstration.

"You spoke of helping me, if you could. Does that mean you cannot help me?"

"Arkus has become a stubborn man. Once he sets his mind on something, you can be sure it will be done. I doubt I will ever truly love him, but I do admire him greatly for that. However…" Orrana said locking eyes with Cassandra. "He does enjoy cutting a good deal."

"I don't have anything I can offer," Cassandra said. "Nothing that a king couldn't get for himself."

"Ah, there are a great many things Arkus cannot get," Orrana said.

"All I have is myself."

"Then offer him something only you can do."

"But what can I do?" Cassandra said. "I've read a lot, but he has scholars and advisors, I know a lot about the Bastion but that's useless now and, as you've said, I've just arrived here so I don't know anyone and no one knows me so — oh." The realisation struck her.

Orrana beamed. "Go, go. Haste is vital in these matters."

"Thank you for the scones," Cassandra said. She bolted for the door and thought she could hear Orrana call out that they ought to do it again sometime.

Cassandra pelted down the corridors of the palace, ignoring the butlers and nearly slammed into a Chevalier as she rounded a corner. She flew down a set of winding stairs that bypassed a couple of floors and brought her to Arkus' council chambers. She arrived panting.

"Let me through," she commanded the Chevaliers. "I must speak to my — my father." They all looked her up and down, hesitated, and then stood aside. She burst into the room, pink faced and hair tumbling down her face.

Arkus was hunched over a map of the city along with Gellick, tapping the area of the Rotting Hill and muttering darkly. They were both taken aback to see her standing there.

"Well, I see you had an entertaining day out," Arkus said looking at her ruined dress. "Gellick, please allow me a moment with my daughter. I will call you back to finish our discussion."

"Your Majesty," Gellick said with a bow. Once Gellick was gone, Arkus looked serious again. He withdrew the map under the desk and sat down.

"Have you thought about what we discussed?"

"I have," she said striding towards him. When she arrived at the desk, she leaned over it towards him. Arkus didn't budge an inch. "There will be no marriage," Cassandra said.

"Oh?"

"I don't expect you to give it up for nothing. What if I deliver Lord Boreac to you?"

Arkus pondered for a while, rapping his fingers across his desk, from pinkie to forefinger, and then back again. "And how do you intend on doing that?"

"I'm not from here," Cassandra said. "Barely anyone knows who I am, which means I can go about the city as a fresh face. I can be a princess when I need the clout and nobody when I need to blend in. And you can trust that I am not part of any circle, which plotted against you. Can you say that of your spies?"

"No," Arkus said. "They are spies after all."

"Well then. Do we have a deal?"

Arkus smiled and leaned back. "You realise that, even if you succeed, it won't change your position or who you are? The problems I have would not vanish, well, other than having Boreac in chains."

"Then keep up the pretence that I will marry Balack until we think of a solution."

"We?"

"Yes, Arkus – I mean… father," Cassandra said.

"Call me what you want," Arkus said, though he said it with affection. "Very well. *If* you can deliver me Boreac, we'll find an alternative. A nice long show trial for him and Annandale will occupy the Assembly for a time. With their positions vacant, I can dole out their lands and titles. That will keep the vultures at bay…" he seemed to drift into his own thoughts for a moment. His mouth twitched and he ran his fingers across the desk again. "There may be some element of risk involved."

"I can handle myself," Cassandra said.

"I wouldn't allow this but I *need* Boreac," Arkus said, as though nothing else in the world mattered. "Don't do anything rash. If you know where he is, you come to me first, understand?"

"I'll find him," Cassandra said. Then she left whilst she still felt confident. Outside the council chambers she allowed herself a smile.

"You can go back in now, Gellick," she said.

Chapter 18

SHADOWS IN DALRIDIA

The Islanders could be wealthy. Being in the middle of the world, they could have controlled all trade. Instead, they've sought isolation, even sometimes from each other.

From Tiviar's Histories

Dukoona – The Splintering Isles – City of Dalridia

DUKOONA WITHDREW HIS blade from the islander's stomach and blood gushed. It fell from the man like the rain around him. The constant rain. With the humans nearby dealt with, he turned to help his spectres cleave an opening in the palisade wall. Once a hole was roughly hewn, demons began to scramble through this latest breach – too few demons in truth. Dukoona saw many slip down high embankments leading up to the walls.

Forward, he commanded to the demons around him. *Do not stop.*

He watched them tear off. They really are such frail creatures, he thought. Small and wispy, the shadows of their flesh were more akin to smoke. And even at a distance, he could see their ribs as the dark mist swirled within them. They lacked sense as well, running in every direction within the maze of walls.

The islanders had built their defences to confuse their enemies. Sure enough, a group appeared from a one-way opening in the wall to fall upon the demons in a storm of axes. At least Dukoona knew about that trap now. Dalridia would not fall without a fight.

"Come with me," Dukoona called to the spectres nearby. "We must create more breaches along the wall." They ran off, unable to find any shadows under the heavy clouds. Dukoona took them right, away from the islanders' ambush, searching for a gap in the inner layers of palisade wall.

A group of islanders ahead were blocking a breach with a stout shield wall. Dukoona swung his dark sword at their backs when he reached them, cutting through leather and mail with ease. The spectres ravaged their flank and the humans broke, running back into the labyrinth. Thrilled, the demons chased merrily after them. Dukoona cautiously followed, thinking the islanders might have broken a little too easily. Around a bend, he saw that the humans seemed to have run impossibly far. They stood bashing their shields tauntingly.

Howling, the demons bounded on.

"Wait," Dukoona snarled to his spectres. He let the demons carry on as bait and, midway, the ground dropped, dumping the demons into a pit of spikes.

It was clever of the humans, but only the rain was saving them. Once enough points along the outer walls were breached, they would be overwhelmed. Still, it was a harder fight than he had anticipated. That was all for the better. It granted a chance to relieve his Master of thousands of demons. Dukoona just hoped his Trusted were not throwing their lives away.

Stay safe, Kidrian. I need you at my side. I can't do this alone.

Trap after trap, dead end after dead end, and at the cost of many of demons, Dukoona pushed his way to the final set of Dalridia's walls. A host of humans gathered to meet him, bloodied, windburnt and covered in mud: the islands' best. To Dukoona's fortune, the clouds finally parted, casting sporadic shadows from shields, bodies, axes and walls.

He reached out to the demons and commanded, *Kill.* They swarmed forwards. The humans pressed their shields together and withstood the impact. Axes arced, spraying smoky blood and chipped demon bone. Demons leapt on top of their brethren to vault over the shields. Just as the first wave was spent, more demons came from behind to join Dukoona. He could always count on having more demons.

Then he felt something twig at the back of his mind. Rectar looked briefly towards him through the bond of master and servant. '*Faster...*' the echoing rumble commanded before he left.

Dukoona froze for a moment, trembling. He rallied quickly and yelled, "Show the humans fear. With me spectres!" And he dove into the thin shadow under the base of the wall, running along it, judging when best to strike. In the middle of the human shield wall, he half-emerged his torso from the shadow to cut at two of the defenders. He melded again before the humans could react and was already half way back along the base of the wall when a shield slammed into his path.

Another thud jarred behind him and he knew his path was blocked.

These really are the islands' finest.

He tore from his shadow, his dark blade carving through the soft leather on the legs of the nearest human. Yet, now he was surrounded. He had to be careful, weaving within the web of ever changing shadows of the melee. One false meld and he'd be caught. Done.

An axe sped towards his face. Dukoona sunk his legs into a shadow to drop under it. He heard a satisfying squelch as the axe continued into the human behind him. He travelled under the axe wielder's legs, sprang up on the other side, knocking men and women aside, and drove his sword through an exposed throat.

Other spectres had been forced to fight in the open as well, melding as fast as they could so as not to be swarmed. One was caught within his shadow and axe cleaved below the surface of the ground to crack at a head that could not be seen.

"Spread out to fight them," one of the humans roared. Quickly, the flickering shadows on the ground grew further apart. Dukoona spotted the one calling orders and made for him. He seemed young, a little stocky, but was quick and raised his shield against Dukoona's dark blade. Dukoona's swing rebounded off a metal coating. "This one is mine," the boy called.

"Lord Grigayne, stay back!"

Dukoona fell back as the boy lowered his shield and rammed him. He melded into the shadow of the shield, taking Grigayne in the chin as he rose. They were so close. Dukoona's cold tendrils of blue flame lapped at Grigayne's face. He switched from his shadow blade to a dagger instead, the weapon morphing in his hand.

He raised the dagger.

He tried to bring it down.

And felt a ferocious blunt blow at his side. Knocked off balance, the dagger scraped into the meat of the boy's shoulder rather than somewhere more fatal. Grigayne screamed, drawing back the butt of his axe from Dukoona's side. Dukoona melded away, under the boy and reappeared behind him. Somehow, the human managed to turn in time to block him.

He was fast and strong this one; he would have to be to carry that reinforced shield. Yet Grigayne's wound would end him and he raised that shield a little lower with each strike Dukoona sent. And then two spectres emerged, grinning their white smiles.

Dukoona did not recognise the newcomers.

That was odd.

Only the Trusted had been brought to Dalridia; he was certain. It might have been the shock that prevented Dukoona reacting to the dark sword coming towards him. The grinning spectre locked eyes with him under hair of long orange flames. Only a slip on the wet earth saved Dukoona, slicing his arm instead. The wound smoked.

So, that's what pain is like. I'd nearly forgotten.

Then he reacted.

The second grinning spectre lunged for him. Dukoona jerked aside then caught the arm of his foe and dragged the spectre onto his dagger. Smoke rose, the grin faded. He threw the body at the first traitor, buying time to switch to his sword. The blade materialised in a whirl of shadows just in time to meet his enemy's weapon. Dukoona pushed with all his might, enough to tilt bend the arms of his foe and impale the spectre upon his own blade.

With the immediate threat over he looked around. Grigayne and humans had pulled away from the spectre infighting. The demons themselves had begun to fight each other Dukoona reached to those nearby and gave the order, *To me.* Many scuttled to his side, yet many also continued killing each other, ignoring the humans entirely.

They're getting conflicting orders.

Spectres were melding in and out of the battle, but they moved so fast he couldn't say if they were friend or foe. Those that leapt for him were clear enough. He knew none of them, they weren't Trusted, but killing them was a blow to him all the same.

Is this how you get rid of us, Rectar? Watching me kill my own kind? Does that please you? But Rectar's power was elsewhere. He wasn't even glancing in Dukoona's direction. Were these traitors acting of their own accord?

A fresh group of spectres emerged from the shadows and Dukoona had never been more thankful to see those guttering purple embers. Kidrian and members of the Trusted came to his aid. Before long, the traitorous spectres were smoking on the ground and the demons ceased fighting each other. Kidrian looked after the retreating humans, ready to give chase.

"Let them go," Dukoona said. "Keep the demons advancing but all Trusted are to fall back. Now."

Miles to the east, with the Nail Head rising behind them, Dukoona gathered his closest Trusted atop the Shadow Spire they had built upon landing. It was smaller, and squatter than the tower back on Eastguard but served well enough. Many galleys sat empty at the coast, their demons either dead, dying or continuing to press Dalridia. Dukoona had ordered the rest to stay on their ships until he got a grip on things. As ever, he needed time to think but it seemed time had finally run out.

"Who were they?" he asked. No one answered. "I made it clear that I wanted no spectre who we did not trust to sail with us."

"Perhaps they came from Skelf," Kidrian said. "Longboats landed to the north of the city to reinforce the defenders. Spectres could have travelled on them, melded away out of sight."

"So Kraz is dead?" asked Sonrid, shuffling forward eagerly.

"We have no idea what's happened on Skelf," said Kidrian.

"We need to know," said Dukoona. "If those spectres were only seeking revenge for being sent on a suicide mission with Kraz then so be it. The alternative is… quite unthinkable."

Again, no one answered.

Then, from the bottom of the spire below, came distant growls from the guards. Kidrian peered over the edge, and then looked to Dukoona. He gave a nod and Kidrian melded away to investigate. Dukoona paced, painfully aware that all eyes were on him: they were looking to him to tell them the answers, but he had none.

Has Rectar, at last, decided to remove me? If so, what do I do? What can I do?

An old haunting memory crept up on him, of when he had first been summoned – a memory of an endless cavern, with demons all around. The demons had charged at him and nothing he had done could stop them. "Know you cannot hope to turn my servants against me," Rectar had told him.

Even the spectres, my own kind, are his servants. Perhaps I could never have turned any against him?

Kidrian emerged from the shadows and Dukoona stopped his pacing. "Trusted have returned to us from the west."

"From the west?" Dukoona said. He had been forced to send spectres to Castallan years ago. "Bring them up." Kidrian disappeared again and returned shortly later with a score of spectres. Of the new arrivals, Dukoona recognised the leader with thick, scarlet flames on his head. "Nordin," he said, dragging out the spectre's name in disbelief. "It has been a very long time."

"I regret that we did not leave sooner," said Nordin in a voice like an angry gale of wind. "Less of our brothers might have needlessly died."

"Why are you here now?" Dukoona asked. "Your timing is both a pleasant surprise and yet, it is also suspicious." He caught Kidrian's eye and he drew a blade from the shadows in case of danger. Other Trusted followed suit.

"We would have come sooner," Nordin said nervously. "We have come because the Dragon King slew the human who kept us down, who sent us in for a slaughter at the town of Torridon."

"Slaughter?" Dukoona said. "How many of you remain now."

"Just over one hundred, my Lord."

Just one hundred, out of the three hundred I sent west…

"Then we shall take a moment, for the loss of so many spectres," Dukoona said. He closed his eyes as did all the Trusted. After a minute, he opened them. "Our people are dying; being sent to death or turning on each other. We are too few now, too few to last another war. Who was this human that you allowed to treat our brothers so, Nordin?"

"My Lord, forgive me, but there was little any of us could do. Castallan's magic turned them into men and women with glowing red eyes who could match a dragon's strength. The wizard's favoured Commander Zarl was the strongest of them all. There were so few of us, there was nothing we could have done. For years, there was no fighting and it mattered little, but then came Cold Point. And Torridon. And finally, the Charred Vale.

"We did what we could; tried to abandon Zarl and let the demons turn rabid. But each time some of us fled, some of us would pay. At the Charred Vale, Darnuir defeated Zarl and so we took our chance."

"And the wizard?" Dukoona asked.

"Dead, for all we care," Nordin said. "The Three Races were moving to destroy him."

"Then the dragons will not be far behind," Dukoona said.

"I couldn't say, my Lord," said Nordin, and his voice petered out in some deep exhaustion. Not a physical tiredness, spectres did not tire. But something in Nordin and the spectres with him looked worn. Their flaming hair was dim and the shadows of their flesh were thin; more like steam than flesh. He caught Kidrian's eye again and nodded. Kidrian dispersed his weapon with a wave of his fingers and all the weapons among the Trusted began to vanish. "I am glad that you have returned, Nordin. We shall need every spectre – every ounce of cunning. All has not been well in the east and all those gathered here should now know."

Kidrian stepped forwards. "Are you sure, my Lord?"

"I am," Dukoona said. "How did you describe these humans, Nordin? That their eyes were red? Another red creature attacked our kind near Kar'drun not so long ago. These things must be linked. The Master does not need us. We've become disposable. Sent to these islands to block his enemies, perhaps to buy him more time."

And even as he spoke, the truth of it dawned on him. He had after all been sending Rectar what he had wanted for decades. And what his Master had desired was dragons.

"I don't want to give him time," Dukoona said. "We're going back to Aurisha."

"What of the demons?" Kidrian asked.

"Leave those already ashore. Those still on board their ships will come with us. It may pass as a tactical retreat to Rectar if it looks like we are trying to split the Three Races."

"And those on the other islands?" Sonrid asked. "Our brethren at Eastguard, Skelf, Ronra—"

"All the spectres that I care about are here," Dukoona said. "Leave the False to serve the Master a little longer."

Blaine – The Splintering Isles – Approaching Dalridia

At the bow of the *Grey Fury*, Blaine looked to the swathe of demons upon the shore. They were another sea, one black and burning, ebbing and crashing against the battered walls of Dalridia. There was no order to them, but there were thousands, stretching as far as Blaine could see.

One more battle and then I tell Darnuir everything.

It was those memories which, had they not been locked away in his gems, might have haunted him every night. He clutched tightly at the chain around his neck, the terrible evidence of what he suspected. Kroener, the betrayer, the cursed, and Darnuir's father had gone to the Highlands, how else could the trolls have come by the necklace? Two had journeyed northwards but only one had returned. Why that was, he would likely never know. But what happened after, he would never forget.

"Are you ready?" Darnuir said, stepping up behind him. The boy was in full armour and his crimson cloak had been repaired. It fit him well; better even than his father and far more than Draconess.

Was it all a mistake? Or is this what the gods intended?

"Blaine?" Darnuir said.

"I am ready."

"If you do not wish to fight… if you are still uneasy after the Bast—"

"I'm fine," Blaine said. It was only half a lie. Physically he was sound.

"You've been quiet of late," said Darnuir. Their ship was now approaching the shore, its shallow hull enabling it to draw right up to the beach.

"The Cascade will not abandon me here," Blaine said. He knew now that was the reason he'd suffered at the Bastion, but it was of small comfort. He'd felt life without magic, without his Blade propping up his aged body. What he couldn't be certain of was whether the gods would abandon him.

Perhaps they abandoned me long ago.

"The city stands," Somerled Imar boomed proudly from the portside. "My son has held the demon filth at bay."

"Good," Darnuir said, drawing the Dragon's Blade and spinning it in his hand. "Let's help him kill them."

The *Grey Fury* beached and men and dragons leapt off over the deck rail. The dragons had removed their armour from their lower bodies to wade through the shallow water. Blaine jumped off with his Light Bearers, Darnuir on the other side with his Praetorians. Hundreds more ships followed in behind them.

The demons didn't seem to know what to do about the landing. Blaine cut through them, the Guardian's Blade fighting the servants of the Shadow once more. It seemed too easy.

Where are the spectres?

"Make safe the city!" Darnuir cried sweeping westwards and rallying dragons to him.

Blaine scored kill after kill; the demons were numerous and vicious, but lacked any direction. He sensed a trap, a false feeling of security. He kept his Light Bearers close and alert, worried that a huge demon fleet might approach from the rear. But nothing came. And the demons were pushed off the beaches, up the land, into the woods, right up against the slope of the Nail Head itself and were crushed there.

It was good that the victory was so complete. After the Bastion, the men needed a win with less of a toll. Blaine basked in the blow they had dealt to Rectar's forces, yet it was a fleeting feeling. The battle had not been as cathartic as he'd hoped. His mind turned again to the conversation he must have with Darnuir: his King, and his grandson.

Chapter 19

A DISH HARD TO STOMACH

Out of every major settlement of humans and dragons, I feel most at home in Dalridia. The islanders' earthern halls are closer to nature than anything in Brevia or Aurisha. There may not be trees but the humans of the Splinters show a deep respect and connection to the world. If only it wasn't so wet.

From Tiviar's Histories

Darnuir – East of Dalridia

DARNUIR LOOKED UP to the top of the strange tower, shielding his eyes against the drizzling rain. It was nothing like he had ever seen before, in this life or his last. He wasn't sure whether to even call it a tower, for it lacked any enclosed space. A multitude of wooden beams criss-crossed upwards to a flat platform under an open sky. The spectres must have built it, yet the spectres had all fled.

They keep on fleeing. Why? Why don't the wretches stand and fight?

He'd enjoyed the battle, enjoyed the feeling of magic in him. The days spent at sea had been dry for he'd had no excuse to draw upon the Cascade. He needed it now. Needed to feel like he had in Castallan's throne room. It wasn't a feeling he relished, and Darnuir feared he was fighting a losing battle with himself.

Each day it was harder to resist. Each day he yearned a little more for it. And each crucial decision he had to make became harder to focus on, for his mind was often elsewhere. He didn't know who to turn to on the matter. Blaine was acting strangely and would only rebuke him.

Brackendon was broken, a terrible sign of what might come to pass. *What can I do? We're in the middle of a war. It can't be delayed just to help me. And if I let them know I'm in this state, they won't follow me.* In this struggle, he could only rely on himself.

Darnuir congratulated himself on his small achievements in this regard. It had been a challenge, for example, to grant Grigayne Imar the honour of destroying the spectre's mysterious tower. It would have made a good excuse to drawn on magic.

To Darnuir's right, Grigayne grunted through the pain in his shoulder and slammed his great war axe down in a two handed grip. It bit deeply into the wood of a supporting beam. Several hacks later and the beam split with a satisfying crack. His men roared in approval and began attacking the tower as well. A groaning soon followed as the first of the twisting walls came crashing down. Darnuir's golden armour was already filthy so he didn't mind the fresh splatter of mud.

"Foul thing," said Grigayne jerking a thumb at the wreckage. His reddish hair was pulled back into a knot and the finer hairs of his beard rolled around his face like the froth atop a great wave.

"A foul thing for foul creatures," Darnuir said. "Your defence of your lands has been nothing short of heroic."

"Has it?" Grigayne said, a touch of frost in his tone.

"I'm sorry we did not arrive sooner."

"We've lost Eastguard, Ronra and Skelf after I had to pull my warriors back to defend Dalridia," Grigayne lamented. "The demons sailed right around Ullusay. Took us by surprise here. There are some smaller villages east of the Nail Head, well there *were*…"

"Demons burned my home," Darnuir said. "There is nothing left in the Boreac Mountains now."

Grigayne nodded wearily. "Rebuilding will be especially hard with winter on the way."

"The demons will be driven back," Darnuir said.

"You dragons never seemed capable of driving them back before," Grigayne said. "Why will this time be any different?"

"Because something is amiss with our enemies," Darnuir said.

"I saw that first hand," Grigayne said. He frowned in some thought. "While I was fighting one of them – a tough bastard with blue flames –

more spectres appeared around me. I thought I was done for. But then, they started to fight each other instead."

"What happened next?" Darnuir asked, intrigued by this new development.

"The one with the blue flames was the target. I disengaged due to my injury and to reform our shield wall. Once one side of the spectres won they vanished. All of them, though the demons did not descend into madness at that point."

"Something similar happened at the Charred Vale," Darnuir said. "They fled the battle and left the demons rabid. The same thing allowed us an easy victory here."

"Why would they do that?"

"You're asking the wrong person," said Darnuir. "Only their leader could tell us."

"I didn't know they had a leader," Grigayne said.

"A spectre called Dukoona, if memory serves." Cassandra had mentioned it to him. She'd witnessed Dukoona informing Castallan about this very invasion. Things didn't seem to be going Dukoona's way.

"A shame you cannot ask him," said Grigayne.

"A great shame," Darnuir said, although the younger Imar had got him thinking.

Why not go east and find out? Going east with all haste would also mean battle that much sooner. Yes, why not go?

"Actually, I ought to go," said Darnuir. Grigayne looked at him as though he had gone mad. "Not a word of this to the Guardian," he added. "Blaine would never approve."

"This could be a ploy of the spectres," said Grigayne.

Darnuir scrambled for some justification. "My gut tells me otherwise. It seems a stretch to think the spectres faked a skirmish in front of you, killing their own in the process, just in the hopes you would survive the battle and tell me. If they even knew who you were. If there is infighting among the spectres, then we ought to take advantage of the situation. Strike hard and fast before they have a chance to end whatever strife there is between them."

Grigayne sniffed. "Your army, your decision."

"You are unimpressed, I gather."

"I'm worn," Grigayne said, rolling his shoulders with a deep sigh. He winced and brought a hand up to his injury. "Worn, tired, beaten and in need of rest. And I thought you might be, well…" he trailed off.

"Different?"

"Something like that."

"This is how my people have been for thousands of years."

"I know," said Grigayne. "Yet the way the dragons are spoken of, it made me think you were something more. A boyish imagination that was never corrected."

"May I ask you something personal, Lord Imar?"

"I'm not the Lord yet," Grigayne said. "But yes, you may ask."

"You speak differently than your fellow islanders, even from your own father. Why?"

"My father wished me to sound more acceptable to the Assembly in Brevia," said Grigayne with a sad smile. "He thought our cause for sovereignty might fare better if I was able to visit Brevia and not sound so foreign. But isn't there a bitter irony in that? I was to give up the voice of my own people to better argue for their separateness."

"And why does your father feel so strongly about this?"

Grigayne shrugged. "It's the way it's always been. Did my ancestors swear an oath of fealty or merely homage to the old Brevian kings? Who is to say? One way makes us subservient and the other makes us respectful. My father would rather not pay taxes and Arkus would rather he continued. Every generation. On and on it goes. Gives my father a goal in life, if nothing else."

"And what do you make of it?" Darnuir said.

"I don't see why we should break apart. Where would it end? First Dalridia gains freedom from Brevia and then the smaller islands become frustrated with my family. Without Brevia to blame it will be those ruling in Dalridia who suffer from disgruntlement, from West Hearth to Eastguard, from Southguard to Ronra in the north. How long until Innerwick and Outerwick decide they will fare better if they rule themselves? How long then until even the people of the Wicks begin to disagree with each other?"

"There is strength in unity," said Darnuir. He was pleased by Grigayne's words.

"So long as it is genuine," said Grigayne. "A shield wall is only as strong as the bond of trust between each warrior. What good would a shield wall be if every man and woman bickered with the person on their right and jostled for a better position? That's the Kingdom more often than not. There's no single answer."

"That is why I have formed my new Praetorian Guard. I hope to make a force of all the Three Races, built on trust and loyalty. A symbol that we can indeed bring unity. But it has proven… difficult. I'd take you and twenty of your best men and shield maidens, if it would please you?"

"I — join your guard?" Grigayne questioned.

"I feel we are of a mind," said Darnuir.

"I'm not so sure," Grigayne said. He took some time. He sniffed again in the misty rain and shuffled his feet a little firmer into the mud. His chainmail rattled softly with every movement. "It's a noble endeavour but joining you would anger my father, and how would that favour you? I'm sorry but I must think of my own people. I cannot abandon them at a time like this."

Darnuir had no answer. *Why do they all resist me on this? Blaine, Fidelm, now the Imar's?* This small dream was already slipping away from him. The two halves of his person battled to dominate his emotions: the old dragon snarled in anger at the human's rebuttal, while the younger man felt cowed and foolish. This time, the young man won. *Some king I am. I'm failing more than succeeding and losing more people than gaining.* He'd left a trail of dead or bitter friends in the west. Arkus would shut his gates to him. East was his only road but he saw nothing on that path but war and hardship. Temptation arose for the Cascade; to draw on it and not feel as powerless for a moment. He bore his hand into a fist so hard that his nails drew blood and managed to resist the urge.

Grigayne did not fail to notice this and raised an eyebrow. Darnuir brought his bleeding palm to his mouth and sucked on his self-inflicted wound.

"I should return to the city," Darnuir said. "There is much to do if I am to take my dragons east and chase Dukoona." Grigayne seemed to understand that silence was required. He bowed courteously then took his leave, trudging back to his warriors by the ruin of the tower. The longship sigil on his shield was barely recognisable under all those notches.

Back in Dalridia, Darnuir tended to what Praetorians he did have. Their bow-work was coming along with practice every day, and their stamina had increased considerably. Lira had found an area for them outside one of the enormous long halls, which dominated the city. Built of loose stone and topped with earth, allowing daisies and ferns to grow wild on the roof.

"We'll work on our shield wall today," Lira announced. "The islanders impressed me, and we can do better. We must be able to make a bulwark against attack."

"Perhaps I could abstain from this training," Raymond said. "Only I fear I might be crushed."

"Harra, Camen," Lira said, nodding at the Praetorians to either side of the Chevalier. "Don't crush Raymond."

"We'll try," Harra said. She slapped Raymond's back plate and he grunted.

Darnuir felt a pang of sympathy for the Chevalier. "Play nice now or afterwards you can sprint against Raymond while he's mounted." The Praetorians mumbled in mock annoyance and some laughed. Darnuir and Lira set up their drill then stepped back to observe.

"Get your shield up to your chin," Darnuir said.

"Cover the person in front of you, don't hit their heads," Lira said.

"Faster now," said Darnuir. "We may need it at a moment's notice."

"Okay, let's try having half of you form a wall and half push it," said Lira. She divided the Praetorians and set them up. "On the count of three. One. Two. Three." The dragons and an exhausted Raymond charged or raised shields as instructed. The wall formed, held, but a section slid back.

"The ground's too wet," the fallen Praetorian said.

"Wet or dry, grass or snow, we must be ready," Darnuir said. Then, more under his breath, "We must be ready because no one else will join us. No one else will help us…"

"What was that?" Lira said. She stepped even closer to him. He noticed some signs of battle on her. A piece of her ebony hair had been cut away, it was now shorter on her left side, and her blue Hinterland leggings had a fresh tear.

"It was nothing, Lira. Don't trouble yourself with it."

"I'm voicing concern as the Praetorian Prefect for my King's well-being."

"Well I'm fine, thank you."

"If you say so," she said. "Look, I'd like to ask for your pardon for what happened at the Bastion, in the dungeons. I questioned your motivations."

"That's part of your job," Darnuir said.

"Rescuing the Princess was important," Lira said. "I only thought you might not be thinking clearly and, well, it does not matter now. Did it help with King Arkus at all?"

"I'm not sure," Darnuir said. "I can only hope that in time he will get over it."

"It's understandable given what Blaine revealed," said Lira.

"He didn't think," said Darnuir. "He should have told me."

"I think he tried, Darnuir," Lira said cautiously.

"I think I would have listened to him if he —"

"You weren't giving him a chance," Lira said. "You were always wanting to train or fight something. I know he didn't treat the hunters very well, but did you have to shut him out?"

"I was just giving him the cold shoulder," Darnuir said. "With something that important he should have insisted, made more of a fuss…" he trailed off. Lira was looking at him again with a worried face. "What's done is done," he said. "Blaine and I can smooth out our differences when we're safely in Aurisha one day."

"That could be a while."

"I intend to sail as soon as possible," said Darnuir. "Take the dragons and seize upon this civil war the spectres are in the middle of."

Lira frowned. "Forgive me, Darnuir, but that seems rash."

Darnuir was beginning to feel his temper rise. It came even quicker these days if he couldn't open the door just a little bit; just by a crack. He forced himself to remain calm. "We could be in Aurisha in a matter of weeks, not months. The spectres are fighting amongst each other. I don't see when we'll have a better chance. And what if we miss our chance before winter comes and it begins to be difficult moving troops?"

Lira did not answer immediately.

"As you will, Darnuir."

Further conversation was ceased by the collapse of Raymond.

"I think Raymond should call the countdowns for a while," Lira said.

"Marvellous," Raymond said. He staggered well out of range of the charging dragons. "By my count then. One. Two Three."

The Praetorians slammed into each other.

"Ooft, that'll be sore t'morrow," came a rough voice. Darnuir and Lira both whipped around to see a wind burnt islander bearing a toothy smile and waving them over with his stump of a hand.

"Do you know who we are?" Darnuir asked.

"What d'you take me for? I 'av one hand, not one eye."

"I'm just used to being formally addressed," said Darnuir.

"Ach, sorry, yer Lordship," the man said. "Lord Imar sent me. Cayn, at yer service." He bowed though it seemed almost in jest.

"Does Somerled have need of me?" Darnuir said.

"Lord Imar has prepared a special meal and invites you and yer Guard to join him."

"Special, you say?" Lira said. "God. We have a lot of hungry dragons here."

Cayn led them towards the heart of Dalridia, over the wide waterways that ran through the city like roads in any other. Islanders navigated these channels on scaled down longships, some rowing, and some propelling themselves forward by pushing a stick behind them into the shallow water. Smoke rose from the centre of each earthen hall or home but the light rain drove most of the smell away. Somerled Imar's own long hall was naturally the greatest. It had a second tier and glass windows, complete with a turf roof covered in bluebells.

"Here ye go, milord," said Cayn. "I'm sure ye can find yer way from here. I 'av tae fetch the other one."

"Does he mean Blaine?" Lira asked when he left.

"What a happy gathering that will be," Darnuir said.

He'd expected it to be dark and drab inside the hall. Instead, galleries of bottles of amber liquid lined the walls, reflecting grey light from the windows tenfold in a golden shine. Chunky tables sat before the bottle stacks, gouged with trenches for food. A fire pit at the centre warmed the hall and whole pigs crackled over the flames. The smell of cooking meat and fat filled the air.

"Darnuir!" boomed Somerled from across the hall, "Welcome, all of you. Please follow me." He swept his way into the semi-darkness at the far end of the hall. Darnuir and the Praetorians caught up with him and took their seats as directed. They squeezed around several tables in the shadow of a protrusion of rock which rose high above at a sharp angle. Smoothed steps were inlaid on the side of the rock to climb it.

Somerled clapped his hands and steaming dishes were brought to their table, although the meat was not what Darnuir had expected.

"Not pork?" he asked.

"That's for my men," Somerled said. "I've had my cooks prepare this specially for you."

What's so special about oversized chickens? Darnuir thought. For that's all the meal appeared to be. Enormous fat chickens, roasted perfectly with a golden skin, but that was it. And then the smell of it reached him. A sudden urge came over Darnuir to feed, to rip and tear and gorge. It wasn't a human feeling. His stomach rumbled desperately, and he swore he heard Lira's do the same. His head began to spin and he lunged for the meat with the rest of the dragons. He tore a leg off the bird, biting through the crispy skin, feeling the hot juice run down his chin as he plunged through the soft sweet meat to the bone. He ate so fast he barely tasted it.

Raymond looked disgusted. "May I request a knife and fork?" he asked of Somerled's staff.

"Glad ye all enjoyed that," Somerled told them.

Darnuir felt very satisfied. The sensation had been almost like a Cascade rush only without the side effects. If anything, he felt sleepy. A horrible thought came over him. *Have we been poisoned?* He shook his head and got to his feet to fight the tiredness.

"What did you put in that chicken?" he demanded.

"That isnae chicken," said Somerled. "It's capon."

"Oh…" Lira said in a dreamy fashion.

"Shall I have more brought out?" Somerled said. The Praetorians grinned and nodded slowly. Some started to rub their eyes. Others lay back, a hand on their stomach. Raymond looked at them all deeply confused and raised his fork to sniff suspiciously at his piece of capon.

"I'd say help yerself tae the whisky an' all but you lot cannae handle yer drink."

Darnuir blinked rapidly. "I found that one out the hard way."

"Would make you all a bit less sour-faced if you could." Somerled laughed at his remark.

"Some watered wine isn't so potent," said Darnuir.

"Then you better return to Brevia for that," said Somerled. "But 'am glad the meat is tae yer liking. A fine reward for saving my city, I dare say. Once Arkus' fleet arrives we'll relieve all of the Splinters!"

"How long will that be?" Darnuir said.

"Depends on how quickly they made it back to Brevia," said Somerled. "At least two weeks from now, maybe more."

To Darnuir, the thought of two weeks felt abominably long. He almost reached for the door in his mind there and then, but he felt more like having a nap.

"Perhaps I could have a word, Somerled?"

"Aye," Somerled said, a little unsure. Lira attempted to get up but only made it half way before her tired legs began to wobble.

"You can stay and eat," Darnuir said. Lira smiled stupidly as though drunk and sat back down.

What's come over us? I need to get out of here.

More capon was being served. Darnuir held his breath to try and avoid the smell. He walked as quickly as he could back outside. Once outside he began to cough and moved to steady himself on the chest high wall overlooking the waterway. He gulped in the cool air; it felt fresh and clean, and cleared the haze of capon from his mind.

"Feeling better?" Somerled asked.

"Care to explain how you've incapacitated my Praetorians with poultry?"

Somerled tapped his brow with a single finger. "We islanders hav'nae forgotten everything about yer kind. My father told me, and his father told him, that if dragons ever come visiting, feed 'em capon. Can't get enough of it he said. Seems to be true."

"I wasn't aware of that," Darnuir said, darkly.

"Nothin' sinister about it. Was that yer first time?" he added mockingly.

"It's not exactly a common dish in the Boreac Mountains," Darnuir said.

"Just thought it was something I could offer, seeing as ye don't drink. When you retake all the islands I'll roast up a whole flock of 'em."

"Ah, about that," Darnuir said. He thought it best to just have it out with him. "I plan to take my dragons east."

Silence.

Darnuir pressed on. "The demons have split their forces and I wish to seize this chance to take back Aurisha before they can regroup in full. Reinforcements will arrive from Brevia soon enough to aid in the retaking of the remaining islands, as you say."

"Soon enough," Imar repeated softly. He slumped over the wall, facing the water below. It rippled under the steady drip of rain.

"I understand your disappointment, Lord Imar but—"

"Can't yer homeland wait a few mer months? Only, and I hate tae mention it, but doing this might only inflame the opinions of those who think dragons only look out for themselves."

"I did not think you were one of those people," Darnuir said.

"Did I say I was?" said Somerled. "I don't despise yer kind, like some. Yet, I don't love you either." One of the little boats passed by then with a family on board; two small girls and a taller lad helping his father propel it along. The two young girls huddling against their mother, shivering in the light rain. The family smiled and waved to Somerled as they passed and he beamed back at them, all trace of disappointment vanishing in an instant from his face. When they passed, his features darkened again.

"They'll be off tae West Hearth, on the island of Nessay," Somerled said gravely. "On that wee boat, out tae our longships waiting for them. We've been sending people west fae months. My own wife is there along with many of my people. Wondering whether they will return home soon, or whether we'll fail and the carnage will reach them there."

"We won't fail," Darnuir said.

"I lost my father during the last war," Somerled went on, as though Darnuir had been silent.

"As did many," said Darnuir. "As did I." He neglected the fact that he could barely remember Draconess. Only the resentment and anger remained. "Rectar and his demons seek the destruction of us all."

"Seems that way," said Somerled. "And yet, when the dragons vanished, when you disappeared, so did the demons. Poof. Gone. Neither sight nor sound of them fae twenty years until you and yer people come back. Isn't that a coincidence?"

"Rectar was licking his wounds after the Battle of Demon's Folly," Darnuir said.

"So, it is just a happy accident?"

"As I do not know the will of Rectar, I cannot give you an answer."

"Perhaps it will be a good thing yer leaving," said Somerled. "Might be we're better aff without ye."

"I am sorry, Somerled."

"You will do as you will, of course. It is yer right."

"I won't be leaving you completely alone," Darnuir said. "Blaine will stay along with Light Bearers and the Third Legion."

"One whole legion?" Somerled mocked, placing a hand over his heart. "Bless the waves but that is kind."

"We smashed a good deal of the demon's strength here," Darnuir reminded him. "They may have more numbers spread across your islands, but not enough on any single island to hold for long; especially when the reinforcements from Brevia arrive."

"The Guardian is pleased with this plan, is he?" Somerled asked.

"I'll make sure of it," said Darnuir, sounding more confident than he felt. Blaine was always quarrelsome and on this issue, he was sure to put up a fight.

"Looks like now's yer chance," said Somerled. He nodded at something passed Darnuir. A group of Light Bearers were approaching Somerled's hall. "I invited them too."

"That's not Blaine," Darnuir said, looking at the dragon that led them. He met Bacchus' eye and they met in person front of the great hall. "Where is Blaine?"

"The Lord Guardian is *indisposed*," Bacchus said.

"He sent you in his place?"

"He sends no one," said Bacchus. "He talks to no one. He shirks his duties and holds up with that elderly dragon. But the work of the gods does not stop."

"And it's work to come for dinner?"

Bacchus sniffed the air and then his face distorted. He ran a hand through his curly black hair as though lost for words. "They would serve us such unclean food?"

"My roosters are well bred and well kept," Somerled said, puffing up.

"It leaves dragons lax and docile," said Bacchus. "It saps us of our strength and wits. It is unclean."

"I allowed my Praetorians to eat," said Darnuir. "Why not the Light Bearers too. They look hungry. Haven't they earned it?"

"You are not a godly dragon, sire, so I am not surprised. But my Light Bearers do not —"

"*Your* Light Bearers?" Darnuir asked. "Last I heard you weren't the Guardian." He stepped right up to Bacchus and his hand twitched near the hilt at his waist. *Oh, go on. Give me a reason. I beg you.*

"You seem a touch violent, sire," Bacchus said. Annoyingly, he remained so calm a fly would not have budged from his shoulder. "Perhaps an indication that you should not eat unsuitable food."

"Nae drinkin' and nae eating yerselves tae a stupor," Somerled said. "It's nae wonder yer all so cranky."

"Stay out of this Somerled," Darnuir said. He turned back to the Light Bearer. "Where is he?"

"Over there," Bacchus said, pointing to a smaller earthen hall closer to the sea.

"Then I shall go and see him now," Darnuir said.

"Dwl'or grant you strength, sire," said Bacchus. "Gods know the Lord Guardian needs it." He smiled next to Somerled. "Lord Imar, forgive my outburst, but your choice of dish caught me by surprise. I should have made dietary requirements of the faithful clear upon our arrival." Then he turned to the Light Bearers he'd brought with him. There were quite a lot of them, now that Darnuir considered it. "Let us pay respect to Dwl'or outside of the city. The woodlands of the Nail Head should offer some shelter from the rain." They marched off.

Darnuir found that his hand had taken hold of the Dragon's Blade without him even realising. Magic was lightly flowing down his arm. He let go, rung his arm, gently closed over the door in his mind, and spat out the bitterness before it grew.

Dukoona better give me a fight.

"I for one enjoyed the food, Somerled," he said. And with that, Darnuir left the Lord of Isles and made haste towards Blaine's hall.

Chapter 20

A MURKIER PAST

Schisms in dragon society have frequently centred on their religion. In each case, the orthodox has won, championing the true way since the time of Aurisha. That is how the Guardian Nhilus summarises it in his accounts written in 1504 AT. Yet, it is clear from the oldest sources available that a formal gathering at dawn was not always practised. The earliest evidence of this behaviour I can find is the year 1362 AT, two years after the quashing of a small sub-set of worshippers who gathered at the tip of the Tail Peninsula. Was this a new behaviour adopted by the Guardians in the aftermath? Perhaps adopted from the very sub-set they had destroyed? We cannot know but I am certain of this. Nothing has remained the same across all of time. Not even The Way of Light.

From Tiviar's Histories

Blaine – Dalridia

"He's coming, Lord Guardian," the Light Bearer announced.

"Bacchus?" Blaine said. "I told him to take service today."

"No, it is the King."

Blaine gulped. "Send him through." The Light Bearer disappeared, back to the main body of the hall, leaving Blaine and Chelos alone in their enclave. One grubby window let in some light and there was space enough for a bed for Chelos. It was tucked away and quiet, and right now Blaine valued that more than comfort.

"We couldn't keep our secrets forever, Blaine," Chelos said. He coughed and spluttered, struggling to regain his breath. Blaine helped him sit upright.

"It pains me to see you brought low like this," said Blaine. At least the room was warm. All that packed earth the islanders used certainly insulated well.

Chelos shrugged. "I'm old, Blaine."

"I'm older."

"Maybe, but I don't have the advantage of a magical sword and I've suffered much in a short space of time. Even a few years ago, I might have recovered more easily. But now…"

"Do not speak like you are doomed," Blaine said. "N'weer will revive you and you shall stride proudly in the Basilica of Light again."

"Won't that be something," Chelos wheezed.

"Have you lost faith?"

"Once you would have found the idea impossible. Are you having doubts?"

"About the gods? No. Never."

"But?" Chelos asked.

"Lately, I find myself wondering whether I am the right dragon to carry these burdens."

Chelos grumbled, pulling the bedsheets tighter around himself. "Draconess too had doubts towards the end." His eyes seemed to shrink away, as though lost in his own tortured memories. "Doubts about Darnuir, about himself, even you, though he'd never show them to anyone else. Never about the gods though, for all the good that did him."

"It sounds like you have lost faith," Blaine said.

"I say my prayers but I learned that faith won't shield me, nor the ones I love, from harm. I saw what Castallan could do. That was true power. And we know what Rectar is capable of. Perhaps our gods are just weak?"

"The gods do not fail us," said Blaine. "It is only we who fail them."

"Then there's been plenty of failure."

"Blaine?" Darnuir had entered their squat little room. His eyes glinted cat-like as he adjusted to the semi-darkness. "This is cosy."

"Get in here," Blaine said. He moved to the doorway as Darnuir shuffled inside. "Everyone is to move to the other end of the hall," he told the Light Bearers outside. "No one is to disturb us." He closed the door firmly shut. Darnuir had taken up Blaine's place at Chelos' side. "So, Darnuir, you've come to hear it all?"

Darnuir looked a little taken aback. "I came to see why you've shut yourself away and let that Bacchus fellow take charge of things. But yes, that as well."

"You asked me once to tell you everything," Blaine said. "I never intended to keep you in the dark forever. Only, there was so much to tell you, and I wasn't ready myself yet." He closed his eyes and felt his heart beat quicker. "Before we begin, know that everything I tell you is to do with our enemy. It is important. Everything I told you about the Champion's Blade; all of it."

"You said you only had suspicions," Darnuir said.

"The visit from Ochnic gave me fresh reason to believe," Blaine said. He fished up the necklace and briefly stared at the little silver 'A' before taking it off. He tossed it to Darnuir.

Chelos leaned over to stare at the necklace in Darnuir's hand. "It's not possible…"

"Who did this belong to?" Darnuir asked.

"It belonged to your father," Blaine said.

"I have no memory of Draconess wearing such a necklace," Darnuir said, squinting at the jewellery and turning it, as though it would reveal its secrets to him.

"It did not belong to Draconess," Blaine said, softly. Darnuir looked at him, perplexed; the faintest shadow of doubt flickering behind his eyes.

And so it begins.

"But you said it belonged to my—"

"Father, yes," Blaine finished. "Draconess, however, was not your father."

So complete was the silence that followed, Blaine thought he heard the worms burrowing within the earth.

"I — I was not expecting that," Darnuir said. "But what has that got to do with anything." Blaine buried his face in his hands.

Where am I to begin?

Darnuir went one. "Perhaps one of your memories would be useful?"

Blaine shook his head. "Memories must be captured in the gems as fresh after the events as possible. I didn't know that these things would become so important. Had I known, I might have been able to stop it. I shall recall as best I can and Chelos can help confirm it. But, as for the matter at hand, your real father was Drenthir, son of Dalthrak. Draconess was his younger brother: your uncle."

"Uncle…" Darnuir repeated quietly.

"That necklace was given to Drenthir by your mother," Blaine said. His voice was already beginning to falter. "Your mother, Arlandra. She was my daughter."

"So, you are — no," Darnuir said, his eyes widening in realisation. He slumped back in his chair, staring dumbstruck at Blaine. For the sake of Kasselle's privacy and dignity, Blaine left her out of it. It occurred to him that perhaps the drop of fairy blood in Darnuir's veins drew him to the Cascade so feverishly.

"Did you know of this?" Darnuir asked, rounding on Chelos.

"I did," Chelos said.

"And you kept this from me all of my first life? Why?"

"Because I asked him too," Blaine said. "Chelos is not to blame for any of this."

"We agreed to it, Blaine," said Chelos. "You, Draconess and I. We all agreed."

"You were barely as old as Darnuir is now," Blaine said. "You followed orders and served loyally."

"To what end?" Darnuir asked.

"Let me explain," Blaine said. "It was so long ago, back when the Black Dragons still lived in the lands around Kar'drun and in their own city. It was a brilliant city, in truth – as splendid as Aurisha has ever been. Too splendid and too strong some said, myself included.

"King Dalthrak, your other grandfather, was ageing, having enjoyed a full reign of peace with the Black Dragons. His line was safe in Drenthir and Draconess. Yet Draconess wanted to be more than merely second in line. I had recently inherited the mantle of Guardian and knew the royal family well. I encouraged Draconess to join my Light Bearers and he accepted. Chelos was very young but a faithful ward. You used to fetch the hot water for my morning shave, do you remember?"

"Of course," Chelos said. "I'll never forget how proud I felt. My parents too. Gods but I'd nearly forgotten I once had parents."

"At the same time," Blaine continued, "there was another dragon showing great promise in the ranks of the faithful. This was Kroener—"

Chelos spat at the mention of this name, narrowly missing Darnuir's boot. "Traitor," he said. "Blasphemer," he managed to add, before returning to a fit of coughs.

"Must you do that?" Darnuir asked. "If he is so hated then why does no one else know of him?"

"Because what happened was kept quiet," Blaine said. "Kroener was just a Light Bearer after all, not many knew of him. I was new to the role of Guardian, and with an ageing King, many extra burdens fell to me. When the time came for an inspection of the Black Dragons, I passed the responsibility on. Kroener was amongst the Light Bearers who travelled north."

"What do you mean by inspection?" Darnuir asked.

"Officially they were diplomatic visits," said Blaine. "In reality, we were ensuring the Black Dragons were complying with the treaty that had secured the long stability we were all enjoying. A certain term prohibited our Black Dragon cousins from raising and training soldiers beyond what was needed to keep order in their lands. Anything further would require the express permission of the Guardian and King in Aurisha. When Kroener returned from that mission, he informed us that the Black Dragons had violated that term. That they were raising a host and planned to make war on us."

"Was it true?" Darnuir asked.

"We thought it was," said Chelos. "Kroener gave a very convincing speech in the throne room. Do you remember, Blaine?"

"In here," Blaine said, tapping at the white opals on his sword.

Chelos sat straighter, seeming more animated. "I'll remember it always. 'Five days with the wind', he kept saying. 'Five days with the wind'. And then he held up an oversized fig." Chelos raised both his own hands in imitation. "It took both hands, so large it was. 'Here,' he said, 'is but one result of Black Dragon sorcery. Larger than life and too ripe. Only five days away with the wind.' Then he let it fall to smash upon the floor." There was almost admiration in Chelos' voice.

"And no one else could vouch for these claims?" Darnuir said. "You said it wasn't just Kroener who went."

"Only Kroener returned from that mission," Blaine said.

"A theme that continued with him," said Chelos.

"He claimed the rest of his party had been killed by the Black Dragons and that only he escaped," Blaine said.

"You think he lied?" Darnuir said.

"I do not know," Blaine said. "Either way we were whipped up into a frenzy. By then Dalthrak was growing ill and his days looked numbered. I stayed in Aurisha and Kroener and your father led the campaign against the Black Dragons. I remember Arlandra begging your father not to leave. She was pregnant with you. She begged him, and then she begged me to tell him to stay. 'You go instead,' she asked of me. 'You go'." The first tears began to distort Blaine's vision. "I — I can see her now, in my mind, in my head, for the first time in years. I hid all the memories away before because it hurt too much. But now I see her again, beseeching me."

The tears fell. He could not remember the last time he had cried. Not even when Kasselle had told him not to return; even then he had stayed strong. But not for this. He couldn't stand this. His nose twitched, turning visibly redder at the corner of his vision. His breath came in laboured, choked gulps.

"I should have gone," he went on. "I should have gone instead. But I told Arlandra that Drenthir had to go. He would be king soon and he had yet to be bloodied in battle; he still had to prove himself a leader… it's all my fault."

He allowed himself this grief. He had ignored it for long enough. Darnuir's face might have been made of stone. His eyes were fixated somewhere on Blaine's chest plate.

"You are not to blame," Chelos said. "You could not have known."

"But my own daughter," Blaine sobbed. "I could never deny her anything except for this. Why? Why did I do it?"

"I agree with Chelos," Darnuir said. "You could not have known."

Blaine breathed deeply, sniffed, and rubbed at his eyes. "Kroener and Drenthir went to war. The first reports were good. The Black Dragons were pushed back mile by mile, till their city fell. We all believed the war was over; a swift victory to put the Black Dragons back in line. And then more reports trickled in. Kroener had sewn salt into the soil. Kroener had ordered the legions to besiege Kar'drun, where the last Black Dragons had taken refuge.

"Months past and Kroener and Drenthir travelled into the Highlands, though to what end we did not know. Each report came with a different story. Then, word finally came. Kroener had returned from the Highlands, but not with your father. There was no word of him. I knew then that something was terribly wrong. I think your mother felt it too. Grief struck her despite the happiness of your birth, Darnuir. Perhaps when Drenthir died it echoed across the world to rake at her heart."

"And you think the necklace is proof that my father died in the Highlands," Darnuir said. He ran the silver chain through his fingers. "Do you think the Kazzek were involved?"

"Kazzek?" Chelos asked.

"Frost Trolls, friend," Blaine said.

"You encountered them?" Chelos asked. "I wouldn't be surprised if those beasts aided the traitor."

"They aren't beasts," Darnuir said. "No more than humans think dragons to be."

"For all I know, they might have been," said Blaine. "When I asked Ochnic, all he would say was 'Da chieftains know dis, not I'."

"Did you ask nicely? Or did you grunt and call him troll?" Darnuir asked. Blaine narrowed his eyes at the boy but it was Chelos who spoke.

"You should be more respectful," he wheezed. "Blaine is your equal."

"And so, I shall speak to him as I will," Darnuir said. "Cassandra loves you dearly Chelos and that speaks volumes. Don't give me a reason to find fault with you now. This tale is one of mistake after mistake, of bad assumptions and your Order gone wrong. Be on with it. I fear it will only get worse before the end."

Blaine did not have a rebuke this time.

This is not the same Darnuir I met at Torridon. And the more I tell him, the worse it will get. Still, I must go on.

The hardest truth of all for Blaine was that Darnuir might be right. Yet, like a poison, the past had to be drawn out.

"Without news of his son, King Dalthrak feared the worse," Blaine said. "His sickness deepened and Draconess and I began preparations for a regency. You were only a baby and, as you well know, the Dragon's Blade will not pass until you are of age. Even as we were deciding how to proceed, legion upon legion trudged back to Aurisha. Battered and spent, the legates told us that Kroener had demanded they travel with him into the depths of Kar'drun. When many refused, Kroener had called them heretics or Shadow sympathisers. Fighting broke out and those loyal to Kroener remained. Rumours spread that Kroener had an unnatural power since returning from the north."

"You think it was the Champion's Blade?" Darnuir asked.

"I'm sure it was," said Blaine.

"But how?" Darnuir said hoarsely. "How could he have been 'worthy'? And how does Rectar come into this?"

"Something must have happened when Kroener entered Kar'drun," Blaine said. "The Black Dragons always said that when one enters the mountain, someone else comes out."

Blaine's hands were shaking now. He clasped them together, rubbing them to try and ease the tremors.

"Arlandra stayed strong for you but I could tell a part of her had died," Blaine continued. Each word was a knife in him. "No smile could cover it up. I promised her I'd make Kroener pay if he was to blame. Then one night, without warning, he returned. He and his companions kept their faces covered with crimson hoods. When word reached me in the Basilica he had already entered the Royal Tower. I tore across the plaza but fighting had already broken out. When I arrived in your mother's room, you were gone. And Arlandra was. She was—"

"You don't have to talk about it, Blaine," Darnuir said.

"It's not quite what you think. I mourn still, of course, but the memory of that day is locked in my gem here." He pointed to the topmost white jewel on the hilt of the Guardian's Blade. "Whilst it is in there, I cannot remember the events other than as a vague impression, like the ghost of a dream."

"I remember what you told me," Chelos said from his corner. "How you confronted Kroener in the King's chambers. Darnuir was in his arms, you said. You must have just saved Dalthrak from being murdered."

"That's right, and as I tried to reason with him, he only said that, 'The one you see is dead. The child will be mine. I am Rectar. The Shadow will fall over your world'."

"And then you fought him," Chelos said, his voice a strange mix of youthful awe and hardened pain. "I watched you from up high in the Royal Tower."

"Down through the tower and out onto the plaza," Blaine said. "The hardest battle I have ever fought. Near enough killed me, drawing on that much Cascade. I thought I might break."

"Well, you didn't lose," Darnuir said.

"I didn't *win* either."

Darnuir leant forward and blew out his cheeks. "You think Kroener must have the Champion's Blade because he fought you to a standstill. Seems to me you could look into that memory of yours and see whether it is the right sword."

"I haven't relived it in such a long time," said Blaine. His hand was shaking so violently now that he could barely fumble his fingers on the gemstones.

"Stop," Darnuir said. "There's no need." He got to his feet, moved to Blaine's side and took his hand in a firm grip. "What happened after this duel?"

"I returned to Dalthrak's side. Draconess was there, injured from the battle in the Royal Tower, but not fatally so. I summoned Chelos to attend as well."

"A witness to the King's Will," Chelos said.

"Only it wasn't *exactly* the will of the King, was it?" Darnuir said. He did not break eye contact and Blaine held it. It was a punishing stare with barely room to breathe between them.

"No, it wasn't," Blaine said. "Dalthrak wished for a standard regency. Draconess would have the Dragon's Blade until you came of age and no longer. Whilst Draconess had the sword its power would naturally dim, as it was not in the hands of the rightful king. Yet, rather than the Blade simply passing upon your twentieth year, we altered the wording so that Draconess would hold onto the sword—"

"Until such time as my rightful heir is fit to rule," Chelos recited. "More open to interpretation. Dalthrak sealed it with a drop of his blood."

Blaine sniffed and tried to fight back more tears. "The Blades are linked. I hoped that by weakening the Dragon's Blade I would also weaken the Champion's Blade, and thus Rectar. I took the armour of the King with me. For without the full power of a Blade, Draconess couldn't wear it. I thought it would buy us some time, and prepare you."

"It might have," said Darnuir, "but it may also have dragged out the war. Why did Draconess not pass the sword along? Why put such a condition on my receiving it?"

"Because we had been wrong about Kroener," Blaine said. "I had, Dalthrak had, Draconess had, and many legions of dragons had. I should have known better than to let one with such a temperament take charge of any army. We had to see whether you would do better."

"Draconess raised you in the Light of Dwna, Dwl'or and N'weer," said Chelos. "But you proved resistant to the teachings. A hot-headed, rebellious young man."

"Was there ever a time when Draconess considered granting me the sword?"

"There was an occasion or two…" Chelos said. "I think he despaired of ever passing the Blade along after the incident with Castallan. That is when Draconess gave up, I think."

"You knew about that, did you?" Darnuir asked.

"One of the few," said Chelos. "Draconess confided in me, but even I lost touch with him during those final years. He spent more time in the Basilica than anywhere else, praying day and night."

"And your gods never came," Darnuir said. "And you did not come back," he added, jostling Blaine with his free hand. Blaine lowered his head, utterly drained. He felt more exhausted than after the battle at the Bastion. And yet, a portion of the crushing weight he had carried all these years seemed lifted.

Darnuir was frowning. Blaine assumed the King would scold him but when Darnuir spoke, there was the softer touch of a grandson in his voice.

"It seems to me you have been punishing yourself for eighty years. Isn't that long enough?" And for the first time, Darnuir embraced him. A true hug, if a little awkward in their armour. "I'll need you before the end. We all will."

Blaine tried to speak but the tears rolled faster and he hiccupped while trying to draw breath.

"I'm taking our legions east," Darnuir said. He pulled away from Blaine but still held his hand firmly. "The spectres have split their forces and the demons with them. I'm going to seize Aurisha while we have the chance and before the wilder winter winds come."

"I will prepare the Light Bearers," Blaine said.

"No," Darnuir said. He was not angry, just firm. "You will stay with the Third to help the humans in retaking the Splintering Isles. Come east when you are done."

"I would fight to retake our city," said Blaine. "Our holy city. I must—"

"Enough," said Darnuir. He raised a hand towards Chelos to prevent him speaking as well. "This time I don't want to hear it."

"Why are you so insistent I stay?" Blaine said.

Darnuir hesitated. "We owe the humans our help. It will go a long way in showing our continued support if the Guardian himself remains to fight."

"That's not the real reason," Blaine said. He'd held back the whole truth for long enough to know when someone else was lying. "Don't go chasing a fight. Don't do what Kroener did."

"You will stay," Darnuir said. As he let go of Blaine's hand, Blaine noticed Darnuir's was shaking. It was only a little, but enough to worry Blaine. His eyes were blinking quickly too.

"You're not well," Blaine said.

"We can't both be absent," Darnuir said. He placed his unsteady hand on the Dragon's Blade and his whole body relaxed. "I'll await you at Aurisha, grandfather." The King moved to the door and pulled it open. Fresh air reached Blaine's face like a splash of cold water. Before he left, Darnuir looked over his shoulder. "Kasselle is my grandmother, isn't she? That's why you hid there for so long."

"She is," Blaine said.

I don't think you should come back...

"I am sorry, Blaine," Darnuir said. Then he left.

A week after Darnuir left, the first of Arkus' forces, along with Fidelm'
fairies arrived, having retaken the island of Skelf en route. Blaine found
himself attending a celebratory feast in Somerled Imar's great hall.

"Tae retaking our lands!" cried the Lord of the Isles.

"Tae retaking our lands!" the cheering crowd responded. Each
islander, man and woman, raised a glass and drained a dram of whisky.
Imar himself stood atop the outcrop of rock, nodding happily as he let
the furore die down.

The humans were growing wilder with each toast. Many dragons
in attendance were slow on capon, slumped forwards with glazed eyes.
Somerled had not offered it to Blaine and the Light Bearers. Further down
the table, Bacchus held a lively court with some of Blaine's best men. Those
closer to Blaine were all taking short shallow breaths to try and avoid the
alluring smell of the capon, Blaine included. The heat didn't help. The
air was close and so thick with the smell of alcohol it felt strangling. His
white linen shirt clung to him with sweat.

The roaring of the humans finally quietened.

"With the help of our neighbours from the mainland, of course,"
Somerled continued. "And the fairies and the dragons as well. We should
make a toast to 'em." He looked towards Blaine. "Lord Guardian, might
ye join me?"

The hall burst into a murmuring of agreement at this request. Few of
the dragons joined in, being so content with their meal. Nor did the Light
Bearers at his table react much, forcing themselves to maintain composure.
Bacchus leaned forward, watching Blaine with a hawkish interest.

I'm still the Guardian, boy.

Blaine rose and walked over to the base of the rock. He'd entertain
Somerled this novelty, even if he disliked the man. Serving up roasted
rooster was a threat in Blaine's eyes; not a treat like some dragons felt. But
he'd hold his tongue for the sake of the relationship between their people.
Darnuir was right on that much, they needed humanity's help now. More
than Blaine cared to let Imar know.

"There's a good sport," Somerled said as Blaine rounded the base of
the rock and ascended the carved steps. He gave Imar the benefit of the
doubt. He was probably feeling the effects of all that whisky.

Blaine had visited the Splinters only a few times in his past, but he'd never been on top of the rock before. He first noticed that Somerled was barefoot, his feet wedged into two smooth gouges in the stone. It was the ancient coronation site of the Splintering Isles. Barefoot in the rock, it connected their kings to the land and the people.

But there is no king of the Isles anymore, only a lord who is subject to the rule of another throne.

Somerled was beaming at him.

"The dragons helped save this city and our home," Somerled said. "Now they fight fer their homes, their lands. From body to rock to land to sea, I wish their King the very best o' luck on the battlefield."

The islanders thumped their tankards approvingly.

"But the Lord Guardian remains to help us in our endeavours. His very purpose is tae rid the world of these wee devils. Why, with him and his Light Wielders—"

"Bearers," Blaine muttered.

"We shall drive the demons off our islands. Send them running back tae Kar'drun. The war shall be over before winter!"

Blaine forced a smile as another round of drinking ensued. The arrival of Fidelm and ten flyers caught Blaine's attention. They looked so small from up here. He leant in closer to speak quietly to Somerled.

"If I may excuse myself?"

"Be my guest," Somerled said in a hushed voice. Blaine turned and was about to descend the steps when Somerled lightly grabbed his arm. "You will sail as soon as possible, yes?"

"As soon as we have the full contingent of Arkus' fleet," Blaine said. He shrugged his arm free. "Fidelm thinks it another week at most."

"Grand," Somerled said. "Waves be at yer back."

Blaine nodded curtly then took the steps two at a time and swept through across the hall. Fidelm met him halfway.

"Enjoying yourself?" Fidelm asked.

"Immensely," said Blaine.

"I hope Somerled realises we aren't ready yet," said Fidelm.

"He does," said Blaine. "He is just eager to capitalise on your victory on Skelf."

"That was barely a fight," said Fidelm. "The demons were fleeing the island as we arrived. Heading east. Oh look," he said, nodding towards the tables of Light Bearers. "Some of your men are trying to subtly look at you without drawing attention to themselves."

Blaine looked back. Bacchus was on his feet, talking to two whole tables at once.

"I shall deal with this," said Blaine. "Enjoy the feast, Fidelm."

So many Light Bearers were listening to Bacchus that they didn't notice Blaine returning and he caught the end of the speech. "...doesn't seem capable anymore. We can't afford to lose the Lord Guardian so perhaps—"

"Don't worry," Blaine said. "You haven't lost me. I'm right here." The Light Bearers' reactions were mixed. Some looked guilty, some looked frightened, and others still bore hard expressions as though bracing themselves for battle. "Bacchus seemed to have you all enthralled there," Blaine added with as much injected confidence as he could muster. Truth was, he was worried by Bacchus' growing appeal.

I might wield the Blade, but I no longer wield their hearts.

"Lord Guardian," Bacchus began. "We are your Light Bearers. We look out for the faith and you are the figurehead of our belief. I was only hoping to express my concern that your recent wounds and hardships might have left you fatigued. Your leg at Inverdorn, the strain you endured in bravely storming the Bastion walls, and enduring our faithless King with such patience. And, as I was hoping to convey to my brothers, there would be no need for you to place yourself in harm's way in the coming battles merely out of obligation. You're too important for that."

"Are you insinuating that I am too weak or old?" *How could they do this to me?*

"Certainly not, Lord Guardian," Bacchus said. His tone was impeccable. Unreadable. Undeniably powerful. "You have carried burdens for longer than any of us can dream. I only suggest that you might wish to delegate some more of those duties, such as—"

"Such as entering battle?" Blaine snapped. He glared at each Light Bearer. He didn't have Bacchus' gift of speech, so he drew the Guardian's Blade and enhanced his voice for sheer volume. "I am not as old and done as you think." With a little help from the Cascade he jumped unnaturally high and landed upon the nearest table. Plates and tankards went flying. The entirety of the great hall was paying attention now.

"That's not what I saw at the Bastion," Bacchus said, his silky voice faltering ever so slightly.

"To lose faith in me is to lose faith in the gods," Blaine said.

He'd neglected a few matters of late, but nothing to deserve this. He was the Guardian. He could barely remember life before he had been the Guardian. And he had no life beyond it. No family. No lover. Only one old sick friend. Darnuir was his flesh and blood, but he was as much a stranger as anyone in this room.

He raised the Guardian's Blade and lit the metal of the sword until those nearby were forced to cover their eyes. This was what he had. This was all he had.

"Allow me to rekindle your faith in me," Blaine said. "The Third Legion will sail for Eastguard tomorrow. Will we break the demons under the light Dwna, Dwl'or and N'weer. All those who wish to sail with us may do so."

Fidelm was running over, waving his hands in protest. Across the hall Somerled Imar got on top of his own table and raised another glass.

"Ah ha, there's the fightin' spirit of the dragons. Tae retaking our lands!" His son, Grigayne, threw back his tankard with a grim expression.

Blaine drank in the atmosphere. He only hoped that he was right. He prayed the gods really did favour him.

Dwl'or grant me strength. Every ounce of it you can give.

Chapter 21

LORD BOREAC'S MANOR

Since the unification of the Kingdom of Brevia with the Splintering Isles, human nobles have continued to compete; not through war but instead through the size of their manor homes. When space ran out in the Velvet Circle, the ornateness of the stonework or design of the garden took over. More recently, size has come back into competition, specifically in how large a Lord or Lady might make their windows. I theorise this constant need for renovation is also due to picking a permanent place to live, rather than roam, as fairies do. You must keep changing your home or else you'll grow bored with it.

From Tiviar's Histories

Cassandra – Brevia – The Velvet Circle

CASSANDRA EASED HER way through the gathering crowds by the water's edge. Balack was making his rounds of the city, Arkus proudly by his side. Today, they were touring along the northern embankment and near the wealthy Velvet Circle. This worked well for Cassandra's needs, for it drew most people to Balack and left the district quiet. Queen Orrana had acquired a set of black leathers worn by Crownland Hunters for her to wear. Cassandra was now black from boots to shoulder guards, with only her skin and the delicate white trim on the leather showing any other colour. She felt it suited her. Kymethra, however, was not as pleased.

"This is mighty uncomfortable," the witch whispered as they skimmed around a group of plump nobles. "It's all tight and constricting. How can they sleep in this?"

"I think the idea is you'll be too tired to care," Cassandra said. She smiled broadly at a passing couple that were wrapping scarves around each other against the autumn breeze. Once the couple passed, Cassandra let her smile fall. She had to keep up the pretence of a dutiful peacekeeper, but her cheeks already ached from today's forced grins alone. She was growing real sympathy for Queen Orrana's unique plight.

Her plight might become my own soon enough.

"Did you give Orrana my right measurements?" asked Kymethra.

"I thought you wanted to help me?" Cassandra said.

"I do," said Kymethra. "Doesn't mean I have to wear something that makes me itch in unflattering places."

This can't all be about the leathers.

"Are you sure you're ready to leave him?" Cassandra asked.

"For the last damn time, yes," said Kymethra, though her voice was a touch higher than normal. "There's nothing more that can be done. Brackers is in fine care. All I can add is a bit of soothing magic if he takes a turn, but the fits have calmed now so... Oh, let's just hunt down the bastards who helped cause this." She stopped picking at her leathers and settled into a stride beside Cassandra.

They finally made it through the crowds and into the Velvet Circle proper. Manor after manor rose along the wide paved streets.

A carriage clopped loudly towards them, likely heading down to the hubbub of Balack's rally. The horses dropped their leavings along the way; a stain on an otherwise spotless street. It barely had a chance to smell before a team of boys dashed from the nearest manor armed with spades, sloshing buckets, coarse brushes and thick brown gloves. By the time Cassandra and Kymethra passed them the street was clean once more.

"Remind me again why we are paying Lord Boreac's manor a visit?" Kymethra asked. "Your father already had it picked clean of anything worthwhile."

"That's what he's has been told but we have no real idea of how deep Castallan's networks ran. He needs someone he can trust to hunt Boreac down."

"And you're the best he's got?" Kymethra said. "I mean no offence, but it seems a little desperate."

"You don't think I can manage it?"

"I just think this could be dangerous," said Kymethra. "I didn't think Arkus would want to put you in harm's way having only just gotten you back."

"He didn't. I insisted. I find Boreac for him and he won't push a marriage on me."

"Well, at least you know how to use that sword," Kymethra said.

"I'm not looking for a reason to use it."

Lord Boreac's manor was easy to find, for it was the one with half its contents spilling out onto its now untended gardens.

"I swear that one is snoring," Kymethra said, flicking her eyes towards one of the soldiers posted at the gates. They wore chainmail over simple boiled leather, with short spears that looked fierce enough, but would be no match for a sword in close quarters. They weren't asleep, Cassandra saw, but they were far from alert.

"Good day," Cassandra announced loudly.

One snapped his head in bemusement at her. "Who are you?"

"Here to help with the clean out," Cassandra said. "Captain Horath's orders." She'd learned the names of a few key members of the Crownland Hunters, but not much beyond. For these two she hoped nothing more would be required.

"Horath was it?" said the other guard, a little dimly. "Didn't he send a message already that we weren't to let anyone else in?"

"I dun' think so, Rob," said the first guard.

"Nat, you can't remember what you ate for breakfast," said Rob.

"Course I can," said Nat. "Bit of watered down porridge, ain't it? Every bleedin' day. Not got much choice with them dragons piling up outside the city, taking all our food."

"True," grumbled Rob.

"Captain Horath made it clear this job was to be done promptly," Cassandra said. She took a step in between the guards.

"Hold it right—" but Nat's words died in his throat. His face glazed over, as did Rob's. They both looked as though they were supremely contented. "Sure," Nat said, his voice wrapping luxuriously around the word. "Go along in."

"Heh," giggled Rob. "No issue."

Confused but not wanting to question her turn in fortune, Cassandra walked into the estate grounds. About halfway to the front door she turned to check on Kymethra. The witch was right behind her, grimacing and shaking her arm as though she were drying it.

"What did you do to them?" Cassandra asked.

"Soothed them," said Kymethra. "Same as I do to Brackendon when he takes his turns. I hit them with a stronger blast of it to move us along. Dranus but I'm thirsty now."

"I thought it was for taking away pain?"

"Numbs everything," Kymethra said. "Including thought. Don't go getting ideas now, it isn't that strong, just a trick. Those two might not have had a full head put together. I didn't even have to touch their heads like I normally—" Kymethra stopped suddenly and looked past Cassandra. There was a creaking of a hinge and Cass turned to see the doorway to the estate open ajar, with a thin woman in a simple pale blue apron looking suspiciously out at them.

"I thought you lot were done?" she said. Her voice gave away that she was a little afraid, trying to cover it up through indignation. "None of us know where he's gone."

"We're sorry to disturb you," Cassandra said. "We just need to ask some more questions. Take a final look around."

"Can't get away from you hunters," the woman mumbled as she pulled back into the manor. Cassandra took that as a cue that she should follow.

The hallway was bare although signs of wealth were evident from the lighter patches on the wall where paintings or tapestries had been hung, while scratch marks along the oak floor showed where furniture had been roughly dragged outside.

"Can I take your cloaks?" the woman asked briskly. "I'm still the head of this household after all. No reason I can't show common courtesy."

Cassandra unfastened her own black cloak and handed it over.

"Thank you, um…"

"Olive, dear," the woman said. "Thought they might have passed along our names at least. Aren't we under investigation and all that?" She took Kymethra's cloak a little gruffly. "Are you okay?"

Cassandra wondered that as well. Kymethra was breathing heavily, her cheeks were flush, and she held her right arm tightly against her side.

"I wouldn't mind some water," Kymethra said dryly.

"Bit hot under those leathers," Olive said knowingly. "Even in the Boreacs I saw them sweat at times. Come through to the kitchens then and may my cooperation show you that the staff and I have nothing to hide."

"Where are the staff?" Cassandra asked. The manor was eerily quiet. Their feet echoed with every step.

"Keeping to themselves mostly," said Olive, leading them down the empty hallway. "Since Lord Boreac took off and armed Chevaliers came bursting in looking for him, everyone has been suspicious of each other. No one wants to be marked a traitor."

"King Arkus has offered a general clemency," Cassandra said.

"So I've heard," Olive said. She turned into a narrow corridor winding to the back of the house and into the extensive kitchens. It felt cold. Not an oven was on, not a cook in sight. Copper pots and pans were stacked up in the basin. Cold grease and mould scented the air. Olive sighed. "Such an embarrassment. Twenty staff used to work here day and night. Often Lord Boreac threw parties for hundreds at a time. And now this."

"I'm sorry for your loss," Cassandra said, although she limited her sympathy. This head of the household could be a traitor for all she knew.

"There's a jug of water by the basin there," Olive said to Kymethra. "The mugs are kept—"

"Won't be needing a mug," Kymethra said, darting to the jug and taking great draughts straight from it. Olive looked startled.

"She's a good bet for drinking games at the station," Cassandra said. "Now, I wonder if I might begin."

"Fine, fine," Olive said. She went to sit down at the servants' rather dirty table and waited expectantly. Cassandra sat opposite her and pushed a plate of mouldy cheese away.

"As head of the household, you must have known Lord Boreac well?" Cassandra asked.

"Well enough," Olive said. "Five years of service, after all. I've already gone through this."

"Please, just answer the questions," Cassandra said. "So, was there ever any odd behaviour?"

"Only in hindsight, I suppose," Olive said. "Back in the spring, a messenger came all flustered, talking about some woman named Morwen over and over. Boreac told him to be quiet, ushered him into his study, then dismissed me. He kept everyone out of his study for hours. After that, he was always a little more on edge, but I would never have guessed he was part of some conspiracy against the throne."

"Morwen you said, not Captain Morwen of the Golden Crescent Hunters?"

"Might be," Olive said. "He got cross when I asked."

That was very interesting news to Cassandra. What was it she had heard one day in Val'tarra? Some burly huntress had claimed that Morwen's body had been found with both human and spectre corpses around it. Morwen had been concerned about a strange black powder being found in shipments that were meant to be fruit from the fairies. Why was Boreac so interested in that?

"Is that the only time you saw him concerned?" Cassandra asked. Olive nodded, looking annoyed already. "How was he behaving while his lands were under attack from Castallan's demons for almost a year?"

"They were — what?" Olive asked, suddenly alert.

"You didn't know?" Cassandra asked.

"None of you lot told me that before," Olive said, sounding frightened. "Tell me. What happened?"

"Why is that such a concern to y—"

"Just tell me."

"Okay," Cassandra said. "The Boreac Mountains are deserted. Its people now are either refugees or dead."

"Dead?" Olive mouthed silently. She ran her bony hands through her thinning hair.

"No one really knew," Kymethra said, coming to join them at the table. "Not up in the capital anyway. Boreac might have been in on it himself if he'd thrown in with Castallan."

"But see this," Olive said, getting a flyer out of her pocket. "This Balack of the Boreac Mountains. This 'Hero of the Bastion', I used to take care of him back when I lived there. It can't be so bad. Or is this all some lie?" She looked desperate as she flung the paper down. It landed upside down and Cassandra reached for it, turning it back up. She had seen these flyers all around the city, proclaiming in large thick print to:

Join Balack, the Hero of the Bastion! Come dockside to hear the story of the great battle in the south where humanity triumphed when dragons failed!

Down in the bottom corner was a picture of a black quill dripping ink onto the words: Tarquill Prints.

"It's no lie," Cassandra said. *Though the real hero is lying broken and deranged in the palace.* She placed a hand on Kymethra's arm and caught her eye to prevent her saying anything. *We mustn't seem to know too much.*

"You raised the Hero of the Bastion?" Cassandra said, feigning awe. *She must know the others too. Darnuir, Cosmo, all of them.*

"It was years ago," Olive said, her hardened demeanour crumbling by the second. "I'd doubt he'd remember me. Don't think I'll be able to help you win any favours or gain an introduction. Although, it would be good to see someone from the Boreacs again. My sister Grace is still there… or she was still there. If all this has happened — Oh, I should have known something wasn't right when her letters stopped; but then I knew she had a baby on the way, and I was so busy here…" she rambled.

The mention of Grace caused another look to pass between Cassandra and Kymethra, an unspoken agreement that there would be no need to mention her death to Olive. Not here and now, at any rate.

"This must be distressing for you," Cassandra said, interrupting Olive in full flow.

Olive sniffed. "It's just another thing to worry about."

"I can only imagine," Cassandra said. "Look, if you answer my questions, I'll make enquiries about your sister."

"Would you?" Olive said. "That's very kind, dear. Very well. Go ahead."

"We'll try not to be too long," Cassandra said. She smiled encouragingly at Olive before starting. "We're obviously interested in any close associates he might have had, people who might be harbouring him. Was there any place Lord Boreac might visit frequently? Friends in the city or country who he might have gone to?"

"Lord Boreac preferred to play host rather than be a guest," Olive said. "He rarely left the city. Said his back hurt too much in someone else's bed. Lord Annandale would visit when he came to the capital, but we know why that is now. The only other person who came around regularly was that hunter. Tall, sinewy fellow. Scythe, I think."

"Scythe?" Cassandra and Kymethra said together.

Olive was taken aback. "Is he a bloody traitor too?"

"I'm afraid we can't discuss that," Kymethra said.

"So, he was then," Olive said. "Curse those men. I built up a reputation, and now no one will hire me. What a waste."

"I understand this is frustrating for you," Cassandra said, hoping to keep Olive focused. "But the quicker we get through this the quicker we'll leave you be."

"Leave me be all on my own. A big empty house and nothing to do anymore," Olive moaned.

Cassandra pressed on. "When was the last time you saw Scythe?"

"Hmm, oh would've been when Captain Tael stopped by. About a year ago." The name wasn't familiar to Cassandra, though she assumed this Tael had been the Boreac Captain before Scythe. "Yes, that was it," Olive continued. "Tael was here, asking Boreac for more hunters, and I guess now I know the reason for that too. Actually, something odd did happen that night."

"To whom?" Cassandra asked.

"To me," Olive said. "That Scythe fellow came looking for me, to talk to me. He'd never so much as said more than his food and drink order before."

"Why?" Cassandra said.

"Just to talk," Olive said. "Nothing in particular, just a bit about me, where I came from, my time in the Boreacs. That sort of thing."

"No specifics?" Cassandra asked.

Olive sighed. "Look it was nearly a year ago, but I suppose he kept trying to worm conversation back to the children I took care of with Grace – the boys in particular, and then the youngest. I didn't know why he was so interested in Balack and Darnuir, but there you go. Well, look what Balack turned out to be, eh."

Cassandra stared at Olive, trying not to look too incredulous or give anything away.

Lord Boreac really did a job of keeping news from you, didn't he?

"Anything more?" Cassandra asked.

"No, that was it. Never saw the man again. Probably dead now I imagine," Olive added. There was a stilted moment of protracted silence during which faint taps and creaks echoed overhead. Olive looked up. "That'll be Milly, the maid. Pacing around again poor lamb. She only started here a month before all this horribleness."

"Unfortunate timing," Kymethra said.

"Will you be needing to speak to the staff as well?" Olive asked.

"It may not be necessary," Cassandra said. "I'm sure they have been through enough." Olive pursed her lips and nodded approvingly. "However, there is one last thing. When Lord Boreac fled, was he in a hurry and what did he take with him?"

"I wouldn't have known he was leaving for good the way he just rushed out the door," Olive said. "He got a letter I remember, took it upstairs. Next thing I knew he was bolting out the door. Barely had his evening cloak strapped on. Went without even a goodbye." She sounded hurt at the memory.

Olive had called her time here a waste and Cassandra couldn't help but agree.

At least I have a way out. A way I can make things better. But she won't be able to bring back the dead.

"I think that will be all for now," Cassandra said. She'd gotten enough out of Olive to be going on with. "Perhaps we could inspect Lord Boreac's study?"

"Your lot already took everything away," Olive said, but she got to her feet all the same.

Cassandra shrugged. "Captain's orders." She rose too, as did Kymethra, and they followed Olive out of the kitchen to a servants' staircase hidden away from the main hallway. They climbed to the second floor where the corridor sliced a neat row of rooms in two. It was as bare as the hallway downstairs and a little dusty. As they walked, one of the room's occupants poked his head out from behind the doorframe; an old man, possibly in his sixties with a white moustache.

"Back in Perkins," Olive said. "They won't be long." She shooed at him as though he was some unwanted dog. The old man pulled back behind the door and closed it with a click. "The butler," Olive muttered. "Of all of them, I'd trust him the least."

"Mmm," Cassandra hummed but said nothing more. Castallan might be dead, but his legacy of distrust would linger on for years.

"Here you are," Olive announced as they arrived at the end of the corridor. "You can let yourselves out when you're done I imagine?" She did not wait for an answer before she shuffled off down another bare hallway, around the corner and out of sight.

"Poor thing," Kymethra said. She gave the door a good nudge and it swung open with a thud. They both stepped inside Lord Boreac's office. Drawers lay torn from their desks and cabinets, ink stained the floorboards and blank paper was strewn everywhere. A fireplace lay cold. "Doesn't leave much for us to go on," Kymethra said. "Don't know what you expect to find here."

"Any clue would be useful," Cassandra said. She started feeling along the walls, tapping with her knuckles at intervals. "By the sounds of it, Lord Boreac left in a hurry. That suggests he wasn't planning on leaving. That suggests to me that he felt safely unconnected to Annandale, Castallan and that whole mess by not having some sort of plan of escape."

"So, what in that letter could have given him such a fright?" Kymethra asked.

"I've no idea," Cass said. "Maybe news that Castallan had been defeated? He might have believed that Castallan really would prevail. Enough people seemed to think so." She paused over another likely spot and rapped her knuckles against it. She tutted in annoyance. *Nothing on this side.*

"What are you doing?" Kymethra asked.

"Checking for compartments or other secret openings."

"The hunters and chevaliers picked the place clean, don't you think they would have already found one?"

"They might not have been looking," Cassandra said. "I used to check every new room of the Bastion I visited." She moved along the next wall, towards the fireplace.

"Boreac likely took anything vital with him," Kymethra said.

"Although Olive said he bolted with barely his cloak clasped on," Cassandra said.

"Alright," Kymethra said. "Boreac can't have been planning on going far then."

"I do think he is still in the city, perhaps with a nobleman who is hiding him," Cassandra said. "His lands are in ruins. The south is under martial law by thousands of Arkus' soldiers. The Golden Crescent is in disarray as are the Cairlav Marshes. Maybe he could have travelled north to the Hinterlands, but Orrana's father is too tied in with Arkus to make the region safe for Boreac. That leaves just the Crownlands and the capital, and I'd wager on the capital."

"But who would take him in?" Kymethra said. "A whole city of people. We need to narrow that down."

"We certainly do," Cassandra said. The third wall was an outer one with two windows, so she doubted there would be anything hidden there. She moved to the final wall behind Kymethra. "You could do something, Kymethra."

"Like what?" Kymethra said, lightly kicking an upended chair to one side. "Nothing here unless you find some secret stash." She began pacing across the study.

This probably isn't distracting her much from her other worries. Please let there be something here.

Cassandra needed a clue to move forwards – one person, one name, one place – anything to point to where Boreac might have fled at the eleventh hour. Halfway along the final wall and her hopes were not high. From the corner of her eye, she saw that Kymethra had settled into a regular patrol of a few square metres.

"When we find him, he'll be sorry," she grumbled. Her steps grew heavier as she paced and the floorboards groaned louder.

Creak, creak, creak, crik.

"Thinks he can get away with it…" Kymethra muttered darkly.

Creak, creak, creak, crik.

The final wall that Cassandra tried proved fruitless. She sighed. She'd have to move onto the floor.

Creak, creak, creak, crik.

"Kymethra, take a step back will you?" Cassandra asked. The witch did so without question.

Crik.

"There," Cassandra said, pointing under Kymethra's black boot. "You've only gone and found the spot." She got down onto her knees. The floorboard seemed well stuck in place. Determined, Cassandra ran her fingers lightly over its surface and along every grain until, at last, she found a thumb size patch that did not conform to the rest of the wood.

This is it.

Her nail caught on the edge of it, digging down a fraction, and then she pulled up the small block, which enabled her to get her hand under the panel and lift it up. Triumphantly, she gazed down and saw a small, bronze strong box.

"Well pluck my feathers," Kymethra said.

Cassandra lunged in for it. "It's quite heavy," she said, puffing as she brought it out onto the floor. She dropped it down with a great thud, and the lid rattled loosely. It was already unlocked.

"Looks like Boreac might have had the time to grab something, but not the time to lock it up again," Kymethra said.

Gingerly, Cassandra opened the strongbox fully. It was empty save for a tiny dark grey ball, which had rolled into one corner. There didn't seem to be room for much inside; perhaps a ledger full of illicit notes could have been slotted in. She picked up the little grey ball.

"What is this?"

"Give it here," said Kymethra. Cassandra passed it over and Kymethra rolled it between her fingers, took a closer look at it and then licked it. Cass raised one eyebrow.

"What?" Kymethra said. "We had to get to know materials for alchemy back at the Conclave. Not that anything more effective than a cough syrup was ever brewed. This is lead, by the way."

"Lead?" Cassandra said. "Doesn't help me much. I'll hold onto it though. Whatever it is, Boreac thought it was important enough to store in a strongbox."

"And take with him when he left," Kymethra said. "I suspect there were far more of these in there."

"Agreed," said Cassandra. She got to her feet, stretched her arms above her head and then let them fall limply. She felt thoroughly deflated. Finding Lord Boreac was not going to be a simple thing at all. Her gaze landed on the fireplace. Back in Chelos' room, it was the bricks of the mantelpiece that opened up the secret passageway. But she was learning that not every large building would have such hidden ways. Yet something about the fireplace itself made her linger on it. There was quite a bit of ash and there were larger white chunks in it. She took a few steps closer.

"He burned some papers," Cassandra said.

"Didn't do a good job of it," Kymethra noted. "He was in a hurry though, I suppose. Likely just ripped the sheets a few times then tossed them in."

"The fire might have already been dying when he did it," Cassandra said. She began rifling through the ashes. She held up a scrap, but all that could be seen on it was a few words, which were meaningless on their own. "Not much to go on though. What was so important to burn? And what was so urgent he had to leave without making sure the job was done properly?"

"Cassandra," Kymethra said excited, pulling out a much larger strip of soot-stained paper. Her eyes ran animatedly over the short piece. "I think this could be from the letter that Olive mentioned."

Cassandra picked it delicately out of Kymethra's hands, hoping it wouldn't crumble away. There was a broken sentence buried under the dirt, the words hastily scrawled.

... I'm unsure about our options. Come to the Station now. R.F.

"R.F.," Cassandra said. It wasn't much, but the initials gave her something to go on. And better still she had a place too. "Looks like we'll be paying the Master Station a visit."

Chapter 22

A FATHER'S PLEA

Garon – The Highlands – West of the Glen of Bhrath

"**F**EELS COLDER TONIGHT," Garon said, as he pressed his face into his fur-lined collar to shield his nose. He had reattached warmer pieces of his leathers.

"Dis is not real cold," Ochnic said. He was crouched down amongst the flora and heather, rocking on the tips of his toes and fidgeting with his dagger.

"Aye, yer right on that," said Griswald. "But it's startin' tae get chilly. Feels like home again."

"Da demons will have burned my home."

"We lost our home, Ochnic," Garon said. "Including many people we loved. I do not wish that fate on anyone. We'll get your family to safety."

"Only daughter," Ochnic said. "My life mate, she passed." He said it so plainly, so matter of fact, so indifferently, yet he couldn't meet Garon's eye. It must have caused him all the pain in the world. A silence followed, as though all three were honouring the dead.

The three of them were sat around a collapsed set of smaller standing stones, upon a knoll overlooking the river of this glen. Marus and Rohka were farther out with a vanguard force in case the demons ventured too close in the night. To the east rose another Principal Mountain, the fourth that Garon had seen since entering the Highlands. Its snow-covered slopes rose above the clouds. The cache of food they sought was in that mountain, in some hall of the golems, kept secret from all save the chieftains and their treasured silver-furred guards. A rush of wind sent another chill through Garon and he pulled his cloak closer around himself.

He realised that no one had spoken in quite some time, so he clasped the hunched troll on the shoulder and said, "We'll get her back, Ochnic. We'll save her and your clan. They are still alive."

"I know," said Ochnic. "Da demons be swarming around da Glen of Bhrath for a reason. But Rohka, Chief-of-Chiefs does not want ta fight through."

"Getting tae yer clan by force would be some task," said Griswald.

"With any luck, we'll only need to fight the demons on this side of the mountain," said Garon. "Rohka says there is another passageway under it, just like there is at the Great Glen. Clearing the demons away from this side of the mountain will allow your clan to use the passages to come to us. Rohka is concerned about the food stores being lost, as he should, but I don't see how he can object to that plan. We'll have a better grasp on things once Pel and her flyers return from scouting."

"Then we go," Ochnic said.

"Then we'll make plans and go," said Garon. "Ochnic, may I ask you something?"

"You ask a lot of questions, pack leader," Ochnic said.

Garon shrugged. "I'm a curious fellow and I wondered about the title Rohka and the Chieftains gave you. They referred to you as 'Shadow Hunter'. Is that what you are?"

"What I was," said Ochnic. "Older now, I am. Those who watch over da borderlands with da Black Rock would stop demons coming through da mountains where we could. I shouldn't have returned but de younger hunters claimed der were many more demons than dey had eva seen. So I went and when I saw what was coming I knew de kazzek could not win. My chieftain, Orrock, tried at first. He gave us warriors and called da other chiefs for warriors. Dey came. Many died. Da demons kept coming."

"And that's when they sent you fer help?" asked Griswald.

"No," Garon said, realising. "They didn't send you, did they? At least not right away. I'll bet my share of the food that we find that it was your notion Ochnic."

"Was it now?" Griswald said.

"It was, I," said Ochnic. "Kazzek be needin' help but Orrock is wary of Lowlanders and said he wouldn't take it to de other chieftains. Dey wouldn't listen at first, but then more bodies came back from da east and da burnings grew so large de clans could see the smoke from glens away. Not all de chieftains wanted me to go. Many said yes to get rid of me, I think. Da eldest, Chieftain Glik, gave me a trinket for da Dragon Guardian. And de rest you know, pack leader."

"Well, your people owe you a great debt," Garon said. "We Lowlanders included."

"These lands might fall still," Ochnic said darkly. "But no debt is owed. I did dis for Cadha. I cannot understand why de others did not think of der little ones, their future, their world, when we are burned to ash."

"It can be a hard thing tae ask for such change so quickly," Griswald said.

"We must change or we'll die," Ochnic said. "Maybe those who don't roam da borders with the Black Rock can pretend but not I; not a Shadow Hunter tired of seeing kazzek fall. We cannot stand alone."

"Many of us in the south have similar issues," Garon said.

Ochnic nodded slowly. "I noticed. I hope dat Lowlanders can settle their grudges."

"You and me both," said Garon. "At least we're trying, eh?" But Ochnic wasn't paying attention. The troll's head suddenly sprung up, sniffing softly at the air.

"Pel is coming," said Ochnic. Sure enough, within half a minute, Wing Commander Pel landed amongst the fallen standing stones with five flyers. In her hand was a giant blue stemmed, blue leafed flower with yellows spots.

"There are kazzek on the other side of the mountain," Pel said. "It must be your clan, Ochnic. Something is holding the demons back though and they haven't managed to swarm into the glen yet. There's still time." Ochnic sprang to his feet and bounded to Pel as though to hug her, but he halted just short, stubbing a large toe on one of the standing stones.

"Dis is well," Ochnic said through gritted teeth. He bent down to attend to his smarting toe, taking rapid little breaths.

"And I found that plant you spoke of," said Pel.

"Ah, chull weed," Ochnic said. He took it from her. "Dis has a few ways but mostly it clears the head of illness. Place da flower in hot water and place your head over it with a cloth to catch da steam."

"Chull weed," Pel repeated. "Got it."

"Class time's over," Garon said. "We need to take this news to Rohka."

"Yes, we go now," Ochnic said and began running down the hillside towards the river. Pel flew after him.

"Think I'll enjoy the night here a for a wee while," Griswald said.

"Very well," Garon said, stretching his arms and legs. "Doubt you'd be able to keep up anyway." Griswald smiled broadly but didn't rise to Garon's bait.

"Right, off I go then," Garon said.

He found it a struggle to keep up as he followed Ochnic and Pel along the riverbank. It ran east through the glen, towards where Marus and Rohka would be stationed with the vanguard. Distantly, Ochnic and Pel halted under the shelter of an overhanging crag, where the fire lit the armour of the dragons and Silver Furs nearby it. By the time Garon caught up, Ochnic was already prostrating himself before the Chief-of-Chiefs.

"Please. Please. Leave dem you can't."

"Sorry, I am, Ochnic, Shadow Hunter," Rohka said. "I cannot open de passage to the other side if der is a chance da demons will enter from de Glen of Bhrath."

"Pel, Wing Commander," Ochnic said, looking desperately around for her. Pel stepped forward a little timid before the towering Chieftain. "Tell him," Ochnic said. "Tell him der is time."

"Great chieftain there is time to act," Pel said. "Something holds the demons at bay. It looked like a storm of earth." All the kazzek turned to each other and began muttering amongst themselves.

"Dat will be da golems," said Rohka slowly. "But even dey cannot hold forever."

"Der are paths, paths on the mountain," Ochnic said. "I know. Long have I roamed these lands. I can take kazzek over and warn—"

"I need my warriors here," Rohka said.

"Pel and da fairies can fly," Ochnic said, more hastily. "She can warn dem and prepare—"

But Rohka shook his great head. "You know dat will not work, Ochnic, Shadow Hunter. Your clan will see fairies as a threat."

"I'm sure Pel and her flyers could carry Ochnic there," Garon said. "Between enough of them, I mean." The Chief-of-Chiefs eyed Garon. The iron bands around his tusks caught a little glow from the fire.

"I do not condemn his clan, Garon, pack leader," said Rohka. "But we must secure the supplies in full. Else we shall all starve. Your people too. Once dat is done, if we can, we shall rescue da clan. But not before."

Garon looked to Marus. "And what do you think on this?"

"Rohka has a point," Marus said, though he shuffled uneasily on his crutch.

"Marus, don't think with your stomach now," Garon said. "We've come so far. Don't let Ochnic down."

"We came to help the kazzek and save the Highlands from being overrun," Marus said. "Rohka is their leader. How will King Darnuir feel if we ruin our relationship with him? I'm sorry Garon."

"Please," Ochnic begged again. He was on his knees, shuffling closer to Rohka. "Please, Chief-of-Chiefs. Don't leave dem to die. Don't leave Cadha to da demons!"

"Dat is close enough, Shadow Hunter," Rohka said. "I have decided. Tomorrow we shall hit da demons on our side of de mountain. We clear dem away and hold dem while we bring out de supplies from da golem halls. If we can still save your clan afterwards, I promise we shall try. But not before." Rohka turned and took his leave.

Garon stood helpless. *This whole mission has slipped out of my control. What should I do? What can I do?* He wished there and then for some power like Darnuir's sword or some title like Cosmo; something, anything that could make them listen. Before he could do anything, Ochnic had risen and was following Rohka, desperately attempting to turn him around.

"I said dat was close enough," Rohka growled. "Know your place, old Shadow Hunter."

"Please," Ochnic said, utterly desperate. He lunged forwards, as though to grab Rohka by the arm; but his flailing hand grasped a patch of Rohka's silver fur instead and ripped the hair from the chieftain's back. Rohka grunted in pain and spun, smacking Ochnic away. But even then, Ochnic did not give up, scrambling back.

"Take him," Rohka said to his guards. "He needs restrainin'."

"What?" Pel shrieked. She started forwards but several Silver Furs got in her way. Garon looked to Marus again but the legate was staring determinedly at the ground.

"This is how you repay the person who saved your life, Marus?" Garon shouted at him. He whirled to face Rohka's back. The Chief-of-Chiefs was stalking away, not watching as his guards manhandled Ochnic and gagged him. "Rohka," Garon called. "Don't do this."

Rohka looked over his shoulder. "You have heart, Garon, pack leader. But you are just one human. Accept dis." And with that the kazzek leader walked away.

Chapter 23

A SHADOW BELOVED, A LIGHT FADING

Dukoona – The City of Aurisha

THE TRUSTED GATHERED in the Basilica of Light. One by one, they emerged. Their cold embers were a wash of colour against the surrounding gold stone. Above Dukoona, the dusky orange sky sent pale light through the opening of the dome roof. He stood behind the three plain stone swords in their stone holders at the centre of the chamber. As the last of the Trusted appeared, Dukoona looked to the cut along his forearm. It had healed over into a black line, but the scar still felt stiff when he twitched his wrist.

All eyes were fixed on him.

"We find ourselves in the greatest of dangers," Dukoona said, elevating his voice to carry throughout the Basilica. "Some of our brothers tried to kill me. Many of you narrowly escaped death as well. Other Trusted did not. We no longer have a choice. To survive, we'll have to work against the Master. We are all bound to Him. If we want to be free, then He must die."

Dukoona was met with silence.

"Our first step will be to weaken His armies," Dukoona said. "The dragons will come to take back Aurisha. We shall let them, but on our terms. We'll bleed the demons slowly until Rectar's army is spent. Only seventy thousand demons remain with us here, the rest dead or still on the Splintering Isles."

"The Master will not allow this," a raking voice called out. "He'll know."

"He will know in time," Dukoona said. "That is inevitable."

"And then what?" another asked.

"We hope our enemies will kill Him for us," Dukoona said. More silence. "You do not think it can be done? Everything can die, even this god of the Shadows. If He were invincible, He would have no need for demons nor us. These gods the dragons bow to are not almighty either. Here we stand, servants of the Shadow, in the very temple erected for them."

He pointed to some spiralling pattern upon the wall.

"Where were these gods when we slaughtered dragons and took their home? What did they do when our Master came to this world?"

He paced back and turned his attention to the carved swords. They looked so old, so old and so worn. "What did they do?" he asked again. Then, summoning his dark blade into his hand, he struck at the closest stone sword. Its hilt crumbled, breaking into smaller pieces as it hit the floor. The bang of falling stone rang in the Basilica. Dukoona looked up to the hole in the dome, arms stretched wide, waiting for the response from the gods to come.

He waited for a full minute.

"They do nothing," he yelled. He turned on the old stone sword again, hacking at it like a sapling until it was too low for him to reach. Then he kicked the final lump away from its holder towards his spectres.

Little Sonrid was there, at the front, hunched low over the broken stone. He picked it up tentatively and Dukoona gave him a reassuring look. Even with Sonrid's diminished strength, he could crush the stone further in his deformed fist.

"Either they have no power here or they do not care," Dukoona said. "Rectar hides in his mountain, as these gods of the dragons hide from the world. They need us to act for them, to serve them; well I am tired of servitude."

I hope that His death will free us. It's all I can believe in.

"No one will grant us this," Dukoona told them. "If we want to escape our bonds then we must act."

"I am with you," came Kidrian's voice from nearby. Dukoona spotted his purple embers and, unexpectedly, the spectre stepped in front of the crowd and got down on one knee. "I am with you, my Lord, until the end."

"Rise, Kidrian," Dukoona said. "And do not refer to me as Lord. None of you will swap one Master for another. If you wish to follow me, do so willingly."

"I will follow you, Dukoona," Kidrian said. He spoke loudly so that all could hear.

"As will I," said Sonrid. He opened his hand and let the powdery remains of the stone sword fall.

"As will I," said another.

"I am with you."

More called out. One by one, then in groups, before finally the last of the crowd cried it out.

"Then we prepare," Dukoona said. "We must be careful in allowing the dragons their victory. If they succeed too quickly the Master will suspect. Beat them too bloody and we might weaken them too much. But be sure of this, no more spectres need risk their lives in this fight. Above all, you live. Let us lure in this Darnuir and his legions. Bring them here. Bring him to me. I mean to speak with their King."

Blaine – The Island of Eastguard

On the island of Eastguard, dragons died, humans died, fairies died.

We should not have rushed here so soon. I have failed again.

Blaine spun, sweeping the Guardian's Blade in an arc at the demons around him. More came pouring out of the former town of Errin. Blaine hadn't even managed to set foot in it.

The back of his head throbbed. He reached behind, winced, then drew away a hand slick with blood.

When did that happen?

He lost his footing and stepped in something hot and squelchy. Death reeked in the air and he saw his foot had landed in the torn stomach of a fallen human. Intestines curled around his boot.

Blaine wretched, as much from the Cascade as from the corpse.

A spectre rose out of the ground, from a crooked shadow cast by their tall spire. Painfully, his arm burning, Blaine blasted it with a beam of strong light from his sword. The spectre collapsed with a smoking hole through its chest.

"Light Bearers," Blaine cried.

No one was near him.

He was alone.

He tried to backtrack across the battlefield but the bodies made it hard to move. There was far more pink and blue than black and purple. And lots of red, of course, spilling across the shore to meet the freezing grey ocean, where longships were already leaving.

"Fall back!" Grigayne roared. Blaine couldn't see him. "Back to the ships."

"Retreat!" many cried.

Blaine found himself running for the sea. When he reached the sand, his heavy feet sunk and he tripped, falling face-first into the gore. He forced himself to his knees, as slimy blood and filth dripped from his face. Heavy clouds that darkened the sky burst and rain lashed down, ticking off his armour.

My hand's empty.

Panicked he scrambled around for the Guardian's Blade, but was still half-blinded by the mess on one side of his face.

A dragon appeared above him, proffering a hand. "Lord Guardian let me help yo—" but he convulsed, inhaling a sharp rattling breath as he died. Blaine saw the shadowy blade rip through the dragon's waist. The spectre responsible turned on Blaine next. He had spiky yellow flames across his head and moved frantically.

"The Master calls," the spectre said. "He speaks to me. You won't take us."

Blaine's hand finally found his sword.

His fingers gripped the hilt.

The spectre cut.

Blaine raised his sword too slowly. He howled in pain, in horror, in shock. His sword hand flailed and the spectre leapt out of his way. Blaine dropped his sword again.

313

His smallest finger had been cut clean away. A broken bone jutted from his palm and blood spurt from the wound. His ring finger was badly cut but still intact.

The gods have condemned me.

"Light Bearers," a voice called, "Protect the Guardian." The yellow flamed spectre saw the Light Bearers running over and thought better of it. He melded away, soaring from every small shadow he could back towards the dark tower.

Blaine scanned the ground for his sword, but someone was already handing it to him.

"I believe this is yours, Blaine," Bacchus said. He puffed madly trying to lift the Guardian's Blade but he managed it and all those around bore witness. Blaine took it in his left hand. It felt wrong there, clumsy, but he had no need for it right now.

He was running; fleeing to the call of "Retreat!" all around.

Chapter 24

THE HIGH PRICE PAID

Captain Elsie was not only the first official leader of the Hunters, she is the only one to ever win unanimous support. She must have been well loved. Still more impressive is that she achieved this long before the Brevian court started meddling in Hunter affairs. Rumours of patronage and rigged elections have grown wilder over the centuries since.

From Tiviar's Histories

Cassandra – Brevia – Arkus' Palace

CASSANDRA GRASPED THE edge of Cullen's cradle. Pudgy faced with rosy cheeks, he was sleeping peacefully beneath a white blanket. She was pleased his room wasn't a blackwash like so much of the palace. Around the walls was a painted sequence of a family with a newborn baby, planting a seed and watching it grow alongside the child with a ceiling of rolling clouds and dazzling stars. Cassandra suspected the artistry was fairy rather than human.

Cullen rolled over. He flexed his tiny fingers against his crisp sheets. Cassandra couldn't help but smile. There was something calming about being around him, her nephew. She'd felt it even when she'd held him during the run from Torridon. Perhaps there was some bond there, unspoken, unforced, but there. *If only it were so easy with Arkus.*

There was a soft knock at the door.

"Come in," she said and was surprised when Balack entered. He'd been given a pristine set of custom white leathers because being a mountain

315

boy was good for his story, as well as a black cloak of fine wool. His beard had been trimmed and oiled, and his auburn hair swept in a wave to one side.

"A bit of pampering suits you," Cassandra said.

He pursed his lips and blushed a little, looking at the cradle. "I hope I'm not interrupting?"

"He's asleep. I come to check up from time to time."

"I do too, when I can," Balack said. He stepped to the opposite side of the cradle and placed his own hand on it. "King Arkus visits as well, though he is extremely busy."

"You've been busy too. All that touring. All those speeches."

"It's good for the people. Good for morale," Balack said, a little pompously.

"Oh, of course. For the people. And for you?"

He shrugged. "It works, Cass. Recruitment has increased by eight per cent."

"Well, I'm glad," she said. "I imagine the guaranteed meals and clothing are also attractive. The refugee camps are stretching things thin."

"A lot of dragons arrived from Val'tarra," Balack said. "Arkus is worried and the Assembly is terrified."

"Why are they so scared?" Cassandra said. "The dragons are waiting to go home. Arkus even invited them to come get a ship."

"They're dragons, Cass," Balack said, as though it was all obvious. "They might be old, women or children but that still makes them far stronger than us. It's all the Assembly talks about right now, especially now that the fleet has sailed with the bulk of our army."

"Balack, the dragons are not going to attack us for food."

"Maybe not now, but what about when the food runs scarce. You know fine well what they can be like. They will take what they want," he ended acidly.

Oh, so that is what this is really about.

"Don't let your feelings for Darnuir lead you to blame a race," Cassandra said. She felt a surge of anger at him then. "You don't even know what happened. He didn't 'take' anything. As if she—"

Cullen rustled and moaned but stayed asleep. Cassandra hadn't realised her voice had been rising. She let go of the cradle and stalked around to be closer to Balack.

"As if she was yours to have taken from you," Cassandra whispered savagely.

"You don't know," he whispered.

"Actually, I do. Darnuir told me back in Val'tarra." She remembered it vividly; the damp leaves, the confiding conversation, Ochnic descending from the trees. "Eve went after him, not the other way around. He was guilt-ridden, Balack."

"Then why'd he break my ribs? A strange sort of apology that."

"Maybe he wasn't in his right mind," Cassandra said. "Maybe having memories from your sixty-year-old self forced into your head causes you to act in strange ways."

"And maybe it just shows that dragons aren't worth helping."

She slapped him.

The clap echoed and her palm stung. Balack reacted slowly, his hand rising to touch his cheek only after several seconds.

"He's made mistakes," Cassandra said. "I've decided to forgive him. You should as well. Grow up and get over this."

Hand still pressed against his cheek, he began to nod slowly as though pushing through sand. "You're right," he said, a little choked. "If there is some way I can—"

He was interrupted by a sharp cough at the door. Standing there, seemingly on his own, was Thane. Small for his age and weedy, Thane was bulked out only by his thick black robes. His skin looked even greyer than usual and there were dark lines around his eyes. When he saw Cassandra, he smiled widely then poked his head back around the edge of the doorframe.

"She's here mother," Thane called, a little out of breath. "In Cullen's room."

A moment later, Queen Orrana stepped into view behind her son, pulling him in close to her in a one armed hug. "You shouldn't overexert yourself, sweetling," Orrana said, planting a kiss on Thane's head. In her free hand was a bundle of letters secured with brown string. A flare of excitement shot through Cassandra. She'd been waiting for this, although she'd need to be alone with Orrana to discuss it.

"But I wanted to—" He coughed again and heaved something up into a large handkerchief before pocketing it.

Well-practiced worry lined Orrana's face but she looked to Cassandra. "I hope I am not intruding? It can be difficult to get acquainted with one's betrothed—"

"Balack was just leaving," Cassandra said.

"Yes — I was," Balack said. He bowed to Thane first, then Orrana. "Please excuse me, my Prince, my Queen, I am scheduled to visit the forges today." As Balack squeezed passed the crowded doorway, the Queen threw Cassandra a quick wink.

"Mother, may I hold Cullen again?" Thane asked.

"Cullen is sleeping, dear. Perhaps later."

Thane trotted over to the cradle, peering fondly down at his, well, Cassandra was not sure what Cullen was in relation to Thane. *If Thane is my stepbrother, I suppose he is Cullen's step uncle? I think.*

"I don't see you in the palace much, Cassandra," Thane said. "Would you like to read with me again one day?"

"Cassandra is very busy," Orrana said. "She's the Princess now."

"I'm a prince and I'm not busy."

"You will be one day," Orrana said. "Why don't you wait outside Thane? Mummy won't be long. I need to speak with Cassandra."

Thane seemed unsure.

"I would love to read with you one day," Cassandra said. "We'll sit in your favourite chair and have cake. But I do have business with your mother for now." Thane smiled again, seeming content with this, then obediently shuffled away. Orrana glanced out, making sure he was out of earshot.

"How's he been?" Cassandra asked.

"A little worse," Orrana said. "He hard a hard time drifting off last night. Anyway, these are for you." She thrust the letters to Cassandra who took the bundle eagerly.

"You know who R.F. is then?" Cassandra asked.

"Ralph Foulis," Orrana said. "It wasn't too hard to narrow it down. The Forsycht's have family members in the hunters, but not stationed here in Brevia, and the Finlays only have two sons, one of whom is a Chevalier. One of the Feweir's daughters is a huntress, but her first name is Maggy so that rules her out."

"Thank you, Orrana," Cassandra said. She took the bundle of letters eagerly and tucked them under one arm. "When have you arranged the gathering?"

"For tomorrow evening."

"That won't seem like too short a notice?"

"I am the Queen," said Orrana. "The lesser houses can't refuse me, particularly as this is the preliminary meeting to one with my husband. Besides, none of them would miss the chance to have their say in rebuilding and resettling the Boreac Mountains, not to mention the many vacant hunter positions in the Cairlav Marshes, Golden Crescent and the Dales."

"Don't the Hunters decide on who gets what position?"

"Ordinarily yes, but the task ahead is such a large one that some formal planning will be required. It's an important matter, one that you can suitably use as an excuse to hand deliver invitations. A nice gesture from the ruling family. Foulis' invitation to the gathering is in the middle of the pile."

"What if Arkus finds out about the gathering?" Cassandra asked.

"He knows," Orrana said. "I convinced him to let me take the matter off his plate, but I didn't mention our real reason for hosting."

"I don't know how to repay you for this," Cassandra said.

"Repay me?" Orrana said in shock. "You don't owe me anything. Repay me if you must by catching Boreac. I don't think I'll feel Thane is truly safe until this is over."

"I will," Cassandra said and, without thinking things through, hugged the Queen. Orrana made a startled little "oh" but returned the hug, lightly patting Cassandra on the back. Now Cassandra just felt too awkward to even let go. She was saved by Cullen waking up and beginning to cry.

Orrana moved to the cradle.

"Was he fed before he fell asleep?"

"I'm not sure," Cassandra said. "The nurse didn't say."

"I think he needs burping," said Orrana, picking Cullen up. She positioned his head on her shoulder and gently rubbed his lower back. "He needs someone who has the time for him."

"There's a woman on Boreac's house staff, Olive," Cassandra said. "Perhaps when this is all cleared up you could bring her on to look after Cullen. If she is cleared of any wrongdoing, that is."

"Why her?" Orrana asked.

"Because she is his aunt," Cassandra said. "His mother's sister." Orrana blinked rapidly, then nodded her head in agreement.

"You should go," Orrana said. As Cassandra left and passed by Thane, who had his forehead pressed in boredom against the wall, she heard Orrana call out after her, "Be careful."

Cassandra returned to her room and found some suitable clothing. No dress or gown, she wanted to be able to move, just in case. What she really wanted was to take a sword, but that wouldn't do. Cassandra was playing princess today. Yet Kymethra didn't have such restrictions and she could play a Hinterland huntress, perhaps a contact of Orrana's sent for Cassandra's protection. She decided on black dress leggings – the sort that huntress captains might wear to formal occasions – combined with a decorative green silk shirt with frilly sleeves. Once dressed, she rolled up the sleeves to free her hands and strapped on her sword. She would pass it to Kymethra when she found her. Pleased with her attire, Cassandra grabbed the bundle of letters and set off to find the witch.

Her first stop was Brackendon's room and she found the door was already ajar.

"Hush, Brackendon," came Kymethra's voice. She sounded exhausted.

Through the open doorway, Cassandra saw Brackendon sitting upright in bed with Kymethra perched beside him. Brackendon's bedrobe was torn in places and there were scratch marks on his arms and neck.

"Gghhnghhm," Brackendon mumbled. His head suddenly swayed into Kymethra's chest where he sobbed and whined.

"Shhhh, shhh," Kymethra said, barely holding back tears.

"End the magic," Brackendon managed to say. "End the magic, end the—" but he broke down again in incoherent babbling.

"It will be okay," Kymethra said. She placed three fingers carefully just above Brackendon's ear, all the while reassuring him, "It will be okay. You'll be okay." On her last words, her soothing seemed to take effect. Brackendon ceased muttering and his eyes glazed over. Kymethra resettled him back down and he fell asleep. That Kymethra only allowed herself one lone tear was perhaps the bravest thing Cassandra had ever seen.

Cassandra felt like a terrible intruder, walking in on the worst form of intimacy. She thought about turning and walking away but Kymethra saw her then.

"Oh, it's you," Kymethra said. "Orrana set everything up then?" Her right arm was shaking as she pointed to the letters and a few more strands of her hair had turned white.

"She has," Cassandra said, suddenly unsure about this. "You don't have to come if—"

"I'm bloody coming," Kymethra said with a sniff and a great shake of her head.

"All right," Cassandra said. "If you put on the Hinterland leathers we can pretend you are the extra protection Orrana has given me, seeing as the Chevaliers are spread so thin."

"Bit of a lame excuse," Kymethra muttered. She started rooting around in some drawers, yanking out pieces of blue leather flecked with pale green.

"I need you to put this on as well," Cassandra said, tapping her sword.

"Why? I can't use it."

"A huntress would have a sword," Cass said softly.

Kymethra nodded, taking the weapon from her. The buckle caused Kymethra's shaking fingers some trouble. She started getting angry again, pulling on the leather strap until it tightened like a corset. Cassandra dove to loosen it and fix the buckle in place as Kymethra wheezed above her.

"I can't imagine what you are suffering through," Cassandra said. "And I know you want to help me catch those involved, but you'll hardly help if you're only half-alive."

"I'm fine. Some cold water and fresh bread from the kitchens will set me straight. Let's just go."

After successfully negotiating the winding old streets of Brevia, the Master Station was a bit underwhelming. None of Cassandra's books had ever described the place and she thought she now understood why. Plain and unadorned, the station took up an entire block near the tanneries, which were now part of the larger Trade District. Though simple, there was something stoic about it. Despite the centuries, the station had refused to change.

There was one huntress stationed at the door, looking bored. She questioned them, but was settled by Orrana's royal seal on the letters and the glaring look that Kymethra gave her.

"Captain Horath is out today," the huntress said, her eyes nervously flicking back to Kymethra. "He's giving a speech along with the Hero of the Bastion, trying to beef up our numbers too."

"That's no matter," Cassandra said, relieved she would not have to deal with the captain. "I only need to deliver these invitations."

"Far be it from me to stop you, milady."

Cassandra smiled pleasantly and she and Kymethra walked inside. Even compared to the dim-witted guards outside of Boreac's mansion that had been child's play. *Playing the princess certainly has some perks.*

The station's interior was not as demure. It was decorated with the most impressive kills the hunters had ever made; enormous stuffed dire wolves, great stags with antlers over four feet long and even a silver-furred bear the size of a carriage. Kymethra didn't seem to be paying attention and occasionally passed Cassandra when she paused before a display. Yet Cassandra couldn't help but admire them, even if it was sad to know that such creatures had been hunted from the world, whether for glory or safety. These animals were likely to be extinct now, never to return to Tenalp. The final display was a collection of thick gold plated armour of varying designs. One suit looked eerily like Blaine's own. A little plaque beneath it read:

The armour of the murderous Norbanus. Gifted to the hunters after the Battle of the Bogs by Dronithir, Humanity's Greatest Friend.

The actual armour of the Guardian Norbanus himself? Why isn't this well known? Perhaps it had something to do with the undiplomatic wording on the inscription. The hunters honoured their tradition well. Dragons were their greatest kills, and not all the displays were of extinct species after all.

Not for now, at least.

"Are you coming?" Kymethra asked.

"Yes, sorry," Cassandra said, striding to catch up.

Room after room, fake pleasantries and seemingly endless amounts of small talk were endured before they finally found the office they were looking for. Cassandra knocked lightly at the open doorway.

"Ralph Foulis?"

"That would be me," the man said without looking up from his papers. "You can tell Horath the transfer candidates still aren't drawn up yet."

"I am not a huntress," Cassandra said. Foulis glanced up then and a look of confusion creased his forehead. At a glance, he was not much older than Cassandra, yet his skin was milkier than most hunters, showing he'd probably sat behind that desk for many years. "I have something for you." She entered the office and dropped the letter on top of the documents he was scribbling at.

"The royal seal?" Foulis said, suddenly nervous. "Who are you? Why would Arkus be corresponding with me?"

"That's the Queen's seal," Cassandra said. "The King knows nothing about this."

"Does he not?" Foulis said, mincing words as though he'd never spoke under pressure before.

"The King seems to be on your mind," Cassandra said. "Any reason? I could inform the Queen herself if it is important."

She'd give him a chance. He looked nervous enough to burst without much pressure.

"If you are so connected to her majesty then why have I never seen you before?"

"Because I spent twenty years as Castallan's hostage at the Bastion." Telling half a truth was easier than a full lie and now she'd dropped another name to make him squirm.

Foulis fidgeted with the letter. "Most unfortunate. Glad that horrible business is all over."

"Is it?" Cassandra asked. "Lord Annandale is to stand trial in the Assembly and Lord Boreac has disappeared. Many seem to think that points to him being involved."

"Well, I wouldn't know anything about all that," Foulis said, without even having the sense to look at her directly. Either that or he found the doorframe very alluring.

"Kymethra," Cassandra said, without taking her own gaze from Foulis. "We'll need some privacy, I think. Go shut the door."

"Hmmph," Kymethra grunted from behind.

Foulis looked alarmed.

And it all happened at once. As Kymethra closed the door with a firm click from the lock, Foulis' chair screeched out from under him. He jumped to his feet, his slight gut already stretching his uniform, and tried to dart around the side of his desk. A slight limp slowed him, but he had one hand on the sword at his belt. Now half-drawn. Steel visible.

Cassandra lunged across Kymethra's waist and ripped the sword there free. She blocked Foulis with a great clang of metal. He stumbled backwards and she buried an elbow into his soft flab. With both arms he clutched at his stomach, groaning, and exposing himself. She jabbed the pommel against his wrist and he dropped his weapon.

"Impressive," Kymethra said, stepping up beside her. She was looking down on Foulis with the contemplation she might have given a juicy rabbit in her eagle form.

"He clearly isn't good at this," Cassandra said.

"I won't talk," Foulis said, trying to crawl back to his desk. "My family needs me – the money. I won't—"

Kymethra swooped down upon the man. "Are you in pain?"

"I'm always in pain," he snorted. "My leg. Tendons ripped. Never healed fully. S'why I'm stuck in here."

"That must be a terrible burden," Kymethra said, in a strangely tender voice. "To have to live the rest of your life like that. In pain. Sat there. It's almost understandable, the things you've done. The people you've hurt. The lives you've ruined…" She was on her knees beside him. Something about the glint in her eye made Cassandra uneasy.

"Kymethra…"

"Well, what could I do?" Foulis said. "I won't rise in rank stuck here, and my House needs support. The King's policies don't allow payments to noblemen injured, even when we're flat broke. There are whoresons wounded in the last war getting compensation. But do I? No. Wrecked on my first night of duty in a tavern brawl. The injustice!"

"Oh, so unjust," Kymethra said. She pushed back a bit of his hair, just above the ear. She placed three fingers there.

"Kymethra," Cassandra said, more pressing.

"Do you know where Lord Boreac fled to?" Kymethra asked.

Foulis shook his sweating head.

"No?" Kymethra said. "But we found a scrap of a letter you sent him. It was you, right?" Foulis didn't deny it. "Did Boreac come to see you, as you asked him?"

"He did, but I don't know where he went."

"You don't know or you won't tell us?" Kymethra asked.

"I can't tell you. If I talk I won't get the gold to help—"

"Let me help you remember," Kymethra spat. Her fingers seemed to vibrate and Foulis froze, his face suddenly struck with horror.

"No," Cassandra cried. Bringing Kymethra had been a mistake. She was too upset, too unstable.

Foulis' mouth opened in a silent scream. His eyes rolled up, showing only white, and he began to tremble upon the floor. Kymethra grimaced as she worked her magic, looking as if the pain from the poison was as great as the pleasure she was receiving from hurting a man who was involved in Brackendon's terrible fate.

Cassandra didn't know what to do, but instinct pushed her to Kymethra's shoulder and she grabbed her, trying to yank her free from Foulis. That was a mistake.

Pain flared throughout Cassandra's body and she fell backwards, colliding with a set of shelves. Paper and scrolls descended on top of her as her vision turned to a revolving blur.

Memories flashed before her. She was nine years old and stuck in one of the Bastion's tunnels with no light or warmth. Trapped. "Chelos," she sobbed. "Chelos, where are you?" She was even younger now, seven and lying on her bed. She was reading stories about children who wanted to run away from home and go on adventures. She didn't understand why they'd want to leave. Everything swirled again, and there was a hand on her shoulder, a scream – and blood was pouring from his chest.

Thud.

Her eyes snapped open. Her head rang in pain. A heavy book lay in front of her; its spine still touched the edge of her nose. With a splitting head, Cassandra got unsteadily to her feet.

Foulis was still writhing and strange foamy saliva trailed from the edge of his mouth. Kymethra's arm shook, yet she held it determinedly in place.

Cassandra looked for her fallen sword and picked it up.

"Kymethra, stop." Kymethra did not. "Stop it now or I swear I'll cut your hand off."

When Kymethra didn't respond, Cassandra raised her sword —

Brought it down —

But she couldn't follow through. *What was I thinking?* She held the cold edge just above Kymethra's wrist, then kicked the witch with all her might.

Kymethra spun away, clipping her head off the desk corner and Foulis regained himself. His eyes were a web of bloodshot lines. All three of them were gasping for air.

"Right," Cassandra panted, feeling winded. "Now we all have thundering headaches; can we go about this more civilly? Foulis. Tell us all you know."

"Why should I?" Foulis moaned. "After that? If this is what Arkus resorts to then what's stopping you from killing me after."

"Arkus doesn't know we're here," Cassandra said.

"Even more reason I am disposable then."

Cassandra glanced at Kymethra who looked thoroughly dazed. A trickle of blood ran down from her temple. *Don't make me regret this, Kymethra.* She tossed her sword well out of reach then raised her empty hands in peace to Foulis.

"All Arkus cares about is Boreac." Foulis still looked unsure. Cassandra slowly crouched down in front of him and he flinched.

What horrors did she make you relive?

"I know a bit about your House," Cassandra said. "I know you once had your time in the sun, that the name Foulis briefly meant something. But that was taken away, wasn't it?"

"What do you know of it?"

"I know an ancestor of yours almost singlehandedly held Brevia from the Islanders when they sacked the city. John Foulis. Just a young man like you; a second son of a third son. A lowly gatekeeper on the city walls. But he rallied his men and barred the doors, and held strong. And when the lords from the Crownlands marched to relieve the city, the gates were open for them."

Foulis nodded along.

"When the White Arch of Brevia was built its sea defences were entrusted to your family, the defenders of the city. But slowly your House declined once more. Little is written, but I can guess what happened."

"Can you?"

"I don't know if your House was ever rich, but it wasn't when such an important duty was placed upon its shoulders. My guess is that you couldn't maintain the costs of the Arch: its upkeep, the soldiers, the staff. Loans might have been taken, but you couldn't pay them back. You couldn't even lean on patriotism once the Islanders had joined the Assembly and there was no need to defend against the sea anymore. So, while other families' rose, yours fell and I doubt anyone cared.

"Maybe Boreac said he cared. Maybe Castallan promised you wealth and power again. Don't you see why they came to you? Why they used you? They played you for their own ends. And now they've met theirs. Castallan is dead. Boreac is on the run. There's nothing to be gained anymore."

"I need the gold," Foulis groaned. "It's not just for me. My older brothers died in the last war. My parents have worked themselves half to death to keep the estate running. They're good to their tenants, which is far more than I can say for most of the Crown Land families. I was their last hope but I'm injured, stuck behind this desk. I'll never be a Captain or rise to anything like this. My sister Ruth is a sweet girl, but homely. She won't marry high in the world. We're done."

Crumpled up, Kymethra finally let loose a groan of her own. Foulis and Cassandra ignored her.

"Boreac promised he'd send word of where he'd stashed some coin for me," Foulis said. "Once he was safe."

"Did he want you to help hide him?" Cassandra asked.

"No. He just wanted some documents I'd kept – letters and such. Secret orders. I thought he would be mad to hear I hadn't burned them, but he was pleased."

"What letters?" Cassandra asked. "What orders?"

Foulis lowered his head. "Look, I'm not talking. My folks need this. I never thought this much bloodshed would happen. Still, it's happened now, and I've made peace with it. So, do your worst."

Cassandra sighed, exasperated. Her knees were beginning to hurt so she sat down crossed legged before Foulis. It was admirable of him, in a way, to risk everything for his parents and sister.

"You must love your family very much," Cassandra said.

"I'd do anything for them," Foulis said. "Wouldn't you?"

"I don't have one," is what Cassandra was about to say. Yet, even as she formed the words in her mind, she knew it wasn't strictly true anymore. Chelos might have been taken from her but she thought of Orrana, and how wonderful and welcoming she had been. She thought of sweet young Thane and even Cullen. Strange as it was to admit, she'd do anything for her nephew. Castallan, Boreac and the rest would probably have killed him if they'd won. That was enough to set a fire in her.

"Yes, I would do anything," is what she said in answer.

"So, you understand?" Foulis said.

"I do, but you need to understand that you're caught," Cassandra said. "Your intentions don't excuse what you've done and I need Boreac to fulfil a bargain with my father. Yet he doesn't need to know all the details. So, if you talk to me, tell me it true, then I'll forget all about you."

"You swear?"

"I swear."

Foulis sighed. "Very well. Don't suppose I have many options…" He massaged his head a little before continuing. "Boreac took what evidence I had surrounding the death of Captain Morwen. He was very interested in the cargo Morwen was carrying. He wanted it intercepted; swapped or stolen."

Cargo meaning black powder, Cassandra thought.

"But something went wrong," Foulis continued. "Everyone sent on the mission died, including the Captain. It was a disaster. I still don't know what really happened. When Boreac asked me for the evidence I thought he wanted to make sure it was destroyed, but he never asked for what I had on that Captain Tael and that was plain murder."

"What haven't you had your greasy fingers in," Kymethra said. She was rubbing her head, nursing her arm, and looked too ashamed to face them.

"Things got out of hand sometimes," Foulis said. "Especially when Scythe got involved. I breathed easier when he took Tael's place in the south. Good riddance, I thought. He always made my blood run like ice."

"And in your position you could arrange for any of Boreac or Scythe's supporters to be placed in any region they wished," said Cassandra.

"That was why they came to me," Foulis said. "I had my uses. Even stuck in here."

"That could be a lot of names to incriminate," Cassandra said.

"You want them?" Foulis asked.

"No," Cassandra said. "Enough blood has spilt, and I suspect many of them died at the Bastion. I'm more interested in why Boreac would want those papers on Morwen."

"He seemed to think it would help him gain sanctuary with the dragons," Foulis said. Then he laughed, in a slightly hysterical way. "Maybe he was losing it. I doubt the dragons would be happy to take him in once it comes out he was involved in all this."

"That's where he's going?" Cassandra asked. "He thinks the dragons will keep him safe?"

"He seemed confident enough," Foulis said. "Must be right desperate to avoid Arkus if he's turning to them." He grinned, perhaps enjoying the thought of Boreac turning up outside a legionary camp, begging for mercy.

Cassandra felt this was coming together. "And you don't know where he might be, right now?"

"Could be rowing with one paddle across the sea for all I know," Foulis said. A droplet of blood seeped from his eye. He wiped it away and his eyes widened in alarm at the red smear on his fingers. "Not sure how I explain this to the healers."

"One last thing," Cassandra said. She pulled out the little lead sphere from a pouch at her belt. "Do you know what this is?"

Foulis squinted. "Not a clue."

Well, he couldn't know everything. He's been through enough.

"We will take our leave now," Cassandra said. She looked to Kymethra. "Can you manage?"

"I can walk," Kymethra grumbled, getting to her feet. She looked a shadow of her former self. No radiance, no cheeky sparkle in her eye – just a lifeless husk where Kymethra had once been.

Cassandra went to pick up her sword. She demanded the belt from Kymethra, strapped it around her own waist, and then sheathed the blade with a satisfying snap.

"I'm sorry for all you've been through, Ralph Foulis," she said. "I'm sorry the world has left your family behind. If it helps in any way, I do not think we shall ever need to meet again."

"And you'll forget about me, yes?"

"The very moment we leave this room," Cassandra said, giving Kymethra a very hard glare. Then, Cassandra turned, and took her leave; Kymethra trailing behind her.

Chapter 25

BLOOD ON THE SAND

Before Dranus led his exiles to settle near Kar'drun, there were no inhabitants of eastern Tenalp. Then came the Third Flight. Forests were felled, cities raised and a great road laid from north to south. The Crucadil Road was meant for trade, but armies have used it more. Some fairies dream of restoring the landscape, but the east has been irreversibly altered, even more so than the west.

From Tiviar's Histories

Darnuir – the shores of the east

GOLDEN SAND, TEAL waters, an autumn breeze; the shoreline might have been a welcoming sight had swarms of demons not marred it. Darnuir squinted against the sunlight reflecting on the water. Demon numbers were impossible to gauge, but the black masses stretched all along the coast. They couldn't know where Darnuir and the legions would land, so had covered as much ground as possible.

Darnuir was glad for the initial advantage that would grant, as it allowed them to press all their force into one smaller point and punch a hole in the demon lines. However, it would be easy for Dukoona to ensnare the legions once they landed, if he wasn't careful.

We'll be harried all the way to the gates of Aurisha and then we'll have to scale the walls of our own city. Unless the spectres just invite us in.

But he didn't want that. Not really.

He needed an excuse to draw on the Cascade. Aside from the mystery of Dukoona's actions, it was why he was here.

He drew a breath, held it and let it go through his nose. A fresh wave buffeted the ship and sent spray into his face. Wiping away the water, Darnuir turned back to his Praetorians, readying themselves on deck. Lira's eyes looked sunken with tiredness and Raymond's were half closed, blinking rapidly to fend off sleep.

"How are the troops?" Darnuir asked.

"As well as can be," said Lira. "It's not been an easy journey."

"The demons are truly without art," said Raymond, picking at a splinter in his left palm. The ships left behind by the demons near Dalridia were crude, unfinished dragon galleys.

"It's been cramped and hard rowing," Darnuir said. "But comfort and war rarely mix. Time is limited. I want to hit the demons before their spectre overlords have a chance to prepare properly."

"Prepare?" Raymond questioned. "I thought there was some schism amongst them."

"That's what we can gleam from Grigayne's testimony," Darnuir said. *Or this is all some ploy, and I've played right into Dukoona's hands?*

Lira opened her mouth as though to speak but stopped herself short.

"Speak your mind, Lira," Darnuir said.

"It doesn't matter. We're here now."

"My gut tells me something is amiss with the spectres," Darnuir said, loud enough for all the Praetorians to hear. "Enough to think we might be able to take advantage of the situation, in one way or another."

Lira pointed behind him, out towards the shore. "If Dukoona wants to talk, he's brought quite the welcoming party."

"We have as well," Raymond said. "Seven legions, if I'm not mistaken."

"Seven legions, but not all at full roster," Lira said. "Not after the Bastion and lifting the siege at Dalridia. The legates—"

"The legionary legates have not voiced any concerns," Darnuir said.

"The legates are good dragons who would never talk back to you," Lira said. She hesitated but kept her head held high. "You told me you wanted me to speak my mind."

"And I do."

"You were a hunter once as well," Lira said. "No squad leader would take risks like this. Not without questions from the rest."

"This is different."

"It is?" Lira asked. "Lives are at stake."

"We're an army," Darnuir said, "Fighting another army, a much larger army. We're not five hunters in the cold and the dark, stalking a lynx that's strayed too far from its den. It's a risk, but one I'm sure we have to take."

"Can we really take such chances?" Lira said. "So far we've pulled through half on luck and half on the efforts of Brackendon." She was looking Darnuir right in the eye. "Castallan wanted you to run right to him and you did."

"If I hadn't, Castallan would have finished Brackendon off."

"Or he could have taken the Dragon's Blade and killed us all," said Lira. "You didn't think. You went to get that girl."

They think I'm being too reckless.

"I told you the reasons why we had to get Cassandra," Darnuir said. A heat licked at his throat and the door to the Cascade in his mind quivered. How he longed to feel it course through every inch of him.

"The alliance, yes," said Lira. "But you risked everything for it. You didn't consider the bigger threat. Or you did but just wanted to get her back." She seemed to know she'd taken a step too far then. Maybe it was the look Darnuir was giving her. His vision had turned to two narrow slits.

Raymond took a brave step between them. "Darnuir took a chance taking the humans from Torridon to Val'tarra. That was worth it."

"I'm not questioning every decision," Lira said. "We'd have failed at the Charred Vale had the spectres not fled, and they did so because you killed Scythe."

"It was reckless, I won't deny it," Darnuir said. "But there seemed to be few options."

"You were angry as well," said Lira. "Because Scythe killed Cosmo. He baited you. Like Castallan baited you. Both wanted your sword. This might be the same thing."

"If I may," Raymond began, "it seems to me that it is the enemy who has taken the greater gamble this time. If this is some manoeuvre, we could have ignored it and focused on retaking the Splinters with ease."

"Something is off, that much is certain," Lira said. "The battle at Dalridia went too smoothly."

"I'm taking another gamble," Darnuir said. "An even bigger one. But it's not all about the spectres. By the time, we have cleared the Splinters and waited on Arkus' full fleet, winter might make the crossing too difficult for a full invasion."

"Yes, the weather can be frightful," Raymond said, if a little stiffly.

Darnuir understood how pathetic that excuse sounded now. He looked around his Praetorians. Armed to the teeth, they stood silently, mouths pressed into thin lines. They would fight, he knew. Lira too. They would not abandon him. Every dragon in the legions would swim ashore if he ordered it. Yet that was the problem.

Have I chased battle and doomed us all?

"Caution drove us from our homes," Darnuir told them. He had not revealed to the Praetorians yet what Blaine had told him. Some knowledge would be best kept among only a few. "I remember my father, kneeling, praying, and waiting. That time has long past. Are we to miss this chance to take back Aurisha?"

"Caution also allowed Castallan to spread rot in the Dales," Raymond said.

Lira gave a short sharp sigh. "One day our luck might run out."

"It won't matter where we are when that happens," Darnuir said. "And it is too late to turn back now. Will you fight?"

"Of course," Lira said, pulling her bow more securely onto her shoulder.

"Good. The legates know the signal?" Darnuir asked.

"Those six who'll be still at sea," said Raymond. "Legate Atilius and the Fifth Legion will be joining us for the landing. They were less than enthusiastic about hearing it from me, however."

"They will learn to deal with you or I shall find new legates," Darnuir said. "To the boats now."

Once on the sea, Darnuir's boat cut towards the shore. He was crouched at the bow, trying to assess the situation. Closer to land, he saw a series of great wooden columns, far taller than a single tree could be outside of Val'tarra. They were well positioned across the land, heading south towards Aurisha.

Those will cast impressive shadows.

He turned around. Praetorians rowed and looked eager now the battle was close to hand. Lira was on another boat on the starboard side, but Raymond was here, encased head to toe in his Chevalier armour.

"One day I shall see you in action with your horse," Darnuir said.

"Bruce shall be happy to get into the action himself," Raymond said. "I spoiled him with apples and carrots for days after the stress of Inverdorn."

Darnuir laughed. "Do you wish you were back in that velvet waistcoat?"

"Never," Raymond said, slamming his visor shut.

Darnuir returned his attention to the shore, itching for the battle to begin. The first stones from the demon catapults launched at them, crashing into the sea. In the shallows before the shore, they sent up torrents of water. Darnuir shielded his eyes against a salty splash that soaked their boat. He spat a mouthful out and pushed wet hair off his face. Far behind came screams and the sound of breaking wood.

Black barbed arrows followed once they were almost ashore. Calls for shields rang. Darnuir brought up his arms to cover his face; the starium-coated armour would provide protection. Yet few arrows came close. As he lowered his arms, keeping his head bowed low and glancing each way, he saw few casualties. Several dark shafts shot into the water between his boat and Lira's.

Are they holding back?

The boat began to slow into the sand. Shrieks met them as demons pelted out from trenches and behind fresh dug mounds. Darnuir rose from his crouch, drew the Dragon's Blade and launched it up the beach. It burst through the closest demons in an explosion of smoke.

"Secure the landing!"

Leaping off the boat he hit the soft sand: the first dragon to set foot in the east since the fall of Aurisha. Praetorians flanked him, loosing arrows against the oncoming demons. The Dragon's Blade returned to his open hand.

Darnuir opened the door to the Cascade and felt a kick at the back of his head; it cricked his neck and he charged up the beach.

Enhanced with magic, he soon outstripped everyone else with his speed. Rusty knives and blades scraped uselessly against his armour. Darnuir carved his way through the demons, letting the Cascade run like a river. But it didn't feel the same. He did not feel the same high as Castallan had pushed him to. His body wanted more; needed more.

With a great effort, he resisted throwing the door open wider.

I must hold back. I must try.

There seemed to be no end of the demons. They leapt frog-like from behind their fellows, flying over Darnuir's head towards where the Fifth Legion would be landing. Even with his strength and speed, advancing up the banks of the beach was becoming a crawl. He thought he heard Lira shouting but couldn't tell over the blood now thumping through his head.

This crush wasn't normal. Demons liked to swarm, spread out, stay mobile, yet here they were pressing against each other. One of the oversized columns cast its shadow right into the horde. A spectre appeared in the middle of it all. Grinning, it motioned for Darnuir to follow before vanishing. The demons descended into a frenzy.

Darnuir swung the Dragon's Blade around to clear room to breathe.

"For Brevia," chanted Raymond, swishing his sword elegantly yet precisely to block two demons at once. The din of battle grew louder behind him. The Fifth were coming in force. Darnuir grunted in shock as a black arrow snapped off the dragon head on his right shoulder. He wanted to unleash fire upon the demons, but the fight was becoming so crushed he feared it might burn his allies as well.

More spectres appeared in the fight but did not get close to the action. Darnuir lunged at them each time, only to watch them flee. One with flaming green hair gestured Darnuir to follow before melding off in the blink of an eye.

Eventually, he waded to the end of the beach. A series of wide, deep trenches was supposed to slow their advance. More rocks fell from the sky. A jagged piece bowled into the demons' own ranks before continuing into the golden line of dragons. The sound of crunching bones and metal was stomach churning.

Or perhaps that was more the effect of the Cascade. Darnuir's arm was shaking now, for he had not let up; drinking in the euphoria. One of the youngest Praetorians went down from two arrows to his neck, and the smell of the blood only pushed him further.

His eyes widened and he no longer blinked. The battle was on him. It was all he could feel.

"Into the trenches," he cried before jumping down. He had no sense if anyone was actually following or how far in front he was. In a fury, he tore through this first ditch, coming across a demon catapult. Its crew barely noticed his sword before it ended them. He took his fist to the machine, smashing it with ease.

He was in a trance, drunk on excessive rage. Every spectre that eluded him only made him reach for more magic and more anger. Livid, he jumped six feet from a standing start to chase spectres over the edge of the trench. They had vanished, but a hunk of rock did collide into the ground in front of him.

He couldn't react in time.

The stone shattered against his armour and the impact blew him back. He landed face down in the trench, tasting dirt and rancid demon blood. Hot pain burned in his lower chest.

A hand took him by the shoulder and he reacted quicker than a beat of his thundering heart.

With a fresh draw on the Cascade, he flipped himself around, then up.

He met Lira's grey eyes.

His hand was at her throat.

She struck his head with the hilt of her sword. He spun away, biting his own tongue and tasting blood. She was screaming something at him but he barely heard.

What am I doing?

He dropped the Dragon's Blade and pressed a foot on it to keep it down. Underfoot it wiggled, trying to break free, but he set all his weight onto it. His arm ached as the poison welled up. And, from nearby, a swirl of shadow arose and a spectre took shape. This one had purple embers on its head.

"Come. Dukoona awaits," it croaked. It melded away before anything else could be said or done.

His senses returned, still amplified by the magic pounding in his veins. Darnuir gasped for air as though coming up from under water. He smelled the very iron of the spilt blood, heard the rattling of demons from far up the beach, saw every hair on his arm shift in the breeze. Turning, his foot still on his sword, he saw Lira gutting one last demon. She mouthed something at him.

Signal. Yes.

Darnuir slid his foot off the Dragon's Blade and it flew back to his hand. Heat rose like a furnace in his throat and he raised the Dragon's Blade, sending a thin stream of fire high into the air. He held it for a good half minute.

When he let go and shut the door, it was all he could do not to be sick.

Lira tossed him a waterskin, which he gulped down too quickly, nearly choking. He swirled another swig around his mouth and spat, but the bitterness stubbornly clung on. His tongue felt drier than dust. The Dragon's Blade was smoking, as was the dragonhead of his armour. Rusty demon blood dribbled from its teeth, looking like it had spewed a fire of its own. Clutching to the Dragon's Blade to process the poison, he slumped against the edge of the trench, looking out to sea. The water churned under thousands of oars.

Lira stepped cautiously towards him.

"I'm sorry," he said. His voice was like a frightened child.

"It's the magic, isn't it?"

He nodded.

"You haven't been right since the Charred Vale," Lira said. "I tried to—"

"I know you did," he said weakly.

She remained standing. Keeping a distance between them.

"I could barely control myself."

"Did the job, though. I think half the demons fell because of you." Despite what he'd almost done to her, she looked concerned for him. She looked him up and down, then turned to check on the demon side of their trench. "They're backing away for now."

Further down the trench, some of the Praetorians let loose a few arrows after them.

"You were right," Darnuir said. "This was too risky. I chased the fight because I was desperate for a reason to use magic."

She crouched down.

"I saw those spectres waving us along. I heard that one tell you to come. The demons threw themselves at us, but like sheep to the slaughter. Whatever the reason the spectres want you to follow them, badly. We'll just have to keep deaths to a minimum." She stalked off.

Ragged breathing and the sound of clanking plate announced Raymond. Darnuir watched him limp along and remove his helmet to reveal his face, which was slick with sweat.

"Tired, my Lord of Dragons?"

"Come take a breather, Chevalier," Darnuir said. He took another long gulp of water as Raymond sat down beside him. "If this keeps up it's going to be a very long road to Aurisha."

Chapter 26

A SIGN

I wish to know more about the Guardians and their Light Bearers. The current incarnation of the Order lacks purpose since the end of hostilities with the Black Dragons. Now there is peace, perhaps the Guardians can find a more positive role – one that aims to better the whole world, not just dragons. Already there is talk of a promising young Light Bearer. I hear his fellows call him 'Blaine' due to the fire of his zeal. If this Blaine becomes Guardian one day, I can only hope he grows to be a wiser dragon than some of his predecessors.

From Tiviar's private notes

Blaine – Dalridia

SOMERLED'S HALL WAS quiet. There was little talk to cover the chewing and grinding of teeth. The fire burned as lowly as their spirits. The whisky racks lacked their amber glow.

Blaine raised his maimed and trembling hand, trying to feed himself with great effort. He took a small bite from the chicken leg, rolled the cold, dry meat around in his mouth without pleasure and slowly swallowed. His stomach turned and he felt cold sweat on his scalp. He reached for his water, awkwardly taking the tankard in a four-fingered grip. It was almost to his lips when he dropped it, spilling water all over the table. What few Light Bearers remained with him tended to the mess while one hastily refilled the tankard.

Across the hall, Grigayne Imar glared at him. He'd suffered a cut across his cheek that had decimated his beard on that side and would surely leave a long scar. When he caught Blaine's eye he drained his mug and slammed it down, so all the hall could see, before storming outside. Somerled avoided eye contact altogether. He had not climbed to the top of his rock tonight.

"Lord Guardian, you should eat something more," one of the Light Bearers said.

"I have no appetite," said Blaine. "Leave me." He then realised that only two had remained for any length of time. When they left, Blaine was alone at the table.

He was done, he knew that. He no longer had what it took to be Guardian. Perhaps he never had.

"You shouldn't sit alone," came Fidelm's deep tones. "Is that gash under your chin fresh?"

"Cut myself shaving," Blaine mumbled.

The General sat down beside him and Blaine lacked the energy to protest. He let Fidelm take his right hand for inspection. "Are you using your Blade to help heal the wound?"

"I don't deserve to use its power," Blaine said. He hadn't touched his sword since sheathing it on the beach on Eastguard.

"Don't be a fool," said Fidelm.

Blaine pulled his hand away and tucked it out of sight under the table.

"At least allow me to apply a paste of silver bark and leaves," Fidelm said.

"No. This is a pain I must endure."

"There is no need to suffer," said Fidelm.

"I was a fool and — and Bacchus was right about me."

"Look at me." Fidelm grabbed him and forced Blaine to face him. "You should have waited for our full forces. Even so, it's war. Defeats are inevitable as well as victories and we had a lucky string of those behind us."

"I threw lives away. Fairy lives too. Aren't you angry?"

"I'm always angry with you," Fidelm said. "A deep, burning fury that I learned to cope with long ago."

"What on earth do you —"

"One Queen, one child, Blaine," Fidelm said. "My race was doomed long ago. The least you can do is not allow this all to be for nothing." He got up and spoke louder. "Most of the remaining Third Legion left an hour ago, heading towards the Nail Head. If you can no longer do this, pass the Blade on to someone who can." He stretched his wings, beat once then took off, flying through the smoke hole in the centre of the roof.

Blaine stumbled through the dark and misty drizzle back to his tent outside the city. Somerled had not been as inviting this time around. He tried to strip his armour. It was so heavy. The oversized suns felt as if they were crushing his shoulders. His useless hand fumbled and slipped at the knot, jarring the stub of his missing finger against the starium coating. A choking gasp of pain left him, and he almost missed the wheezy cough from the entranceway.

"They've all left with Bacchus for service at the Nail Head," Chelos said. He'd recovered enough to walk freely now. At least that was something amongst all Blaine's misery.

"I know that, I'm not blind," Blaine said, more cruelly than he meant. "Wait," he pleaded. "I am sorry, my friend. Could you give an old dragon a hand with his armour?" With a wrinkled, thin smile, Chelos came to his aid.

"They'll come back, you know," he said, tugging at a strap at Blaine's shoulder.

"Why should they?" said Blaine. He tried to help Chelos by holding the rivets of plate still. Chelos' waxy skin brushed over his own. It felt overly soft, malleable and frail like a silk sheet.

So, weak, yet I am weaker.

Together they freed Blaine from his metal cage. With the removal of each piece, he sighed in relief as his skin felt the kiss of cold air. He donned a fresh white shirt and washed his face at the basin though he was unable to cup his right hand properly. Water leaked from the gap of his lost appendage and he reluctantly switched to his left hand. It took far longer than it ought to and foolishly he'd gotten his bandages wet. Changing those would have been impossible without Chelos' help.

"What does he say to them?" Blaine asked.

"You should go and hear for yourself," Chelos said.

"I'm afraid," Blaine said.

"Why? Because you've taken one little knock," Chelos said. "You faced a god and lived."

"I'm afraid because our gods have deserted me," Blaine said. "How can I face Rectar again if I cannot even win back one small island?"

"And will Bacchus do any better?" Chelos asked. "Darnuir still needs you. You'll face Rectar together."

"I can hardly grip my sword," Blaine said.

"I never dreamed I'd see you like this," Chelos said. "It would break Draconess' heart if he were still alive."

"But he isn't," Blaine said. "He failed. We failed. I failed. It's time I stop pretending I have the grace of the Light. I have nothing left now."

"You'll do what you think is right of course," Chelos said. "But think hard, Blaine. I'd hate if after all this time, after all this struggle, you just gave up. I'd hate to never see the Basilica in its full glory again." Chelos took a moment to press a fist into his own back. There was a crack and he sighed in relief.

"Chelos, if I give up the Blade, I don't know how long—"

"Blaine, don't you dare —"

"Goodbye, old friend. Just in case," Blaine said. He took Chelos by the shoulder and then stepped forward to an embrace. "Thank you for believing in me all these years. You will learn to place faith in another." He took his leave, lacking the strength to look back at Chelos as he left.

The stars and moon were bright enough to see by. He wouldn't draw the Guardian's Blade save for the final time. He was sure he could see where Bacchus was holding his congregation by the fire glow someway up the lower slope of the Nail Head. Blaine traipsed towards the base of the mountain, glad to reach the woodland of birch trees and inhale the scent of leaves, of moss, of wildness; to hear the warbling song of the night birds and have the time to savour it. A sense of calm had come over him. This at least he could not fail at.

This close to a Principal Mountain many of the birches had an odd black branch or a silver dusting to their narrow white trunks. In his state of clarity, he could almost sense the Cascade in the air and ground, where it had seeped into leaf or insect. A slight swell formed from behind the door in his mind. It almost seemed to call to him for he heard something, ever so faint, like a distant whisper carried on a light breeze.

Not now Blaine…

But it was likely just the wind. It was so quiet out here at night. The sea still roared despite being so far away, as though in constant battle with the land. He heard it even as he climbed the Nail Head, heading towards the orange haze. The incline was steeper than he had anticipated, and after a while his calves began to burn. The fact he felt the exertion only proved his time was over.

Finally, he reached them all. Bacchus had formed his congregation in the shelter of a mini-valley between the jagged slopes of the Nail Head. Three large braziers lit the clearing, one of which stood at the head of the crowd. A sole dark silhouette moved beside it. The golden armour of the dragons glittered brightly. Blaine quietly descended to join them, half-sliding on soft earth. As he approached the back of the crowd, Blaine paused for half a heartbeat.

I must do what is right.

Then he took a very deliberate step forward.

And he took another.

Bacchus was projecting his voice well, reaching even Blaine at the back with clarity.

"The Lord Guardian vanished for years and we suffered. He returns, we suffer still. He withdraws from us, shaken from his first real battle in decades to spend his days with an old dragon none of us know."

"What are you saying, Bacchus?" someone called.

"I'm saying that we deserve a stronger Guardian. Dwna, Dwl'or and N'weer deserve a stronger Guardian. Light must be brought back into the world. The Shadow has grown dark indeed. It's touched the hearts of wizards and humans; it's lain across our homeland unchecked for twenty years. What I am saying is hard to hear, but I do it out of love for every dragon. It might be time for change."

Blaine hadn't stopped moving. He gently eased his way through the congregation. Soon the dragons were parting for him, creating a road directly to Bacchus. When he made it to the front, he stepped out, turned and faced thousands of twinkling yellow eyes.

"It is the Guardian who decides when to pass the Blade on," Blaine said. "It has always been this way. Through millennia, long before demons ever crawled into our world."

"None of us can remember such a time," Bacchus said. "All we've known is war and death and endless demons." There was much agreement at this from the crowd.

"The Guardian has always decided," Blaine said again. With some difficulty he took hold of the hilt of the Guardian's Blade. His grip felt weak and clumsy but he drew it out and held it high. He looked to Bacchus and the Light Bearer took a careful step back, perhaps fearing that Blaine would strike him down. Blaine did bring the Blade down, with all the might still left to him and thrust it into the earth at Bacchus' feet.

"But I am no longer fit to be Guardian," Blaine said. "If this is your will then I shall pass the mantle on. Bacchus, you may take the Guardian's Blade. I grant it to you without reservation. Only the gods themselves can object now. And if our Lords Dwna, Dwl'or and N'weer do not wish this, then I ask them for a sign."

He let go of the Guardian's Blade.

He turned his back on it.

The dragons in front of him turned wide-eyed and fearful.

Light, purest most radiant light, began emanating from behind him. Blaine watched his own silhouette cast forwards in a dark shadow. His arm shook though he felt no rush down it. Then came a strident cry like a hundred dying owls. He went deaf.

His shadow darkened as the light from behind grew brighter. And his breath caught in his throat. Invisible cords constricted his neck and tightened their control, suffocating him.

Is this how I die?

Something was clogging his mouth and Blaine recovered enough wit to spit saliva, thick and blue. The light intensified, growing so bright it removed his shadow altogether.

It is a sign!

Spinning, he faced the source of the blinding light and squeezed his eyes shut against it.

If this is truly a sign, it will not harm me.

He opened his eyes and searing pain did not come. His skin prickled as though bathed in the summer sun and a childish vitality returned to his muscles and joints; his mind felt clear and alert. In that moment, he forgot what tiredness was. He forgot all memory of hunger. He forgot pain.

Grasping, Blaine's hand found the pommel and slid down to take the handle. He gripped it strongly and pulled the Guardian's Blade free.

His arm seared then, as though dipped in molten steel, and the world darkened. Braziers went out, even the moon and stars, as all light in the world was sucked into the Blade. It held for a heartbeat in which Blaine heard a voice.

It is not yet time to give in. Never forget our power, Guardian.

Then, with the boom of a thousand powder barrels, the light radiated out in a single golden wave. Blaine watched it race to the horizon before it passed from sight. Slowly, the moon and stars returned and Blaine looked to the crowded dragons. Many had averted their eyes, crouching down and facing away. Those brave enough to turn back gawked at him, flexing their fingers as if they had felt the same freshening of their bodies. Others looked stark white as though they'd also heard what he had.

Bacchus traipsed up beside him. "I heard a voice in my mind," he whispered. "It told me, 'It is not your time. It will never be. Never forget our power, Bacchus.'"

"And we never shall," Blaine assured him quietly. His finger was still missing but the gods had made themselves clear. He turned to the dragons assembled there and cried, "Never forget. How could we now? Never forget!"

When next they landed on Eastguard, things went very differently. The gods favoured them with the weather, driving back the wind and rain, if not completely banishing autumn's cold. Despite heavy resistance, the demons folded swiftly under the new fury of the Third legion. On the beach, in the overgrown streets of the town of Errin, at the foot of the great twisted spire, Blaine's dragons were a white-hot knife of the gods.

The humans and fairies were out there, somewhere, helping however they could. But he and the Third did not need them.

Even among the shadows of the spectres' mighty construction, the dragons did not falter. This was the reward for faith, for zeal; this was why they, dragons, were the Light's own chosen.

Blaine waded in. He stopped a spectre mid-meld with an intense beam from the Guardian's Blade, obliterating the shadow in which the creature hoped to flee. He kept the light aglow at all times, embracing the burn down his arm, spitting on the face of each spectre he killed to rid the bitterness from his mouth.

Before long they were running up the rickety walkway of the spire. Blaine guessed it was there for regular demons to climb. But it was precarious and weak, cracking under the weight of armoured dragons. Blaine was forced into a Cascade enhanced jump to hurdle a widening gap. No one else could make it. He saw a Light Bearer try, fall, and descend three storeys to the battle still raging below.

"Return and kill every demon you find," Blaine called to them. "I shall flush out the devils at the top." He continued his charge upwards. From this height, the jagged extensions to the town of Errin looked like a thicket of thorn bushes. Arrows filled the air from the Brevian forces who had finally joined the fight, their spearmen crawling up from the beaches, too far away to make any real difference. The islanders fought better, their axes rising and falling like shiny teeth. They pushed into the town at points where the Third had stormed passed

Blaine climbed higher.

A spectre with shoulder-length orange flames burst from a shadow to his side, howling with the full-blown shrillness of the insane. Blaine spun, quicker than a viper, and caught the spectre by its throat. He squeezed. The orange flames went out. A cloud of smoke puffed up as Blaine dumped the body. Nothing else tried to stop him before he reached the top.

Up here a fierce cold wind bit at him. He waited for his foes to reveal themselves. When they did not, he flashed the Guardian's Blade brightly and cried, "Out demons. Out foul servants of Rectar. Out and meet your end." From a sliver of a shadow across the platform emerged a wounded spectre. It clutched at its side, smoke rising between its fingers, and stumbled to face Blaine. It had peculiar flaming hair; short spikes and lemon yellow in colour. Blaine recognised it as the one who'd taken his finger.

"Struggling, scum?" Blaine spat.

"The Master lied to me," it said in a high, scraping voice. "Lied," it repeated, in some pain. "I shall watch over you, Kraz. Always, he said. I remember. You can't forget a voice like that. Not one in your mind." He grinned madly. A few teeth at the front had been chipped or knocked clean out. Blaine looked around warily, wondering if this was some trap. The spectre babbled on and Blaine doubted there was any semblance of control left to even prepare an ambush. He stepped forward, Blade raised, and was within reach of the spectre when he spoke again.

"Everything's a lie," Kraz cried. "The old one lied to me as well. Curse Dukoona. Master, curse him." Blaine halted. That name was familiar. Kraz wouldn't stop his wailing. "He tried to have me killed. Curse him for abandoning us. Lies. You lied."

"Silence!" Blaine's voice brought the spectre back to reality. Kraz focused his black eyes on him and gasped. "I will give you a quick death, wretch," Blaine went on, "if you tell me about this one you call Dukoona." He prayed that the gods would not be angry at him for talking with this spawn of the Shadow, but he had to know.

"Dukoona?" Kraz said, eyes popping. "Dukoona. The old one. He led us, led us all for years."

"And then what?"

"I know," Kraz said, unhelpfully.

"Know what?"

"Why he left," Kraz said. "Clear now. So, clear. We tried to stop him. We failed."

Blaine seized Kraz with his free hand. "Tell me why he left," he demanded, shaking the spectre. Kraz's wound smoked more profusely smelling of rust and death.

"He hates the Master," Kraz said. "The Master told me so."

"Your own leader? Dukoona works against Rectar?" Blaine asked. This was surely some lie, something to distract or disarm him. But if it was true, then Darnuir might—

"Why," Kraz shrieked. He stumbled back from Blaine, dripping blood. "Why Master have you left us to die? Did I displease you? Do you not need us?" He was stepping unwittingly close to the edge of the platform.

"Wait," Blaine said, lunging for him.

"No," Kraz screamed, swiping wildly with a conjured dark dagger. He did not stop creeping backwards. "The Master only spoke when he needed us. To use us."

Then he fell.

Blaine moved carefully to the ledge and peered over. Kraz was falling, a black speck soon lost against the writhing mass of demons and dragons below. If that was their leader, or one of them, then this battle would be over soon.

Blaine pulled back from the edge and extinguished the light on his Blade. Within seconds he felt nauseous from the magic he'd used. Lack of sleep hit hard as well, now there wasn't a burn of Cascade energy fuelling him. Phantom pain from his lost finger flared. Days away from that transcendent moment upon the Nail Head and his grip had begun to feel lax again. He'd have to train or learn to switch hands; not something easily done.

For now, he stole a precious half-minute to collect his breath and let the poison drain down his arm. All the while his thoughts were fixated on Kraz's troubling words. This spectre lord, Dukoona, had gone rogue and fled east. Would he seek to cut some deal with Darnuir? His sympathetic grandson, so concerned about alliances, might very well listen. The gods would not tolerate that. He'd known Darnuir was in no fit state to lead either but he'd not stopped him. Another failure, but one Blaine would rectify.

I should not have let him go alone. We shall forgo rest and sail east to Aurisha with all speed.

For the idea of Darnuir meeting this Dukoona worried Blaine.

It worried him more than anything.

Chapter 27

JUST ONE MAN

Garon – West of the Glen of Bhrath

GARON HAD NOT wasted his time before dawn. He sharpened his sword and dagger, brought out his bow from storage, re-strung it, checked the fletching of his arrows, trimmed them where necessary, filled his quiver, tied on his harder leather shoulder guards, making him appear about three inches broader and splashed his face with freezing river water to awaken him, and calm his nerves. The river ran in a clear ice blue from the mountains. Its water tickled his skin in a gentle burn that washed away the dirt of his travels and left his face feeling supple and fresh. Then morning came.

A layer of mist rose to meet the soft light and reddening leaves fell in pairs from the trees of the glen. He closed his eyes and listened to the sound of lapping water. He breathed in deeply and exhaled slowly through his nose.

What should I do?

Ochnic was being restrained by the Silver Fur trolls. Marus seemed decided on appeasing Rohka and without the dragons behind him, Garon had little sway on his own. He tapped the scroll still at his waist. *What would you do, Darnuir? What would you do, Cosmo? What's the right thing?*

Ahead at the eastern edge of this glen, Garon saw the first waves of dragons and kazzek warriors begin to move, heading to engage the demons under cover of the morning mist. Pel had kept her fairies back; the hunters remained as well, waiting for Garon to decide. They'd need their full strength against the demons if they were to succeed. But if the demons were pushed back, they were likely to turn their full attention on the Glen of Bhrath. Ochnic's clan would be lost. His daughter killed. Garon had to decide.

'*On patrol, you never leave a squad mate behind,*' Cosmo's voice reminded him. '*Dead or dying you bring them home, just as you would want to be.*'

"That's well and good, Cosmo," Garon muttered to himself, "but Marus has a point. Rohka is the kazzek leader and Darnuir wants unity. It's not down to me to jeopardise that."

He paced through the heather, torn. Then he remembered it was Darnuir who had risked all to bring the humans safely from Torridon to Val'tarra. He wouldn't have been able to live with so many deaths on his hands.

'*You never leave a squad mate behind.*'

Ochnic is my friend, Garon thought. *He's the best of us.* And Garon made up his mind.

Half an hour later, Garon had made his plans and was approaching the Silver Fur guarding Ochnic with as much confidence as he could muster. The Silver Furs had camped by the edge of the treeline that ran towards the peak of the nearest hill. Distant sounds of battle from the east reached Garon. Marus had engaged the demons. There wasn't much time. The Silver Fur didn't seem to notice him coming. He was too busy looking in the direction of the battle, though nothing could be seen from here. He rustled around and kicked the nearby heather.

Ochnic was sitting crossed legged on the ground. His arms were tied behind a stake planted in the earth and he was still gagged.

"Why, hello there," Garon announced loudly.

The Silver Fur snorted and whipped around. "Der is no need to be here, pack leader. Der is a battle to be fightin'."

"Wouldn't you rather be out there?" Garon asked.

"My Chief-of-Chiefs gives me this task," said the Silver Fur. "Watch over Ochnic, Shadow Hunter, I must."

"Ochnic is no threat," Garon said. "He's just worried for his family. Let him go. Who will fight the demons harder than him?" The Silver Fur furrowed his brow in thought and Garon took the moment to check the treeline behind the kazzek.

Ochnic moaned incoherently through his gag.

Garon snapped back to the Silver Fur. "You see? He's very eager."

The Silver Fur curled his lip up to reveal his fangs. "He stays here. Rohka commands it."

"Well, I didn't expect anything different," Garon sighed. He drew out his skinning knife. "I'll just let Ochnic go myself then."

The Silver Fur laughed a low, guttural sort of laugh. "No further, pack leader. You Lowlanders without the golden clothes are not so strong. I don't wish to hurt you."

"You're right," Garon said. "We aren't *that* strong. But we're quite good with a bow." He looked to the treeline again and whistled loudly, a sharp, oscillating signal of the hunters: three short blasts to call an ambush. Griswald and a score of hunters materialised from behind the nearest trunks, their bows raised. Fairies flew out in a torrent of leaves from the trees as well. Pel lead them down to surround Ochnic and keep him safe.

The Silver Fur was aghast. "Der's no need," he said. He grasped his tusks, crouched and bowed his head to Garon.

"No need at all," Garon said. He nodded to Pel and she cut Ochnic free. They replaced him with the Silver Fur guard.

"Rohka will be angered by dis, pack leader," Ochnic said as he nursed his wrists.

"He can't push the demons back without us," Garon said as he sheathed his skinning knife. "He'll deal with it. Now, we have to move quickly. You mentioned mountain paths into the Glen of Bhrath. Can you lead us to them?"

"I can," Ochnic said.

"What of the demons?" asked Griswald. "Paths like that in the Boreac's were steep slanting treks with sheer drops. I don't much fancy having tae fight up there."

"We will walk high," said Ochnic. "Da demons should not notice us, if dragon legate is fighting dem."

"Marus is fighting already," Garon said. He hesitated for a moment. "You must try and forgive him, Och. He is only doing what he thinks is best for everyone."

"As is Rohka, Chief-of-Chiefs," Ochnic said. "But not you, pack leader?"

"I couldn't bear it to let you down," Garon said. "Not after we've come this far. I'm not sure I was ever cut out to lead armies and play nice in negotiations."

"But Darnuir, Dragon King, chose you," Ochnic said. Pel giggled.

"What?" Garon asked in mock indignation. "Think I was a bad choice?"

"A hunter with no experience of large scale command?" Pel asked. "You were the perfect choice."

"I'm thinking you might have been more agreeable when you were hungry and cowed, Wing Commander," Garon said. Pel flapped her wings playfully. "Look, Darnuir is expected to lead large armies and he never even got around to leading patrols first."

"Aye, but that's different innit," Griswald said. "Magic sword, a wizard companion, long lost ancient mentor figure and all that."

"Yes, a different set of rules," said Garon. "I, however, am a hunter not a commander of armies. My experience is in hit-and-run, in quiet ambushes and toiling across hard terrain. And after coming this far you'd have to think me mad not to see this through to the end with you Ochnic. You're our friend and we're going to save your daughter."

The troll broke into that toothy smile of his. "Glad for de help, pack leader."

"Alright then," Garon said. "Let's go join Marus. There are demons to kill."

They gathered the full might of the fairies and hunters and sped to the battlefront. As they came into view, Garon saw that Marus and Rohka had already cleared enough of a space to begin entering the mountain passageway. To the right, dragons stood in tight ranks with shields raised, holding back the demon horde in the narrowest corridor between the mountain slopes. Behind the dragons, the kazzek warriors dealt with stray demons that managed to worm their way over or around the Ninth Legion. To the left, a great archway was already materialising in the mountainside. Silver Furs were disappearing into the dark passage.

This will be our chance.

"What's the plan?" Pel asked, drawing up beside him.

"We'll need to hold the bulk of the demons here and secure this side of the mountain. I'll take around a hundred hunters with Ochnic to warn his clan. The remaining seven hundred will stay here to fight."

"What about the doorway on the other side?" Pel asked.

"Chieftain Orrock will know," Ochnic said. At the battlefront, Marus' line of dragons took a very visible step back.

"We need to move now," Garon said. "Pel, help Marus. The moment things look stable here you fly to us and let us know it's safe for the clan to leave."

"Stay safe," Pel said, then she took off. All her flyers followed her into the sky and hovered high over the demons, waiting for the hunters to send their arrows first. The dragons took another step back.

"Hunters!" Garon cried. "Into position behind the dragons. Three volleys then let the fairies descend." Word spread around the hunter forces and their arrows cleared some ground, enabling the dragons to inch forwards again. Garon kept close to Ochnic as they weaved through the back ranks of the battle, towards the beginnings of the mountain path. Ochnic was already leading the splinter force of hunters up it when Garon heard his name over the carnage.

"Garon. Garon, turn around." It was Marus, breathing hard as he limped to catch up. He had perhaps two score dragons with him.

"You don't look bloodied yet," Garon shouted to him.

Marus scowled. "I can hardly fight directly." He looked up towards where Ochnic was climbing. "He shouldn't be free."

"I had to do it," Garon said. He pulled out the scroll from Darnuir and threw it at Marus' feet. "Orders are to help Ochnic and *his* people in any way we can. His people are trapped on the other side of his mountain."

"That's interpreting my King's words very loosely," Marus said. "You know what he really meant. I won't be the one to cause discord between us and the kazzek. Now come back or I'll have my men take you."

"Rohka can take any anger out on me," Garon said. "Ochnic saved your life, Marus. He saved both our lives from that red-eyed huntress. We both owe him."

"I hate being reminded of that," Marus grunted.

"Let us go and the debt's repaid," Garon said. "Give us the chance to save his only child."

Marus pressed his lips together, ruffled his brow, and ground the heel of his crutch into the damp grass. "Go," he said. Garon smiled and turned. He was about ten paces away when Marus called, "Wait!"

Garon halted. Revolved slowly on the spot. And saw Marus shuffling towards him.

"Yes?" Garon asked.

"Take care out there, human," Marus said. He grasped Garon's forearm. "Don't die on us."

Garon took the legate's arm in return. "Why thank you, Marus. You stay alive too. Don't get any more limbs sliced open." Marus made a sound, which orbited a laugh, and Garon took it to be his equivalent to a delighted roar from Griswald.

On a narrow ledge, high above the battle raging below, Garon tried not to look down. He inched carefully along the ledge on his heels, back to the mountainside, arms pressed against it for dear life. He tried not to peer down and see where he would splatter onto the rocks, but he couldn't help a glance or two. Their combined forces had gouged a chunk from the black mass of demons now, but their advance was slowing somewhat as they spread out. Mercifully, the demons had not noticed Garon and his company's progress on the mountainside. Garon was even more grateful when the ledge widened out at a sharp turn, taking him out of sight of the battle.

Hours passed until Ochnic announced he was in sight of the Glen of Bhrath.

"Cannot waste time," he called. "Da golems work without rest."

"Golems?" Garon said under his breath. And then he saw their work. At the southern pass into the glen the earth churned. Boulders broke off the mountainsides and crashed down to form a blockage or crush demons. The golems themselves stood just below the height of the surrounding trees, upon limbs of dark stone webbed in blue lines like veins. Three in total, their silver eyes were the size of arched windows and they leaned forward, pressing giant hands, glowing in a silver-blue light, into the ground.

"And I thought I'd seen all the extraordinary things the world had to offer this year," Garon said.

"Bloody hell," Griswald commented.

"Dey cannot keep dat up forever," Ochnic said. "Let us hurry."

On their descent, Garon saw the golems weren't enough to hold all the demons at bay. Many made it through the tossing earth and were met with grey-skinned warriors of the kazzek, moving sluggishly compared to others of their kind.

How long have they been fighting for? It's a wonder they can even stand up at this point.

Ochnic's own energy seemed to redouble as they entered the valley, and he started running off to where smoke was rising.

"Ochnic," Garon called but it was no use. "Come on then," he said resigned to Griswald and the other hunters. They followed the troll up the glen. When Garon first saw the camp his stomach sank, as 'camp' was a generous word for what he saw.

Old trolls with thinning tusks and wrinkled hide lay unmoving under the sky without shelter. The children looked thin and shivered against the cold. Their blankets were worn and damp. One group was segregated from the rest. They were paler with patches of fur missing and Garon feared a sickness had begun to spread.

"Now that's a sorry sight," Griswald said.

"That it is," said Garon. "I'm glad we came. Seeing this — it's what it's all about. What hunters should be all about: helping people. And I've never seen a group more in need, not even us when we were fleeing the Boreacs'." Sadness and anger flared within him. He felt like crying and hitting something all at once. He looked away from the emaciated trolls and felt cowardly for doing so.

It was just so hard to see.

Ochnic was busy scanning the area; his eyes darting madly left and right, up, down, until his ears visibly pricked.

"Papa!" a pitched voice squealed from amongst the refugees. "Papa."

"Cadha!" Ochnic cried. He spun madly to find her.

"Papa," came the voice for a third time and a small kazzek with short tusks like baby teeth came running into view.

"Cadha," Ochnic said half-weeping, falling to his knees as his daughter jumped into his open arms.

"Papa," Cadha sobbed into his fur. "Miss you. Miss you, I did."

"We were needin' help," Ochnic said between planting kisses on her head. "But I back now, Cadha. I will never leave you again."

Garon felt a tremor underfoot and saw another great golem plodding through the camp towards them.

"Garon," Ochnic was calling. "Come here. Cadha, my sweet, this is Garon. He is a human who has brought many Lowlanders to help us fight da demons." Cadha looked up apprehensively to Garon, her wide, wet eyes as cold in colour as her father's. He thought she looked terrified at seeing flesh that was not hard and grey. She clung to a hairy, three-legged toy as though it would defend her from this foreign creature.

"Where's his fur?" Cadha asked.

"Same place as your papa's," Garon said. "Just not so much of it on me. I wear clothes to stay warm, see?" He tugged at his leathers. A moment passed in which the girl contemplated him, then she giggled.

"Cadha," Ochnic began, "what has happened?"

"You left," Cadha accused.

"Cadha, I had to go," Ochnic said. His daughter looked no more appeased. "Cadha tell papa—"

"You left," she said again, "and Chief Orrock died—"

"Orrock is dead?" Ochnic asked.

"And demons chased us, and I nearly lost dolly and..." but her words muffled as Ochnic hugged her close. Garon suddenly felt sorry for any delay he might have caused on their journey.

She is far too young to have been left alone. Ochnic must have believed in his mission like that Blaine believes in his gods.

"I will never leave you again, sweetling," Ochnic was telling her. Father and daughter remained embraced when the golem reached them. Its enormous eyes had no pupils but it swivelled its head and tilted it downward, seeming to gaze upon Garon. It extended its boulder-sized hand, palm up. Instinct told Garon to do the same and he placed his hand upon the golem's own. His view of the world began to change: rock and stone became brighter, more colourful, more than just black and grey and yet he could not comprehend it. He saw faint blue lines run through the hillsides, through the earth, and felt pulses from underfoot like many slow beating hearts. After a moment, a voice spoke in his mind.

It sounded older than the mountains and tired in a way beyond his own comprehension.

'It has been an age since I have seen your kind, human.'

What is happening to me?

'Do not be alarmed. Our senses have joined to form this connection. What is your name?'

I am Garon. What can I call you?

'These kazzek call me the Stone Father. That will suffice. You bring warriors, young Garon?'

A hundred or so, not many but we'll fight hard.

'My brothers and sisters hold the southern pass but will not last.'

My hunters and I shall aid them. Can you open the mountain passage on this side and let the clan through?

'I can open it now, if the way is clear?'

No, not yet. I await word on that. Ochnic will prepare the clan to move. Ochnic? Ochnic? Oh, right I'm talking in my mind...

Garon pulled his hand away from the Stone Father, feeling dizzy. His vision cleared, returning to a human's again, and the golem lumbered off.

"Uh, that's disorientating. Ochnic, you need to get your clan ready to move."

Ochnic, at last, looked up from hugging his daughter. "Dis I will do, pack leader."

"Right then," he turned to Griswald and the rest of the hunters. They were a mix of Cairlav Hunters, of Crescent Hunters, of Boreac Hunters, some of the last of his white-leathered friends. Each looked determined, likely masking fear, just as he was.

"Hunters, this is why we're here. We've got a clan of kazzek to save and a southern pass to hold. Fight harder than you've ever fought in your lives. Aim true and earn your leathers. With me!" He bolted south and they followed. No one challenged the need to help these poor creatures who were trapped, hungry, despairing and no different from any human or dragon or fairy at heart.

Amongst the woodland at the southern end of the valley they came across kazzek from Ochnic's clan; wounded and exhausted. Garon thought their defeated eyes regained a small spark when they saw the hunters coming. They didn't even question humans showing up. They just rejoiced at the arrival of aid. One ran off to inform the golems. Groans of exertion from the golems carried through the very ground. Garon felt it more than he heard it and saw trees pushed aside as two of the three golems began to fall back.

"The demons will take advantage of this," Garon called. "Into the woods. Let's set a surprise for them." He was one of the first in. Those kazzek who could still fight joined the hunters, climbing tree trunks into the canopy with all the speed of squirrels.

Drawing his sword, Garon wedged himself between two trunks and peered through the narrow gap between them. His heart pounded, his breathing increased, his fingers twitched with a nervous energy. He could just make out the final golem ahead, still maintaining a churning stretch of earth which blocked much of the pass. Yet, with two of the golems gone, a portion of the ground had become still and demons were spilling in over it.

Normally, before a fight, Garon would turn to Cosmo for a reassuring nod, just like he'd had done since he was fifteen. This time, it was hunters who caught his eye and he nodded to them, grinning in a way that only the insane or the patrol leader ever did. He could not seem downcast. He smiled just like he had to Darnuir, Balack and Eve the first time they had come across a fully grown and angry wolf; the same smile he'd seen from Cosmo, and the same one he'd seen old Captain Tael give Cosmo many years ago.

The demons drew closer.

They crossed from tossed soil to the red and yellow leaves of the woodland floor.

Closer still.

A few ran passed the trees Garon was pressed against.

He let another heartbeat pass. "Now," he roared.

"Get stuck in," bellowed Griswald.

Garon picked his target and came out hacking. He caught the demon and smoke spiralled upwards from the wound. He kept moving, shouldering into another. He stamped on its small foot and smashed the pommel of his sword into its howling face.

As the second wave of whooping demons reached the hunters, the kazzek descended from the trees, crashing to the earth in a blaze of knives and orange leaves. Garon felt a burst of newfound energy and battled on, rushing at the nearest demon, thrusting his sword at its neck. The demon's dying body stumbled backwards, stepping in front of a running kazzek who flipped over the demon, landed, and continued to run.

Demons kept coming and the day wore on. As the light began to fade, the death toll of the hunters steadily rose. Garon stumbled on a red-leathered body and the act of balancing himself took him out of his tempo. Suddenly, he felt his exhaustion hit him and found it hard to breathe in air now thick with smoke. He fell to one knee, panting. *We cannot last much longer like this.* Even as he thought it, a kazzek fell from above with two black arrows in his chest.

More demons were coming.

There were always more coming, but strangely no spectres yet.

Garon clenched his fist amongst the wet leaves and blood squelched between his fingers. He rose to meet the demons and saw he was not alone. A fairy landed and struck at two of their backs with her spear. Garon cried from the exertion of blocking the third demon. He held it in place and the very tip of a spearhead punched through its stomach.

"Pel," Garon gasped.

"It's done," she said. "The western exit is secure. The demons are falling back."

"Fly up the glen, tell Ochnic." She took off at once and Garon summoned what strength remained in his voice. "Back! Back now. We're getting out of here. Hey," he yelled at a passing kazzek, grabbing him by his arm. "Tell those golems we're going."

"Dey will know," the troll insisted, nodding his head vigorously. Garon ducked to avoid being shredded by his long tusks. Sure enough, the ground began to shake, signalling the golems were on the move.

Garon joined the stream of hunters and kazzek fleeing the area. He could no longer feel his legs but he ran. Closer to the camp Ochnic ran out to meet them, his daughter sitting on his shoulders.

"Lead da demons away. Da clan are still moving into de passageway."

Garon nearly collapsed at Ochnic's feet. Doubled over, he was helped up by an enormous set of hands.

"Up ye get lad," Griswald said. Even his beard looked drenched in sweat.

"You're older than me," Garon said. "How am I the one struggling?"

"Who said I wis'nae struggling?" wheezed Griswald.

"How many of us made it?" Garon asked.

"About half," Griswald replied.

Garon supposed it could have been far worse. "We need to give the kazzek more time."

"Come," Ochnic said, bounding off towards the mountain pathways he had led them on. "We distract da demons dis way, draw dem off."

"Ochnic, what about Cadha?" Garon cried.

"I won't leave her."

"But—" Garon tried.

"Don't bother," said Griswald. "We hav'nae the time."

"No, we don't," Garon said. "I'm surprised they haven't caught up to us already." The sound of demon cackling was certainly louder than before, but not as close as it ought to have been. Garon looked back to the southern pass and realised then that only two golems were retreating with them. "Where is the third?"

"Must have stayed behind to buy us time," said Griswald.

"If only we had half its courage," Garon said.

"If only we were that big and made of rock," said Griswald. "Let's follow Ochnic, c'mon."

They did. The remaining kazzek warriors and hunters dashed up the mountain path. The last golem was doubled down at the southern pass, its feet and hands were dug deeply into the earth, drawing up raw Cascade energy in luminescent pools. The blue liquid steamed and smoked, turning the grass and trees silver or burning them black in a slowly growing radius. In what seemed a final effort, the golem pressed deeper into the earth. Deep cracks appeared in its stone body. It wasn't in vain, for the ground quaked and broke in an arc before the golem, swallowing demons whole or crushing them beneath a flood of soil. Some demons still made it through, swarming over the hunched form of the golem. Garon had no idea how long the golem might last like that. Already the smoke and steam of the raw Cascade was blocking it from view.

Garon reached over his shoulder and was pleased his bow was still intact.

"Hit the demons in the flank," Garon yelled. "Draw them away from the clan."

Bow strings twanged as quickly as the hunters could draw and release. It worked a little too well. The demons changed course to chase them.

"Move!" Garon called. "As fast as you can. Move."

It was precarious trying to run along the narrow path with a sheer drop on the left. A full moon and starlight helped but not by much. The kazzek's natural agility served them better than the humans. One hunter ahead stumbled and fell, tumbling out of sight.

At some point, wings buzzed overhead. "The clan is safely in the tunnel along with three golems," Pel shouted down. "The doorway is sealed behind them." The battered kazzek warriors running with Garon and the hunters rejoiced, throwing their fists into the air. "Move fast. The demons are finding their way onto these trails and we've seen spectres popping out of shadows cast by moonlight." The celebrating stopped at once.

"Thanks for the encouragement," Garon said. Pel descended to Garon's level, fluttering beside him, an arm's length off the safety of the path.

"You're welcome," said Pel quietly, not catching the sarcasm. "I'll bring more flyers back with me." Then she was off, and in his delirious exhaustion Garon had a nightmarish image of spectres emerging all along the narrow path, their dark razor sharp swords cleaving at their ankles.

He slapped himself in the face and carried on.

An hour passed, then two. Their progress heading back was far quicker than it had been on the approach. Pressure from demons at the rear kept Garon's legs working. He could still hear the tumult of the demons. It never grew louder, but nor did it fade away, a constant reminder of what hunted them. His vision was blurring and shifting as though he were drunk. He kept focused on Cadha in front of him. She was on Ochnic's back, her little arms and legs wrapped tightly around her father.

Then something appeared below at the base of the mountain. It seemed to be a new shimmering river. No, that couldn't be right. He tried to focus on it but the golden glint stung his sore eyes. *Golden.* His mind worked slowly. *Golden — that's no river... Dragons! It's the dragons.*

"We've made it back to the other side," Garon blurted out.

"Just a little further, pack leader," Ochnic shouted back.

The path began to descend. When they were about thirty feet from ground level, Garon could make out the Ninth Legion more clearly and the fairies alongside them. Ranks of dragons ran right up to the base of the cliff face below. Many were pointing up at Garon and the others. Yet even as he looked over their allies, the glint of the dragon's armour vanished. A jagged cloud had cut across the moon and shadows spread along the mountainside. And like a drunkard suddenly forced to cope with some harsh reality or danger, Garon felt alert in an instant.

"Spectres!" came the cry.

They came up from the path underfoot just as he'd feared. They came with axes, swords and maces, swirling in purple shadows. They came like smoke caught in the wind. And they came screaming.

"Kill, kill, kill," the spectre closest to Garon screeched. "The Master calls. He caalllllsss—"

Garon silenced him with a sword in its gut. More spectres were emerging from the steep slope of the mountain, sliding down towards them, shouting incoherently.

"The voice it calls."

"In our minds."

"Killll," they screamed.

"Kill us!" One roared and even attacked another spectre.

What precious space there was on the mountain path quickly disappeared. Garon swung his exhausted arm and his sword caught on a spectre's heavy axe. Griswald boxed the spectre off the ledge but more came. The tendril of cloud blocking the moon seemed unwilling to move on.

"We are sorry," the spectres cried. "Sorry to disobey you, Master."

"Master, master, master," others pleaded.

"PLEASE," said another, even as it tried to skewer both Ochnic and Garon. Ochnic slashed at its throat and Garon steadied the troll with a helping hand. Cadha clung bravely to her father, not uttering a word. A spectre rose in the sliver of a shadow between them. Garon and Ochnic were shoved aside as it sprang upwards. The force of it knocked Cadha from Ochnic's back and Garon stumbled, lost his balance, and fell from the edge of the ledge.

Below, the dragons were still battling with the demons. Garon fell towards them for a second, and then a rough hand caught his forearm.

Ochnic grunted. The troll had fallen flat on his belly and was being pulled closer to the edge of the path by Garon's weight. Garon tried to swing his free hand up to grab the ledge. His fingers brushed the dirt but he couldn't gain a grip.

"Papa," Cadha yelled. Ochnic was holding onto them both but the battle with the spectres was not over. A kazzek body fell past Garon as he tried for the ledge again.

He missed.

"Ochnic, I can't make it. Let go of me." He didn't need to think it through. It was the only choice he could make. And he meant it.

"Don't say dat," Ochnic said in evident pain as his chest scraped a little further over the ridge. Cadha was sobbing.

"Ochnic, don't be a damned fool. She's your daughter. She's why you did all this. Let. Me. Go."

Ochnic moaned from the effort.

Garon felt his hand slip.

"Papa, I can't hold you," Cadha wailed.

"Let me go," Garon said. "If she falls this has all been for nothing. We came to save your people. We weren't all going to make it."

"Be quiet," Ochnic said. "Cadha, sweetling, hold me. Hold on, you must." He began pulling Cadha up, every muscle fibre on his sinewy arm shook under the strain. Garon felt himself slip a little more and Cadha dropped her doll to grab onto her father's arm with both hands. But she wasn't strong enough to cling on and she slid down Ochnic's arm.

Garon met the troll's eyes, and his fear was plain. Ochnic's lip trembled but he unfurled his hand from Garon's arm.

"Bye, Och."

Garon let go too.

There was a great sense of freedom just falling through the night. He saw Ochnic grab Cadha with his unfettered hand. Saw him pull her up. Saw the flash of a spectre swing its sword above Ochnic, down into his back.

No!

Ochnic's hands unclenched and Cadha fell.

No. This isn't right. Only Cadha's silhouette falling after him remained visible. And the thing that caught her.

A blue streak blew by so fast Garon almost missed it. It caught Cadha, swerved wildly around and headed west, away from the fight.

That's better. That's right.

The rush of wind blocked out all other sound.

He closed his eyes.

Crunch.

Pain. There was definite pain. Lots and lots of pain. But if there was pain, he could not be dead. Not yet at least. He was on top of something metallic and solid, and decided it was best to roll off it. His face landed on cool grass and he sighed. Even sighing hurt. Slowly, as slowly as he could, he opened one eye.

"Marus?" Garon couldn't believe it.

"Not a word, human," Marus groaned. He too was lying on the earth, spread-eagled with pieces of his crutch by his side. "Saw you lot up there. Couldn't let you die."

"I might have preferred it to this," Garon said. "I think everything is broken."

"You'll mend," Marus said.

Both of them lay there, taking laboured breaths, enjoying something close to a respite. Before long there were dragons and fairies all over them like a hot rash. Garon felt himself being lifted and carried away. Marus had fared a little better and could and least be pulled to his feet. It was a pleasant weightless feeling being carried like this. A pleasantness sorely interrupted by the appearance of Rohka. The Chief-of-Chiefs loomed over him as his carriers continued to bear him away from the battle.

"You went against my wishes, Garon, pack leader."

"You got your food and we saved the clan as well," Garon said. "Are my people up on the ridge? Is Ochnic —"

"I sent my Silver Furs up to aid dem," said Rohka. "As for da demons below, they're going mad. Wild. So are de spectres. Dey are dying quickly."

"Everyone wins then," Garon said.

"Everyone but you," Rohka said.

"Well, I don't matter much," Garon said. "After all, I'm just one human. Aren't I?"

"Rest, you should," Rohka said. Starlight flashed against the metal on his tusks and he left. Garon moaned softly, though the pain wasn't so intense when his body didn't have to carry its own weight. He closed his eyes. He did not intend to open them for a long time.

Chapter 28

A SHEEP AMONGST DRAGONS

The First War between humans and dragons began at the Rump Coast, to the east of Deas. Enough sources confirm that a dragon trading galley was shipwrecked there late one autumn. Dragons claim the humans refused to feed the survivors. The humans claimed their harvest had been poor and so they had little to share with ravenous dragons. Tensions mounted and sadly, blood was spilt. A human child was supposedly the first victim. Those shipwrecked dragons were all cornered and killed in revenge, save for one who managed to flee. When he reached Aurisha with the news, war was inevitable.

From Tiviar's Histories

Cassandra – Brevia – Arkus' Palace

I KNOW WHERE LORD Boreac is.

Cassandra tossed and turned in bed, kicking off her sheets despite the cold night. The howling wind and lashing rain might have been blamed for disturbing her, had her mind not been racing.

I know where Lord Boreac is.

She had repeated that to herself and Orrana for days now. The words echoed in her mind as she drifted from sleep to near-sleep. In her broken dreams, the thought floated above her like a butterfly she couldn't catch. Then her hands caught it, crushed it, and its wings turned to ash.

She woke in a start.

367

Sitting up in bed, she rubbed her eyes, grinding the crust of her disturbed sleep away. She reached for the half-drained cup of wine at her bedside, hoping the heavy red would weigh her mind down and let her dream in peace. The windows rattled in their lattice frames. Then a more unsettling sound reached her – a baying of pain. Brackendon was not sleeping well either.

Cassandra finished off the rest of the wine. She hadn't been allowed much at the Bastion, but here she was offered it daily. She could even make demands here, have things brought to her, done for her. She'd gotten used to it quicker than she cared to admit. She'd got more used to wine as well, and after some weeks of wincing at the taste, she was enjoying it. Already, she felt more settled.

I know where Boreac is.

The words came song-like as her head hit the pillow.

She was sure; in her gut, she was sure. The trouble would be finding him amongst all the dragons. Tomorrow was her chance. There might not be another. She just had to trust that Balack would come through.

At last, she slept.

In the morning, Cassandra threw on black leathers again and pulled back her hair in a ponytail. She ate breakfast with Orrana in her colourful parlour. It was becoming a habit of theirs. Even the clash of colours had become welcoming; a burst of brightness within a gloomy palace. Thane would sometimes join them when he had slept well enough to rise early with the rest of the palace. Today was just such a morning.

"Mother," Thane said, pushing his scrambled eggs around his plate. "Will father join us?"

"Father is busy meeting the lower houses, darling," Orrana said. "Come along. Eat up." Thane pushed a forkful of glistening egg into his mouth and chewed slowly.

"You know my stomach feels wriggly in the mornings," Thane said.

"Just have what you can manage," Orrana said.

"Arkus will be busy all day then?" Cassandra asked.

"All day," Orrana said, her voice full of knowing. "I doubt he'll have time for anything else. Especially the dragon refugee camp."

Cassandra smiled and helped herself to another strip of bacon. The fat was perfectly seared. Arkus being kept out of the way was one part of the plan. Cassandra had been tempted to go to him and tell him everything but thought better of it. He would not want her to go alone, and would insist on sending the hunters in force while she stayed safe in the palace. Cassandra had weighed those options but flooding the refugee camp with hunters to look for Boreac would only increase tensions there. Worse still, it might spook Boreac into fleeing further afield. The missing lord might not even be there, of course, and so a lot of effort might go to waste. Better to catch Boreac and come to Arkus bearing the fruit of her investigation all at once.

"Your talks with the houses went well, I take it?" Cassandra asked.

"Well enough," Orrana said. "The MacKenzies and the MacKinnons both think they should take the lion's share of Boreac's lands. The Erskine's have agreed to bring their extensive constructing assets to help rebuild the worst affected areas, for a pretty price I will add. It's tricky but we might be able to come to an amicable arrangement in time. Everyone feels reconciliatory and polite right now, the scoundrels."

"Mother!" Thane exclaimed. "Father says we are to be nice."

"I am," Orrana said. "But some of them must have been tangled up in the plots against us. Forgive them, Thane, but do not be so foolish as to forget." She turned to Cassandra. "More shimmer brew?"

"Please," said Cassandra. She'd need the energy. "Thane, could you pas—" But Thane had already taken up the pot and was at Cassandra's side in an instant. He began to pour, filling the cup dangerously close to the brim.

"Is that enough, Cassandra?" Thane asked brightly.

"Perfect," Cass lied, cautiously taking a sip to lessen the chance of a spillage. Thane beamed then returned to his breakfast, attacking it with a little more gusto than before. Cassandra couldn't help but feel a pang for him whenever he took ill – a protectiveness she had never felt before.

"I should take my leave," Cassandra said. "Thank you again, Orrana."

"For the breakfast? Nary a thought child. Don't mention it. Go on now and be safe."

"For all your help, as well," Cassandra said. "Goodbye, Thane." The Prince waved at her with a slice of toast dangling from his mouth.

The parlour door opened just as she was reaching for it. Gellick's tall frame loomed on the other side of the doorway. He pulled himself back in a great show of humility, bowing his head and saying, "Princess," ever so solemnly as she walked by. She heard him step inside the parlour after her.

Down in the palace courtyard, Cassandra waited for Kymethra, but after twenty minutes of feigning interest in the artful work of the hedge trimmers, she moved on. She slinked casually out of the palace grounds without anyone paying her a passing notice. Brevia was quiet now that the troops had sailed. Many soldiers were still in the Dales, leaving only the hunters to keep watch on the dragon refugee camp. As the camps sprawled, the nerves of those inside the city strained. The people of Brevia had drawn a collective breath. Waiting.

The quicker the war is over and the dragons can go home, the better. For everyone.

To her relief, Balack was already waiting at the southern gates, surrounded by a baggage train to support a small army and an eclectic entourage – hunters and huntresses, merchants and giggling admirers. Balack stood a little apart from them all, looking nervous.

"Quite the retinue you have these days," Cassandra said.

"The extra hunters are to help keep order," Balack said. "And many of the city's traders were interested in helping me in this endeavour."

Cass thought them sycophants hoping to absorb a splash of the honour and prestige now associated with Balack. At least they were helping, she supposed. A beefy man with a red face in a red doublet smiled hungrily beside a stacked cart.

"If nothing else, the poor dragons will eat a little better today," Cassandra said.

"Humans need to eat as well," Balack said. "If this keeps up for long, even the palace will have to start rationing."

"Well, I'll live. It's not the dragons' fault they're stuck here like this."

"It might not be so drastic if Arkus hadn't issued an open invitation for them to sail home." Balack stepped closer to her then and glanced quickly around before continuing. "Arkus may well have made a mistake. He's trying to appease the Assembly but such a huge migration to Brevia is putting the city under pressure. Lord Esselmont says that his harvest in the Crescent will fall short with all the damage and disruption."

"Yes, the Kingdom is a wreck," Cassandra said. "We'll just have to pull through it. Complaining won't help, nor will blaming it all on the dragons."

"I know, but it's easy for people to blame others, as it was for me." He turned to look at the city gates, staring intensely, as though seeing through the iron and wood to the refugee camps. "Arkus won't be pleased when he finds out what I've done. But I want to help. I find myself without my home as well. The Boreac Mountains are deserted, the people I knew dead or scattered. I won't claim to have it as hard as the dragons out there, but I can sympathise with them, I think. I should have done so sooner."

Cassandra looked at him when he turned back to face her; really looked. Under all the pampering, Balack was hurting. His eyes gave it away. They lacked their full colour and he seemed distant within them, as though still tethered to the sorrow and pain of his recent heartbreaks.

"You're doing the right thing now," Cassandra said. "And don't worry about Arkus. If I find Boreac, he won't care."

Balack nodded. "I hope you're right. You should have told me sooner. We need to get that ridiculous engagement cancelled."

Cassandra gasped in mock anger. "You'd reject your Princess in such a manner?"

"I know how hard you can slap a man," Balack said. "I just wouldn't feel safe, Your Highness. Besides you wouldn't want me. Too many damned issues of my own to sort out." He smiled, then stepped back, put two fingers between his teeth and whistled loudly. The cogs above, twice the size of cartwheels, began to grind with the effort of moving the enormous gates.

An hour later, they were at the centre of the refugee camp. A podium had been hastily thrown up at Balack's request. Grim-faced dragon after grim-faced dragon had gathered with an eerie stillness. Most were female, with children following dutifully at their heels. The few men were the old or wounded, scowling from their loss of dignity. Cass felt a tension here as well. It wasn't the quiet brewing fear inside of Brevia, but a grief at fallen pride.

They were bitter, these dragons and it only intensified each day. They'd been sent from Val'tarra by Kasselle or travelled on their own volition, all under the promise of going home. Instead, they'd been penned in. The number of hunters out in force for Balack couldn't be helping. It gave an impression of herding animals. At least this stunt was having the desired effect. The city-sized-camp was pooling in the centre with the promise of food, dragging even the most distant dragons in. After the night's storm, the chill morning and freshly sodden ground, some thought of relief would be welcome. If Boreac was indeed here, she reckoned he would stay well away. There were too many hunters, who, as far as he knew, could be chasing him down.

Balack took to his stage, not as confidently as he had been doing for human audiences. There was no Arkus to back him now, no resplendent Chevaliers to add glamour. The eyes of the dragons looked not to him but to the sacks, carts and barrels collected behind him.

"I have been called the 'Hero of the Bastion'," Balack began. He'd grown skilled in projecting his voice and it carried towards the back where Cassandra was lurking. "But I did not storm the walls alone. How could I? It was dragons who took the walls, who fought on them, bled on them, bled for us all."

Arkus would not like this at all. Cassandra wondered whether the hunters cared, whether they would trip over each other to report it to the King or his Chevaliers. *I better find Boreac after all this or I'll find a white gown and veil in my room at the first opening in Arkus' schedule.*

Something sharp nudged at her ankle.

Cassandra felt relief at seeing Kymethra behind her. The witch would be invaluable in covering the camp quickly. Cass held out her arm and Kymethra settled there, delicately placing her talons into the thick leather vambrace. The weight made Cassandra's knees buckle before she gained her balance. Kymethra's big bird eyes looked imploring at her.

"I'm glad you came," Cassandra told her. Kymethra opened her beak and tilted her head playfully. It sufficed for a smile. "Are you feeling up to it?" Kymethra nodded. It was singularly strange to see a bird make such a movement. The witch lifted a wing and stretched it to its impressive length behind and around Cassandra's head. *Is this a hug?* There were equal white feathers to brown now, but they were soft, comforting, like the taste of butter on hot bread.

"I forgive you," Cassandra said through a mouthful of feathers. She ran a finger down the back of Kymethra's head and the witch closed her eyes in some pleasure. Afterwards, Kymethra pulled her wing back, snapped her beak happily, and turned with those penetrating eyes to stare across the camp.

"Look for any man on his own," Cassandra said. "He'll be older and likely staying as far away from the hunters as he can."

Kymethra took off in a flurry of beating wings and Cassandra began her search the only way she could. One tent at a time. One row at a time.

Most of them were empty, but some were occupied by women with infants or newborns at their breasts. Cassandra hoped someone would bring them some of the food. One growled, low and threatening like a mother wolf when Cassandra peeped behind the tent flap. Cassandra ducked out immediately, hardly wishing to come to blows with a dragon. Two children passed her looking especially dishevelled, their clothes ragged with neglect and dirt, and their bodies were little better. Thin, with wild hair and sharp long nails, the children looked feral; starring at her as though sizing up a meal.

Poor half-starved things. Are their parents even here? Are they even alive?

"Haven't seen an older human wandering around, have you?" she said. They just gazed blankly at her. *I guess not then.* "You should follow the crowds," Cassandra told them. "There will be food. Here," she added, tossing them the oat biscuits from her ration pouch. The children descended greedily upon them. Within seconds the biscuits had been devoured.

"There," one of them pointed through the camp to the south-east. "A white-haired man. He doesn't run so fast when the food comes."

"And he stumbles in the dark," said the other. Then they scampered off. Cassandra looked to the sky and waved her arms around. Kymethra eventually saw her and she descended, blowing a rush of air over Cassandra's head before landing in front of her.

"Try the south-east portion," Cassandra said. "If those children were right there is at least one human there." Kymethra cocked her head at her. "What? We don't have many other leads." The witch snapped her beak and took off again.

Cassandra wove her way towards where Kymethra was flying. Already there were dragons returning from the rally, looking disgruntled, perhaps at a failure to secure more food or let down that the announcement was not for ships to take them home. She didn't think Balack would have finished so soon but neither could he keep them all interested for long.

Come on Kymethra. Find him.

As though hearing her plea, Kymethra let loose a shrill squawk and dove downwards. Cassandra's brisk pace turned into a jog and then a sprint as Kymethra's cries grew louder. She covered herself in wet mud and splashed through dirty pools. She leapt over tent pegs and cookpots, over ash grey dead fires and bedrolls exposed to the elements. Kymethra rose out of the sea of mismatched cloth and hovered over one spot. Breathing hard, Cassandra arrived beside Kymethra, now in her human form.

"I got a bit overexcited," the witch said. "He got a fright and ran inside." The tent before them looked thoroughly dishevelled. It was greyed with time, patched and no longer taut; the very worst of the old ruined stock the hunters were handing out.

"I'm certain it was a human," Kymethra said. "He was slow and weighed down carrying a sack, as though his whole life was inside it."

"Might well be," Cassandra said, puffing slightly, "if it is him, of course. That or you've just scared some poor old dragon half to death."

"Shall we?" Kymethra said.

"You keep watch," Cassandra said. *We don't need a repeat of last time.* Kymethra nodded slowly and did not protest. "If anyone seems to be heading this way give three sharp screeches," Cassandra added. Kymethra morphed back into the eagle and took flight.

Carefully, Cassandra approached the tent at a crouch, then lay down at the edge of the material. She gently lifted a section of the tent wall. It was empty save for the brown sack near the back. Boreac might be a smart man, but he can't have been used to anything physical like this, not least because she was sure she could hear his panicked breathing from the corner to her left.

Waiting with something heavy or sharp to strike me with?

She inched silently along the ground and lifted the tent wall just enough to glimpse the soles of some bare feet. Then she heard a foolishly loud sigh of relief from the owner of the feet. Cassandra sat back up in a crouch, drew out her sword, and then struck hard with the flat of her blade at where she thought the knees would be.

There was a heavy grunt of pain and Cass doubled back and barged in the tent's entrance. She was on him then, pinning him with pressure to the small of his back and twisting an arm up behind him. He had white hair as the children had described. It was thick but matted and filthy. Entire tufts had fallen away. His face was cleanly shaven although she spotted several small bristles under his jawline.

"Lord Boreac?" Cassandra whispered into his ear.

"If you're here to kill me then be done with it," Boreac muttered. At least that is what Cassandra thought he said. His speech was muffled with his mouth half full of grass.

"Oh no, the King wants you for trial."

"Dranus' hide he does."

"He was quite insistent on finding you." She took both his hands and bound them together with a strand of strong silver silk. She moved to do the same to his feet.

"I'm not going to run," Boreac said. "I'm too old to try and outpace you and I have no weapons to speak of. Wouldn't have gotten into the camp otherwise."

That's true enough. "What's in the sack?" she asked, eyeing it up.

"The last scrounged up possessions of a fleeing man," said Boreac. "Some clothes, some trinkets of my ancestors—"

"Some papers on the suspicious death of a hunter captain?"

"Found Foulis, did you? Look, why don't you let me sit upright and you can fling accusations at me in a more civilised manner?"

Cassandra increased the pressure on his back. "Don't try anything."

"I assure you I am too old, too tired and too weak to attempt much."

"No sudden moves," Cassandra said, keeping a hand on the hilt of her sword just in case. She stood up and allowed Boreac to rustle himself upright. With the entrance flap shut the tent was dim inside, but the material was worn so thin that a gloomy light seeped through. Aside from the brown sack, there was only an aged bedroll, another handout from the Master Station.

On the ground, Boreac groaned again. His dirtied tunic was torn in places and vibrant purple-blue bruises were visible on his shoulder. Every muscle was defined due to his emaciated flesh and the smell was quite potent, like vomit outside a tavern on a hot morning. He tilted his neck to one side and there was a crack like breaking stone.

"Gahh," he gasped. "It's crick after crick sleeping this rough."

"How long have you been out here?"

"When did the Bastion fall?"

"Just over two months ago."

"Then that long," Boreac rasped. Cassandra unclipped the waterskin at her belt and threw him it. "Thank you," he said, taking two long gulps and dribbling some of it down his chin. "That's a kindness."

"We're being civilised," said Cassandra. He chuckled and took another sip of water. "The sooner you come with me the sooner you can regain some of your dignity with a bath and clothes."

"Give an old man a moment." He stretched out his legs lethargically, seeming utterly disinterested in the idea of movement. "I didn't think I'd be found here. Reckoned the camp would be a blind spot for Arkus."

"Arkus doesn't know," Cassandra said. "Not yet, anyway. I might never have guessed you were here had you not told Foulis you intended to go to the dragons. That was your biggest mistake."

"I was in a rush," Boreac said. "And how did you find Foulis? We were careful about him."

"There was a scrap of a letter in your fireplace."

"Hmmm," Boreac mused. "This is my first grand escape, I was bound to slip up."

"You didn't have a plan in place to flee?"

"All our plans were ruined the minute Castallan died," Boreac said. "And you know, I'm glad he's dead. I planned to stop one man gaining too much power and instead helped one far worse – one far less predictable. What poor choices I have made."

"You haven't asked me who I am."

"Does it matter?"

"I might be able to have you treated better. If you're cooperative." Boreac looked at her properly for the first time, squinting in the gloom of the tent.

"Ah," he sighed, realising, "there is much of Ilana in you. We were close once, your mother and I. Once I would even have named Arkus a friend.

How times change. Here I am defeated and here you are, looking so much like her. Yet I feel there is more Arkus in you than your appearance would suggest. You're clearly cunning and resourceful, just like him."

"Is that an insult?"

"Far from it," Boreac said. "Although it depends on whom you ask these days. Once your father was a good man, if not a great prince or king."

"Or so you say," Cassandra said.

"Believe what you wish. He changed when Ilana died."

"Are you a good man, Lord Boreac?"

"No more or less than most, I'd wager," Boreac said. "What did you do with poor Foulis in the end?"

"I agreed to forget all about him," Cassandra said. "He can go on living a normal life. You're the real prize."

"I assume there's no way to persuade you just to forget about me as well?"

"Wouldn't count on it."

"Such loyalty to a man you barely know."

"I didn't do it for Arkus. I did it for me. That would have been enough. But I've seen the trail of broken people that your failed revolution has left and I was there at the heart of the Bastion. So many died because of you. So many lives ruined."

"Arkus has ruined lives as well," Boreac said.

"Not in the same way."

"More slowly perhaps, less obviously," Boreac said with an exaggerated shrug of his shoulders. "Still, he has been just as ruthless. Houses rise and fall on his whim. Forgive me if I wanted to be on the right side of a power shift."

"The Assembly holds much power," Cassandra said. "We aren't like the dragons."

Boreac raised his eyebrows. "I forgot you were an expert having arrived in the city two months ago. You may not believe me, but it's true. Each year Arkus takes more control, subtly of course. Oh, he's very good, but taking power and influence still; a little here, a little there. There's no use in an Assembly that is under the King's thumb and I'm afraid our failure has only accelerated that. What?" he added, smiling at Cassandra's confusion, "you don't think I'm right?"

"You're all just power grabbers," Cassandra said. "Are you trying to say that Castallan would have shared power equally?"

"You make a fine point," Boreac said. "Getting caught up with the wizard was a mistake as well, but Scythe and Annandale got more radical as the years went by. They began listening to Castallan and blamed the dragons more and more, an easy scapegoat I suppose. It worked so well because there is a grain of truth to it. But Dranus take them for their bloodshed. I never wanted it to come to that. I wanted to fight Arkus at his own game, stop him upending our world to forge his new one. He's won now though."

"Unless you get to the dragons," Cassandra said. "That's why you're here. Do you really think Darnuir will listen to this tale you're weaving for me?"

"There is always a chance the dragons will see how far they can kick my head from Aurisha's plateau. My actions have condemned me, but what I have to tell them should save me. I'm confident of that."

"Which has got something to do with Captain Morwen, black powder and this," Cassandra said, pulling out the little lead sphere. It left a trail of dark grey on her skin where she rolled it between her fingers.

"From my lockbox?" Boreac said.

"You must have dropped one. Why would Darnuir care about this?"

"Because it could mean a change in power across this world like we've never seen before," Boreac said. "And with the dragons already weakened it could mean—"

A sharp screech came from outside. Cassandra turned to face the tent entrance and heard Kymethra's piercing cry two more times.

She rounded on Boreac. "Help coming for you?" Her stomach sank. Boreac might have been keeping her talking on purpose.

"No one knows I'm here, I swear it."

"Get back then," she ordered and Boreac hobbled to his feet and stepped back, closer to his precious sack of goods. Cassandra resisted drawing her sword. If it were hunters on patrol they might just pass by.

She tried to calm herself. *That's all it will be, surely?*

Voices were muttering outside now. They weren't moving on.

Stay calm.

"Definitely the witch," a man's voice said.

"Stay out here in case she lands," said another. "We'll go in."

Cassandra drew her sword as five hooded figures entered the tent. Black cloaks hid their bodies, but links of chainmail slinked out from their sleeves and a glint of dark steel was visible at their collars.

"Not with you?" Boreac asked.

"Not with me," Cassandra said.

"Put your sword down, Princess," the lead man said coolly. "You aren't going to die for him."

He was right. She couldn't win this fight. A scuffle came from outside and then the last hooded men joined them, Kymethra in tow. Her hands bound behind her, a gag cloth had been shoved into her mouth and a long dagger pressed lightly at her back. Kymethra looked to Cassandra, her eyes pleading. She could almost hear the witch's thoughts of "*Magic! Let me use my magic.*"

But it wouldn't help.

Cassandra might take one, maybe two, and Kymethra another but there were six opponents in this cramped space. No room to move. They wore armour and she did not. And Boreac's life wasn't worth her own. She'd caught him. The deal with Arkus was done.

Cassandra dropped her sword on the grass.

"Wise move," said the lead man. He drew back his hood to reveal his dark blond hair and pristine skin. Gellick smiled at her. "You've done very well, Cassandra. Your father will be pleased."

"Gellick Esselmont," Lord Boreac said with disdain. "Unsurprising to see you padding alongside Arkus like a good pup. Quite young to be positioned so close to the King."

"He needs men he can trust," Gellick said. "You've proven false, Geoff Boreac. A pity, I always enjoyed attending your feasts as a boy. Your cooks had a way with guinea fowl."

"You've been following me?" Cassandra asked.

"Dranus' hide, no," Gellick said. "Someone like me would have drawn too much attention. You said it yourself. You could do this because you aren't known yet. We only knew where you were today because Queen Orrana came to me in confidence. She was worried for your safety,

Princess. Asked us to keep an eye on you. We nearly lost you in this dragon cesspit but Kymethra conveniently flew overhead for us. And, well, this will make matters cleaner than back at the palace."

"Cleaner how?" Cass said.

Gellick smirked. "I must ask you not to scream. Do you promise, Princess?" But he didn't give her time to answer. "Do it," Gellick barked. One of the chevaliers pulled out a slender knife, stepped up to Lord Boreac and stabbed him in the gut. Boreac's wheeze of surprise faded as he fell into the fabric of his killer's cloak. The knife plunged wetly for a second time.

Cassandra stepped forwards. "No!" She looked to her sword, bent to pick it up, but Gellick's steel encased foot weighed it down. He hoisted her up by the leathers at the nape of her neck and flicked out his own dagger, pointing it at her.

"I said, no screaming."

Chapter 29

RETURN TO AURISHA

For those not fortunate to have journeyed to the dragon capital, allow me a moment to describe its splendour. Everything gleams there, from the stone at night to the eyes of dragon children, so comfortable and assured in the most powerful city of the most powerful people in the world. Contentment is high and life is stable. Lemons, plums, figs, quinces, melons from the peninsula, and every sort of nut and grain overflow in their markets. Smells of cooking meat are often on the air, though that does not please my tastes as much. Every home and street is spotless.

From Tiviar's Histories

Darnuir – West of Aurisha

EVERY MILE TO Aurisha had been with plagued with demons. They put up little resistance, but they were still in the way. Each time Darnuir thought to deviate their direct southern route the demons would harry them, just enough to get them to move onwards, closer to the city. It seemed Dukoona wanted them to reach Aurisha in good time. He wanted it badly.

Darnuir thought his heart would swell when he laid eyes upon Aurisha, but he was disappointed. He didn't feel anything. He just saw a city he had to take. It didn't feel like it could be or should be home. The plateau still commanded the landscape, the walls were still high and thick, fanning protectively around the northern edge of the city from shore to shore. But it was the demons that stirred emotion in him. Their host sat idly outside the walls, uncharacteristically still.

I must be wary. I must try to think clearly… One false move and twenty thousand lives will be on my hands. His head throbbed with want of the Cascade. His fingers twitched, longing for his sword, to enter battle, to let the power flow. With a great effort, he shoved the impulse down and took a drink from his waterskin to cool his urges. Something of his struggle must have shown on his face for Raymond looked down in concern from atop his horse, Bruce.

"Are you not exhilarated to gaze upon your ancestral home?"

"Brevia might be the black city," Darnuir said, "but Aurisha looks dead."

"Your people will return Aurisha to her former glory," Raymond announced, clenching his fist dramatically. "Why look, the demons have been gracious enough to leave the gates open."

"Not open but broken," Damien said. The outrunner was sitting down, rubbing his bare feet. He had been tireless in scouting ahead on their march south.

"Broken suits us fine," Darnuir said. "We can walk straight in."

"There are a lot of demons barring our way," Lira said.

"Sixty thousand at a rough gauge," Damien said. His thumb reached a particularly tender spot under the arch of his foot and he sucked through his teeth in pain.

Lira looked to him. "Are you alright?"

"I'll get back up, Prefect Lira." Despite his smile of assurance, he sounded strained. "We're so close to home to now. Then I can rest."

"Outnumbered, three to one, however," Raymond mused.

"We faced those odds at the Charred Vale," Darnuir said. "But there we had no choice. One lucky chance cannot stand as the basis for our plans. I've driven us on into this, but that does not mean we should hastily press further." He glanced to Lira for confirmation but she did not acknowledge him.

"The demons have offered precious little fight so far," said Raymond. "Practically asking to be slain."

"That does not negate the possibility of some ruse or feint," said Lira. "Lure us here, let us drop our guard or our senses, then crush us."

"I agree," Darnuir said. "Although it is likely such a move has cost them the Splinters. If it's all to try and reel me in, then it would be a foolish move. As foolish, I dare say, as chasing an army triple your size on a hunch alone."

"Some would call it bold, sire," said Damien. "The men respect your audacity. Your father lost too much of that in his later years."

"And gained too much caution, I'm aware," said Darnuir. "My former self certainly thought so, but then he got himself killed in the end. Following my old self's example would not be wise." But he'd like it too. He'd rather have the fight there and then, of course, as his thumping head reminded him. His right arm began to shake and he tried to hide it by tucking it close to his body under his cloak. Lira met his eye then but held something back through flattened lips. He pretended as though nothing untoward had occurred. "A part of me wants to believe that we could walk up to the gates and be welcomed in, but if Dukoona truly wished to meet with me then he could have come himself already."

"What is to be done then?" asked Raymond.

"Nothing for now," Darnuir said. "I need time to think."

Dukoona – Aurisha

"I cannot see them from here," Sonrid said. "Forgive my poor eyes, my Lord."

"Neither Kidrian nor I can see them," Dukoona said. "It is just nice to get out of the Royal Tower on occasion. A change of view."

"They are out that way I assure you," Kidrian said. "Less than a day westwards, still close to the sea." Sonrid gripped the edge of the balcony and gingerly hoisted himself up on his toes to peer out west. The bottom tier of the city was hundreds of feet below, a sheer drop from this terrace, which protruded from the face of the plateau. Many of Aurisha's fine homes had such balconies. This one had a table and a set of chairs, beaten roughly by years of wind and rain. Dukoona imagined dragons sitting here, eating supper, peeling a grape or picking at olives, and watching day fade to night. Now he watched to see if Darnuir would come.

"We did not manage to kill enough demons," said Dukoona. "More should have died to tempt Darnuir to seize the city."

"They've been crawling along since their landing," Kidrian said. "It's been rather vexing."

"I imagine it seems too good to them to be true," Dukoona said. "I'd move our forces well away but that would look even more suspicious and not only to the dragons." Rectar's vast presence had paid fleeting glances in Dukoona's direction. They had usually been harassing the dragon army during those times, so it had always looked good. However, were Rectar to glimpse the dragons inside Aurisha while sixty thousand demons ran merrily in the opposite direction, a passing glance would quickly become a fixation.

"Why not just send the demons to attack?" Sonrid asked. "Get it over with. Let them die."

"My dear little Sonrid," Dukoona said. "You cannot control our mindless cousins at the best of times so you won't understand how hard it is when they are whipped up into a battle frenzy."

"Especially that many," Kidrian said.

"Many more dragons would die than we now wish," Dukoona said.

"So, all we can do is send smaller groups?" Sonrid asked. "Like we have been doing?"

"For now, that will have to suffice," said Dukoona. "Kidrian, send one hundred demons every hour towards their camp and empty the city of every demon. Make a big show of it. Let's see if we can provoke them into an attack."

"Yes, my Lord," Kidrian said. He placed a hand into a nearby shadow, submerging most of his forearm, but hesitated. The purple fires on his head had dimmed.

"What troubles you?" Dukoona asked.

"Even if we manage this and Darnuir comes, and takes the city, what then?" Kidrian said. "He might simply kill you."

"I'll ensure there are plenty of shadows. He'll find me hard to kill."

"The Master then," said Kidrian hurriedly. "One day he'll find out. And then what?"

"I'd have it so Rectar does not find out until it was too late," Dukoona said. "But should the worst happen, then I hope the punishment does not last for eternity." He took Kidrian by his shoulder, squeezing hard and the shadows of his flesh swirled energetically underneath. "We will be free."

Kidrian nodded then melded fully into the shadow on the balcony.

Darnuir – West of Aurisha

Darnuir scooped up the last fistful of silver alderberries from the deep copper bowl and rammed them into his mouth. He chewed frantically and swallowed. His armour had felt suffocating, so he'd taken it off but his white shirt clung to him with cold sweat. He paced in his tent. Up then down, up then down, to his bed, back to the table. He needed an answer to their plight but he couldn't think. He needed the Cascade. Just one drop. In a nervous fidget, he reached for the empty bowl.

"No," he wailed. "No, no, no…" Unabashed he licked the bowl, covering every inch with his tongue, tasting nothing but the tang of metal. In a rage, he bent the bowl out of shape and hurled it. The crumpled copper hit his armour stand with a clatter.

Sucking in choked breaths, he surrendered. He could barely keep his hands still, yet he forced one onto the hilt of the Dragon's Blade. He nudged the door open in his mind. And he sighed. During one, long, luxurious exhale through his nose, he closed his eyes to enjoy the relief. His throbbing head ebbed away. All his troubles seemed to—

"Darnuir," Lira said. Her voice was like needles on his ears. "Stop."

"I can't," he whispered. Then he felt her hand fall bravely upon his own. He opened his eyes and looked at her. She wasn't afraid.

"You must," she told him. The memory of standing over her during their landing, a stroke away from killing her, brought a wave a shame. It was strong enough to out burn his need for magic. Each finger suddenly felt made of rock and protested as he unfurled his grip. With a great effort, Darnuir released his hand, drawing on a last quick stream of power before his pinkie left the hilt.

"Can I at least get more silver alderb—"

"You've ate them all," Lira said. "They aren't easy to find, you know."

"I'm sorry. I know I keep having to say that lately, but I am. I'm not so stubborn that I can't admit fault."

"Our people need a king with a clear head."

"I know. But there is little I can do about it right now. I can't cleanse myself of it before the war is over, before we are on the other side of Aurisha's walls." He breathed heavily again.

"The demons came again," Lira said after a few moments. "On the hour, just like the last five."

"Think we could kill them all if we waited long enough?"

"Do you think you could wait that long before offering battle?" Lira asked. He didn't have to answer. "He's baiting us. It reminds me of tracking this huge silver dire wolf back in the Hinterlands. We were used to setting traps for white wolves from the Highlands that strayed too far when hunting. White wolves can be large, but this silver one was something else entirely. We stalked it, laid out meat to lure it away from the villages and quarries but it didn't run back north. Once a civilian lost their life, we had no choice. But killing it wasn't easy. I think it enjoyed the sport. It was fast enough to grab the carcasses and bolt before we could take clean shots. Some of us were brave enough to wear extra padding and plate armour, and stand near our offerings to catch it that way. Obviously, it didn't come close then.

"Eventually, we took down all the game in the area. The wolf started to grow hungry. And as it grew hungrier it dared to come closer, a little more each day. Finally, it couldn't wait anymore and came for its food. Even with the iron traps in its hind legs, more than twenty arrows and two spears it still killed those brave men in the armour. Its teeth could bite through the steel. But it got hungry and it came at us and it died."

"Are we the wolf in this scenario?" he asked hoarsely, abruptly aware of how dry his throat was. He looked to his jugs but he'd drank all the water as well.

"You're the wolf," she said. "You said it yourself, you're craving the fight to draw on magic. How long until you grow too hungry?"

"Not long at all. I can't think straight. I don't trust myself to make decisions anymore."

"I've always thought that had the wolf run away, we would have chased it," Lira said. "If you're the wolf then the demons will follow."

His head was pounding again. "We should run from Aurisha?"

"Not all of us," Lira said. "We'll do something the silver beast could not. We'll split in two."

Dukoona – Aurisha – The Royal Tower

Dukoona was lounging on the throne of the Dragon King, his head dangling over one stone armrest, stretching out his neck with one foot lopped over the other. Many of the Trusted were with him, waiting. Sonrid crouched at the base of the stairs to the throne. Most spectres were out with the demons, trying to keep them in line. They were growing restless; Dukoona could feel their agitation even atop the plateau. He wondered if Rectar would be able to feel it soon, all the way at Kar'drun. If his Master checked in now things would not look good at all, but Dukoona tried to keep his fears to himself and not worry his spectres.

"Have any of you ever wondered what it would be like to eat?" Dukoona asked the room at large. The two dozen or more spectres in the room all looked taken aback.

"It is an advantage not to require regular provisions," one spectre said. "We do not need to stop or rest."

"An advantage to whom, though?" Dukoona asked. "It makes us better killers, better soldiers but does it make our existence any better?" No one answered. "I feel we're missing out on the ability to taste. Humans, fairies and dragons gain some pleasure from it."

"A temporary pleasure," another spectre said.

"I once found killing to be a temporary pleasure," Dukoona said. "A brief glimmer of satisfaction. Do you think it is the same feeling?" Again, no one answered. "I'm not seeking a definite answer, I merely—"

"My Lord," came the croak of Kidrian. He called as he sprang from a shadow upon the wall, landing in a kneeling position. "The dragons are moving."

Dukoona flicked his legs around and jumped to his feet. "Do they approach the city?"

"They stole a march in the night when our melding is hindered," Kidrian said. "Heading north, my Lord." All the spectres present growled low at the news, a mixture of excitement and disapproval.

"North," Dukoona repeated quietly. "How many?"

"Seven dragon standards were seen," Kidrian said. "It could be all of them."

"To what end, I wonder?" Dukoona said. "Send our army in purs—" He felt it then – a burning at the back of his mind; the feeling of being watched, magnified a thousand fold. Rectar was glancing his way.

"My Lord?" Sonrid said in concern.

"Send our army in pursuit of the dragons," Dukoona said forcing confidence into his voice. He could not let them know. "And reserve five thousand demons inside the city in case of any trickery on the dragon's part," he added, looking right at Kidrian as he gave the order, willing him silently to understand, to not ask questions. For a nervous second, Dukoona thought Kidrian would not realise what was happening. Rectar's gaze was lingering.

"At once, my Lord," Kidrian said, bowing his head deeply, overly so. He had understood.

"Go," Dukoona told them. As the spectres melded away, Rectar's piercing presence left him as well. They had made it through another passing glance. Dukoona hoped it would be enough.

Darnuir – West of Aurisha

Half a morning's march north from camp, Darnuir awaited news on the demons. He stood with Raymond and five Praetorians, armed with sword and bow, neither in sight of Aurisha nor the sea, under the shading of a small collection of stone pines. These trees were the sad remains of a larger area the demons had likely cut down for their ships. With clear skies the land was free of shadows cast by clouds, meaning the fear of spectre attacks was minimal. Still, the wait was dragging on and Bruce flicked a hoof impatiently, sending up a muddy-red dust cloud.

I know how you feel.

Raymond comforted his steed by gently scratching his great neck.

Darnuir was still itching for magic, and he absentmindedly ground his foot into the ground as a poor means of release. More reddish, dusty earth puffed up. Beneath the grass, much of the land was cracked like dry lips. The closer they were to Aurisha, the more it appeared.

"There," Raymond announced, pointing and elevating himself on his stirrups. "I do believe it is Damien." Sure enough, the outrunner materialised within the minute, pelting at a great pace from the north.

"Take a moment to find your breath," Darnuir said.

Damien groaned. "No need sire." His feet were swollen.

"Damien, I do not require you to run yourself to death."

"It's just my time approaching, sire," Damien said. "Runners don't last forever, and there's fewer of us now, so we're each doing more."

"Soon we'll have our city and you can rest," Darnuir said. "You've earned far more."

Damien smiled, painfully. "Once we've won back our home, I hoped to start a farm down on the peninsula."

"You would choose the life of labour?" Raymond said.

"Better than my feet becoming bloody stumps."

"You shall have your farm," Darnuir said. "Now, as for the demons?"

"It's working. The host chases Prefect Lira. They are now well removed from the city."

"A fine plan," Raymond said. "I just hope holding back an extra legion's worth of dragons does not cause Lira any more danger."

"She just has to take the demons as far from the city as she can," said Darnuir. "After two days, they are to wheel about and return to the city with every ounce of speed and strength left to them. As for our extra men, I thought it a prudent measure."

"Well, I shall not complain to have more dragons around me," Raymond said. "It will be a victory to savour."

"I hope so," said Darnuir. "Back to camp for now. We move at nightfall."

When the sun set and darkness fell, Darnuir and his two legions set out quietly as they could towards Aurisha. Stars appeared and the city shined faintly despite its state of disrepair. Darnuir's starium lined armour began to sparkle as well. They headed for the main gate, a large gaping hole in the otherwise indomitable walls. Chunks of the old gate lay broken and untouched in the courtyard beyond.

Darnuir was the first to cross the threshold. It was dark and bleak, lifeless and soundless. Even the sea was calm and could barely be heard. He turned his attention to the plateau and there he saw a sole red glow, high above the plaza. It could only be coming from the Royal Tower. Praetorians formed up around him and followed his eyes, staring up at the sinister light like a beacon calling to them.

"If this Dukoona is here then he is unlikely to be alone," Darnuir said. "Stay vigilant."

They encountered no demons as they advanced along the northern thoroughfare. The Great Lift would have made the trip to the plateau painless, but it looked hoisted and tied up and, in any case, it would be too risky. It would be the long walk for them, first south to the harbour side and then up the switchback streets of the sloping side of the plateau. Darnuir had met his end running down that way, caught by demons and stabbed in the gut. He would not let that happen again.

"Stay close," he ordered. "Shields up."

All was quiet as the masts of the demon's ships came into view and they drew closer to the harbour.

And then they came.

Shrieking demons fell on them, from above, from the side streets and alleys, from every doorway and window like black ghosts. But the dragons had their shields raised and the demons did not work in a swarm. They fought alone and died alone, each one falling quickly to a sword or a crushing fist. More demons sprang on them a hundred yards down the road and again they were soundly beaten.

"Small waves," Darnuir noted to those around him. "He's trying to kill them off." He couldn't keep the hint of anger and frustration missing from his voice. This was no real fight and he had no need of the Cascade. Just easy kill after easy kill, a laborious grind. So few demons came that sometimes he was robbed of even that satisfaction.

Ahead spectres began to appear. Hundreds lined the streets, stood out on rooftops and half-emerged from moonlight shadows, midway up walls or the rock of the plateau. The array of coloured fires was a sickening rainbow, and Darnuir had the unnerving sense that they were all looking to him.

"Come," many raspy voices called.

"Come, Darnuir."

"Come, Dragon King."

"Come, come, come," they chanted. Praetorians took shots at them but the spectres vanished only to reappear after more waves of demons. At the harbour, they began to scream at him, some clinging to the masts of their ships.

"Come. Come. Come."

Their calling didn't cease, not when Darnuir reached the incline of the plateau, not even as they cut their way through the demons on the switchback roads. And as the night wore on, so did Darnuir's patience. He fought against the impulse to throw open the door to the Cascade and tear off after the spectres. It was harder with each turn in the road, with each cautious but safe step that the dragons took, leaving a smoking trail in their wake.

At the summit, the demons finally abated. The final hunched creature, all swirling flame and dark mist, leapt towards Darnuir. It cackled, entirely happy to fight alone. Darnuir killed it with a well-timed lunge. Across the plaza, the spectres gathered. They smiled and their perfect white teeth appeared to float in the darkness.

"Come, Darnuir," they said. "Come alone."

When Darnuir stepped forward they vanished into one shadow or another cast by the moon. All that lay before him was an empty plaza and the red glow from the Royal Tower.

No more games, Dukoona. Blaine gave me answers and so will you.

"Form up," he called to his dragons. "Take count and take rest, and rejoice for today we have won back our city." There were no cheers or celebrations. After more than twenty years, it was too simple to just walk in the front gates; to have it politely handed over. Perhaps the slow march through their dead city had sapped their spirits. Darnuir wished he knew what was going on. He didn't even raise his hand to tell them to stay because it was shaking again. "Wait for me," he said. "And do not follow."

The marble archway at the entrance to the tower was fractured at elbow height. It felt cold inside and Darnuir lit a fire on his sword. His grateful body sucked up the magic as he let light and heat flow from the Dragon's Blade. He moved up the grand staircase, one echoing step after another, and reached the spiralling stairs. They wove upwards for a long time. It was all vaguely familiar. Impressions from the memories left to him began to surface as he passed hallways, statues and rooms he used to see every day but could barely remember.

Eventually, the red glow indicated he'd reached the right place. The doors were opened and inviting. To his surprise, he discovered he was sweating. It ran from his brow and stung at his eyes. He wiped it away, even as the bitterness grew in his mouth, and entered.

This was the war room, he remembered, with the great crescent moon table and carved seats for the King and Guardian. Candles were everywhere, on the tabletop, on the floor and hanging from lanterns, along with a dozen torches lashed onto the balcony outside. Shadows crossed everywhere in a black mesh.

"I've been waiting," a sly voice spoke.

"Show yourself, spectre."

"I think not. What advantage would I have if I were to step out of my shadow?"

"Then I shall set this room ablaze to find you," Darnuir said.

"But I only wish to talk," Dukoona said.

"Is that so?" Darnuir said. "How can I be sure of that?" He took a few measured steps deeper into the war room.

"Because, if I wanted you dead—"

An ice-cold hand gripped his throat and a razor-edged knife materialised under his nose.

"You already would be," Dukoona said gently in his ear. Darnuir wrestled forward but Dukoona tightened his hold of him, keeping Darnuir's arms down. "I am strong myself."

Let's see how strong then.

Darnuir shoved the door in his mind open and pushed his arms outwards against Dukoona's locking hold.

"Gah," the spectre cried as he was knocked back. Darnuir spun, poison shuddering down his arm, but Dukoona was already gone.

"Melded away again?" Darnuir taunted, though it was nearly a gasp. He slammed the door to the Cascade shut. "You've made your point, Dukoona. If you want to speak with me, then speak." Still there was no answer. "I know you've been holding back. Your spectres fled at the Charred Vale after I killed Castallan's commander. You abandoned your siege of Dalridia and I've seen spectres vanish in the midst of battle since landing in the east, leaving their demons exposed."

There was still no answer.

"Why?" Darnuir yelled.

"Where is your other half," Dukoona said from some unknown place.

"Blaine would call it blasphemy to even hesitate in killing you," Darnuir said. "But I'll hear you out."

There came a sound like wind blowing, and Dukoona appeared in the chair of the King. The carved dragon atop the chair looked down on the spectre menacingly. Dukoona rested his feet lazily up on the war table and held his blade of shadow across his lap.

"Come, take a seat," said Dukoona.

"You're in my chair."

"Oh," Dukoona said, looking up as though to check. "Force of habit." He melded into the shadow cast by the snout of the carved dragon and rematerialised on the chair of the Guardian. "Does this suit better?"

Darnuir couldn't help but smirk. "And your weapon?"

"I'll keep it ready, I think," Dukoona said. "I imagine you shall do the same." The spectre pointed his sword towards one of the dusty chairs across from the great stone seats. Darnuir drew up behind it but did not sit down.

"You seem to have put yourself in a difficult position," Darnuir said.

"You cannot begin to comprehend."

Darnuir frowned. "Why this ruse?"

"I want my people to survive, as many as can be saved. Too many have fallen already."

"Those still on the Splintering Isles?"

"They are nothing to me now. Only those I trust most dearly are with me."

"Seems callous," said Darnuir.

"Loyalty is worth more than anything when you live forever," Dukoona said. "So far as I am aware, I shall not decay. I will only die in battle, by my Master's wishes or by a traitor's knife. I very nearly did."

"You were ambushed at Dalridia," said Darnuir, remembering Grigayne's words of a blue flamed spectre being attacked by several others.

"I was and so I left those who I cannot trust to rot on those islands."

"The Guardian will see to them," said Darnuir. "And with the help you have provided we have made incredible gains with minimum losses. The end will come soon."

"Yes, but unlikely in the manner you intend," said Dukoona. "I do not know when but my Master is almost ready."

"Ready for what?"

"To release his new servants," Dukoona said. "I believe my kind are no longer as valuable to him as we once were. There have been deaths, disappearances, strange red creatures with incredible strength leaving Kar'drun."

"What new servants do you speak of? New demons?"

"That is the frightening question," Dukoona said. "I only have a theory, though I am certain there is no other explanation. Especially since reuniting with those spectres who were long under Castallan's tyranny."

"Why are you telling me this?"

"To warn you for one," Dukoona said. "And offer you my help in killing him."

"Your help?" Darnuir said, quite taken aback. "Why should I believe you?"

"Sonrid, come here," Dukoona called. A twisted, hunched over creature hobbled out of a dark corner of the war room.

"What is that?" Darnuir said.

"This is Sonrid," Dukoona said. "A Broken spectre, the result of my Master's lack of power following the taking of this city."

"Does it speak?" Darnuir asked.

"Yes, I speak," Sonrid said, trying to pull himself up another few inches. "I also think and feel."

"I can hardly believe I'm even having this conversation," Darnuir said. "So, Rectar failed to summon more spectres properly. Forgive me if I do not grieve."

"He treats us like tools to be worn into disuse," said Dukoona. "Sonrid's suffering is uniquely painful but all spectres suffer. We are slaves, not servants. And we want to be free."

Silence reigned for a few moments.

"What is coming?" Darnuir asked. "What are you afraid of?"

"Castallan experimented on humans with his magic, making them stronger," Dukoona said. "He was successful, I am told."

"Too successful," Darnuir said.

"Strong, were they?"

"As tough as a dragon. Some, such as Scythe, he made even stronger."

"Hard to fight?"

"Hard enough," Darnuir said. "Get to the point, spectre."

"For years Rectar commanded me to capture dragons, not kill them." Dukoona seemed to weigh up his next words. "They were sent to Kar'drun as prisoners. What he did with them, I never knew…"

Darnuir gripped the chair more tightly, crushing through it, even without reaching for the cascade. "No," was all he could say. It was unthinkable. To face such enemies would be impossible. Fighting Scythe had been difficult enough.

"What can we do?" Darnuir asked softly.

"I'll do what I can from Kar'drun," Dukoona said. "But their army will be your trouble."

"As will killing your Master," said Darnuir. "I'm not seeing what I gain from this truce."

"Kar'drun is a labyrinth," Dukoona said. "You could spend a lifetime and never find your way. But I know and if you can make it to the mountain, then I will take you and the Guardian straight to Him."

"That's it?"

"I am a demon and he is my Master," said Dukoona. "There is little I can do in truth. But I want him dead. I do not see a place for my kind once Rectar's new servants are ready." Dukoona spoke more urgently, all pretence at intimidation gone. It was almost a plea. "I do not see a… a—" the spectre stuttered and then paused, as if he had been struck dumb. "No!" Dukoona wailed, then vanished again, reappearing moments later by the balcony facing north. He clutched at his fiery head with one hand as he stumbled out to the balcony's edge.

"What is going on?" Darnuir said, rushing over to him.

"He's re-retaking control," Dukoona said, the agony evident in his broken speech. "The forces I sent away from the city—"

"They're coming back," Darnuir finished for him. "You must stop them."

"I can't stop Him," Dukoona said. "Not when he—" Dukoona burst into a scream. It was a sound Darnuir had never heard before, chilling him beyond all the cold of the Boreac Mountains; a sound not of this world. Darnuir bent and took hold of Dukoona, thinking he might help, but not knowing how, nor why he should truly trust him.

"Fight him," was all Darnuir could think to say.

"We must go to the mountain," Dukoona said meekly. The dense shadow of his body began to swirl, unravelling a little, revealing glimpses of pristine white bones underneath. "I cannot resist…"

"You must!" Darnuir implored. "How else will you fight him?"

"Do you trust me now, Dragon King? Do you trust me?"

Darnuir did not answer. He could not answer. He could not be sure.

Dukoona pulled him in closer with one of his dark purple hands, the other groped for a nearby shadow. "We do not have to be enemies," he whispered before his finger found a shadow and he was gone.

Chapter 30

UNTO THE DAWN

Humans and fairies will rarely settle in Aurisha. For the fairies, there is precious space to attempt cultivating a silver tree, while humans feel they have no place. Military service lies at the heart of dragon culture but a human could never hope to join a legion. Intermarriage is scarce and children of such unions are considered unfit for service. And how can the new human baker or tanner or shoemaker compete with the established businesses that have been running since before they were born and will continue after they die? It is a wondrous city, something all should see. Yet the future of our alliance won't be served in such an environment. However, I am merely a chronicler. I do not have the solution.

From Tiviar's Histories

Darnuir – Aurisha – war room of the Royal Tower

DARNUIR REMAINED ON his knees after Dukoona left. When he got up, his muscles felt stiff and tired. He went to the balcony's edge and leaned forward, as if he might see across countless leagues to the demon horde heading back to Aurisha. He'd been killed in this city once before. A second death now looked possible. *I've gambled too much. I've caused this.* Darnuir could only hope that Lira would discover what had happened and return in time.

He wrenched himself away from the ledge and strode back into the war room to be greeted with the sight of the little spectre.

"Why are you still here?"

"The Master did not call me," Sonrid rasped. "He never calls the Broken."

Darnuir contemplated killing the half-formed spectre. He looked in pain after all.

Wouldn't it be a kindness to put him out of his misery? He drew the Dragon's Blade just enough to show an inch of golden metal.

"I do not wish to die," Sonrid said.

"Oh? Why is that?"

"I asked Dukoona once to end my suffering," Sonrid said. "He refused. He said it would be better to live and seek revenge on the Master. Dukoona has shown me I have worth to him. I've aided him and he has given me hope. I wish to do what I can."

With a loud snap, Darnuir sheathed his sword. "You have a lot of respect for Dukoona."

"He looks out for the Broken; the Master does not."

"I've never seen your kind before."

"Most of us cannot escape from labour in Kar'drun or the Forsaken City," said Sonrid. "I only got away because of the red creature I witnessed. Dukoona's closest, those he calls the Trusted, brought me here to tell my tale."

"Trusted…" Darnuir said. "This rebellion sounds like it has some weight behind it."

"Dukoona has gathered spectres to him for many years," said Sonrid. "He means what he says Dragon King. He wants the Master dead."

"Then we share that goal." He crouched down to Sonrid's level and looked into his small twitching eyes. He held out a hand, palm upwards, and after a moment of confusion, Sonrid placed his own crooked hand upon it. "Your body is freezing. I never knew that before."

"And I never understood how warm your kind is," Sonrid said.

"I suppose I never stopped to think much about spectres," Darnuir said. "When I was young, I had a sword thrust in my hand and told to kill demons."

"We are spectres," said Sonrid. "Our lesser brethren are beyond help."

"It's a curious thing. I've been trying to bring the Three Races together to stand strong against Rectar. I've not enjoyed a lot of success. Everyone has a grudge or wants something in return. Dukoona asks for nothing. He offers help instead."

"We want to be free," said Sonrid.

"One day, I hope you are," said Darnuir. He withdrew his hand and rose. "Will you meld and travel back to Kar'drun as well?"

"Melding causes me great pain," Sonrid said. "The Broken struggle with it. I will return to Kar'drun though. I have nowhere else to go and Dukoona might have need of me."

"I'll escort you to the city gates."

Sonrid dismissed the notion with a wave, as high as his tightened shoulder would allow his arm to rise. "You will have much to prepare. I will meld my way to beyond the walls then make my journey from there."

"Then I wish you luck, Sonrid," said Darnuir. "If we ever meet again, may it be over Rectar's corpse."

Sonrid sniggered, unable to form a full laugh. He shuffled over to the balcony and staggered towards a shadow on the ledge. When he melded it was slowly done. Spectres normally zipped into their shadows in an instant but for poor Sonrid it appeared to be a lengthy process. He groaned and winced as his hand vaporised, then his arm, then a leg and torso. After about five full seconds he had finally melded and Darnuir was alone in the war room.

He stood frozen for a moment in the grip of fear.

Over Fifty thousand demons. Six thousand dragons.

This time there was no Scythe to kill. No head of the beast.

Darnuir sat down in the King's chair. The pressure of his armour as he sat instantly made him uncomfortable. The stone chair as a whole was rather uncomfortable. He was just a little out of reach of the crescent moon table, meaning he couldn't even lean on it. So, he slumped back, tired, craving magic, bitterness building up again in his mouth. This moment should have been triumphant, instead he was alone amongst the candles and flickering shadows. Darnuir placed his head in his hands and sighed, feeling his hot breath on his skin and tugged at his hair.

He sat there for a long time.

In the daylight, Aurisha looked even worse for wear. Most haunting of all was the plaza. The stone was charred black from some great fire, and there was a red tinge to it that was too close to blood to be anything else.

"Something terrible happened here," Raymond said. He rubbed his eyes furiously, revealing dark lines when he withdrew his hands.

"And it could happen again," Darnuir said. He felt as energetic as Raymond looked. Small bursts of the Cascade had fuelled him through the night while they gathered their supplies, equipment and, of course, Bruce. Morning came in the middle of their toils and a fatigue had settled over the legions. Darnuir couldn't sleep in his current state, but did not wish to be alone. Raymond kept him company by the pulley of the Great Lift, taking in the view and soon-to-be-battlefield.

"I assume we will be defending the plaza in lieu of the walls," Raymond said. He gestured to the six working catapults they had managed to salvage from the demon warships.

"That is my intention," said Darnuir.

"A necessary step," Raymond said. "Blocking the gate would prevent Lira from entering as much as the demons."

"And if we're stuck inside we can't help Lira in turn. Fleeing on the ships left by the demons is not an option either. Lira and her legions would be caught in the open. No, we make a stand here. Bring the demons into the narrower streets, break up the horde, and with some luck Lira might be able to smash those caught outside against the city walls." He felt the bite in his own voice and his pulse quicken just thinking about it. "We've been tiptoeing around avoiding battle for weeks. It's time to fight. I ache for it. I need—" he stopped himself.

"Lira told us about your… condition," Raymond said. "Sickness is not your fault."

Darnuir sniffed and looked to his boots. "I'm not entirely innocent. The consequences of my actions could lose us the war. And I've caused enough pain to those I care about already."

Raymond straightened his back and stood tall. "If it helps at all, Darnuir, I'm glad I joined you. You are still in need of some refinement, but your intentions are right. I'm used to refinement but from those who are selfishness and manipulative. It took you to show me what honour really is."

"Me? I've not been so honourable of late."

"Daliridia would not stand, were it not for you," Raymond said. "I would still be Gellick's whipping boy. Lira might not be with us at all. And then there was Torridon, where I grew to admire you more than any Chevalier who's ever reigned above me. You do improve the lives of those you meet. You have done good, don't forget that. Right now, you're sick, but you'll get better. And we'll be there for you."

Darnuir allowed himself a half-smile. He felt his back and shoulders unwind some tension and he actually sagged from the relief. "Thank you, Raymond. I didn't know how much I needed to hear that. Go get some rest."

Raymond yawned. "You will not sleep?"

"I'll sleep when this is over."

Raymond bowed and took his leave. Darnuir turned to stare out across the city and the Crucidal Road running straight to the north.

He had omitted to tell Raymond that his decision to forgo sleep was also due to fear. He doubted his body would rise in time for the battle, if he rose at all. Only the Cascade sustained him and he dreaded going without it for any length of time. Withdrawal would cripple him. Of course, breaking would be worse. The image of Brackendon wrapped tightly in blankets like a baby reminded him of the consequences. Despite this, his shaking hand could not help but find the Dragon's Blade for another reassuring drag.

Run, Lira. Run faster than you ever have before.

The demons appeared at twilight, kicking up a cloud of dust as they trampled onwards. Darnuir forced life back into his stiff limbs, stretching and rolling his shoulders. He'd never gone so long without sleep, not even before the battle at Cold Point. He could hardly believe that had only been earlier this very year. Now here he was, a king atop his hill, preparing to face an equally dismal fight.

I wish you were here Cosmo and Brackendon and Balack too. I wish you were all here to help me again.

He wanted to turn back time and save Eve, to not act so foolishly with Cassandra, to get to Cosmo's side in time, and never have to see his dying body pinned against that tree. More than anything else, right this instant, he just wanted to rest.

Seven hundred feet below the demon army began to converge, forming into a thinner stream at the city gates like water flowing to the path of least resistance.

It was time.

He stepped forward to address his six thousand dragons. The two legates were at the front, the red plumage of their helmets ripped or frayed in places, and they called the men to attention. Flanked by tall colonnades, the dragons barely filled a third of the space of the plaza and seemed so small beside the Basilica of Light.

"This will be the longest night of our lives," Darnuir cried. "But if we can hold until the dawn, then we few will have held where our whole race once fled. This is not our grave. This is our city, our home; and Rectar and his demons have held onto it long enough." He raised the Dragon's Blade and let a jet of fire pour forth. "Unto the dawn!"

Unto the dawn? I'm beginning to sound like Blaine.

The response was comforting; each dragon roared their ascent to fight.

"Rain stone upon them," he said to a group of outrunners. They dashed off to inform the catapult crews. Four had been placed on the western edge of the plateau while the other two were stationed upon flat roofs facing south over the switch back road, down which the legions were already marching.

Darnuir dashed to the head of the column, leading them into position. Halfway down the first road, he heard the clunk and whoosh as the catapults let loose their first loads. With the steepness of the plateau's slope and the buildings all around him, Darnuir didn't see the rocks land. But he did hear the demons' death shrieks, and their hissing, howling and shrill, chilling cries as they grew closer.

"Shield wall," he ordered and the front ranks held their barriers with strong arms. The second row moved forward and raised their shields to cover the heads and shoulders of those at the front. All had short swords in hand for the crushing melee and stood ready as the first demons came scuttling into view at the bottom of the road.

If the creatures felt tiredness they did not show it, running uphill with an enthusiasm of a routing army. Many tried to jump at the golden shields, failing, and tumbling back. But on they came and the battle was quickly upon the dragons.

402

Weapons scraped like talons against shields, screeching with each strike and pricking the hairs on the back of Darnuir's neck. Beyond the front wall of dragons, the demons piled up as they found their path blocked. They began leaping upon one another without concern until the tottering demons looked likely to hop over the shield wall.

Darnuir twisted his torso then threw the Dragon's Blade towards the boldest demons. Before he even saw the bloody results, he looked to the red-slated roofs above and cried, "Javelins."

His order was repeated throughout the legions. Dragons appeared with steel-tipped shafts in hand. In unison, they pulled back, held, and threw. Javelins ripped into the demons, spraying smoke and chipped bone. More followed, raining down like oversized arrows. But still the demons stacked upon each other, caring little about trampling their comrades underfoot. They seemed driven to overcome the shield wall at all costs.

And many did.

Darnuir met the first one with fist alone, cracking its chin to ruin with an upwards blow. The second to land near him was killed by the hilt of the Dragon's Blade, caving into its skull as it returned to Darnuir's hand. Yet more came. Darnuir gutted one, snapped the weak rusted sword of another, but quickly their numbers were overwhelming. Without resistance, they began savaging the shield bearers from behind. Bile rose in Darnuir's throat as he saw his dragons fall within a swarm of hacking knives. Amidst the agonies of the dying dragons and the delight of the demons, calls for, "Next line forward," were bellowed, and Darnuir found himself surrounded by a new shield wall.

It will just keep happening.

Through the gaps between the shields, he saw the demons scrambling up their extra few feet of hard-won road and begin the construction of a new body pile to climb. Crunches and cracks cut across the battle as those at the bottom of the heap were weighed down.

Rectar must be forcing them on. Even the spectres would not do this.

Darnuir shoved the Dragon's Blade through a gap in the shield wall, skewering the already dead demons on the other side, and threw the door to the Cascade open. His head cleared, his arm tensed with the flow of energy and searing flames gushed from the Blade. He swept the immediate area in a wave of red fire. His exhausted body protested quickly under the strain of it. He closed the door over, leaving it open by a crack.

He stumbled back from the shield wall, his vision a golden blur. The shredding, zipping sound of arrows passed by in both directions. One unfortunate dragon was taken in his left eye and Darnuir felt a flash of pain from the side of his neck. An arrow had ripped his skin. Another two arrows rebounded off the thinner plate around his forearm and he groaned from the bludgeoning.

Even as his senses refocused, the second shield wall was being enveloped by the horde.

Something had to be done.

"Third wall," he cried and a new line was dutifully formed. "Hold and step back on my order. Stay strong. Ready — Step. Step. Step." The third wall took careful, but sure steps backwards, maintaining their defence. Demons scrambling up from the carnage of the second wall were caught off guard. Some tried to make the jump, fell, and rolled backwards, tripping others, and caught more in a gathering crush.

The blockage granted Darnuir precious time.

He tore back through his own ranks, praetorians hurrying to keep up as he made for the top of the final road before the summit. Somehow, the sun had set without him realising. Night had fallen and the city had begun to radiate its dim glow under the stars. The legate of the first legion met him.

"My King," he shouted, slamming a fist over his heart.

"We'll need to try our plan sooner than expected."

"Sir," the legate yelled in understanding and moved with intent towards the buildings lining the edge of the road overlooking the assaulting demons. On top, the javelin throwers were still launching their attacks while the third shield wall began to falter.

"Fall back," Darnuir called. "Fall back to the plaza." As word spread, the dragons began an orderly retreat. Those keeping the brunt of the demons at bay bravely held their shields high. If a gap appeared another dragon hastened to take his place. Step by step, they pulled back to Darnuir. "Hold," he bellowed.

And hold they did.

The line steadied against the onslaught and the demons pressed forwards with a single-mindedness no free-thinking creatures could have, creating a new build-up of demons before the wall began in earnest.

Darnuir held for long as he dared.

The stack of demons grew.

He held a little longer.

A couple of demon heads appeared above the shields.

"Now," he roared with the enhanced power of the Cascade. His voice boomed loud enough to make the demons flinch. And from the building at the bottom of the incline, where the curve of the road turned down a level of the switchback road, dragons charged into the flanks of the demons. They formed fresh walls, three men deep, facing both towards the bulk of the horde and back towards Darnuir, trapping the demons stuck in-between. A second wave of dragons emerged from buildings all the way up the road. A full three-hundred-man cohort slammed into the demons like golden spikes.

"Forward!" Darnuir cried, his voice cracking under the strain of the Cascade. He kept the magic flowing as he leapt over the wall of his men, crushing both demon and paved stone as he hit the ground. He cut down every demon within reach, embraced the blood pounding between his ears as the Dragon's Blade burned white-hot. The smoke from his flames and the demon blood grew so thick it was almost blinding, yet through the haze the dragons pushed down the road.

Darnuir left them well behind, working himself up into a bloodlust he hadn't felt since their landing weeks ago. He half-slid his way towards his men at the bottom of the road, facing the entirety of the demon army. With a mad draw on the Cascade, he sprang over the new shield wall with the power of an unloading catapult.

He sent the Dragon's Blade flying on another murderous journey when he landed, letting fire lash freely from it. With his empowered muscles, he swept his arms and bowled demons over. One he missed, but the demon was close enough for him to headbutt. Its skull exploded in a shower of rusty bubbling blood. A splash entered Darnuir's mouth and it was honey compared to the rancorous Cascade residue.

He stood alone in front of the shield wall, awaiting the Dragon's Blade. As the sword sliced its way back through the demons to his hand, the draining of the poison continued. Unrelenting, the demons swarmed forwards again. Darnuir blew his out his cheeks at them like a snorting bull. He raised his arm.

But found couldn't lift it passed his shoulder.

Something in him finally gave out.

He froze. His legs were leaden and he couldn't move. Dragons were around him immediately. Praetorians had fought there way out to his side, forming a defence around him. Some began pulling at his waist. Pulling him back. He let them and they hastened back behind their shield wall.

Darnuir dragged himself back up the road. At the summit, he collapsed panting. Praetorians closed in and someone handed him a waterskin. Even Raymond was amongst them.

"Our rocks bombard them," Raymond said, "but it doesn't disrupt their ranks. Shall we continue?"

Darnuir swirled, gargled and spat. He sat up but remained bent over for a second, fighting back the urge to retch. "Nothing else we can do," he said to the ground. His head was making a strong argument for detaching itself and dying peacefully elsewhere.

"They aren't going to flee this time, are they?" a Praetorian asked. He was one of the youngest and blood dripped from his left arm, which hung wounded and limp.

"If that didn't encourage them to back off nothing will," Darnuir said. "It must have always been the spectres who felt the fear. Rectar controls them directly now. He won't stop until all his demons are dead or we are."

The shield wall took another cautious step backwards, javelin throwers warned of dwindling supplies and the demon army began to laugh hauntingly as one; as if Rectar were relishing his victory through more than fifty thousand cackling creatures. Their laughter filled the night, filled the city and filled Darnuir's ears.

Survival seemed a distant thing.

Lira – North of Aurisha

Lira ran.

Her legs screamed, her muscles burned, but she ran. She'd been running for so long she'd almost forgotten what it was to walk. Behind her, fourteen thousand dragons stampeded through the night.

When the outrunners had reported that the demons had wheeled around, Lira had gathered the legates, hastily got their bearings and tore after them. It had been almost impossible to tell where they were in the dark but since finding the Crucidal Road, they had followed it south. It would lead them back to Aurisha.

How long ago had that been? A few hours? It had all vanished into the grind.

We should break soon or we'll all collapse before even sighting Aurisha.

But stopping a run like this would be tricky; if she suddenly stopped she'd only get trampled. So, she slowed her pace, very carefully, gradually, and the Praetorians near her slowed too, as did the legates, and eventually their speed was close to a human's jog. She called a halt and, exhausted, the dragons wound down.

"We should remove pieces of our armour," she suggested to the legates assembling around her.

"Lady Lira," Quintin, Legate of the Fourth began, "we cannot weaken ourselves just to make the run easier."

"We'll still have our shields and our strength, or what's left of it," Lira said. Quintin was a hulking figure and she craned her neck to speak to him.

Another beefy legate spoke up. "We understand this is your first command but—"

"But nothing," Lira said. "Legate Quintin, you will refer to me as Praetorian Prefect. I outrank you and I say we strip our armour. This is a chase, not a lumbering march. If we don't reach Aurisha quickly we'll lose the King. Keep your breastplates if you feel the need but have the men strip their greaves, vambraces, gauntlets, anything unessential. With any luck, the spectres will turn tail if we smash their army in the rear. Well," she added when no one moved. "Go. Now."

The legates exchanged looks before leaving to spread her orders. They did so begrudgingly, Lira knew. This had been her idea and it might have backfired. But there was no time to waste on worrying or pandering to the egos of old legates. She'd hit Darnuir across the face. The legates were nothing on him.

She hadn't expected this, of course, when she had left her mother behind to go join their people gathering in Val'tarra. Lira hadn't thought she'd be made the head of Darnuir's guard. She never thought she'd be shouting down dragons nearly three times or more her age. Yet here she was, the Praetorian Prefect, whether she could believe it or not, and Darnuir was in sore need of protection. She'd bring him his five legions, weakened as they were. She would do her job.

Lira returned to the few Praetorians she had brought with her. It was a relief to sit and she unpacked her rations. The mutton was cold and chewy with fat, the bread hard. She'd never tasted anything half-so-good. A Praetorian nearby, Sabina, removed her boots to inspect the growing blisters, releasing a rancid smell of feet baked in days of sweat.

"Don't touch them," Lira told her. "It's tempting but you'll only risk infection if you break the skin." Sabina gritted her teeth miserably. "Eat," Lira implored, "and elevate your feet if you want while we rest. It won't make getting up again any easier, though." Sabina took the advice, propping her legs on top of her ration pack and shield whilst she lay exhausted on the flat of her back. Wrinkled and swollen, her feet almost throbbed with bulbous green-yellow puss balls on her heels. Lira turned away, not daring to inspect her own feet. She wanted to keep her food down.

I'll have to remember to be more in awe of Damien in the future.

After devouring every morsel, Lira began removing her armour and the Praetorians followed her lead. The pieces clunked one by one to the ground. She hesitated with her breastplate but took it off and breathed easier. All she wore was basic leather padding, britches and a white shirt; no protection at all. Hunter leathers would have been preferable. But this would get her to Aurisha with some energy left to fight, and that was all that mattered.

She rubbed her eyes, fighting back a yawn.

And mother used to worry I wouldn't get tired enough during training and reveal I was a dragon. If you could see me now. I'm going back. I'll find our old home.

Lira rose with determination and within half an hour the legions were running again, less encumbered by armour and provisions. They had their shields, their swords and, for now at least, their will.

When they reached Aurisha the demon army was pressing towards the bottleneck at the gates. It was impossible to say for sure whether they even noticed the legions approaching from behind. Some did, slowly. Fiery eyes began to turn to face Lira and move in her direction as the legions manoeuvred into a giant wedge formation. Distant sounds of a battle indicated Darnuir's men were still alive. There was a slim chance. They had to take it.

As the number of demons turning grew from a trickle to a substantial wave, Lira called for the charge.

Sword out, shield raised, throat ragged from cheering, Lira was the first forward. Her legs wanted to buckle, her shoulders stung deeply at the joints but she ran. With the last scrap of her strength, she ran. This was it: the last great battle. And the ground shook, and the demons came on, and the dragons roared with such might as to be beasts of old once more.

Lira hit the first demon so hard it burst. She hit the second just as hard, and the third harder. She careened into the meat of the demon host and none held under the fury of the legions' thunderous boots. No demon withstood her until the momentum of the charge died. Lira felt herself slow as the press of the demons became thick and unyielding. Somehow, she found herself standing still and blocking attacks from angry shrieking demons.

They haven't broken. The realisation almost killed her.

Dragons closed in around her, but they were now bogged down. Before long the dragons were falling and they were all taking a step or two back.

It didn't seem right.

She scanned for shadows, anticipating spectres but none came. Only now she realised she hadn't seen any spectres. None. Only demons, howling, laughing, squealing like frightened pigs but swarming like a nest of hornets. The dragons hadn't even made it close to the walls. Lira assumed she and all around her were doomed. But she kept fighting.

In the east, a red dawn broke to usher in a bloody day.

Darnuir – the plaza of Aurisha

Darnuir slipped in blood pooling underfoot. Fresh red rivers flowed down the switchback roads, filling the air with a coppery stench. He watched demons enter each building on the final road, overwhelming the dragons there. His trick of feigning retreat to the plaza had worked a second time. It had not worked a third.

Now he really had pulled back, but they could only retreat so far before the width of the plaza would stretch their formation too thin. And this was it. They could give no more ground.

Darnuir remained at the front, all his focus directed on the next demon; the next demon; the one after. Time vanished. Nothing else mattered. Just the next foe. He'd heard his men cheering from far behind at some point but he didn't know why.

When it became too much, he stumbled back through the legions to catch his breath. He'd drawn on as little magic as he could, but the culmination of it hit him hard as he closed the door. He lurched towards a marble column, steadied himself with one hand, and then vomited behind it. He gasped as the acrid taste lingered. He peered worriedly at the back of his right hand. His skin had turned white but not yet black.

Looking up, he found Praetorians close about him; fewer now than when the sun had set. Dawn had come without his noticing and towards the north he saw Lira's legions surrounded, like a golden coin on a black field.

Darnuir pointed to them. "When did they arrive?"

"Just before daybreak," Raymond said. "Yet they have the same problem as ourselves. Without the demons breaking—"

"They'll be swallowed up," Darnuir said. The cruel fact was that Rectar did not need to keep his demons. Their final task would be to weaken the dragons if not outright kill them, softening them for this new threat warned of by Dukoona. He stared blankly out at Lira's forces. The golden circle contracted with each heartbeat.

"We're out of ammunition for the catapults," Raymond said. "Darnuir?"

"Yes," Darnuir said, snapping back to the situation. "Out of stones, yes." He paused again, looking from the Royal Tower to the Basilica. They could try setting a defence within one of those stout buildings, but eventually they would die.

That is not the way I will go. That is not the way we will go.

"Sire!" The call came from behind. Darnuir whirled to see a member of a catapult crew waving him up. "Flyers," the dragon called with childish glee. "Flyers in the air."

"It can't be," Darnuir whispered. He sprang towards the announcer with fresh spirit, leaping in a Cascade enriched jump to the roof of the villa. What he saw from the south pulled his lips into a broad grin.

Fairies were indeed approaching, their wings invisible blurs, and further beyond, so small in the distance but unmistakable, the black and white sails of Brevia were making for the harbour.

"We might survive this," Darnuir said. The catapult crew were smiling too, looking half-mad from sleep deprivation. "Join us below," said Darnuir. He turned and hopped back to the ground. "We will survive this," he told the Praetorians and those dragons in the back ranks nearby. "Raymond, fetch your horse. We push back."

"With pleasure," Raymond said.

Darnuir felt life return to him, his aches seemed to dull and he felt the blood rush to his cheeks, so jubilant was he at this moment. Dragon's Blade in hand, he opened the door and pulled on magic to enhance his voice.

"Dragons," he bellowed, moving back to the front. "Unto the dawn, I told you. Well, the dawn has come and with it comes your Guardian with all our allies from the west. I say we venture down and meet them. What say you?" His men bellowed their assent; a chorus of song-like joy at their salvation. The demons didn't comprehend their change in fortune. Perhaps Rectar did not know. They kept up their attack but found their way blocked more aggressively. The dragons took steps forwards rather than back.

Across the plaza, Raymond came cantering upon his great steed. Darnuir called, "Let him through," and the Chevalier drew up by his side. "Today we take back our city alongside humanity," Darnuir told them. "Today we win this fight as we should have years past, united and stronger together. Let us usher in that future. For dragons, for humanity, for fairies, for the Three Races!"

And so, they charged.

The demons were unprepared. They were knocked aside or trampled as the dragons ran. The natural descent of the sloping roads made leaping over the body piles of the fallen shield walls easier. Darnuir and Raymond spearheaded the counterattack, Bruce the horse scoring as many kills as his master. Halfway to the docks, the first of the fairy flyers dove down into the fray, helping to clear the way. Darnuir spotted Fidelm's inky skin whiz above, twirling his double-ended spear in smoky spins. He met the General when they reached the harbour's edge.

"Blaine landed with the Third Legion and the islanders while we sailed around the peninsula," Fidelm informed him.

The demons were hit with precision by the mangonels of the human fleet and soon their own spearmen and archers were disembarking and the demons could not hope to withstand an assault from three sides.

Darnuir led the push through the city, scouring every street and alley. The demons refused to flee. At the city walls, he ran up to judge the battle beyond.

Blaine was coming. A new golden formation, small but compact, and driving on with purpose approached the remaining demon flank. A dazzling light issued from the figure leading them.

When Darnuir rejoined the slaughter, he forgot to check how much Cascade he was relying on. The door in his mind pulled free of its hinges and when he tried to spit out the bitterness it was more like dry retching. His stomach was empty. The heaving brought on muscle spasms. And as the last demon fell dead on the dry earth, he thought he saw Blaine stepping cautiously towards him. He thought but could not be sure.

Then, he blacked out.

Chapter 31

REVELATIONS

The Champion's Blade is an enigma. Dronithir is the only person to wield it. Many have tried to theorise why he was 'worthy'. Did he give up Elsha, the woman he loved, for the greater cause? On and on it goes. In the end, it is naïve to place our own conceptions about 'worthiness' onto Dronithir's story. With each generation, the theory shifts as values change. And even then, the story that the Blade shall appear to 'those who are worthy' comes from a time little better than legend. If we take a leap, and believe it all, then the gods of the dragons blessed the creation of the Blades. And if the Champion's Blade was blessed by gods, would it not be for their Champion? Who is to say how they would judge who is worthy to them? It could not be for us mere mortals. I've said it before, but it could be a myth; a story invented to give hope in the darkest of times. I'd prefer that. Hope saves us from despair. It saves lives. I've never known a sword to cause anything but pain.

From Tiviar's Histories

Garon – the Great Glen

RAIN DRIZZLED UPON the Great Glen. Garon struggled through the thick mud at his boots and his waterlogged cloak weighed uncomfortably on his smarting body. The splint rubbed roughly on his forearm, his sling pulled painfully at his neck, his shoulder throbbed, a rib or three were bruised and he'd suffered a concussion, but otherwise he was fine. And so while the weather wasn't the most fitting return for the

413

victorious, it didn't dampen his spirits much. He was alive, walking and, given the circumstances, very, very grateful.

A little rain didn't stop the kazzek from celebrating either. Music filled the glen from kazzek blowing into long pipes attached to swelling bags under one arm, sending out high-pitched blasts at a thunderous pace.

"Daa-daa-dee-da," Ochnic hummed.

"Know this one?" Garon asked.

"De song? It is familiar," Ochnic said. He winced loudly, sucking air through his large teeth. Tenderly, he placed a hand at his back.

"The wound hasn't opened," Garon remarked as he checked the linens for signs of fresh blood.

"I will mend," Ochnic said. Then he returned to humming. "Daa-daa-dee-da."

"Papa you're not keeping in time," Cadha said. Ochnic's response was to hum louder and even more offbeat. Cadha laughed and thumped his leg with her tiny fist. She hadn't mourned the loss of her doll.

"Foul water," grunted Marus. "Your people know how to cope though, Ochnic."

"We hadn't had da rains yet," Ochnic said nonchalantly. "So now we get dem all at once."

"Look at us three now," Garon said. "The walking wounded. Ochnic bent at odd angles with his back, I'm favouring my right side so much I might tip over and Marus limps along as usual."

"Just means we've done our duty," Marus said.

"And then some," said Garon. "Where has Pel gotten to? Has she acquired any debilitating injuries since the battle? She can't be flying in this rain, surely?"

"She isn't," came Pel, sloshing up in between Garon and Ochnic.

Cadha jumped for joy at her arrival. "Can we fly again, Pel?"

"Later, I promise," Pel said. "If the rain ever stops. Could we hurry up and get out of it?"

"We can only go so fast as our broken bodies will carry us," said Garon. "You're young though and mostly unscathed. Run ahead if you like."

"And sit in a room with those Chieftains alone? No, thank you."

"I don't blame you," Garon said. "Rohka hasn't seemed too angry though, am I right Ochnic?"

Ochnic gave a rather large and rather unhelpful shrug of his shoulders. "We'll face them together," Marus said.

"Marus," Garon said in mock exclamation. "Are you telling me that you will stand by us? Are you saying we're one solid tea—"

"I should have let you fall," Marus muttered darkly. He smirked and Garon returned the gesture. Then he grunted from fresh jolts of pain as they began to descend farther into the valley.

The ancient set of standing stones looked even larger than Garon remembered them, dwarfing even the Stone Father standing sentinel at their front. The blue lines on his rocky body pulsated lightly. When Garon reached him, the golem proffered a vast hand, palm up, and Garon placed his own upon it. His senses morphed as they had done back in the Glen of Bhrath. He saw all rock and stone in great clarity, saw the presence of magic lining the mountains and felt the strange heartbeats from deep within the earth.

'We owe thanks to you, Lowlander. You and all those who came with you.'

We failed one of your golems. I'm sorry for your own loss.

The Stone Father sighed deeply. It echoed around every crevice of Garon's mind.

'My kind has accepted our fate. The day the Dark One came to the Black Rock the blue of our halls began to fade. There is no point in clinging on when other creatures might live and carve out their own path in earth or stone. Your coming made my sister's sacrifice mean something. For that, I thank you.'

Sister? Garon thought but the Stone Father's presence was already retracting from him. The golem withdrew his hand and took his leave, heading for the eastern mountainside, and leaving large muddy pools in his wake.

"You don't look well, Garon," Marus said.

"It leaves you disorientated for a moment," said Garon. But it was more than just discomfort from the strange sensory experience. The Stone Father's words had left him disheartened. A golem had died for them, and there were so few left. He took a moment of silence and listened to the pit-patter of rain on Marus' armour. The arrival of the Chief-of-Chiefs forced him to smile.

"Da kazzek owe you thanks," Rohka said a little stiffly. "Our food stores are filled and a clan was saved, even if you risked much." Although Rohka

415

was intimidating, Garon held his gaze. "Da chieftains insist dat you come now and eat with us." He led them towards one of the more lavish homes surrounding the ancient stones, the one with smoke rising from four chimneys. Stepping across its threshold was a relief Garon hadn't realised he needed. Crackling fires and the smell of roasting beef warmed him to the marrow, and a portion of tension in his back unknotted. A young kazzek in black tartan took their cloaks, paused, seeming unsure what to do with them, then tossed them roughly in a pile by the doorway. Garon couldn't help but laugh. The young troll looked confused but Garon gave him a wink and carried on.

How will I ever return to stodgy civilisation after this?

It seemed this floor of the house was one large gathering area. A feast was arrayed hapzardlay in stone dishes upon the floor. Kazzek were merrily helping themselves, using their hands to place food on their boards of wood which they used for plates, and using no cutlery to tear or mash their meals. Many stood but some were on stools fashioned from thick blocks of wood, cut in whole cylinders from tree trunks.

Garon picked a stool and helped himself to one of the small round golden vegetables he'd seen before in Pel's soup. He bit at it tentatively and blew fiercely as steam rose from inside it. Its skin was crisped and coated lightly in salt and garlic, yet its inner flesh was light and fluffy.

"What are these little wonders?" Garon asked.

"You don't have dem in da south?" Cadha gasped.

"Potatoes," Ochnic said. "Dey grow well up here."

"I'll have to bring some back with me," said Garon. "After we see out the winter."

"Hmmm," Ochnic mused.

As Garon went to examine some more of the fare, he saw a kazzek presenting Pel with a separate deep wooden dish, which looked filled to the brim with a mashed gloop of carrot, neeps and cauliflower, glistening with butter. Pel accepted it happily.

"Mmmmm," she said, taking a second bite. The kazzek looked even happier and bowed his head. He walked away with pride on his face.

Their fellow guests consisted of the chieftains and some assorted staff or higher-ranking clan members. Occasionally, they stared at Garon, Marus and Pel, and put their heads together to talk more quietly. Even Ochnic received a few looks. After sufficient time was granted for everyone to eat their fill, the Chief-of-Chiefs called for silence and moved to address them.

"Today, we remember those kazzek lost to us. Orrock was a chief like us, and he is no more. Many more kazzek have gone unburned and I hope da blue poison will let dem rest."

"Let dem rest," muttered the rest of the kazzek, including Ochnic and Cadha.

"Now der is a decision ta make," Rohka said solemnly. "Will da Lowlanders stay?"

Silence reigned.

"Where else would you like us to go?" Garon asked. He felt a bit bold, perhaps due to the first proper hot meal he'd eaten in months. "Winter approaches and the demons may yet return. You'd really send us marching off in the cold?"

Rohka's nose twitched. "You have great spirit, Garon pack leader. But you were also reckless and dis decision cannot be made lightly."

"Lowlanders should not be in da Great Glen," said the chieftain in the pink and green tartan.

"Dey have earned a place," Ochnic said. He did not bow his head or hold his tusks this time. "My clan would be dead if it weren't for dem. Da Stone Father too. Chieftain Rohka would not have helped us."

"I took a risk, yes," Garon said, "but I did it because I felt it to be right. Now, I know the kazzek have bad history with the fairies—"

"And da dragons," someone called out.

"Dat was da work of one mad dragon," said Rohka. "It was agreed. The Wise Ones declared dis long ago."

"Dragons?" Marus said. "What have we ever done to your kind?"

"Dey do not even know," bemoaned the chief in yellow and black.

"What is this all about?" Garon said.

Ochnic set Cadha down from his lap and got to his feet. "Dey have earned der place. Dey have righted da wrongs of da past. Let it go."

"Who was this dragon?" Marus said. "I know nothing of dragons in the Highlands."

"It was before even your birth," came a wizened voiced. "Before even da demons came." A very old troll stepped forward from between two concerned bodyguards. Her tusks were worn down to the roots, her white hair was cut closely to her scalp, and she was wrapped in an extra layer of tartan.

"Chieftain Glik, der is no need to trouble yourself," said Rohka. "Please sit."

"It is no trouble," said Glik. "I fear da truth is forgotten. De years will have worn at the tale despite my trying." She was shaking a little in the effort to stand, so one of her guards produced a chair. He slid the cut tree trunk underneath her and she sat down. "It was over eighty years ago. I had only seen my tenth summer when dey came."

"Who came?" Garon asked.

"Drenthir, Dragon Prince and Kroener, Cursed One," said Glik. The kazzek chieftains responded to the last name in their own choice way. Some spat on the floor, some gnashed teeth, some growled lowly. Others simply seethed in silence, pressing their lips into thin lines.

"Wait one moment," said Marus. "Eighty years ago, the then prince was surely Draconess."

"Der was no Draconess," said Glik.

"You are mistaken," said Marus.

"Chieftain Glik never forgets," said the Chief-of-Chiefs.

"Never," Glik repeated. "It was Drenthir and Kroener, Cursed One. Dey came in search of da Black Dragons, those who had fled their homes after Kroener slaughtered the rest of der people."

"Slaughtered?" Marus said. The colour was rising in his face. "The Black Dragons were our sworn enemy. Agents of the Shadow, they—"

"Marus," Garon snapped. He grabbed the dragon and pulled him closer. "What happened to you not truly believing in all that religious stuff?"

"This — this is different," Marus said.

"I'm not so sure it is," said Garon. Then, for the room to hear, he said, "Let Chieftain Glik tell her tale."

Glik carried on without even a momentary pause. "As I was tellin', Black Dragons were fleeing north into our lands. We took many in. I remember helping a young boy who was sick and underfed. Each day I mashed up potato and fed him spoonfuls until his strength returned.

But Kroener came for dem, and that little boy, the one I had helped, was rounded up and slain like a beast.

"Dark days followed and Kroener came down hard on us kazzek who had tried to help da Black Dragons. My mother and I were taken by da dragons, chained and held for questioning. Kroener marched as far as da Glen of Bhrath, though it had another name in those days. Der was only one who spoke against Kroener, as I remember, and that was Drenthir, Dragon Prince."

Glik paused then and signalled for a drink of water. As she drained her mug, Garon chanced a glance at Marus. The legate's cheeks were ablaze and growing hotter with each second. To Garon, the whole story seemed well rehearsed. Doubtless, the old troll had told it hundreds of times. Glik passed her mug back, wiped her mouth and continued.

"Kroener found out about de roads of da Stone Men and thought he could enter Kar'drun through dem. Black Dragons eluded him in its depths. Drenthir tried to change his mind. I remember, one night in my pen, the two of dem were close by, hoping to talk away from der men. Drenthir told Kroener he was wrong, that having fought the Black Dragons he saw dey weren't different. Dey were not the enemy, and nor were da kazzek. Drenthir spoke of dark creatures from Kar'drun, which the Black Dragons had been trying to keep in check. Now dat the Black Dragons were all gone, what was to stop these new creatures? Drenthir told da Cursed One dat he thought dey had made a great mistake. Kroener disagreed.

"Two nights later, Drenthir came around da holding pens. He broke our chains and set us free. He told us dat a mighty weapon had been granted to him, a sword of great power. He said a guiding voice had spoken to him whilst on da mountainside, telling him he was right. He told us not to fear da Cursed One anymore. But I was scared and did not move even as my mother called me to follow her. I sat curled in my pen, not trusting dat Drenthir could stop Kroener. As de others fled, Drenthir walked over to me and knelt by my side. He pulled out a chain of silver from around his neck and told me it had been given to him by da woman he loved. She was the daughter of a powerful dragon. Da dragon Guardian. Drenthir said da Guardian would listen to him because of this and not Kroener. He said dat together they would stop Kroener. And so, I got up and ran with my mother to safety.

"Da dragons did leave in da end. Once we were sure dey had gone my clan went back to check for more prisoners or see what the dragons had left behind. What we found were dead dragons. Many of dem. Drenthir was one of them. He was lying on a sleeping roll, with ruins of da camp all around him. His throat was cut open. When I saw da necklace, I thought it too precious a thing to throw away. I picked it up and it remained with my clan until I gave it you, Ochnic, Shadow Hunter."

"You remember all that?" Garon asked incredulously.

"We told you, pack leader," said Rohka. "Glik does not forget."

"If that is all true…" Marus began but he didn't seem able to finish his thought.

"All of it," said Glik.

"But this — this," Marus said. "I may need a moment."

"You see why we are distrustful of Lowlanders," said the chieftain in yellow tartan.

"And what of my people?" asked Pel.

"I think you already know," said Rohka.

"Fairies are told that Frost Trolls – the kazzek, that is – used to hunt and kill our kind if we ever ventured north," Pel said.

"And why did da fairies come to our lands?" asked Rohka. "To seek da blue poison and—"

"And those who found it snapped like I did," said Pel. She seemed to ponder for a moment. Her wings fidgeted, buzzing in short bursts. "You could have warned me, or at least explained. Instead, you decided to hate me." She spoke to Rohka but it was old Glik who answered.

"Not hate, young one, but fear. Fear of what fairies will become when dey touch da raw blue. In times past, our people tried to warn you, tried to stop your kind reaching it but you would not listen. We defended ourselves and then we tried to prevent you reaching it. Perhaps we were wrong. It was long ago. I say," Glik added with sudden volume, "I say we forgive da Lowlanders. Ochnic, Shadow Hunter, is right."

Marus stood up suddenly. He wobbled on his bad leg and placed a hand on Garon's last good shoulder to steady himself. "For what it's worth, I am sorry for any crimes my people have caused. One day I hope King Darnuir will make amends on behalf of all dragons."

"I believe he will," Garon said.

"What do you know of da Dragon King?" asked Rohka.

"I know more than most," Garon said. "I was there when he was a baby born again. I was there when he learned to walk, learned to talk and learned to hold a sword. He's a little rough on the outside but I know he has a good at heart. A good man. A good dragon, despite what may be happening to him. Could anyone alive claim to understand what it is like to have lived two lives? No, of course not. But I do know this. He is trying to make a better world, one where all the races can work together. And if he is trying in the south then we should be trying in the far north."

The chieftains and their attendants descended into muttering again, whispering in their earthy tongue. This would be it. Garon's mission would hinge on the next few moments. He wondered if there was anything more he could say, anything more he could do and then his shoulder, arm and chest throbbed to remind him of what he'd already done. It was enough, surely. Yet even if it wasn't, he felt proud. He'd hauled his grumbling force northwards and saved the family of a friend. Val'tarra and all human lands were safer for it. Even if no one ever thanked him. Even if no one ever knew or cared; they'd done it.

It was Ochnic who made the first move. He stood by Pel, swelling up his hairy chest and announced, "Da pack leader is right. From now on I call Pel, fairy friend."

"Me too," squeaked Cadha. She took Pel's arm and hugged it tightly.

"Well, I for one am touched," Garon said. "While we're all sentimental, I guess I should say Marus that you're not as grouchy as when we first met."

"Thanks," Marus said coolly.

"And I suppose I owe you my life now," Garon said. "I should probably stick around until I repay that debt. Friends?"

"It is one's duty to save one's commanding officer," said Marus. Garon frowned at him. "Very well," Marus said. "Friends it is, human."

"Thank you Marus," Garon said. Something about the dragon's moment of humanity touched him, and then he realised that very word was wrong. Marus hadn't become more human because really he and the others weren't so very different in the end. Garon addressed the room himself now. "You kazzek refer to me as pack leader, and that's flattering, I think. But that makes me sound superior or special, and I'm not. None of us are. Not Marus, not Pel, not Ochnic; we're actually mostly the same. We care about our loved ones and families. We'll do ridiculous things to help those we care about and even set aside our pride and duty in some circumstances." He looked to Marus at that. "What I'm trying to say is we're all really much the same. I know the thought of thousands of outsiders coming into your homes is frightening, but know we've been just as frightened. So what do you say, Rohka. Can we stay?"

All eyes began to turn to Rohka. "You can," said the Chief-of-Chiefs. "For now," he added. "We do owe you much." That seemed to settle the matter. One by one all the chieftains gave their consent and a drink was called.

Mugs were brought out on oversized trays. Garon lunged for the closest one, looked at its contents, and found not beer, nor ale, nor harder spirit, but something white. *Is that milk?*

"To new friends," roared Rohka. He raised his own mug and some of the milky drink sloshed over the side.

"To new friends," repeated everyone; the chiefs, the guards, the servants, Marus, Pel, Ochnic, Cadha and Garon too. He tilted his head and threw back the mug. The drink was ice cold and tasted of creamy milk sweetened with honey. It was delightful. It felt clean. And then the kick came in the aftertaste, a bitterness that plunged down his throat and set a fire in his stomach.

"Phwoa," Garon said, shaking his head, enjoying the immediate tingling around his body. Pel gasped; Marus already looked drunk and hooted loudly. The kazzek chuckled at their intolerance.

"More," Rohka called. Their mugs were refilled with the hazardous milk and a pair of kazzek took up instruments that looked like long curving fiddles. A soaring wave of music filled the common room and Garon felt his aches and pains lessen.

He had not felt this good in years.

Chapter 32

THE WAR IS WON, THE WAR IS JUST BEGINNING

There is a simple saying among my people: 'rotten to the roots'. Aborists use it when a tree is beyond saving and should be cut down, burned, its very roots dug away. The poison runs so deep, even the roots must go to give the best chance for new life to grow. As I investigate the history between the Aurishan Dragons and the descendant's of Dranus, I am inclined to say it. Rotten to the roots. With humans, it is only marginally better.

From Tiviar's Histories

Darnuir – Aurisha – The Royal Tower

DARNUIR WAS RUNNING through the snow. It was freshly fallen, soft on top and crunched pleasantly underfoot. He came across a golden stone table, perfectly round, with chairs set at equal intervals. Instinct made him place a hand on it, sit down slowly in one of the chairs.

"What are you doing?" Cosmo asked. He was leaning on the table, whole and healthy, looking down at Darnuir.

"I asked them to come join me," he found himself saying. "Arkus, Somerled, Blaine, Fidelm and Kasselle. But they're not here yet. I'm waiting for them."

"I'm hardly surprised," Cosmo said. "Better you than me."

"Will they come?" Darnuir asked.

"Hopefully," said Cosmo. "You invited them and you are the Dragon King. Don't they have to?"

"I think so," Darnuir said looking down to his knees. "Cosmo, what if I can't do it. What if I—" But Cosmo was not there. He'd vanished.

The falling snow thickened and Darnuir felt a chill run from his ears to his toes. He wrapped his arms about himself, rubbing his chest and puffing out steamy breaths.

"Well, this won't do," said Brackendon, appearing from nowhere in the space Cosmo had been. With a thud of his silver staff, a ball of warming fire materialised, bobbing in the air between them.

"Can you help me?" Darnuir asked.

"Castallan must pay first," Brackendon said.

"He's dead. You killed him. Don't you remember?"

Brackendon's eyebrows shot upwards. "Gracious, really? Well, then we should be moving on."

"On?" Darnuir said. "But I have to wait here."

"Oh no," said Brackendon. "There's worse out there. Who do you think is causing all this snow? Come along now my tamed dragon." Darnuir stood and everything started to spin. When the world righted itself he was at the base of a huge mountain, the rock of which was burned black. "He's in there, Darnuir."

"Rectar?" Darnuir said. He reached for the Dragon's Blade at his waist but the sword was stuck fast in its scabbard. "Brackendon, help me."

"I can't help you in there. Not anymore. You burned my staff." And as he spoke the silver wood in his grip turned to ashes.

"I thought you wanted me to," Darnuir said. "Kymethra told me."

"I did," said Brackendon.

"It is I who should break and not you."

"A generous offer, Darnuir, but we'd all be better off without magic."

Darnuir craned his neck looking up at the black mountain. His heart quickened in fear. His palms felt sweaty. "How can I fight Him without magic, without you?"

But like Cosmo, Brackendon had disappeared as well.

A doorway opened from the mountainside and Darnuir walked towards it. Over the threshold, he fell, into an utter darkness. He saw nothing. He felt nothing. Not even a rush of wind against his skin. He hit cold stone with a wet thud. And he lay there, flat on the ground, unable to move. Someone shook his back and he rolled over, got up. He couldn't see his saviour's face for they were looking downwards, half veiled in shadow. A red glow came from where their eyes should be. The person, whoever they were, drew something from their waist, bringing it up to Darnuir's chest and —

Bang.

Darnuir's eyes flew open.

"Careful, human," Blaine said in his most condescending tone.

"I did not intend it, Lord Guardian," came Raymond's voice. "Those doors are rather heavily designed."

"I think he's awake," Grigayne said. Darnuir blinked painfully, the sleepy crust felt like cement on his eyelids.

"Yes. He yet lives," intoned Fidelm.

"Darnuir?" Blaine said. "Darnuir, can you hear me?"

He tried to speak but only croaked something incoherent. He was parched. His throat felt like he'd swallowed sand and his eyes seemed determined to squeeze out from his skull, as though trying to escape the pain in there. His head hurt so much he considered yanking his mind out through his nose and letting it writhe in pain elsewhere. He was lying on a hard, unforgiving bed. The sheets were clingy and damp, and he wished dearly to die there.

"He needs water, surely," Raymond said.

"He needs magic," Blaine said. "Darnuir. You haven't broken, but you came very close." He seized Darnuir's hand and pressed it against the hilt of the Dragon's Blade. "Your body depends on the Cascade. Draw on a little, quickly."

Darnuir fumbled at the door in his mind.

"Do it now, Darnuir," Blaine said, squeezing Darnuir's hand to the sword. Darnuir felt the door give and the magic pour in. For a moment, it rushed through him, thrumming towards the Dragon's Blade and just as he wished to rip the door apart and drown in the ocean beyond, Blaine yanked his hand away.

"What?" Darnuir gasped, feeling a modicum of his strength return.

"That's enough for now," Blaine said. "You'll need to be weaned down from this overindulgence."

"Overindulgence? Blaine, I didn't mean for this to happen. At the Bastion I —" What was the point in making excuses? He bowed his head feeling too ashamed to meet Blaine's eyes. "How long was I out for?"

"Just over two full days," Raymond said.

"Then I should see the city," Darnuir said. He painfully managed to rise to a sitting position.

"Take rest, Darnuir," Fidelm said. "The war is won and your city will still be here when you are better." Darnuir's thoughts turned to Dukoona's warnings.

"No," he grunted. "There is much to be done." Shakily he stepped out of his sodden bed, the same one he slept in when camped. A larger bed was next to him, with a frame of carved starium and a dragon looming above a ripped old mattress. "Where is Lira?" He asked. Then the horror struck. "She isn't—"

"She's alive and unharmed for the most part," Raymond said. "Cuts, some deep, some not. Remarkable, considering she had no protection."

"Foolish girl," Blaine said.

Raymond ignored him. "I believe she is taking care of some personal business in the Lower City."

"Very well," Darnuir said. "I shall need to thank her. All of you, as well. I owe more thanks than I can possibly convey in words. For standing by me, Raymond; for your timely arrivals, Blaine, Fidelm; for bringing your own people to my aid, Grigayne, even after they have endured so much."

"Yes, we have endured much, haven't we Guardian?" Grigayne said bitterly. Darnuir noted the animosity Grigayne shot Blaine, knowing he'd need to ask about that later. Grigayne looked back to Darnuir more kindly. "There is no need to thank me, Darnuir. You rescued me and my city; I've helped secure yours."

"I may have to ask even more of you before the end," Darnuir said, "of all of you."

"The demons are defeated," said Fidelm.

"But not their Master," said Darnuir. He looked to Blaine for support.

"This will not truly be over until the Shadow of Rectar is banished from the world," Blaine said. "But Fidelm is right in a sense. With his armies destroyed Rectar will fall soon."

"His armies are not gone," Darnuir groaned. Fresh pain stabbed at his stomach, chest and kidneys at once, as though several fists with ragged nails were clenching his organs.

Blaine's brow creased. "I believe we saw to the demons and the spectres for that matter. I saw none in the battle."

"Ah," Raymond said, raising a finger. "The spectres vanished, Lord Guardian."

"They fled again?" Blaine said.

"Not exactly," said Darnuir.

"And how would you know?" Blaine said. He narrowed his eyes at Darnuir, searching for the cover-up, the lie. Darnuir stared right back, quite willing to have it out.

"Because I had words with Dukoona," said Darnuir. The colour of Blaine's face grew closer to beetroot.

"But Darnuir, many of the Brevian forces are already setting sail for home," Fidelm said.

"What?" Darnuir snapped. "No. They can't. I need them to stay here."

"Arkus will require the ships to send your people across the sea," Fidelm said. "He won't take kindly to his troops staying here while dragons —"

"We can negotiate with Arkus later," Darnuir said. "For now, I need those troops to remain. Fly, Fidelm. Prevent more ships from sailing."

"What shall I tell the Admiral?"

"Tell him he has to stay," Darnuir said, clutching his head. "Tell him the war is not over. Tell him anything..." he trailed off into another headache, squinting down against the array of colour assaulting his vision. He gently massaged the side of his eye to little effect and did not see Fidelm leave.

"I must consult with my father," Grigayne said. "I'll send a message to Dalridia but our warriors and shield maidens will remain for the time being." More footsteps and the loud closing door signalled he too had left. Darnuir had his eyes fully shut now.

"Might I have some privacy with my King?" Blaine asked.

"I leave only if Darnuir commands it, Guardian," Raymond said with more defiance than his usual bearing.

"Thank you, Raymond," Darnuir said. "But I shall speak to Blaine alone." A quiet scrape of metal meant Raymond had bowed.

"Careful with the door," said Blaine. No bang followed this time. Darnuir risked opening his eyes again but kept massaging his skull.

"What's gotten into you?" He demanded of Blaine, albeit weakly. "You seem back to your old self and I don't know if that's for the better." It was then he noticed Blaine's maimed hand. "Dranus' scales, Blaine. What happened to you?"

"Did you want to see the city?" Blaine said.

Back to avoiding questions again too, I see.

"I'd like one last walk while I still feel capable," Darnuir said.

"You'll have to enter a period of rehabilitation," Blaine said.

Darnuir sighed. "How long?"

"It can take ninety days," said Blaine. Darnuir winced. "But," Blaine continued, "as we've caught it early on, and the Dragon's Blade is second to none at processing, you may recover faster…"

"And if we forced the issue?" Darnuir asked. "Cut me off for longer stretches and really hastened things?"

"It could kill you."

"I know you won't let that happen."

"Let's go for that walk," Blaine said, placing a gentle guiding hand on Darnuir's shoulder and they went in silence down through the Royal Tower. Passing the war room, Darnuir saw the half melted candles left by Dukoona had been cleared.

"We found another scrying orb in the throne room but it was smashed," said Blaine. "Luckily, Fidelm brought us the spare from the Bastion. Arkus has the orb I found among Scythe's camp."

"Good," said Darnuir. "You'll be able to communicate with Arkus in my absence." They continued their descent, still in the grip of silent discord. After a while Darnuir felt compelled to speak. "You might start with a full apology regarding the Bastion. You might then inquire about the rest of our people back west. See they are treated well and get as many home as you can. It's a task I don't envy. Arkus is sure to want his own men home for late harvests and for sowing in the spring, but Rectar does not work to the seasons. Well? Nothing to add, grandfather?"

"I shall make these demands, if you wish."

"Not demands," Darnuir said.

"Would you accept an alternative?" Blaine asked.

"Within reason but, broadly speaking, no. We need their soldiers."

"Then you are demanding," Blaine said.

Darnuir wanted to shout, to scream at him but his head was spinning again. He lost his footing on the stairs and scraped his arm to a pink flaky ruin against the coarse stone railing.

"Draw on a little more magic," Blaine said curtly. "Just half-a-second." Darnuir did and steadied himself. For now, he focused on making it down the stairs. The pain from his arm barely registered amongst everything else.

One step at a time. Just one step at a time.

"You should not have conversed with a spectre," Blaine said. "They are full of madness and lies."

"Not this one. I won't apologise for speaking with Dukoona. I'll apologise for the recklessness, for my addiction, for a lot of things but not that. It was worth it. We'd never have found out about this new threat otherwise."

"And what threat is that?"

"The very thought frightens me."

"You need not be afraid, Darnuir," Blaine said, pausing to face him. That momentary stop made Darnuir lose his hard-won rhythm in tackling the stairs. He began to feel dizzy. "Come to the Basilica with me," Blaine urged. "I'll show you why you ought to start believing."

Gingerly, Darnuir began moving again.

One step at a time. Just one ste—

His hand slipped and his feet gave way under him. A solid edge of rock dug into his hip when he went down.

"Ugh," he moaned, but the greatest pain of all was the yearning to open the door. "I can't do this, Blaine. I need more magic. Please," he begged, spittle spraying from his cracked lips. "Please. Just let me draw on more. I can't — I can't go on like this." Blaine stared down on him, lying spread-eagled and pathetic. He bent down to Darnuir's side and reached out a hand to cup his face. Blaine's eyes widened and for a moment, he was a concerned grandfather. Then the Guardian returned.

"Back to your chambers."

Lira – Aurisha – the Lower City

Lira picked her way through the streets at the foot of the Great Lift. This had been the poorer part of town, this cramped, tight maze of wooden extensions upon ancient stone homes. The wind was prevented from freshening the air and it was often in the shadow of the plateau. Aurisha had been constructed thousands of years ago, so Lira supposed there had been more than enough space for the dragons at the time. But not as the city grew. Those extensions rose six storeys in places and many now looked tilted and unsafe. Yet she could ignore those. Her old home would be at street level, the one home with the green door. A bit of green to liven the city, her mother had said.

She found it on a narrow street four doors down from the base of the plateau. Her mother hadn't exaggerated. Every other doorway was a pale yellow but not hers. It didn't even look damaged. Lira pushed it in, crossed the threshold and half-choked on the stale air.

A feeling of being unwelcome came over her, as though the abandoned rooms had grown accustomed to their solitude and wished her gone. A layer of dust covered everything, from the ceramic pots on the low built shelves to the still set table at the centre. Three plates were laid out: one for Lira, one for her mother; and one —

She looked away, feeling foolish at grieving for a father she never knew. An urge to leave washed over her. She'd just find that damned doll her mother always talked about and get out. A last memento of her father. He'd made it for Lira, apparently. Not that she could remember. She found it flung unceremoniously on the child-sized bed in the tiny room off the kitchen. Its limbs were bent at bone snapping angles, the wooden joints frozen in time like the rest of the place. She picked it up, admired the carved detail of the women's face: the broad smile and the happy blue eyes. Something gave inside her and an unwanted tear splashed on the wood.

Doll in hand, she left the house with the green door. She glanced back once then retraced her steps towards the Great Lift. When she arrived, the lift had just finished a downward journey and dragons pulling carts of dead bodies from the plaza trundled out. They marched, stern-faced, towards the broken city gates, taking the corpses out for burial. The dead had been stripped of anything useful and left virtually bare, their skinned exposed to the elements. Already, an awful smell of rotting meat followed them.

And Lira felt more tears well in her eyes, and she knew it wasn't all for some doll or a promise made to her mother. It was this, being paraded right before her. Nothing but death, death and more death. Out of the heat of battle, it was sickening, terrifying. How much blood had been spent taking back the city? How much had been spent since the first demon crawled out from Kar'drun, and how many tens of thousands before that in every war ever fought by every king or guardian.

She was exhausted. She had been exhausted even before she had run for a full day to crash into a horde of demons that didn't break. Everyone around her was tired as well – just no one would admit it. Tired of fighting. Tired of death. At least for now they might rest and, with the demons defeated, begin to dream of peace.

She looked up to the plateau where all the greatest of her kind use to dwell. Up there, amongst all the marble and the finery. Yet, while Darnuir recovered and Blaine droned on about his divine experience, the Great Lift brought more bodies down.

Two waves of carts passed Lira before she finally moved on.

Darnuir – the Royal Tower

Darnuir sat shaking in a starium chair. The Dragon's Blade lay sheathed across his lap, the hilt just a little out of reach. His hands, arms, shoulders, waist, thighs, calves and feet all bound.

"I'll likely rip out of these bonds," Darnuir said.

"I'll have stronger steel chains brought soon," Blaine said.

Darnuir nodded, breathing hard. He'd been allowed one final draw before the real recovery began. Already, he felt desperate to feel the Cascade in his veins again. Failing that, he just wanted to scream.

"Before this begins," he said, practically panting. "What's made you so sure of yourself? What happened on the Splinters to bring you back?"

"I asked our gods for a sign and they answered," Blaine said. His expression did not betray any twitch of a lie or coercion or anything except the plain truth. Blaine believed every word he said.

431

"And your trouble with Bacchus?" Darnuir asked.

"Gone. He has returned as a devout Light Bearer and follower."

"A follower of your religion or of you?"

"When you have recovered, ask any of the Third who were there at the Nail Head. It was a holy event. Why else do you imagine the demons have crumbled before us now?"

"Because the spectres let them die," Darnuir said. "Because Rectar didn't care for them any longer. Because something worse is coming."

"Don't trust a spectre's word."

In his frustration, Darnuir bit on his lip and tasted blood. He could move nothing else. "Damn it, Blaine. Dukoona wants to *help* us. He's warned us. Rectar has dragons, enchanted like Castallan's red-eyed humans. You must prepare. You cannot ignore this."

Blaine wrinkled his nose. "How can dragons fall to such a thing? We are the Light's chosen race. We shall prevail."

"Of course, we can fall," Darnuir said. "One of your own did. Have you forgotten?"

Blaine leaned in, right up to his face. "I am nothing like Kroener."

"Of course, you only have nine fingers," Darnuir said. "Did your gods give you comfort when you lost it?"

"I'll forgive that based on your current condition," Blaine said. "If only you believed."

"It's not that I don't accept there is something powerful out there," Darnuir said. "Rectar has power. He reaches out to the minds of his minions. He summons them to this world from somewhere — somewhere else. Kroener alone, one dragon, even with a Blade, could not have this much power. There is something we don't understand, but I don't think we'll have any help in this fight. We're on our own Blaine, but we don't need to be. Let the humans in. Let the bickering and the hate end. Look at what we've achieved in one year together. Let your prejudice go. Please. There's no point in it. Please…" He hung his head and licked his lips, attempting to regain control of his breathing. Muscles in his back twitched, threatening seizure.

"N'weer watch over you, Darnuir," Blaine said, taking his leave and slamming the door behind him.

Chapter 33

LIFTING THE VEIL

The First War between humanity and dragons was bravely fought, but bloody. Humans hoped to match the dragons by breeding warhorses of immense power and size, even larger than destriers used by present Chevaliers. Mighty they might have been, but when the humans charged at the Battle of Deas the dragons stood there, allowing it. Some say they even laughed as the first ranks dodged the steeds with ease, cleaving into their legs and knocking them down with plated fists. In response, the earliest Hunters were formed. Humans set aside the notion they could beat the dragons with brute force. Leathers and mail replaced armour, bows would kill from afar and dense spear formations absorbed the brunt of a dragon charge. Where dragons have been content to rely on their physical prowess, humans have sought other means to fight and I suspect they always will.

From Tiviar's Historiesr

Cassandra – Brevia – dragon refugee camps

CASSANDRA HAD NOT anticipated feeling this distressed by Boreac's death. For what seemed an aeon, she stared at his corpse. His blank, terrified, still open eyes looked up at her in shock.

Gellick remained before her, waving his fine dagger in a vaguely threatening manner. He didn't mean her harm, but he would not allow her to act either. There was nothing she could do.

Does it matter? What's one more killing when the whole city, the whole kingdom, has been backstabbing, plotting, scrambling over the top of one

433

another. And all for what? For this? A dead old man running half-starved from his home. It's over. I shouldn't care. She looked again to Boreac's body. *No. It's wrong. He was caught, cornered. He would have come quietly.*

Gellicks' crisp voice snapped her back to reality. "Search him. We'll take these possessions he deemed most dear back to the palace. I dare say a reward will be in order, gentlemen." His voice was fat with triumph. The other cloaked Chevaliers murmured their agreement. Kymethra had stopped trying to break free from her captor. Boreac's murder had left her just as still and confused as Cassandra.

This is wrong…

"This isn't right," she finally said aloud and was pleased to hear she sounded calm and still together, when the opposite was true.

"Nor is plotting to overthrow the King to whom one is pledged," Gellick said.

"You can't," Cassandra began. She stepped towards him with no real plan. She tried to gently push his knife aside but he whipped a leather-gloved hand across her face, leaving a stinging scrape on her cheek.

"It's done. Take it up with your father, Cassandra. We're leaving. Now."

"What about the body?" the man who had done the stabbing asked. His face was still hidden beneath his hood.

"Leave it. King's orders. Now, let us depart, *quietly*," he added with a fresh flourish of his dagger at Cassandra and Kymethra.

Back at the palace, their small company moved without a word to each other. Kymethra was escorted off to her quarters, still gagged. Cassandra was forced to follow Gellick towards Arkus' council chambers. The Chevalier had a bounce in his step and his blond hair flopped with each rise and fall. He had Boreac's worn sack over one shoulder and something in it clanked against his armour. There were no guards outside the council chamber.

"Arkus will be meeting with the minor houses," Cassandra said. Gellick didn't acknowledge her. He sniffed and began leading her upstairs to the doors outside Orrana's parlour. There were five Chevaliers there, all with their visors up. They saluted Gellick as he approached.

"You're dismissed," he told them and the men marched off without dispute. He knocked once, twice, still no answer. "My King," he called. "I have urgent news of—" But from the other side of the door came laughter, a mixture of low voices and high tenors. Gellick pushed on the door revealing a scene of Arkus and Thane guffawing at some private joke. Arkus was kneeling by Orrana's regular tray of overly sweet cakes with purple frosting spread across his nose. Thane stood in front of him, with pink icing and crumbs in his hair, wielding a purple covered sponge in one hand like a mace.

Their laughter took Cassandra by surprise. It was a happy, joyful, songful noise, the sort of laughter that might have forced a smile across the dourest faced dragon. Neither father nor son noticed Cassandra and Gellick's arrival.

"My King," Gellick said again. This took Thane by surprise and he half choked in turning to face the Chevalier. His caught breath sent him into a fit of coughs, hacking loudly into a white doily cloth that Arkus snatched up from the tray. The King rubbed the Prince's back and gave Gellick a look as though he wished the Chevalier to boil inside his steel. Cassandra dashed forward and poured a cup of water from the jug beside the cake tray, ready for when Thane surfaced from his episode. After half a minute, Thane calmed and yellow-green mucus clung like tar to the now ruined white doily. Cassandra offered him the water and Thane sipped it, sighing heavily between gulps as he sought to steady his breathing. A lone tear left Thane's eye from the exertion and Arkus pulled him in for a tight hug.

"Go on and find your mother now."

Thane nodded and left. Cassandra thought she saw Gellick flair a nostril in disgust before arranging his expression into one of deep concern. The moment Thane was out of the parlour, and the door closed behind him, Arkus rounded on Gellick.

"Is it done?" he asked brusquely.

"It is," Gellick said. He dumped the sack at Arkus' feet.

"This is all of it?"

Gellick nodded.

Arkus bent down and rummaged frantically in Boreac's last possessions before pulling out an object that Cassandra had never seen before. It looked like a hollow wooden tube with a slanted handle and some mechanism fashioned from metal pieces just above where Arkus held it. He let loose a shivering sigh as though overcoming some powerful trepidation.

"Hiding in the refugee camp..." Arkus said, more to himself. "Nearly had me there Geoff. Nearly got away with it." He turned to Cassandra. "You cannot know how much of a relief this is. You've done so well, Cassandra."

"You never said Boreac was to die. What about the trial?"

"Annandale will suffice for a trial," Arkus said. "And you have no idea the danger Boreac might have placed us all in. We're not yet ready. We're—" He had seen the cut on Cassandra's cheek. "Did Boreac do that?"

"Ask the young Lord Esselmont here," Cassandra said.

Arkus whirled, rose and asked, "You did this?" Each word was a bite as if chewing wood.

"Just to move things along, sire," Gellick said. His aura of pomposity suddenly shaken. "The Princess and the witch were—"

Arkus struck Gellick's face with the bronze butt of the handle. Gellick snorted in pain but had the grace not to clutch his bleeding and swelling face. He took his punishment well.

"Never harm my daughter again."

"Never, my King," Gellick said, a little thickly.

"Leave us, before I rethink your approval to the White Seven." Gellick did not need to be told twice and was careful to shut the door gently behind him. Arkus turned the strange weapon over in his hand, inspecting it and a tiny chamber which opened at the ridge of the handle.

Cassandra shifted her weight between her feet, looking from Arkus to the thing in his grasp. Boreac had believed that Darnuir would be so grateful to hear about the weapon's power, he would keep him safe from Arkus. And Arkus had been desperate for Darnuir not to find out. Desperate enough to hunt Boreac down. The old lord had died for this thing.

The parlour seemed dull and lifeless now, the colours less vibrant without the early morning sun. Brevia itself looked grey under the overcast sky, half shrouded as though veiled in some secrecy.

Brevia, the palace, the Queen, Kymethra, Thane; it had started to feel comfortable. She'd dared to hope she'd found a home. Had this changed anything? *No, this is all Arkus. I might be caught up in his games but the others are genuine, right?*

"Your betrothed caused quite an upset with his speech to the dragons," Arkus said, still inspecting the weapon. "Or should I say, your former betrothed?" He glanced over to her. "We made a deal after all."

"And you'll honour it?"

"Of course," Arkus said. "I do not think you need to be bartered off. My grip on the Kingdom is firm now. The minor houses have been easy to appease with so much to be divided up; lands, titles, positions. You've helped, of course."

"Me? All I did was find Boreac."

"And ended my fears of the dragons catching wind of my activities. Annandale broke quickly. He thought information about his fellow schemers would make me more lenient. He was wrong. But he did go on about Boreac's obsession with a secret project of mine here in the city."

"Were you always going to kill him?"

Arkus tapped his fingers over the ridge of the device. "Yes, does that bother you?"

"That's why you wanted me to come straight to you, because—"

"Because I didn't want you to come to harm."

"How do I know that's not another lie?"

"I like to think of it as omission," said Arkus.

"So, what happened today with Gellick? He said Orrana spoke to him, does that mean she—" This time her voice broke. She didn't want to ask. She didn't want to risk knowing Orrana had been lying to her as well. Arkus' expression softened, his lower lip rose and he cocked his head by the smallest tilt.

"Orrana was worried about you. Like me, she understood there might be some danger in hunting down a wanted man. She acted out of affection and then Gellick came to me."

"But she knew I was looking for Boreac."

"Yes, but like you, she didn't know the full reason why," Arkus said. "Just as she knows nothing of the weapons I have been producing here in the city. And even though I recruited hunters from the Hinterlands to be retrained; Lord Clachonn never let Romalla know their purpose. I have found it is… safer that no one person knows everything. Easier to track betrayals."

"You seem to trust Gellick," Cassandra said.

Arkus shrugged. "Gellick's one of the best at what he does."

"Which is?"

"Serving me," Arkus said in his most kingly tone. "Keeping our family alive."

Cassandra lightly touched her stinging cheek. "I wouldn't trust him. If he's an Esselmont, then the only thing making him less fickle than others is his sister's betrothal to Thane."

"I'm more than aware of that," Arkus said. "I am under no illusion whatsoever. Gellick and his father will be loyal so long as they have a stake in power. This can be carefully handled. Dangerous rivals are those who have nothing to lose and everything to gain by changing the balance of things. Boreac, old and childless, was one of them. Humans I can deal with but the dragons…" he trailed off ominously.

"The dragons are our allies," Cassandra said. "They destroyed your enemies for you. And now they're outside your walls, cold and hungry. Feed them, shelter them, and what will they have to hold against you?"

Arkus took a moment to think. He strode to the windows with the whole city in view and tapped the wooden tube lightly against the glass.

"Pride," Arkus said, as though addressing all of Brevia. "Dragons will be accommodating and grateful whilst they need humanity. Yet, if the dragons regain their former strength they'll dominate us again. You have a mind for the past, Cassandra. You of all people should know. The dragons have either made war upon us or dragged us into them. That Guardian, Blaine, is of the old ways and he is a walking warning. The tunnels of the Bastion prove we have never been safe. I cannot tell you how many contingency plans against dragon invasions relied on the Bastion holding strong.

"And I remember the old Darnuir as well. I could never have felt secure around him. He seems to have changed, I grant you, but it may be an act. Even if it isn't, even if Darnuir is sincere, and all the good things a fellow ruler could be, he won't live forever. So how long, Cassandra; how long until another fanatical dragon decides humanity must be purged? My predecessors were foolish in keeping to the status quo. They voluntarily remained weak, a second-rate race. Castallan would have made us stronger I have no doubt, but then we would have been reliant on him and not even Castallan could have lived forever.

"I have secured our future through craft and intelligence, through ingenuity and creativity. Humanity will no longer have to fear the dragons. That is the only way a true alliance can ever be formed." Arkus ended his speech a touch breathless. There was spittle against the window.

Cassandra had taken several small steps back without being conscious of it. Her calves pressed up against one of the plush sofas and she was sorely tempted to fall into it. This was the real Arkus. Stripped of any need to perform. This was the man – a cunning, careful planner who worked in decades, not mere years. And he had everyone either fooled or under his thumb.

"Is that thing your grand solution?" Cassandra asked. She pointed to the wooden tube.

"This is just one small piece," Arkus said. He let the weapon fall into the sack. "If you come with me. I'll show you everything."

Night had almost fallen and so, under the cover of darkness, Arkus and a guard of Chevaliers headed by Gellick, spirited them through the palace, to the back courtyard where there was a postern gate in the perimeter wall. Heavy vines hid the door in the wall but it only led out to a nondescript segment of the city.

Cassandra wondered where on earth they were heading. Before long, the back alleys began to reek of piss and vomit. A tavern rumbled far to their right and lanterns covered in a red film winked at passers-by. This was the outskirts of the Rotting Hill, only now there was no tower to guide one's way. Arkus and the Chevaliers made their way without discussion. They had clearly walked it many times before.

Deeper they went into the rundown borough until no citizens of the city could be seen or heard. And still they walked on. Cassandra felt the land begin to rise as they approached the hill where the Conclave tower had recently stood. For a wild moment, she thought they might be taking her to the ruins of the site. Perhaps this wasn't a trip of trust after all.

She felt exposed, foolish, unarmed and unable to run. Boreac lay dead and the dragons were neatly setup to take the fall for his murder. Her own body could disappear here without incident.

"Cassandra," Arkus gently called. He had taken down his hood and was standing in the doorway of a crumbling building. "Are you coming?"

She looked to the hooded Chevaliers around him and then to the ruined frame of the building. "Will I come back out?"

Even in the weak starlight Arkus looked hurt. "I would never harm you." He stepped a little closer. Cassandra mirrored with a step back and drew an inch of steel. Arkus raised his hands and said, "You are my daughter. I'm so proud of how strong you are, despite all you've gone through. I lost you once, Cassandra. Never again." He didn't come any closer or move to embrace her but she could see into his eyes from here. Small and narrow though they might be, they swam with an honesty that no one could feign. She'd only seen that before in Chelos when she was frightened or injured or upset, and he'd hold her and tell her, "I'm here for you, my girl. I'm here."

And Cassandra believed him.

She sheathed her sword, along with her fear. She was safe, even if others weren't. Yes, Arkus was a killer, yet half the world were killers, for one reason or another. Arkus strove for power but also for survival and to defend his family. And they were her family now too: Thane and Orrana. She would fight for them, if she had to. Many who fought gave the same reasons as Arkus and were called heroes. Was there really such a difference? He was flawed, but he hadn't done anything irredeemable. Not yet, anyway.

Arkus was beaming. "Not long now." Together they returned to the Chevaliers and filed into the wrecked building. Two great ovens, cold and lifeless, indicated this had been a bakery. The wood was wet, parts were rotting away, and yet the door above the cellar looked new. Heavy iron locks held it in place. Gellick took out a set of keys and opened it.

"Come," Arkus beckoned, "Gellick and his men will guard the entrance."

They descended deep into the earth, for how long Cassandra was not sure. It was surprisingly well lit and clean and soon a faint rumbling sound came drumming from the end of a long corridor. Arkus led her towards it.

As she walked beside her father, Cassandra realised the true extent of what Tiviar had meant when he said that most of what we read about the past is a lie, a trick, or a condensed and simple narrative. Arkus had proved frighteningly good at retelling events already. He'd become a butcher, cutting away all the sinew and mess from events at the Bastion, to leave an easier tale to swallow. One of human triumph and dragon failure. Boreac was growing as cold as his namesake; his story would not be told. As for Annandale, Cassandra guessed his word would be twisted beyond recognition, and who would stop it? Arkus had won. He had control and he had Lord Tarquill to print and spread any story he liked.

Another round of loud cracks came, like breaking rocks echoing in a valley. She could make out many individual ones now, coming close together, but not at the exact same moment. They reached what she hoped was the final door and Arkus pushed it open.

If there could be such thing as a horizon underground, then the space before her reached out to it. A vast cavern, supported by pillars and beams, not roughly constructed but laid with a stone floor. There were even carpets, desks, chairs, and beds stretching off. It might have been a hunter's lodge. Men and women sat working, scratching at pages furiously as though they had no concept that night had fallen and the day was over. Two soldiers in black uniform sprang up when they saw the King.

"Your Majesty," the female of the pair said. "We were not expecting you."

"No matter," Arkus said. "Take me to General Adolphus. I can hear he is at drill."

"You have soldiers living down here?" Cassandra asked. "Shouldn't they be fighting in the war?"

"They will be soon."

In another equally vast chamber, columns of soldiers paraded around, carrying weapons like the one Arkus had shown her only far longer, which they propped up on one shoulder. Others cleaned theirs, others practised some art with the latches on the ridge of the weapons while blindfolded. More soldiers were placing those little lead spheres into black pouches.

Ahead, some of those who were marching stopped to raise their weapons straight with rigid shoulders. Deafening bangs followed. Smoke rose from between their hands, rising towards a series of shafts that must have led up to the borough above.

Behind the marching troops, a light-haired fellow with an oversized moustache and wispy goatee was yelling orders. When he saw the King, he approached them briskly, long strides, arms swinging like pendulums at his side. "My King," he barked in greeting, snapping his feet together.

"General," Arkus nodded. "Circumstances have contrived that my daughter must be shown our work here."

"Very good," Adolphus said, without as much as a glance at her. "I shall continue with the drill." The general returned to his troops and resumed his flurry of orders. A fresh round of the weapons went off. A hundred yards opposite them stuffed targets exploded with straw. The targets were replaced and armour placed over the top of them. "Fire," cried Adolphus and the metal plates gave way at the force of the projectiles. More straw spewed to the floor.

"What's causing that?" Cassandra asked. "You're using black powder to propel something. But—" she realised what it was. She reached into her leathers and pulled out the little lead ball. It rolled in the dip of her palm.

"You found a musket ball as well, did you?" Arkus said.

"Muskets," Cassandra said slowly. She was taking everything in.

"Igniting the powder proved more complex than we originally thought," Arkus said. "The first designs required a match cord to be lit, fastened into a spring catch, which used to be above the trigger – where the soldiers are pulling their fingers back," he added for clarification. His eyes were alight. She had only seen him more animated when playing with Thane. He continued. "But that was cumbersome and too dangerous. Now there are pieces of flint secured to the hammer you can see them cocking back. When the trigger is pulled, down it comes, sparks, and—"

Bang. Another round of the weapons fired. The musket balls and punched holes into the thick metal plates over the targets, ripping the metal like steel through leather. It was only now that she paid attention to the plate, she realised the armour was golden; of dragon make and design.

Who do you intend to be aiming at Arkus?

"Why use that armour?" she asked.

"Strongest in the world," Arkus said off hand. "Why test on anything less. I'd like to see how it fares against starium stone, but our testing with granite would suggest the weapons have little impact. At least, not our hand-held muskets. Larger units are being finalised for that."

"Larger?"

She thought she saw one of these larger muskets. A team of four was slowly pushing around a long thick bronze tube on wheels. Fear and awe took her, imagining the damage that thing might do.

442

Cassandra's apprehension only grew as she scanned the rest of the compound. She saw an armoury, stockpiled with weapons. Row upon row of muskets glinted in the depths, their polished wood barrels catching the orange lantern light. Mountains of black ammunition pouches must have carried enough shot to block out the sun a thousand times over.

Drill sergeants and Adolphus each shouted their orders in rhythm but the men and women were a fraction ahead, already confident units firing, marching, loading, and firing again.

Those at the front took their shot, turned, marched to the rear of their five-man columns and began to reload. They bit at white rolls of paper, poured black powder into the weapon, closed the hatch, sank the remainder of the powder down the muzzle, loaded a ball, stuffed the paper in after it and, from the side of the barrel, pulled out a thin rod to ram it all down. This whole process flashed by, the soldiers ready to fire again by the time they reached the front, keeping up a steady barrage. Within one rotation, the targets were nothing but shreds of metal.

"So, this is your alternative to Castallan's magic?" she asked. "This is how you will make humanity strong?"

"Yes," Arkus said, as though there was a great weight to his voice. "This is how I'll keep our family safe."

"Fire," Adolphus called.

And bang went the muskets.

Bang.

Bang.

Bang.

EPILOGUE

Dukoona – in the depths of Kar'drun

PAIN. HAD SUCH pain ever been felt?

Dukoona howled into the crevice of rock he had been plunged into. Or was it an endless cavern? Nothing had made sense. There had only been darkness. And the flames. There had been the flames.

He slipped in and out of consciousness. One moment had felt like a lifetime, and cognizant moments between hallucinations were precious. Yet, when they stopped, there was only darkness.

And the flames. He could not forget the flames.

Mercifully, he closed his eyes.

"Awaken," the voice rumbled around him, through him, in his very mind. Dukoona felt his eyes wrench open to a blue light. It came from a great shimmering something in the distance. Its size was hard to gauge. He felt like he could be worlds away from it. Whatever it was, it was opal in shape and a bubbling blue substance boiled within it.

Against the blue glow, the outline of a body began to form. Its darkness was utter and complete. It seemed to suck light into it because the cavern dimmed further as the figure took shape. Floating, the dark form drifted towards Dukoona. It looked down upon him with a faceless head.

Pain seared within him, but he no longer had the energy to scream. His thrashing limbs were locked in place by some unseen force.

There came a loud crack and before him stood a spectre. Dukoona thought he recognised this one; a member of the Trusted, with curling green flames upon his head. The spectre spun wildly until he caught Dukoona's eye. There was no point in reassuring him. Dukoona could do nothing, say nothing that would save him.

I have failed them all.

The dark figure descended gently down behind the spectre and placed a hand upon his shoulder. In a cry of anguish that might have split the

445

earth, the spectre smoked inch by inch from existence. First his hands and feet, then his arms and legs, then only his torso was left fizzling out of the world. As his throat smoked away, his last scream echoed on until he and it were gone.

Dukoona watched it all.

"Kill us and be done with it."

"Your service has been lacking," droned Rectar's voice. Slowly, the dark figure began to solidify. When it finished, there was little to see, as a shredded crimson cloak wrapped its entire body. Its head was shrouded by a hood, though a few blond strands of hair poked down at the neck. Just visible through one of the tears in the cloak was a pale hand, gripping the steel hilt of a sword covered in fine black and gold cloth.

"We should never have granted your kind such freedoms and powers," Rectar said. "We should have chosen our servants more wisely. The Others should have chosen more wisely as well. Dragons were strong. And now they are mine."

"I have been your slave," Dukoona said.

"I am the Shadow," Rectar said. That seemed to be his answer.

"And I have destroyed your armies," Dukoona said. It was his one victory. His best act of defiance.

He fell back into agony again. A hundred small cuts suddenly appeared on his body, the dense purple shadow ripping apart to ooze his smoking blood. Beneath the flaps of his torn flesh, he could glimpse his pristine white bones.

"You have caused me a great setback," Rectar said. "But you have not destroyed my armies. Not all of them."

Dukoona's pain ceased. His cuts healed over and he hung his head, exhausted. Done. Defeated.

There was another terrible crack and all light was taken from the cavern. A moment later, heavy footsteps crunched towards him and even heavier breathing came from above. Dukoona brought his hanging head up, looking for whatever it was. He could barely see anything, but he was sure it was there. The breathing sounded higher still. He craned his neck to look upon the thing. A long red-scaled face snarled at him with fire bright eyes.

Rectar's voice rung through his mind; a fierce, amorous whisper.

'The end is nigh for all'.

A NOTE FROM THE AUTHOR

Please leave a review

If you've made it this far, then I certainly hope you enjoyed the read.
If you did enjoy the book and wish to support me, one of the best ways you can help me out is by leaving a review on Amazon. Reviews don't have to be long or in depth, but each one is beneficial. Not only does it make the book more appealing to other readers, but it can help kick the Amazon algorithms into life, thus leading to more sales. If you're willing to leave a review, you can follow this universal link to the book's page on your regional Amazon site. viewBook.at/VeiledIntentions

Book 3 is on the way

The Dragon's Blade is a planned trilogy. It's really one long story split into three parts, mostly because a 450K+ word book would be impossible to publish. I'm hard at work on book 3 with the working title of, *The Last Guardian*. It will be released into the world just as soon as I can get it ready! If you're eager to hear updates about my progress then you may want to join my mailing list.

Let's keep in touch

One of the best things about being an indie author is having the opportunity to connect directly with readers. More importantly, as I'm in full control, I can also give away FREE goodies without anyone telling me 'no'. By signing up to my mailing list you'll be the first to know about progress on my books, special guest blog series, the first to receive free chapter samples of upcoming works and get the chance to win FREE paperback copies. If that interests you, why not sign up by following this link http://thedragonsblade.com/michael-r-millers-mailing-list/

ACKNOWLEDGEMENTS

I FOUND IT SURREAL to write an acknowledgements page for the first book. Doing it again feels even stranger. I find I have even more people to thank this time around. Perhaps by my tenth book I'll have a movie's worth of people to credit.

Firstly, thanks goes to my family, who have continued to be supportive and eager to help out in any way they can. The amount an indie author has to take on board can be overwhelming at times, but my parents in particular are generous and help to lift that load wherever they can. A broader thanks to all my extended family and friends who have supported me through buying the book, and boring other people to death telling them about it. Every little helps!

My editor, Leila Dewji, deserves another round of applause. Without her, a certain character might have been left a bit lifeless. After some headaches and editing rounds that character became a beta reader favourite, but I'll leave it to you, dear reader, to try and figure out which character that was.

Thanks must go again to all those who beta read for me. Their feedback was once again invaluable and really helped me in the final polishing and editing stages. Those fantastic people are Eirik Røsvik, James McStravick, Walter & Linda Miller, George McCloghry, Kalyani Nedungadi, Rachel Norman, Samiha Bham, Rebekkah Ormel and Ross Ferguson.

Another fanfare please for Rachel Lawson (now an award-winning designer!) and her spectacular work on the book's cover and maps. I can't wait to see what she comes up with for book 3.

I'd also like to acknowledge all the amazing people I've met over the past year while attending conventions and groups such as the Super Relaxed Fantasy Club. Fellow authors and readers, you have all helped to keep me buoyant during the times when writing and publishing can feel like drowning. More specific thanks goes to all involved in the Self-Published Fantasy Blog Off. There isn't a more supportive or friendly online environment, nor one championing indie books to the same degree. To all those out there writing, I wish you the very best of luck.

Printed in Great Britain
by Amazon